PRESIDENTIAL INDISCRETIONS

Sandy,

You are a joy to know.
Best wishes always,

Turner Joy
November 30, 2005

PRESIDENTIAL INDISCRETIONS

Turner Joy

iUniverse, Inc.

New York Lincoln Shanghai

Presidential Indiscretions

iUniverse books may be ordered through booksellers or by contacting:

iUniverse
2021 Pine Lake Road, Suite 100
Lincoln, NE 68512
www.iuniverse.com
1-800-Authors (1-800-288-4677)

ISBN-13: 978-0-595-30883-5 (pbk)
ISBN-13: 978-0-595-66215-9 (cloth)
ISBN-13: 978-0-595-75705-3 (ebk)
ISBN-10: 0-595-30883-X (pbk)
ISBN-10: 0-595-66215-3 (cloth)
ISBN-10: 0-595-75705-7 (ebk)

Printed in the United States of America

CONTENTS

▼

Rose 1

Cintura 10

Paula 20

Traci 35

Marinia 50

Crystal 55

Pam 60

Alberta and I 72

Dilly 78

Diane 81

Tammy 91

Taylor and Teal 117

Lori 121

Shamanda 131

Michelle 134

Jessie 155

Andrea 180

Stephanie 192

Joyce 206

Maggie 210

Melissa 218

Nudyi 269

Albee and Cintura 278

Traci's Epilogue 285

Acknowledgment

This book is dedicated to three very special people in my life. My soul mate taught me how to laugh at adversity and cry at success. I love her with all of my heart, body and soul. My two children's boundless love and energy are the glue that holds my life together. They give me the daily impetus to value each moment and live each day to the fullest.

I deeply appreciate the prayers and well wishes from my family, friends and colleagues. Special thanks to my parents, grandparents and great grandmother for their legacy of diligence and perseverance that gave me the inspiration to author this novel.

Some say that "Presidential Indiscretions" is not a fictional story, and the names have been changed to protect the guilty. Others say, let public opinion be the ultimate judge.

Rose

I've got the best job in the world with the world at my fingertips. That's because I work for Robert Jordan Nelson, the 45th President of the United States. Thanks to President Bob (PB), I've seen more action in the back of my motorized office than at my favorite Washington D.C. strip joint, The Honey Station. That's where our President met Rose, The Honey Station's number one attraction, who tried to wear out the back seat of my limousine just last week. President Bob was introducing her to what he considers one of the finer things in life (his sexual prowess) as I drove slowly on Interstate 495. At one point, I thought the "oohs" and "aahs" emanating from the back seat were due to the excellent manner in which I was handling the unmarked presidential limousine around the curves. I later learned these noises were noises of passion. PB chided me for not driving more carefully, saying that he might have injured himself doing erotic exercises in the cramped quarters of our motel on wheels. This baby blue, revamped, accessorized and extended Lincoln Town Car is a chameleon on wheels.

I told him later that I couldn't understand how, in his position, he could see around the wonders of Rose's 44-D chest. He gave me a cat-that-swallowed-the-canary grin (the same one that ushered him into the White House) and said, "You don't have to see around that 5-foot-8-inch brunette. That miraculous 44-26-36 body would make any man melt like butter. We have a give and take relationship, you know. I give as much as I can and take as much as I can. It's the American male's dream, and I've got it." I never quite understood what this meant, but who cares?

President Bob says there are three things that make a good President: commitment, integrity, and personality (and he ought to know). Be committed and true to your ideals even if others don't agree. If it sounds sincere, people just might support you. Second, you should ooze integrity, regardless of the consequences of your actions. President Bob says that no man makes the right decision all of the time. Not a very original thought, since Abe Lincoln said that very same thing, but President Bob willingly adopted Honest Abe's philosophy. President Bob feels that a good leader makes the right decision at the right time. He also must have a people personality. You can't even get elected dogcatcher if you can't attract people with a winning smile and gracious charm. People want to identify with their candidate. If you want to win, show the people you support them. If they cannot see themselves in you, the game is over.

Bob also thinks a leader must find time to play. If he's not able to relax and let his hair down, then stress takes over, and one makes decisions hastily usually with drastic consequences. "Even at play," he says, "you can never lower your guard. Always be prepared for the onslaught of negative criticism from the opposition. Sometimes, you even have to play with those who are adversaries hoping they will lower their guard and allow you to find their weaknesses. That way, you can do some of your work, even while at play."

Women comprise seventy percent of the electorate and are a joy as well as a curse for a male politician due to the "Power of Presumption." If the official is accompanied by a female other than his wife and is not in a compromising position, it's assumed that the woman is a family member, member of his staff, dignitary or member of the press. Reporters fear the price they would pay if they reported that a mysterious female accompanied the President somewhere, and it turned out to be a Secret Service agent.

President Bob sees Rose once or twice a month but never on the same day of the week. After all, he loves his wife, Diane. He says Rose is his spice and Diane is his sugar. Rose loves his blue eyes, athletic body and 6-foot-4-inch frame. The prestige of sleeping with the President just makes her bubble with joy 'cause she knows that her friends would love to have the opportunity to sleep with President Bob.

She loves his sense of humor. The two of them are always laughing, as they relish what they've done together and look forward to what's in store for them. The excitement of their affair keeps them coming back for more.

Tonight, Rose wore a sexy, black, slip dress with a thigh-high slit (the easier for President Bob to get where he's going in a hurry). We picked her up at her friend Tiffany's condominium. By the time we got two blocks away, the dress was off, the tinted windows rolled up and the black glass between the driver and the passengers was shut tight. I knew the route to take, which was anywhere out of the way with not too many cars and not too many people. The President's unmarked limousine is not easily recognized. After an hour, I called back to see if they were ready to go to the Kennedy Center because the show was scheduled to begin in twenty minutes. President Bob was a little out of breath; however, he was cordial as always and told me to proceed to the show. He opened the inside window and the fog dissipated. I heard Rose ask him to hand her the red lace panties. "You know," he retorted, "I always like to keep a souvenir, and since possession is nine-tenths of the law, I'm confiscating them as presidential panties." He tucked them neatly into his inside coat pocket as I pulled in front of the Kennedy Center.

As I opened Rose's door, I could see those perfect, silky smooth stockingless legs. She held President Bob's arm as he escorted her into the Kennedy Center and into the presidential box. Rose had an air of pride about her that was unmatched. After parking the car, I joined them. I sat at my station to the rear of the box as they sat in front of me side-by-side, gazing out onto the stage while their hands performed a private game of hide and seek. I decided to give them some privacy and took a stroll to the concession stand for a drink.

After finishing my cool drink, I returned to my station, reflecting on Rose and President Bob. Inside the box I am a blind observer, while the Secret Service is outside the box all seeing, all knowing and knowing nothing. This isn't an oxymoron; it's a moron that knows nothing. Yet only I can chuckle because other than the participants, only I know the tale about how they met.

One night several months earlier, while riding in the limousine, President Bob lamented about a tiff he had with the First Lady. Gazing forward, as if he was glancing into the mirror of time, President Bob relayed the conversation. As usual, he seemed oblivious to the fact that I had heard it all. While I was waiting as usual, patiently, and silently nearby, President Bob watched Diane pet their dog and commented chidingly, "Diane, you show more passion for our black cocker spaniel than you do for me."

"At least the dog knew whom to come to for love and affection."

President Bob snarled back and said, "Well I'm not going to lick your hand or lick your feet, and I certainly will not kiss your…" But before he could utter another word she cut in.

"Well," she retorted, "you enjoyed doing just that when we first met, before all day meetings and late night meetings. Recently, everybody seems to get a piece of you except me. And I guarantee you, you won't get a piece of me until I can have more of you."

"It comes with the territory honey," he advised. "You knew what you were getting yourself into when I told you I was going to play the game to realize my lifelong dream. Damn right, politics is a game! You have winners and losers. The losers are the ones who don't have the foresight or aptitude to pay the price to become winners." He eased over to her, put his arms around her, and kissed her tenderly as he said, "And even after the game is over, I'll still love you, and you will love me. You will finally admit to yourself it wasn't my game; it was our game, and we won."

He edged over to the solid oak bedroom door, turning the handle firmly. "I'm going out for a drive. I'll be back a little later. Why don't you slip into something sensuous, and I'll wake you up when I get in?" She just smiled as he walked down the stairs and beckoned me to get up from my seat in the den and follow him out the door.

As I drove off with him in the back, he asked me to take him to one of my hangouts. I told him I enjoy going out to jazz clubs and a few strip joints. It was 1:00 a.m., and a little late to catch the last jazz set, so I suggested The Honey Station. I told him most patrons would be so wasted that they wouldn't recognize him. Just in case, I gave him a false mustache and goatee that I kept in the glove compartment since a Halloween party. He looked like a count after he put on the disguise. The club's red neon sign beckoned passersby with its nude silhouette six blocks away. Bouncers were perfectly positioned outside to shoo away riff-raff and usher in their clientele. I found my usual vacant parking spot across the street in Kings Automobile Dealership. We squinted as we entered the dimly lit club. Cigarettes burned in ashtrays and smoke swirled while lips were wet with expectations. Eyes roamed from torsos, to hips and lips. They passed but seldom met because their soul's view was blocked by years of promiscuity.

As we walked into The Honey Station, President Bob's eyes lit up when he saw "honeys" mingling with the patrons. He bought them a few drinks, but refused their offer for a "lap dance" until he saw Rose. She was different from the other women. At a glance, one could easily tell that Rose was the star attraction because she was very beautiful and sensual. Rose could go home with any man whose pockets were deep enough to fulfill her monetary needs, a man who was also smart enough to treat her with respect. She came on stage dressed in a rose-colored swimsuit. Rose did a magnificently hot dance routine, moving gracefully across the entire length of the stage, so everyone could get a good look at her offerings. She took off her top to reveal the tassels on her dark nipples, and just as quickly eased off the thong that barely covered her moist crotch. Rose finished her second dance number, sauntered down three steps leading to the stage-bar and allowed the patrons to put dollar bills in her garter belt which was high on her thigh. She smiled as each man placed the money in her belt and glanced out of the corner of her eye to note the denomination of each bill. President Bob drew deep into his pocket then gently placed two crisp $100 bills into the pink-laced belt and complimented Rose on her dancing ability. She smiled and moved on.

After she moved off toward the dressing room, Bob clumsily tore a sheet of paper from a notepad and wrote, "I'd love to buy you a drink at your convenience." He gave it to a barmaid to pass on to Rose. To my surprise, she accepted his invitation.

As we walked away from The Honey Station, Rose did not give any indication that she knew her latest gentleman friend was the President of the United States. She rode with us in the limousine, and Bob fixed her a drink. I wish I could have seen more, but President Bob closed the inside glass.

I knew which route to take, so I waited at least an hour before I disturbed their romantic interlude. When I called back, the President calmly gave me Rose's home address. I proceeded to the massive structure located in the heart of the nation's capital. These condominiums were home to Washington's elite. Although they were located on a corner with a drive-in parking lot below, I pulled over and parked near the curbside entrance.

I dutifully opened the door and waited for President Bob and Rose to get out. As the two of them exited the limousine, I noticed that President Bob did not have on the mustache and goatee. He held her hand as they embraced and kissed. As President Bob escorted her to the door, they walked hand-in-hand, looking like a couple of teen-agers after a date. Both were beaming, as if they had raided the cookie jar. Rose spoke first, cooing, "Call me, soon," as she smiled and made her way into her condominium.

President Bob smiled at her and replied, "For a flower as lovely as you, I'll be back to settle your petals."

As we drove home, President Bob rambled on about how bright and energetic Rose was. He respected her for her honesty and choice of profession. She was a woman who knew her limitations, was comfortable with her status in life and was making a great life. Rose didn't worry about tomorrow but respected the energy of the moment.

I told him I did not understand his energy level. It was late at night, and he's still talking intelligently without a stimulant.

"Albee, I get my energy from Club P." You've heard me talk from time to time about Club P.

Nodding affirmatively, I told him that I recalled him occasionally mentioning something about needing five cents to play. I assumed he was referring to a golf course; but at most fancy courses where he played, the annual membership began at $15,000.

"If you don't know what P stands for by now, you better hand your girlfriend over to me." He laughed heartily and continued. "Most people in Washington would think this refers to the fancy Pinewoodzy Golf Club. Albee, Club P is The Pleasure Palace in Takoma Park, Maryland. It's an exclusive erotic club inside the Department of Quintessential Studies, a fictitious department where governmental officials grease the wheels of government and conjure favors from world and business leaders."

As he was talking, I remembered the place he was describing. I had taken him there a few times; however, I was never allowed to go inside. The club was inside a five-story office building, and the first two stories contained a 100-space parking lot that was usually full. There was a two-foot sign on the building's exterior that said "Department of Quintessential Studies."

I dropped the President off at the side entrance to the White House near the Blue Room. This was the closest door to the sleeping quarters. He thanked me and proceeded inside. As I drove to the White House garage, I thought to myself that President Bob was an all right guy. He told the "truth" as only he could tell it and as a good performer who never disappointed his audience. He knew Diane would be anxiously awaiting him, and he would come through.

Several months later, I realized that President Bob and Rose were connected by passion and found meaning in the craziest things. Their zest for life and desire for self-fulfillment was something special. They looked at life through rose colored glasses. One day I drove President Bob to Baltimore to attend a Unity Day Festival at the Washington Monument. As he stepped out of the limousine, an Irish setter darted out from the crowd and came to President Bob wagging his tail. I commented that the dog was friendly.

"No, the dog is smart. He knows damn well that I have to pet and cuddle him because if he senses that I'm afraid of him, he will act on it and tear my head off. However, if he senses I'm friendly, then he'll respond in kind," said President Bob.

Last month, Rose said something quite similar. She said that men are like dogs. When they wag their tails, I know they're interested and can be easily controlled. When they don't wag their tails, they're more appealing but dangerous. They're in the position of control and can read you. If you pass their scrutiny, they will show their gentleness. If you don't, they will rip your head off and not worry about it. It's all about who's in control and how the control is maintained.

That same day Rose was discussing her childhood with President Bob, but he did not roll up the inside window. She said, "I don't know whether most people are too dumb to notice or too smart to care but when it comes to relationships, I have to give it to my mom. On holidays, she used to make a toast to my stepdad. 'To a man who has an open mind, wallet and bank account. May he give me all I want quietly and generously!' That philosophy worked okay until shortly after my seventeenth birthday. She came home late one night after being out with a male friend and found my stepdad showing me the finer points of sex education. He was a little quick on the trigger, so she caught us a little too late. It took her about forty-eight hours to get over it. She put me out for trying to steal her husband and threatened to put him in jail for statutory rape if he divorced her or saw me again. I took the little money I had saved up working the previous summer and went to stay with an aunt in Connecticut.

"My stepfather still sends me money every now and then. So, he's not exactly spineless but is close to it. My high school physics teacher used to say, 'It's not the light you shine on an object that makes the object visible; it's the object's size, shape, texture, density, etc. that gives it status. I don't know. He also said that guilt is like a penny; it's not worth much whether you or someone else holds it. So spend it or get rid of it; don't keep it. If you do, it will become you."

Rose also commented that she loved her mother. She believes she helped save her mother's marriage. Her mother was not attending to her husband's needs. If she didn't perform her wifely duties, some other woman would have. She also mentioned her stepfather wasn't bad looking and was financially independent. He had become wealthy by perfecting an intelligent computer chip. Her stepfather had made $17 million from it twenty-one years earlier at the tender age of 42 and was still living off of the interest. He wasn't much of a lover, and that's why her mom sought affection elsewhere. However, Rose tried to make him happy during the short time they were intimate.

I have a deep respect for Rose's ability to separate her sense of family, duty and intimacy. She sacrificed herself sexually to enable her mother to see what she would lose. Some would say that her cool exterior masked a lot of pain. However, a closer look would reveal that she has handled her past well, accepted that it happened and moved on with her life. Rose realizes that life is a continuum of choices. Some are good and some are bad. One has to live with the choices one makes and learn from them. So, reflecting on the past is okay because you learn from history. However, glaring incessantly at the past is bad because it won't allow you to see the present and look towards the future.

I wish many of the women in and around Washington were as honest and in touch with themselves as Rose. Several White House cabinet and staff members have been inside the "loop" too long. They've lost themselves in their desire to succeed. They've forgotten that success comes to those who are prudent in conduct, passionate in desire and prepared to handle success. Most of them only have passion.

CINTURA

Cintura Richmond is a perfect example of passion. She is the executive secretary to the White House Chief of Staff, Barton Craig. Cintura is a 43-year-old, extremely fair Nubian, hazel-eyed, bleached blond who stands 5 feet 8 inches tall and weighs about 120 pounds. Friends and colleagues consider her to be a shapely and attractive feminist who has excelled in a male-dominated, white, Anglo-Saxon, Protestant environment. Her biggest asset is that she is a "spin" queen. Cintura's job is to divert attention from negative issues involving the President and cabinet members. She is the darling of the media and can hold them at bay with a smile and her quick wit.

Cintura does whatever it takes to get her job done. Several years ago, a prominent news reporter was hounding the President about an old high school sweetheart who became gay shortly after their relationship ended. Cintura conveniently found some old high school photos of the reporter in a wig, wearing female clothing and holding onto a very athletic classmate. Apparently, the reporter played a female leading lady in a play at his all-male high school. A competing news station aired the pictures without mentioning that the reporter was dressed for the play. They also showed some recent photos of the reporter in a shirt and tie. It gave the reporter's name and ran with the title, "Then and Now." Cintura's tactic was very successful, and the reporter was embarrassed to the point that he no longer covers the White House. He was transferred to the sports department.

Immediately after the incident, Cintura obtained three, 12-inch, ultra-plasma flat screen, laptop computers, with dual capability of personal computer and television technology for the President, herself and me. Each sleek silver device was connected to a satellite that monitored foreign and domestic adversaries who posed a threat to United States security and/or White House initiatives. Cintura instructed me to place the laptop in any vehicle in which I transported the President, so he could have instantaneous access to intelligence.

Cintura was always an expert in manipulation. Twenty years ago, Barton was running for mayor in their hometown of Austin, Texas. She was an unemployed legal secretary and thought he had enough savvy to win. Barton was 34, attractive, and extremely naive regarding the political process. During her job interview with him, Cintura discussed strategic maneuvers Barton needed to make in order to win. He was surprised by her insight and agreed to incorporate her ideas into his campaign strategy. One of her suggestions was for him to marry Nudyi Sorienson, a woman he had dated over the years. Since Barton was running in both a majority Catholic and Democratic district against a state senator who was both single and Republican, their union would attract married voters.

Nudyi and Barton had been high school sweethearts. She was class valedictorian and won a four-year scholarship to Stanford University. She majored in microbiology, and her demanding college schedule took its toll on their relationship. After her freshman year, she asked Barton to place their relationship on hold until after college. Nudyi said that she didn't have time for the late night calls, letter writing, and rushing home on holidays and semester breaks to spend time together. Barton did not like the idea of her having access to other guys. He suspected that she was looking for an excuse to fool around with someone else and told her so. Nudyi told him that if this was how he felt, not to bother writing or calling her. Barton became angry and vowed never to date again. He felt as though he had given his best effort to make their relationship work, but Nudyi no longer wanted to be part of his life. His ego was bruised because Nudyi was his first love.

Although Nudyi missed her family and friends, she spent the next four years devoted to her studies. She attended a seminar on dentistry in her senior year, became fascinated with the subject and concluded that she wanted to become a dentist. Nudyi knew if she was going to attend graduate school, she wanted to go to a university close to her hometown. She applied, and was accepted, to the University of Texas School of Dentistry. Although they hadn't talked in two and a half years, she called Barton and invited him to her graduation. Her phone call caught Barton completely by surprise. He listened attentively as she extended the invitation. She ended by saying, "If you have a girlfriend and can't make it, I'll understand." After she finished, Barton told her that he hadn't dated since she dumped him. Nudyi always held the keys to his heart, and he wouldn't settle for anything less than what they once had. They both could no longer hold back their tears. They felt closer at this moment than they did when they first dated.

Barton was an outstanding pitcher with major league potential. He was the only high school athlete to throw three consecutive no-hitters. Barton won an athletic scholarship to the University of Texas and played there for two years. Then a batter's line drive hit his left leg and shattered his fibula close to the knee. It did not heal properly and cost him a promising baseball career. Barton does not walk with a noticeable limp; however, he can not run normally. He completed his degree with a double major in history and political science. After teaching school for eight years and feeling disgruntled with the lack of political support for public education, Barton decided to run for mayor.

Cintura used radio commercials to entice Barton's students and their parents to show support for him. One spot said, "Barton Craig has given years of public service, taught our children to be good students and citizens, instilled good values in them that they can utilize in all aspects of their lives, and has what it takes to be our next mayor. I urge you to support him with your voice, volunteerism, and vote! Let's all pitch in and help." Shortly after the announcement aired, 230 parents and kids volunteered to distribute leaflets in the community and work at polling places around town. Cintura's strategy worked; Barton won with 63 percent of the vote, and she has worked for him ever since.

Barton's marriage to Nudyi worked out extremely well. They are still together after twenty years and three kids. Terri, the oldest, is in her first year of medical school. Barton Jr. is playing left field for the New York Yankees, and Terrence, the youngest, is a freshman at Harvard. Both Terri and Terrence graduated at age 16, magna cum laude. Barton Jr.'s first love was sports; his second was the ladies. Education was not high on his list. He graduated at the age of 18 with a 3.0 grade point average and 1000 on the Scholastic Aptitude Test. That was enough to qualify him for any Division I NCAA school to play sports. However, he turned down eight scholarship offers for an opportunity to play for America's team, the New York Yankees. Barton Jr. could tell you the day, inning and which at-bat Babe Ruth had hit his 713th home run. He could also recite when Mickey Mantle hit two home runs in a game, when Thurman Munson threw two runners out trying to steal in an inning and the date Billy Martin was hired and fired by the best and most controversial owner in sports, George Steinbrenner. Barton Jr. always came to Mr. Steinbrenner's defense. He felt that George got a bad rap. Mr. Stienbrenner was an owner who viewed his team as a business and he loved baseball.

Nudyi is a very successful dentist. However, Cintura taught her long ago how to be a political wife. Her philosophy is that the politician must appear to be a good father, a loving husband, head of his home and the breadwinner. Although feminism has brought America a long way, we still live in a very chauvinistic society.

As White House Chief of Staff, Barton makes $180,000 per year. As a dentist, Nudyi makes $375,000 annually. She is content staying in the background and letting her husband get all of the publicity while she enjoys her career. Although she has a maid, she finds time to cook breakfast and dinner four times a week. Nudyi and Barton send one another love notes at least once a day by e-mail.

A year ago, a summer female intern tried to seduce Barton in hopes of manipulating him to secure her a permanent job. Cintura found out and had the young woman dismissed. Since the woman had been counseled several times for being away from her assigned work area, she was dismissed citing that as the reason. Cintura always took the politically correct position in decision making.

Cintura seems to have been beamed down from another planet. In governmental circles, she's viewed as being a spinster or lezzie because of the hundreds of luncheons and dinners that she has coordinated. A male friend has never accompanied Cintura. With a body like hers, I can't imagine Cintura bumping bones with another woman. Although she and a recently hired administrative aide have been a little too friendly, that's none of my business. They are both over 21 and can hug and feel as much as they want.

Cintura has always had a knack for keeping her social life separate from work. She has no relatives other than a young lady she introduced some time ago as her niece, Barbara. Barbara was petite, had light-blue eyes, sandy brown hair and a quick wit. She was raised in boarding schools and had never been to the White House; however, she has been to some affairs on the Hill. A few years ago, I heard her talking about attending graduate school. Barbarahad full scholarship offers from Harvard, Yale, University of Southern California and Princeton. She chose Harvard because the average salary was $75,000 a year for the previous year's graduating seniors. Barbara expressed a desire to work for a prestigious law firm for one year and then run for political office. Every few years she came home for the holidays but seldom visits now.

Most wives would be jealous of Cintura. No woman wants an attractive woman working with her husband. However, Nudyi and Cintura came to an understanding the first day they met. Back then, President Bob was a young, 34-year-old senator supporting his high school teammate, Barton, at his first fund raiser. Senator Bob, Diane, Nudyi and Barton were sipping champagne and discussing the mischief they had gotten into during high school. Cintura came in to summon Senator Bob because it was time for him to present the welcoming address. Nudyi was a little bit perturbed by the interruption and wore a scowl on her face. Cintura escorted Barton to the stage then promptly invited Nudyi to go with her to the ladies room. Nudyi told Cintura that she didn't appreciate her taking her husband away when she wasn't done with him. Cintura appeared amused and responded coyly, "I don't want your husband because I don't deal in leftovers." They both had a good laugh and joined Barton at the podium. Since then, Nudyi has considered Cintura a good friend.

Later that night, as Cintura was leaving the hotel ballroom, she noticed Senator Bob sitting in the hotel lobby. She asked him why he was by himself. Senator Bob said that his wife had taken the car and driven herself home. He was waiting for a staff member to discuss a pending bill. They were supposed to have a late night drink at the hotel's bar. He invited Cintura to sit and talk. They exchanged political ideas and were surprised that they held similar views. After about twenty minutes, one of the hotel staff informed Senator Bob that he had a telephone call. He stood up to take the call, telling Cintura that he'd be back in a minute. As the Senator tried to get up, he slipped, fell forward, landed face down in Cintura's lap and split his pants. He inadvertently grabbed her right leg to brace his fall. After Senator Bob caught himself, he said with a grin "This is the first time I've fallen for a woman in a hotel lobby."

"This is the first time a man has gotten under my clothes without permission."

"At least you have all of yours intact. My pants are a little breezy at the moment." They had a nice chuckle, and then Senator Bob took his call. He returned shortly and informed Cintura that his colleague couldn't make it. She agreed to take him home, but first she wanted to change her shoes and slip into some pants since Senator Bob had created a run in her pantyhose and scuffed her heels.

When they got to her home he escorted her inside. Cintura asked him to make them both a drink while she changed clothes. As he was making a drink he heard a loud thud, as if someone had slipped and fallen. Senator Bob ran upstairs while yelling, "What happened?" He entered the bedroom and saw Cintura sprawled on the floor wearing only her blouse and panties. The heel on her shoe had broken as she was taking off her skirt. Cintura had always worn her hair up, looking like a schoolmarm. However, it was now flowing down her back, and that air of professionalism that she always had was gone for the moment. This was the first time he saw the feminine side of Cintura. Senator Bob apologized for coming in, telling her he was concerned for her safety. Cintura heard the sincerity in his voice but for some reason was paralyzed by her own vulnerability. As Senator Bob helped Cintura to her feet, Cintura's hands made their way around his waist, while simultaneously her lips met his. They both gave in to the passion of the moment. After an hour of intense lovemaking, they snuggled on the bed for several minutes gazing into one another's eyes. Both knew that it must never happen again because they had too much to lose. They showered and dressed, never uttering a word but reflecting on their moment of bliss.

While Cintura was driving Senator Bob home, she asked him what he would tell his wife. He pondered for a second and commented, "I'll say that a staff member arrived late for a meeting and presented me with some alternative solutions to a problem. His assistance was invaluable in review-ing the critical issues and putting them in perspective. We were so engrossed in the issues that we lost track of time. After much soul-search-ing, I concluded that it was well worth the time invested; however, due to my hectic schedule, I could not follow through on it again. The cost of fol-lowing through was prohibitive."

Cintura just laughed, telling President Bob, "You're full of…" But before she could utter another word, he kissed her on the right cheek and stroked her right hand with his left. Cintura drove on until they arrived at his home. She did not bother to drive up the massive driveway to his man-sion in the distance, which was hidden by trees and well-kept shrubbery. Cintura parked along the curb, and Senator Bob released her hand. As Senator Bob walked up the driveway whistling a wayfarer's tune, Cintura drove home.

President Bob knows that to this day Cintura hasn't told anyone. How-ever, he has confided in me, as he often does from time to time because he knows I won't repeat anything.

Tonight's the big party for Barton, Jr. The Yankees begin a four-game series at Camden Yards and although most people in attendance will be die-hard Oriole fans, there will be plenty of Barton Jr.'s friends and family pulling for him to do well. Thankfully, this affair is by invitation only, so the groupies will not have easy access to Barton Jr. and his teammates in attendance. At the last affair we had at Water Circle Towers, there were more groupies than invited guests. It was the oldest game in town called, "Find a man with deep pockets, get pregnant, and then you and your child are set for life." The only problem is this game doesn't work on the Hill. A woman quickly discovers that the deeper the man's pockets, the less she receives. And, the bigger the controversy you cause, the slimmer your chance of surviving the scandal.

A famous author, George T. Thompsoner, once said, "The world is neither black nor white—it's gray. The average man will never see it, and that's why he remains average. The brightest man will never see it because his head is in the clouds. But the fox of a man will clearly see it because this is his domain." What that has to do with the tea in China, I don't know.

It's time to go, and the President, First Lady, Barton, Nudyi and their children are resting comfortably in the back of the limousine. I have the stretch limo today. All of the cars are steel-plated with bulletproof glass and a high tech security system. However, this limo has the smoothest ride of the cars in the fleet and can accommodate up to 10 people comfortably. The inside window is drawn, but I know Barton Jr. is spinning a tale about his longest hit. His batting average is .310 this year. Barton Jr.'s home runs are of the low, line drive variety. On each drive if you look at his lips closely, you'll see him praying that the ball clear the fence. You can tell how much of a relationship he has with his deity because out of his 217 hits, he only has 14 home runs.

As we pulled up to the Hilton Hotel, there was a crowd of paparazzi poised like cobras in the Thailand countryside, ready to have the satisfaction of striking and disarming the first passerby. As always, I waited for the Secret Service to secure a pathway for the car to the hotel. Sixteen dark-suited soldiers with sunglasses stood at attention, all ready to take a bullet for President Bob.

They ushered us in without too much commotion. As we walked inside the Hilton's ballroom, I saw someone I hadn't seen in years—Alberta, my fraternal twin. We had been inseparable in our youth. Even with her crown removed, she looked every bit the Miss Arkansas she was eighteen years earlier. There were 15 to 20 men in the lobby, all with their eyes on her. Some men were with their significant others; however, Alberta's beauty and innocent smile were understood by the jealous hearted and accepted by the secure ones. She wore a blue, chiffon, strapless dress, matching blue four-inch heels and diamond studded earrings resting on her ears like the sun's reflection on water. Her light brown eyes caused men to drool and become tongue-tied as they attempted to say "Hello" as they passed by. Little had changed since a quarrel separated us about seven and a half years ago. She still could cause conversation to stop when she entered a room. Even if she were not my sister, I would still call her a true Hispanic goddess.

Since I was on duty, I took my position in the rear of the hall and became inconspicuous. Professor Lynch, Director of Philosophic Studies at American University, was nearby explaining to five young men his reason for choosing philosophy over writing. I only caught tidbits of what he was saying.

"I wanted to be a writer to shape the minds of men and develop new theories through observation of the human spirit but found it perpetually boring. To view others through a foggy microscopic lens of interest is a wasted activity because the only thing that's seen is a fleeting picture captured in your consciousness for a brief moment in time. The picture is only real for the moment you view it. It's not permanent."

I totally disagree. If something is in your consciousness, it's not temporary. Do mountains get up and walk away just because one views them for a brief time? No. Professor Lynch is so smart that he doesn't have sense enough to know that he's stupid.

Now look who's on the other side of the room talking to Terri—Bart Millersby. His Yankee nickname is Batting Bart. He has averaged hitting a home run every 5.6 times at bat. If he stays healthy, he'll crush Hank Aaron's home run record. He's what every woman wants in a man. Bart's honest, religious, doesn't have a girlfriend and hasn't let success ruin his personality. Last season he signed a multi-million dollar contract in spring training but got hurt. Bart insisted that Yankee management pay him the minimum salary for a year and give area youth groups 150 free tickets for each home game. His unselfish actions endeared him to the community, and he is becoming an icon. Bart's having a tremendous season this year, but he's the most down to earth player on the team. During interviews, he talks more about his teammates than about himself.

I guess Bart is just being kind to Terri. Terri has a cute face and a nice personality, but she has a pancake body and no life outside of work. She always wears her naturally blond hair down to her shoulders when she's not in school. I saw Bart write something down to give to her. I thought it was his autograph. I discovered later that it was his phone number. They danced a few times, but he spent most of the evening showing appreciation for the cook's hard work. After his fourth helping of the main course, he decided to try the dessert.

Barton Sr. and PB both made short speeches, encouraging the guests to finish their repast and join the others on the dance floor as the Shimmering Light Connection played the current top 40 tunes.

PB was Barton Jr.'s godfather. He made a point of discussing how he took Barton Jr. to his first little league game because his father had a previous engagement. Barton Jr. hit a ball over the third base bag, but the umpire called it foul. He cried until PB slipped him five dollars and promised to get him some ice cream. PB said that he didn't know if it was the five dollars or the cute 13-year-old girl serving the ice cream that eased Barton Jr.'s pain.

We stayed at the Hilton for another hour before getting up to go. Barton Jr.'s coach gave their team a 10:00 p.m. curfew, and it was already 9:00 p.m. As we were leaving, Paula Stillson-Barnes entered the room on the arm of Trent Morrison, the Senate Majority Leader.

PAULA

Paula's the kind of woman that you don't need as a friend or want as an enemy. She uses her friends and has innovative ways to get rid of her enemies. The rule of thumb is to always walk beside her. If she's behind you and you cross her, you will feel a nice long dagger in your back. Last summer she was on PB's short list to be appointed the United States Ambassador to Italy. She has a bachelor of arts degree in sociology, master of science degree jurisprudence and a Ph.D. in public administration. Paula worked ten years for the Justice Department and three years as chairperson of the Equal Employment Opportunity Commission (EEOC). She received Presidential Citations for outstanding administrative service for each of the last three years. Nevertheless, Chester Lorton, the Speaker of the House, opposed her nomination due to her lack of international experience. Paula was furious and got even with Representative Lorton. The Gay & Lesbian Alliance of News Professionals was giving a bridal shower for its president, Peter Renaldo. It was scheduled to take place in the Chateau Room at the Paradise Hotel. Paula asked Representative Lorton to be the keynote speaker at a news media professionals' meeting. She was quite cordial, so he assumed that she was being conciliatory to garner his support.

Mr. Lorton knew the importance of keeping the media under control, as well as an ally, so he agreed to speak. Paula arranged to meet the Alliance president and Mr. Lorton at the entrance of the Chateau Room. They arrived at the Chateau Room as scheduled. Paula immediately introduced Mr. Renaldo, cited his full title as President of the Gay and Lesbian Alliance of News Professionals and then opened the door. Mr. Lorton's staunch conservatism rose to the surface. His face turned cherry red, and his mouth dropped open as if he was having a tooth extracted. Flashbulbs were going off all over the room. He was only at the door for a moment, but that moment must have seemed like a lifetime. Newspapers had a good time with this story. *The Westonian Post* wrote, "Speaker Becomes Speechless While Escorting The Bride." *The New York Minute* headlines read "Lorton's Conservative Cover is Pulled Left, Showing Liberal Underwear." *The Dallas Sensorship* wrote, "Lordy, Lordy, Lordy, Chester is Real Naughty." As a result, Mr. Lorton took a two-month leave of absence to let the fever cool down. He knew that Paula had set him up, but there wasn't a thing he could do about it. Mud slinging wasn't his forte, and she threatened to bury him with a harassment accusation if he pursued her in retribution.

Paula met Trent at the inaugural ball last year. Trent Morrison, Mr. Liberal, is a native of Massachusetts. He's bright and dedicated to improving the lives of his constituents. His district is composed of black, Hispanic and Asian lower- and middle-class voters. He ran on a platform promising to improve education, increase jobs and protect the Social Security program. Trent and his wife, Sylvia, have been separated for twenty-three years, but she refuses to give him a divorce for economic reasons. They have an informal agreement that Trent will give her one third of his total income. Trent's deceased father's will stipulates that he will continue to receive $1.5 million annually from a $132 million trust fund as long as he and Sylvia remain married. If they divorce, Trent will only receive $250,000 annually until he remarries. If Trent remarries, his stipend from the Trust will increase to $500,000 annually. Trent also receives a Senate salary of $175,000 annually.

During legislative sessions, he lives alone in Salvador's Executive Condominiums in Alexandria, Virginia. Trent and Sylvia still share his father's home in Massachusetts but not the same bedroom. It's easy to lead separate lives in a 17-room mansion. Trent's father had been a builder and spared no expense on his home. Eight plush bedrooms with full bathrooms attached, a sunroom at each end of the house, living room, dining room, a 30-seat theater, an indoor swimming pool, and sauna more or less complete the huge interior of the estate. Their two children, Justin and Marla, never approved of their living arrangement but have accepted it.

When Paula met Trent, he was suave and debonair. Trent came to the affair with June Thomas, a popular singer. She had a petite model-like figure and wore a size 4, sequined red, strapless evening gown. June's chest seemed firm but was also held in place with a size 34 push-up bra. Paula wore a similar red sequined dress. Except for Paula's dress back being bare and her size 40 breasts beckoning onlookers with their natural position, Paula and June seemed to be wearing the same dress. However, Paula's size 8 dress and 5-foot-8-inch frame made her stand out.

When June went to the restroom to freshen up, Paula made her way over to Trent and struck up a conversation.

"You look stunning in that dress," he told her.

"I think it would look even better, off. Why don't you see after you take your date home?" She handed him her address and walked away as June returned. As always, Trent's curiosity got the best of him. June soon became history, and Paula had captured another fly in her ever-expanding web. She maintains there's nothing wrong with lust; it's love she has problems with. So Paula doesn't love for long; she loves for lust. If it's Trent today, it'll be Tramp tomorrow.

Trent is the Senate Majority Leader, a moderate Democrat, and lately has been opposed by members of his own party. His party considers him a closet Republican because he tends to be conservative on most issues although he is liberal when it comes to democratic issues that positively affect his constituents. Trent has asked Paula to use her influence to assist him in retaining his seat as his Democratic colleagues have threatened to oust him. In exchange for her support, he has agreed to support Paula's nomination for the ambassadorship to Spain. Trent has already made calls on her behalf. Paula agreed as long as he pays her three to one. Three to one on Capitol Hill means three favors for one. Every man can be bought because every man has his price. The only issue is, "Are you willing to pay the price?"

Three months ago, Paula's nephew, Simon, needed a summer job. She asked Stuart Peters, Director of Personnel at the Department of Justice, to give him a job. Mr. Peters resisted until Paula reminded him of his long-time relationship with her brother and that his wife and three children could quite easily be made aware of this. Simon was immediately hired, with strict instructions from Paula to report any departmental mischief to her. He was a diligent worker. Simon received an outstanding evaluation at the end of the summer and presented a journal to Paula before he returned to the University of Virginia at Charlottesville for the fall semester.

Simon's journal detailed Mr. Peters' questionable hiring practices. He had two of his children and his wife on the payroll, but none of them had ever come into the office. The most shocking entry was that Mr. Peters had spent three weeks at meetings in Lanai, Hawaii with his Uncle Timmy, although the government has no office there.

Paula's brother, Timothy Stillson, has never worked. He has been openly gay since the age of 17, when his parents found out his sexual preference and sent him packing. Timothy was quite promiscuous and had a penchant for well-to-do, white, Anglo-Saxon Protestant men. Whenever a relationship ended, he rarely left empty-handed. For three years, he lived with his 31-year-old lover, Tony Masters. Tony treated him well and paid for him to attend junior college. Timothy majored in fashion design and did a little modeling in his spare time. He then had a brief affair with one of his instructors; unfortunately, Tony found out and asked Timothy to leave within two weeks.

Although Paula doesn't approve of Timothy's lifestyle, he has always been useful in getting dirt on her opposition. He crosses male and female lines as only he could. Timothy isn't overly feminine, so both men and women like and accept him. His natural good looks and surfer-like features make him attractive as well. He is always the life of the party and can tell the dirtiest joke in the most tasteful way. Paula allowed him to move in with her on the condition that he would do the three for one. Timothy agreed, so he moved into her spare bedroom. While he was unpacking, she asked Timothy to drop by her office the following morning and convince Trent Morrison to pose with him for pictures and find some dirt on the White House Chief of Staff as well as the President. Since his choice of living quarters was limited, he agreed and showed up at her office as requested. He greeted Mr. Morrison with a hearty handshake and told him that he had always admired his work and followed his political career. Timothy then asked Paula to take a picture, so he would have a memento. Paula looked at Mr. Morrison smiling as he enjoyed the flattery and nodded in agreement. After the photo, Timothy excused himself explaining that he was going sightseeing and then proceeded to his next assignment.

Paula kept the film for protection. She told me once that if a gal doesn't cover her tail, she usually doesn't have one for long. I guess she was right.

Timothy did not come home that night. Since he was 26 and had been on his own for a number of years, Paula didn't worry. However, she didn't hear from him the next day either, so she called his friends and most recent lovers, but they said they hadn't heard from him. When she talked to Tony, he pleaded with her to have Timmy call when he got in. He said that he wanted to patch things up. Paula returned home about 9:00 p.m. and to her surprise, two uniformed police officers were waiting for her. Before they could say anything, she said, "What has Timmy done now? He's my only sibling, but he gets himself into so much trouble."

One of the officers cut her off and said, "Ms. Barnes, we have some bad news. I'm detective Michael Johnson, and this is my partner, Fred Strivinski. The couple next door has been on vacation for the last week and when they returned home earlier today, they discovered your brother's body floating in their pool. Apparently he drowned."

"But my brother doesn't swim. He never learned how to swim." Paula covered her face with her hands and sobbed uncontrollably. The detectives asked her if there was anyone else who should be called. She said, "Timmy is my only brother. Our parents died years ago."

"Is there a friend or acquaintance nearby we can call for you?" asked Detective Johnson.

"Yes, there is." Paula gave them Trent's name and phone number.

Detective Strivinski called him and explained that Paula's brother was recently found dead, and Paula needed a friend to help console her. Trent assured the officer that he would be right over, then hung up the phone and quickly drove to Paula's house. The police cars and crime investigators were still outside when Trent arrived. He appeared genuinely concerned and stayed with Paula throughout the night. Trent slept on a chair in the bedroom while she slept on the bed.

Paula tossed and turned all night as if wrestling with the devil. Finally, at 4:30 a.m. she woke up screaming, "Timmy, I'm sorry." Trent leaped from the recliner and held her trembling body. Her sobs touched his heart, but his lips failed to utter anything to comfort her. In her heart, Paula must have known that nothing would ever be the same. She had put her brother in harm's way and had hastened his demise. At the tender age of 37, she was left without parents or siblings.

In an effort to take her mind off the tragedy, Trent told Paula about the guilt that he had felt when he lost his parents. "I grew up a spoiled little rich kid. I never wanted for anything. As a matter of fact, I used to pray for my parents' early demise, so I could spend the fortune that they had amassed. However, when they died, I blamed myself for my selfish thoughts and quality time lost with them. But after a while I realized that thoughts couldn't kill anyone. I would always have the memories of the love we had shared as a family. As I went off to school or summer camp, the hugs I had gotten from them were priceless."

Paula's tears ceased, but she knew of no such days. Her parents had not done a great deal of hugging and kissing. Paula resented her brother when he was born because he took all of the attention she had been receiving. She dried her tears and focused on what angered her most. Paula suspected that someone in the White House had her brother killed, and now she had an insatiable need to find out who it was.

About 6:30 a.m., Paula told Trent to go home. Reporters might be lingering around the next few days, and he didn't need their unwanted attention. Trent agreed, noting that he had to shower and change. After Trent left, Paula took a warm bubble bath, then called Simon and John Stillson to inform them of their cousin's death. She reached Simon in the dorm.

He said that since it was Friday, he would drive to her house after his final class ended at 3:30 p.m. and would be there by 6:00 p.m. Paula was unable to reach John but left a message for him on his home answering machine. Then she drove to the Washington, D.C. Police Station on I Street and New York Avenue to inquire about the circumstances surrounding her brother's death.

The desk sergeant could hear the swift clicking rhythm of Paula's heels about thirty seconds before she arrived at his desk. Her grimace caused the sergeant to ask, "How can I help you miss?"

Paula pulled out the tentative police report from her purse and said in a sharp tone, "I want to see Detectives Michael Johnson and Fred Strivinski!

"Wait a minute; I'll get them."

Within minutes, Detectives Johnson and Strivinski came strolling out of one of the adjacent offices. They informed her that they had little additional information. Timmy was discovered with his driver's license in his swimming trunks; there were no other clothes or identification found. The medical examiner had performed an autopsy, but it would be several days before the results would be known. Paula said that she had to make arrangements for her brother's memorial service. She explained that he had requested his body be cremated and his ashes spread over the AIDS Memorial in Washington, D.C. They told her that she was free to have a funeral home take the body; however, it would be a federal offense if she defamed the memorial by pouring her brother's ashes on it. However, Paula was free to open an urn containing his ashes and allow the wind to blow it on the memorial.

Paula left the station and immediately called Barton. She told him she knew someone murdered her brother. Barton denied knowing what Paula was talking about but offered his condolences. He told her that she had a lot of enemies that may be returning some favors three to one, so she had better watch her back. Barton advised Paula to contact Cintura before she took any additional action.

"Barton, it's Friday, and I'm going to have a small memorial service for my brother tomorrow. I can't deal with the White House or Cintura right now. I'll take care of her the first thing Monday morning. Mortimer Cravitts Funeral Home located at 1529 Connecticut Avenue will do the cremation and has agreed that we can hold a brief memorial service tomorrow at 11:30 a.m. Afterward, we will dispose of my brother's ashes per his wishes."

Barton sighed as if exasperated by the whole ordeal and said, "Fine. I'll try to make it. The President has me scheduled to meet with gun lobbyists to discuss his stance on gun control and responsible gun ownership." They both hung up the phone muttering and questioning the other's motives.

Barton dutifully called Cintura and warned her. Paula called the mortician and her cousin, John. It was a hectic twenty-four hours, but Paula managed to pull it off. About 25 close friends and relatives came. Even three of Timmy's former lovers came to say farewell. There was no clergy present, so she allowed two minutes to everyone who wanted to talk about Timmy, and then she spoke last.

"The reason there aren't any clergy here today is because my brother requested that none be present. He also requested that I read this letter." Paula's speech stumbled as she fought back the tears. She read, 'Hi, as you can see I had to make a quick exit. I asked that no clergy be in attendance because I don't want to appear a hypocrite. I did not attend church regularly and to tell you the truth, I don't know if I'm going to heaven or hell. Yeah, I know a lot of clergy do not approve of my lifestyle and quite frankly, I don't approve of theirs. I've done what I've done, lived the way I lived and given the way I've given. I wasn't perfect, but who is? Paula, I know I've been a pain in the ass most of the time, but deep down you really love me. By the way, you told me once that you thought that I hated all women. Well, to be truthful, there was one young lady that I've been crazy about and looked up to all of my life. She's the best sister a guy ever had. Tell any of the guys that show up "hello and sweet dreams." Thanks for remembering me because I'll never forget you. Timmy.'

By the time Paula got to the end of the letter, there wasn't a dry eye in the building. Even the mortician's helpers were unable to maintain their humble, stoic and impartial stance, dabbing their eyes with handkerchiefs as other mourners grieved. After the memorial service, the audience followed her by car in a procession to the AIDS Memorial where Timmy's remains were scattered about by the wind as the urn was opened. The mourners greeted Paula with hugs and whispers of support and then quietly drove to their own homes leaving Paula alone in front of the Memorial.

Paula called Cintura the following Monday and asked to meet with her at 1:30 p.m. at the White House. Cintura indicated that she was going to be leaving early but reluctantly agreed for Paula to come to her home at 1:30 p.m. She gave Paula her address and told her that it was imperative that she arrive on time because at 4:30 p.m., she had another engagement.

Paula taped a small tape recorder under her clothes beneath her right breast and went to meet Cintura. Cordial and composed, Cintura greeted Paula at the door with an extended hand. They shook hands, and Cintura escorted her to the den, which was her home office. She sat in front of her credenza in her black executive chair, while Paula sat in one of the two leather armchairs facing her. After they exchanged pleasantries, Paula asked Cintura what she knew about her brother's death. Cintura admitted to knowing about Tim's death and offered her condolences.

"I understand that he was doing a little research. Unfortunately, he didn't have the opportunity to complete his assignment. Maybe someone else will be more successful," Cintura said coolly with an intimidating glance.

"Maybe Timmy couldn't complete his assignment; but I will because I have a lot of three to one favors I can call in." Paula stomped toward the door and angrily said, "I will get the damning evidence I need to put you away forever!"

Cintura impeded her exit, slapped her and told her that she was making a foolish mistake. Paula fell backwards, and her blouse opened wide enough to show the tape recorder. Cintura snatched the tape recorder as Paula struggled for the door. Paula pushed Cintura away, ran outside, jumped in her car and sped away. As she crossed the second intersection, a car cut her off. Paula lost control of her car as it hit the concrete median railing, flipped several times and burst into flames. Unfortunately, the fire department and paramedics arrived too late to save her.

The two detectives, Johnson and Strivinski who had been assigned to investigate Timothy's death went over to Paula's house the day after her death to see if they could find any clues. All of the furniture, clothes and household items were gone. They then checked with most of the moving companies in the area but couldn't find a trace of the furniture. However, they found a pound and a half of cocaine in the toilet tank in the first floor powder room. A review of Timothy's banking records indicated he had $650,000 spread over several checking and savings accounts with his sister named as the primary beneficiary and John Stillson, a cousin, named as a secondary beneficiary. The detectives informed their captain of their findings and expected him to initiate a full investigation. However, he said, "The FBI has assumed jurisdiction of the case due to national security. Timothy was the brother of Paula Stillson-Barnes, a highly respected federal employee and ambassador nominee. There is a suspicion that unscrupulous governments are behind the deaths surrounding Timothy and Paula's demise." The official file noted that Timothy's investigation was closed due to insufficient evidence. The file had a sub-conclusion that read: non-determinable but drug related. Paula's death was noted as accidental.

Shortly afterwards, a highway patrolman found Simon Stillson's body in his car with the motor running. The patrolman had received a CB radio call from a motorist who noticed a man slumped over the steering wheel of his car. The police deduced that Simon had pulled off the road to catch a few hours of sleep on his way home from college. Carbon monoxide had seeped into the car from the engine, and he never awoke from his nap.

John Stillson was devastated by the loss of his brother and cousins. He was 25 years old and in his final year of medical school. In a few short weeks, his world had crumbled around him, now he was Paula's only living relative. Since the police could not connect the money to drug profiteering, they gave the money to John, the only surviving beneficiary.

John's sudden wealth did little to soothe the misery he felt, but it did allow him and his wife the ability to arrange separate funerals for Paula and Simon. He contacted the Dean of Student Services, Mable Watermate, at the University of Virginia and requested to use their campus chapel for Simon's funeral service. She told him, "This was highly irregular. To my knowledge, the chapel has never been used in that manner." However, after fifteen minutes, Ms. Watermate reluctantly agreed to allow John to use the chapel on Saturday from 1:30 p.m.–4:00 p.m. John contacted all of Simon's teachers and gave them a flier inviting everyone to the funeral.

Two days later, the chapel was packed with 250 students, faculty and John and his wife. The campus chaplain, Reverend LeRoy Wright, gave the eulogy. The most significant portion of Reverend Wright's message was when he said, "Simon was an excellent student and everyone at the University of Virginia will miss him. He not only left behind a brother and sister-in-law, Simon left behind a University of Virginia family that loves him. This young man was simply a good down-to-earth student. No, Simon never made the honor roll or the football or basketball teams. He never skipped class nor was he disrespectful to a fellow student or faculty. Simon never cheated at chess, cards or on an examination. He gave of himself and even worked summer jobs at the Federal Building and the White House. Simon will be remembered as a young man who lived his life learning what he could do to make life for others more fulfilling and meaningful."

Paula's funeral had to be held in Grace Baptist Church in Northeast Washington, D.C. because it could accommodate the largest number of attendees. Most of the Senate, House of Representatives, and Cabinet members were in attendance. Even President Bob came and gave his condolences. John was very quiet but cordial. The only family he had left was Traci, whom he had married during his junior year in medical school. He had never told his family about their marriage since Paula made him promise not to marry or get seriously involved until after he graduated from medical school. Of course, this was so Paula could "check out" his choice. John did not want to live in the house where his deceased cousins had lived, so he sold the home and bought a three-bedroom condominium. Traci was an associate in the firm of Samson and McKnight, a prestigious criminal law firm that only took high profile criminal cases. Usually their clients were affluent, albeit guilty, but they invariably were acquitted due to their capable lawyers. The facts surrounding Paula's death bothered Traci. Although she had never met Paula, John had frequently talked about her. He explained how she had made her way from being a tomboyish aide to an excellent student and very astute politician, respected government servant and successful investor. The facts surrounding her death just did not add up. However, John could not get the police to reopen the investigation. They told him that there weren't any leads.

John and Traci agreed to hire a private investigator, feeling it was the least they could do for Paula. Not wanting to hire someone locally, they decided to go to Philadelphia. They hired James Carson, a hard-nosed former attorney, famous for solving unsolved murders for police departments across the country. Two ex-marines (Johnson Carter and Prestis Sorrenson), a former Navy seal (Alton Cummings) and an ex-con (Kennedy James) comprised the team. They all went by initials except for James Carson. They called him Car.

Car was a tall, slender, black male, handsome, cool and extremely polished. He could talk easily and in depth about politics, medical issues, and proper investigative techniques. Car listened attentively to John and Traci as they told their story. He told them it would cost about $150,000 if they found the killer and another $50,000 if they assisted in the conviction. After a brief private discussion, John and Traci signed a letter of agreement. Car brought in his team as well as a tape recorder and asked John to repeat his story. Car then told John and Traci to go about their lives as if nothing had happened and cautioned them not to discuss his team's involvement in the case. Car said he would contact them as soon as they had any tangible information.

Several weeks had passed and John hadn't heard anything from Philadelphia, so he called Car. Car told him that he had set Prestis up in an apartment in Rockville, Maryland and sent her to Pressing Secretaries Temporary Services, Inc., a private company that provided secretarial services to the White House. Car had hoped that she would be able to obtain a job at the White House near Cintura's office. Since Paula had been scheduled to meet with Cintura shortly before her death, Prestis was assigned to find out the purpose of that meeting. It had only been a week, and she hadn't reported anything. However, Car advised he would check with Prestis that evening.

Car waited for Johnson Carter, a.k.a. JC, to arrive at PS's apartment, but she didn't show up. He then went by Cintura's office, but it was closed. The next day he had JC pose as Prestis's boyfriend and contact Cintura. Cintura informed him that Prestis had been arrested by the security guards for drug possession and had been taken to the 48th Precinct police station. JC called Car and asked him to meet him at the station. When they got there, JC asked the desk sergeant how much Prestis's bail was. The sergeant informed them that PS had committed suicide in her cell the night before by hanging herself with her sheet, and her body had been taken to the morgue for an autopsy. They immediately went to the morgue to retrieve the body. The medical examiner on duty said that he had received a call earlier in the day that it was going to be sent; however, the body never arrived.

Car then called John and Traci and asked them to meet him at Jonily and Nobility Bookstore's reading room in Northwest Washington, D.C. When they arrived, he asked them who they had spoken to since their cousins were killed. Both denied talking to anyone except the police. Car explained the circumstances surrounding Prestis's death and asked permission to search their home with special equipment to detect listening devices. Both readily agreed, and Car called his men on a cellular phone and instructed them to debug John and Traci's home and call him when they were done. Car's men were already parked outside of their home. Thirty-five minutes later, they called Car and reported their work was completed. Nine listening devices and three cameras were found. They found listening devices in the telephones in both guest bedrooms. A telephone and a lamp in the master bedroom concealed two others, as well as the medicine cabinet knob in the adjacent bathroom. They discovered four more in the living room, the kitchen telephone, and under a chair. They found cameras in the master bedroom's mirror, the living room wall's portrait of Katherine Mansfield and the kitchen's ceiling vent.

After Car's team disabled the devices, Car told John and Traci that they were in danger. The seriousness of the tone in Car's voice got their undivided attention. "Whoever killed your cousin would not hesitate to also kill both of you. These people are very good and very well connected. Do you want to involve the police or do you want us to drop the investigation?"

Car said that he never withdraws from a case unless the clients become fearful for their lives. His team knows that death could be part of their job. Car agreed to give John and Traci 48 hours to make up their minds. They thanked him for his assistance and walked out the door with him. On their way to the car, Traci asked John to drop the investigation stating, "We're both over our heads in this and don't know whom we can trust."

John said he was not afraid of anyone, and he'd die before he gave up. He'd never rest comfortably knowing his cousins' deaths remained unsolved. His cousin and brother had left all of their life's possessions to him. John never wanted their money, just their love. As John was opening the car door, Traci noticed that she didn't have her purse. She sighed and lamented that she must have left her purse inside the bookstore. Traci asked John to pull the car in front of the bookstore while she got her purse. John did as Traci requested while she scurried back inside the store. As he turned the ignition to start the car, it burst into flames, killing him instantly. Traci saw the flames from inside the bookstore and began shaking her head and sobbing.

After a brief investigation, the police mechanics determined that one of the fuel lines was worn and leaked a little fuel on the engine that then ignited. It was an unfortunate accident. Upon hearing their report, Traci remained silent.

Car attended the funeral. John was burned beyond recognition, so they had a closed casket funeral. Traci informed Car that she was moving away. She had lost two cousins she had never met and a very good husband. Traci paid Car $150,000 and told him she was moving back to her hometown, Austin, Texas.

Traci instructed her bank to transfer her funds to a new account and called Cintura on her digital car phone stating confidently, "I did as you suggested. John wouldn't listen to reason. He insisted on obtaining a $2 million insurance policy on himself and me after we inherited the money.

Well, it will be a month before the insurance money comes through. I'm going to take a two-week vacation from the firm and go to St. Thomas to mourn my loving husband. When I get back, I'll put half of the money in your special account. Mom, I'll talk to you when I return."

"You can go to St. Thomas or Morocco, but you better have an air of mourning about you. All you need is an overly zealous reporter getting a shot of you sunbathing and entertaining the natives when you're supposed to be grieving." Traci heeded her mother's advice. She knew well the consequences of crossing her.

TRACI

Traci Barbara Richmond Stillson was cold and calculating like her mother. She never knew her father but hated him because he had left Cintura to raise her alone. Her mother never discussed him. Traci doesn't remember her mother ever dating anyone. When she was in school, her mother always talked about money, position and power. Cintura's philosophy was in order to make money, one had to obtain a position of power. Once you were in a position of power, it was up to you to utilize all means necessary to retain and enhance that power. That's why the haves have and the have-nots don't have.

Cintura had sent Traci to get close to John and find out what he knew about Paula's activities. The plan was for John to relocate to another city after he had received his inheritance. Traci would stay with him six months and then seek a divorce. They'd split their assets and hopefully, John would go on with his life. However, once John had pursued the investigation, he had signed his death warrant.

After Traci returned from the islands, a $2 million check from Universal Insurance Company of Washington was in her mailbox. She deposited the check and divided the funds: half into her new account and the other half into her mother's account. Cintura's special account was a non-taxable, golden investment trust. The government allows individual family members to donate an unlimited amount of funds into the trust. It is invested in mutual funds of the trust owner's choice. The trust is then taxed at a 10 percent rate when funds are taken out. After age 60, there is no tax liability.

Soon afterwards, Cintura met Traci for lunch and told her that her next assignment was to become involved with Justin Morrison. "He is being transferred from the accounting firm of Smearling and Ables in New York to their office in Washington, D.C. His job is to procure additional business from private and governmental sources. Justin plans to have his firm act as a holding company for governmental funds that are sent monthly to Social Security and Welfare recipients. If it works, his firm could realize up to $500 million annually," Cintura informed Traci.

Justin was scheduled to be at the White House for an affair that evening, and Traci's name was added to the guest list. Cintura showed Justin's picture to Traci, giving her a list of his attributes and favorite activities.

Traci arrived conveniently late for the party. She wore a short, black, after-five dress with a deep V-neck. Her voluptuously firm breasts looked like two small cantaloupes suspended in air. Traci's makeup was very modest and her manner was shy. She coyly scanned the room for Justin, finding him standing with his sister, Marla. Traci approached Marla, asking if she knew where the restroom was. She glanced at Justin as Marla pointed to a small corridor across the room. Justin smiled at her and extended his hand as he introduced himself and his sister.

"It's a pleasure to meet you. I'll see you a little later." Traci smiled and quickly walked away. She could feel Justin's eyes follow her down the corridor.

When Traci returned from the restroom, Justin was waiting patiently. He started a conversation by explaining he had just arrived in town, did not know anyone other than family, and was looking forward to getting to know Washington and developing business opportunities. She listened patiently then volunteered to show him around the city. The two of them hit it off, spending the next two hours exchanging bits of their personal histories. Justin offered to drive her home, but Traci declined; however, she did give him her phone number. Over the next few days, Justin tried unsuccessfully to reach her by phone. On the third day, he stopped by her office unannounced with two dozen yellow roses. He invited her for dinner, but she opted for lunch instead.

At lunch, Traci explained, "My husband was recently killed in an accident, and I haven't been on a date since then. It is still painful, but I'm taking it one day at a time."

"I'm sorry for being so forward and thoughtless."

"I accept your apology, and how about having dinner tomorrow?"

Justin was captivated by her charm and honesty and then shared many of his business ideas with her. "If you ever want to leave your law firm and make some "real" money, let me know," he offered.

Undaunted by his comment and wanting to shift the conversation, she replied, "My husband left me financially secure, so that isn't a concern. It's nice that you enjoy the challenges of your job."

They spent the next six months going to the theater, lunch, dinner, basketball games, poetry readings, and dancing. One day, after having dinner in his private suite at the Remington Hotel, he had a violinist serenade them at their table. Justin got down on one knee bubbling with joy, pulled out a two and a half carat diamond engagement ring and said, "I love you Traci and want to spend the rest of my life with you. You are the joy in my sunshine, laughter and success. Will you marry me?"

As he gently reached for her left hand to place the ring on her finger, Traci withdrew her hand with a cautious look of regret on her face. She eased the ring out of his hand and explained, "I care for you and do love you, but I can not accept this ring. However, I will keep it until I can. It is too soon in our relationship to consider marriage, and I need you to be patient."

"My parents already gave me their blessing. I will be patient as long as we spend quality time together, just as we have since we met."

After he took her home, Traci called Cintura on her mobile phone and informed her of what had transpired. "A public marriage is out of the question. Reporters are nothing but dirt diggers, and they'll try to find something in your background to make headlines," Cintura responded. Their mother/daughter connection must lie dormant until it was time.

Cintura instructed Traci to take a leave of absence from the law firm, accept a position with Justin's company, and learn all she could. She was further advised to copy all critical company records.

Traci followed her mother's advice and used the information from Cintura to start an accounting firm, AB Cartel International. Since it was illegal for Cintura to own a firm that did business with the federal government, Traci hired four female Wall Street investment brokers to head her firm. The company records that were filed with the Federal Commerce Commission indicated Traci owned the company. The government didn't know that Traci's will stipulates the following: "Upon my death, Cintura Richmond, my mother, is bequeathed 100 percent of my real and personal property."

AB Cartel International's financial backer was Chastity Bank of Manhattan. They gave AB Cartel International a $15 million line-of-credit because of their sound business plan and $5 million in assets. The Senate Finance Committee had the power to award contracts under $50 million in order to satisfy minority government participation requirements. The committee voted to allow a Washington firm to be their holding company. There were twelve proposals submitted, and AB Cartel International and Smearling and Ables were the top two. AB Cartel International was selected because it satisfied the minority governmental regulations involving minority hiring and awarding of contracts under Section 8(a) of the federal regulations pertaining to small businesses.

Justin was crushed because he had worked so hard and couldn't understand where he went wrong. His company seemed like a shoo-in because it had 25 years of excellent experience in finance, and an Asian family held 51 percent ownership. He was so distraught that he went to a bar after work and spent the rest of the evening drowning his sorrows in alcohol. The next day he called Traci to apologize for missing their date.

"A few weeks ago you professed to love me and wanted to marry me. Just because one little deal didn't go your way, you expect me to take a back seat to a bottle," Traci said curtly.

The more Justin tried to make excuses, the less headway he made. Traci submitted her resignation and returned to the law firm. Justin sent flowers and gifts, but all of them were returned unopened. In his despair, he transferred back to his Massachusetts office.

Traci was content with the knowledge that in less than a year she would make $10 million. Occasionally, when she was alone, she would pose in front of her bedroom mirror reflecting on her hidden income and comment, "That can buy a lot of happiness." Traci still drove her 2002 Lexus and now lived in a $135,000 condominium. She was a team player at work and received the respect of her colleagues. Traci was content to remain in the background as others took credit for the outcome of successful cases, even those to which she contributed the most legal expertise.

A few months later, Traci received an e-mail message about a two-hour seminar that President Bob was presenting at Jefferson-Washington University. He was going to lecture on "Ethics in Politics/Ethics in Business," so she signed up for the course. When Traci arrived, PB was talking about a college schoolmate.

"If there's something she wanted to do, she did it. If there's something she wanted to say, she said it. She didn't push for affection but expected affection and respect from people she cared for. This young lady believed that her friends should respect her right to make choices regardless of cultural mores. Cynthia does not always embrace the old adage that respect is earned, not given. If it is given to her, and not earned, she won't refuse it. Cynthia's philosophy on life is simple but problematic. She feels that the Creator put us on this planet with one mission in life: to get all we can, keep all we get, and wisely and aggressively invest all we can. That's the American way: capitalism in its purest form. Once, she asked candidly, why the President sucked up to leaders of major corporations. Cynthia thought corporations had a big fish/small fish mentality. Big companies buy smaller companies to become even larger. I explained to her that the majority of businesses try to accumulate wealth. It's not a big fish/small fish mentality; it's really a big fish/similar fish mentality. Whether a corporation is big or small, it wants to garner all areas of its market. If it can undercut the price of products to drive out its competition, it will. If it can buy the competition and absorb it, it will do that as well. Competition is good for the consumer and bad for business. Most corporations' allegiance is to the bottom line. They will do whatever is necessary to appease their stockholders, ignoring the mom and pop store on the corner. The controlling margin of error is the profit margin."

Traci sat attentively hanging on his every word, suspecting that this might be the villain who had caused her mother a lifetime of pain. She began to reminisce about all the times growing up and she had read the words on her birth certificate: Traci Barbara Richmond...father unknown...

During the question and answer period, she raised her hand and asked, "Mr. President, do you support corporate interest or competition?"

"I support the American people because that's who elected me. Corporate America is the driving force of commerce; however, it's the American people that comprise corporate America."

Traci thought that his response was a typical political non-answer.

Later that night, Traci called Cintura and requested a meeting with her the next day. Cintura agreed to meet her for lunch at Apple Blossom Mall's Twisty Tyme Restaurant in Washington's business district, on 14th street. Both showed up in front of the restaurant precisely at noon. Cintura always dressed professionally and looked exquisite in her gray shoes, gray pleated skirt with matching jacket, and pink blouse. Traci wore a navy blue pantsuit that accentuated her girlish figure. Her V-neck white chiffon blouse made her breasts appear inviting but were hidden from view.

Mother and daughter greeted each other with a peck on the cheek, complimented each other on their attire, proceeded into the restaurant and found a table. A waitress spotted them and brought menus and two glasses of water to their table. She returned several minutes later to take their order. Cintura ordered a BLT on wheat with coffee, and Traci ordered broiled rockfish, broccoli and tea.

"Is PB my father?" Traci asked Cintura.

"No! And if he were, I wouldn't tell you. I told you long ago that your father was in an awkward position prior to you being born. He could not be committed to us because he had a family. So drop it! We have work to do." Forcing a smile and in a stern voice, Cintura added, "I didn't send you to the best schools in the world, so you could sit around and worry about some bastard that never knew about you or cared if you're living or dead. Now I suggest that you drink this glass of nice cool water to cool your little ass!"

Traci backed down feeling content because at least she got something. She now knew her father never knew about her. Her anger now turned to curiosity. She'd be careful but would find out on her own. Unfortunately, Traci did not know the depth of her mother's distrust and suspicion. The metal buttons on Traci's purses and belts were bugged. Even her home was bugged and had cameras strategically placed, so Cintura could constantly monitor her behavior.

Although the restaurant was filled with patrons, their tables were spaced far enough apart from each other that no one else could hear Cintura's comments. The waitress brought their food within ten minutes, and they ate their meal in silence. When the waitress came to ask if they wanted dessert, Cintura said snidely, "I've had as much sweets as I can tolerate for one day. Do you want anything Traci?"

"No, just the check."

The waitress walked to the cashier's desk, calculated their bill, returned with one check, and gave it to Traci.

"Thanks for lunch dear." Then Cintura got up and walked away while Traci reached in her wallet for her credit card.

Later that day, Traci scanned the Internet searching for anything she could find about PB's background. She pulled up pictures of his children and compared them with her own looks. She surmised that there was a distinct similarity between Arlen, PB's only son and herself. Their eyes and eyebrows were very similar.

Arlen was a rancher, but he never liked politics or the limelight. He was content to stay on his ranch in Willow, Texas. His wife died of colon cancer a few years ago, so he ran the ranch with his two kids Jason and Denise, seven and eight years old, respectively.

Traci told her mother that since she had no pending assignments, she would take a week or two off to travel across the country. This was something she never before had the opportunity to do. Cintura suspected something was up but granted her permission to go.

Traci flew to Dallas, rented a car, and drove 127 miles to Willow. She stayed at a bed and breakfast inn called Pete and Gladys' Breakfast Home. Both Pete and Gladys were 72 years old. They were delighted to have such a young and charming resident. Gladys talked about local events and ran down the list of single men she might see at the local dance on Saturday night. The fifth eligible bachelor she mentioned was Arlen. Pete and Gladys said he was a nice guy but stayed to himself. They cautioned her that Arlen had taken his wife's death very hard and hadn't dated anyone since then, except for a brief two-week fling with Natalie Kamen.

Gladys peered over her wire-framed glasses and said, "Natalie has dated most men in the area at one time or another. She doesn't know how to keep her skirt-tail down. Arlen found out how she was one Thursday night after she agreed to watch his kids for a few hours. He came by to get them a little early, and she opened the door scantily dressed. Arlen discovered one of his drinking buddies fast asleep in her bed. Natalie is simply wicked."

Traci wanted to find out if she had another blood relative. She had grown up alone and so had Arlen. They might have been good friends if they had known one another growing up.

On Saturday night, Arlen came alone to the dance. Traci recognized him right away because he had his daddy's smile, and his eyes and eyebrows were just as she had imagined. Traci wore a simple jean skirt that was just below her knees and a white blouse with a blue-jean collar. Due to the heat and humidity on this August night, she went out without pantyhose or stockings. Her skirt and blouse fit in with the other women in attendance. For some unexplained reason, Arlen was drawn to Traci the minute he noticed her.

"Hi, I'm Arlen. I'm glad to make your acquaintance." Although he owned the biggest ranch in town, he didn't mention it.

"I'm Traci Stillson. I'm new in town and it's a pleasure to meet you," she said, extending her hand. Arlen offered to buy her a glass of lemonade or beer. Traci opted for lemonade. Arlen quickly got her some lemonade, sat down at a table and explained where everything was located in town, telling her a few things about the town's history. He never asked her any personal questions.

After about an hour, Arlen said he had to get back to his kids since a neighbor was keeping an eye on them. Arlen offered to take her horseback riding the next day, and she accepted. Then he followed her in his truck back to Pete and Gladys' Breakfast Home and walked her to the steps that led to the front door. Traci thanked him for being so hospitable and mentioned that she had a wonderful time with him. He extended his right hand as he smiled shyly and replied that it had been his pleasure. Arlen appeared completely smitten by her.

"Let's get started early, maybe 7:00 a.m."

"Okay, but let's go get breakfast first."

Arlen nodded in agreement as he turned and walked to his truck. On the way home, he whistled an old flirtatious love song and reminisced about the evening's events.

To her surprise, the next morning Arlen took her to his ranch for breakfast. They had bacon, grits, scrambled eggs, toast, coffee and orange juice, which he had prepared himself. His kids were up and introduced themselves prior to saying grace. As they ate their breakfast, they eyed Traci intensely. They found it strange that their father had invited a lady to breakfast. Usually, their guest was the widow Hatherway, who lived next door. As they left the table to do their chores, they told Arlen that Miss Traci was different since she was younger than old Mrs. Hatherway. They said she smelled good and was very pretty. Traci smiled, beaming with gratitude, in response to the children's compliments.

Arlen blushed from embarrassment and then asked Traci to go with him to the stable to saddle their horses. As they walked hand in hand to the stable, Traci felt a little awkward. After all, he might be her brother. She remained calm while asking Arlen questions about his background. Arlen's shyness during her tacit interrogation was evident, as he appeared to be blushing while responding truthfully to her inquisitiveness.

He assisted her in mounting a frisky, gray mare, and then Arlen mounted a perky, red stallion. They rode several hours around the ranch.

Traci had never been on a horse before so by the second hour, she could feel that the ride was taking a toll on her thighs and buttocks. She discreetly tried to reposition herself in the saddle; however, out of the corner of his eye, Arlen noticed her squirming.

"I guess Sally has a little too much bounce to the ounce." This was Arlen's sole comment as they neared the stable. Traci saw little humor in the statement but forced a grin anyway and mentioned that she needed to relax awhile after she got back to his home. With a short tug to the left, on the stallion's reins, the horses turned and headed home. The last 15 minutes of the ride seemed like an eternity. After they arrived at the ranch, Arlen gave Traci some Calamine lotion to massage on her legs and buttocks. She went into the bathroom, immediately disrobed and administered the balm.

When Traci returned, Arlen pulled a few albums from the shelf in the den and showed her pictures of his family. His father PB and his mom Diane were cheek to cheek and holding hands. There were also pictures of PB and Diane's wedding. Another album showed PB and Barton in elementary, junior high and high school. The last picture in the album was of President Bob, Barton, and two young ladies in elementary school. One was blond and the other was a brunette. The brunette had a striking resemblance to Traci's mother. Traci told Arlen that he had a nice looking family. She also told him that she worked in Washington and would be in town for a few more days. Traci said she would like to see him again before leaving. He then leaned forward to kiss her, but she turned her cheek and gave him a hug instead.

While Traci was driving back to the bed and breakfast, she noticed a car had broken down on the road. She stopped, rolled her window a quarter of the way down and asked the driver if he wanted her to get help. The male driver calmly walked over to the car and told her that Cintura was giving her 24 hours to return to Washington, unless she had brought a black dress for Pete, Gladys, and Arlen's funerals. Traci then called Arlen.

"I was called back to the office for a very important case. It was nice meeting you and if I accrue some additional vacation time, I'll come back and visit." Then she caught the first flight home.

When she got to her condominium, her mother was already inside. Cintura grabbed her by the neck and slapped her so hard that she stumbled to the other side of the room.

"What the hell were you doing in Willow?" Cintura demanded, with her piercing eyes and pursed lips.

The chilling coolness and seriousness in Cintura's voice caused Traci to tremble while wishing the floor would open up and swallow her whole. Traci knew better than to lie, so she reluctantly told her the truth.

"I wanted to find out if Arlen and I were related."

"I told you that Arlen is not your brother, and you didn't believe me. Now you've made his children orphans. Tonight he was cooking dinner for Natalie Kamen, and the kitchen curtains inadvertently caught on fire. He fell and hit his head on the steel stove and died instantly. Natalie died due to smoke inhalation trying to pull Arlen out of the house. The only reason the children survived is because they were next door at Mrs. Hatherway's.

"Now I'm going to tell you once and for all. You don't have a father. I've been a mother and father to you all your life. I brought you into this world and damn it, if you cross me again, I'll take you out of it. I've made you, and I can break you. I'll see that Gladys, Pete, Jason and Denise have a one-way ticket to join Arlen. Do you understand me?"

Traci wanted to respond, but her voice was suppressed by fear. Cintura, angered by Traci's lack of immediate affirmation, grabbed her by the throat with one hand and by the hair with the other and asked forcefully, "Do you understand?"

"Yes," Traci muttered, as she gasped for breath and shook her head affirmatively.

Traci had a cold exterior but never the depth of hardness that her mother exuded. Cintura's rage made Traci think that she could snuff out her life in an instant and then go to the depths of hell and do it again. Whatever the source of her mother's rage, she preferred not to know, so she ended her search.

The next day's chilling headlines read, "President's Son Meets Fiery Grave in Lover's Arms." The article read, "The police indicate that there are no signs of foul play...The children will be cared for by their grandparents, the President and First Lady." Traci was reading the article and commented snidely, "My mom's good. I have to give her that." Traci touched her neck and browsed through the rest of the paper.

This caused quite a stir in Washington, and expressions of sympathy came from around the world. Cintura sent President Bob a fruit basket with a card that said, "I know it's tough on you now, so leave the grandchildren with Pete and Gladys. That way, they'll be out of the limelight and able to lead normal lives."

It's interesting that even with the death of PB's only legal child, his public efficiency ratings improved. Diane and PB held a small funeral in Texas with members of their immediate family, Barton and his wife and Cintura. They left Jason and Denise in the care of Pete and Gladys after the funeral and returned to Washington grief stricken.

For about a month, the President and First Lady became almost total recluses. In one of PB's most troubling moments of despair, he confided that Traci and Arlen were fraternal twins. Diane and Cintura were pregnant at the same time. Cintura never wanted any children but could not find a physician in the United States who would do a late term abortion. They told her that she might not survive an abortion. When she told PB that she had found a physician in Mexico that would terminate her pregnancy, PB protested and told her that he wanted his child. He agreed to pay for her hospitalization and the child's upbringing if she agreed to carry the pregnancy full term. Cintura protested until PB mentioned that he would set up a $1 million trust fund in the child's name with Cintura as executor of the trust.

Diane gave birth to a stillborn male child several days before Cintura had the twins. When Diane discovered her child was stillborn, she suffered from post partum depression. Shortly afterwards, PB convinced Cintura to let them adopt Arlen, and she could keep Traci. She immediately agreed to the arrangement because this meant there was one less person she had to share the trust fund with. Their arrangement worked out well, and Diane loved Arlen from the first time she held him. The media was not informed of the death of her natural son or the adoption of Arlen. PB had a judge draw up, process, sign, and seal the adoption papers. His secret remained dormant until now.

After a month of seclusion, PB and Diane decided to get away for a few weeks to mourn the loss of their son without interference from family, friends, colleagues or the media. PB left the White House and country in the capable hands of Vice President Spencer Leon; however, he did not have President Bob's savvy. But he was politically astute enough to follow the President's agenda to the letter and not make any new proposals.

Spencer was married to Stella Estavan, his money ticket to public life. He was a sociology professor from Brooklyn, New York, who decided to run for Congress six years ago. Stella was a popular soap opera and movie star. For two months, she campaigned tirelessly for her husband. She used $2.75 million of her money to finance his campaign, and he won by a landslide. At Stella's urging, PB selected Spencer as his running mate. PB needed someone who would help him get the Northern white vote as well as the black and Hispanic vote. Spencer was a fair-skinned black male, and Stella was an attractive Hispanic woman with European features.

Stella urged her husband to talk to his constituents about economic empowerment and educational opportunities. Being an actress, she could anticipate questions the media would ask. Stella prepped him with standard answers, and he followed her advice to the letter.

Political BS is a language very few politicians' wives grasp and respond to because they are either elitist snobs or are too inexperienced in life. Coming from an impoverished background, Spencer possessed the insight he needed to navigate around Washington's pitfalls. He knew the BS game and had played it successfully the last six years. The only direct responses you give are the ones that are favorable to you. The people who ask you questions, whether they are the media, constituents or the opposition, already have the answer in mind before they ask you the question. So, the substance of your response doesn't matter; it's the manner in which you deliver the response that does. Jokes are always tasteful unless it involves a death, ethnicity, or religion.

A very irritating journalist, Stu Simmons, once asked the Vice President, "Do you mind that your wife sleeps with other men on TV?"

"Sure do. The least they could do is go into the bedroom and hand me the remote." This type of smug response kept the journalists honest, and the questions kept the vice president on his toes.

When PB returned to office, he was quite subdued the first month. However, by the second month, he was back to his jovial self. Spencer and Barton tried to shield PB from the press as much as possible. It's always important that the President appears strong and in control. If he shows any sign of weakness, the vultures will be waiting to swoop down on him.

Spencer is one of the few politicians who never fooled around on his wife. He was too scared of the consequences if he got caught. He's the first African-American Vice President, and he knew what price his people would pay if he let them down. It would take another hundred years before any white person would consider supporting a member of his race again. It would be back to politics as usual: White male first, white female second, Asian American third, Hispanic fourth and African American fifth. If you listen hard enough, you will always hear a rattle from the chains of racism. Everyone knows that the myth about African Americans is not true; however, they are convenient distractions to the majority race. The myth indicates that African Americans are less intelligent then any other race. African American men are more athletic than any other race but remain far less intelligent than African-American females. History has proven that African Americans have the oldest civilization known to man.

African Americans have innovated more inventions than any race in Europe or America, but I've never seen a TV show indicate the real contributions black Americans made to this country: Joseph Nichols and Lewis H. Latimer invented the electric lamp in 1881; Granville T. Woods invented the relay-instrument in 1887; A.E. Longand and A. A. Jones invented caps for bottles and jars in 1898; Payton Johnson invented the swinging chair in 1881; George W. Kelley invented the steam table in 1897; Alexander Miles invented the elevator in 1867; John Love invented the pencil sharpener in 1897; Frederick M. Jones invented the air conditioning unit in 1949; and, the list goes on and on. The only thing kids are taught in school is that George Washington Carver invented several hundred products from the peanut and Benjamin Banneker invented a clock.

But no one talks about Charles Drew and blood plasma. Sure, they will talk about Jessie Owens' athleticism, but what about Dr. Benjamin Carson's skill in pediatric neurology. Yes, the myth of the black man's ignorance has been dead, but someone just forgot to tell the media and KKK to bury it.

I know if I make the above comments, I'll be labeled a nigger lover. Yes, I said it. It's out there, and I don't care. I'm just commenting on what I see. I'm just an observer, but I have a conscience, too. When Spencer ran for political office, the first article didn't comment on the Purple Heart awarded him for his military performance in Desert Storm or the commendation he received for resuscitating a drowning victim. The article read, "Black man seeks to be the first Congressman from Brooklyn." Printed underneath was apparently the darkest picture they could print.

I'm convinced the old adage is true: "Men who achieve greatness do not make great achievements. Great men make great achievements." Speaking of great men, President Bob once amicably chewed and shipped out Marinia Marconi for harassing him.

MARINIA

One day President Bob was in the Oval Office taking a catnap. Marinia
was temporarily assigned to be his secretary that day since Dorothy Con-
nors was on a well-deserved vacation. Marinia was young and opportunis-
tic and found President Bob irresistible. As President Bob was catnapping,
Marinia entered his office, crawled under his desk, unzipped his pants and
proceeded to perform oral sex. When President Bob felt what was going
on, he ordered her out of his office. As Marinia got up from her knees, he
could see that although she wore pantyhose, she had no panties on.
Marinia grabbed him hard as she pulled herself up.

"Is there anything else I can do for you?"

President Bob blushed from embarrassment. "No, but I can't let this
sort of thing happen again. I won't report you, but I will have you transferred to a more fulfilling position with Ms. Cintura Richmond in the
White House Chief of Staff Office."

"I hope my new assignment will be as fulfilling as this one, and I hope
I'll have another opportunity to show my gratitude." She glanced at his
eyes, then his torso and walked away. President Bob's eyes followed
Marinia as her skirt accented her every movement as she left his office.

Cintura interviewed Marinia in the conference room. She asked
Marinia to describe her background and assets she would bring to the
department.

"I have a bachelor of arts degree in English, graduated with a 3.5 QPA and am fluent in French and Spanish. My hobby is drama, and I have performed in a few summer community plays."

"What other talents do you possess?"

Marinia smiled and said, "I have no other talents."

"That's not what I heard. I understand you're an expert at fellatio!"

Marinia became nervous and uneasy in her seat. She crossed her legs and grasped the arm of her chair as if to brace herself for an attack. Marinia had never been at a loss for words but the more she tried to speak, the more nothing would come out. She always put men on the defensive with her flirtatious mannerisms. However, at that moment, she was scared and wanted to crawl in the nearest hole.

Cintura looked at her with a stone cold glare and said, "I don't give a damn who you suck, feel or fuck on your own time but while you're in the White House, you will keep your mouth closed, your ears open and panties on your ass! Have I made myself clear?"

Clearly shaken, Marinia squeaked, "Yes."

Cintura reached her hand inside Marinia's blouse and searched under her breast for a concealed microphone. Then she reached under her skirt and continued her search between her legs. After not finding anything, Cintura told Marinia that she would be assigned as a congressional runner. Her job would be to run messages from the White House Chief of Staff to the Speaker of the House and Senate Majority Leader.

"I want to know of any impropriety that goes on. If someone asks sexual favors of you or anyone else, I want to know. If anyone flirts with you, I want to know that also. If anyone feels you on your ass or hot spot, I also want to know that. You will be paid 25 percent above your current salary, and I expect you to earn every penny of it. If you cross me even once, you won't be able to get a job shoveling chicken shit. Now go sit by the desk in the rear of my office and file those folders away in the cabinets adjacent to your desk!"

Marinia did as she was told without comment.

Marinia reported that Senator Gallah offered to take her to St. Thomas for the weekend. Senator Matilda Morris invited her to a pool party the next weekend. Although Marinia was tempted, she declined both invitations. Cintura instructed her to accept Senator Gallah's invitation and suggest that they stay at the Hotel de Grande. Cintura gave Marinia a pin to wear on her blouse and ordered her to put her blouse on the bedroom chair nearest the bed. Her last instruction was to encourage the Senator to give her some spending money.

Although she suspected that something was up, Marinia followed Cintura's instructions to the letter. Unbeknownst to her, the pin had a camera in it. When Marinia and Senator Gallah arrived at the hotel, they were given Suite 713. Marinia and the Senator dropped their bags off in their suite and had a quick meal in the hotel restaurant. They discussed their upbringing, likes and dislikes, desires and interests. He also told her not to call him Senator Gallah. His full name was Richard Gallah, and he did not want to be called Dick or Dickie. They both got a good chuckle out of that. He said most of his friends call him Rich. To her surprise, Marinia discovered that the Senator was single.

After they returned to their suite, Marinia told him she was going to get a little more comfortable. She took off her clothes and placed her blouse on the chair as previously planned. Then Marinia put on a red teddy nightgown and called for him to join her in the bedroom. Once he saw her waiting expectantly for him, Senator Gallah quickly undressed and made mad passionate love to her sweetly and tenderly. When they awakened the next morning, Marinia told Rich that she didn't bring that many clothes but would find something to put on. He reached in his trousers on the floor and gave her $800 to go shopping while he set up a scuba diving excursion. Marinia started to protest but reluctantly accepted his gift. They had an exquisite weekend.

After returning home, Marinia reported to Cintura what had transpired. Marinia said that she really liked the Senator and did not want to be deceitful with him. Cintura encouraged her to continue seeing him but told her to report any information regarding the Senate Finance Committee. He's the Committee Chair, and there are a few bills on his agenda President Bob needs to move forward.

Marinia and Rich became an item. They had lunch together in the congressional cafeteria several times a week and dined together almost every night. Marinia began talking about their relationship with her mother and younger sister, Cybil, who lived in Pittsburgh. They were glad to hear Marinia was finally settling down in a stable relationship. Marinia's mother Ester was widowed twice. Her last husband had died in a coal mining accident twelve years earlier. Cybil had married her first love, Brian. They had met in tenth grade and immediately hit it off. They soon concluded that neither one wanted anyone else and dated exclusively. By the time they graduated from high school, they were inseparable. They married shortly after graduation and currently have a spoiled 2-year-old daughter.

After about four months, Marinia could not conceal her love for Rich any longer. One day she reported to work early, so she could speak to Cintura alone. She informed Cintura that she wanted to quit her job since she and Rich were getting close, and she suspected he was going to propose soon.

Cintura listened attentively as Marinia detailed her fairy tale romance. Marinia went on to say how much she loved and adored Rich.

Cintura snarled and with a calm cold demeanor said, "Honey, the only way that you get out of this area of government service is to get carried out. I have a little background information you forgot to share during our last heart-to-heart interview. Do you remember James Florentine? He said you made love with him one night, and then he found his wallet missing the next morning. And, you must remember Professor Anita Cerio. She hired you to baby-sit her children on weekends, so you could earn a little extra money for college. Professor Cerio discovered her husband back-dooring you in his office after work. Now, I know you remember Coach Saunders. He broke off a two-year relationship with you to save his marriage. To get back at him, you slept with his 15-year-old son. When the son found out about his father's previous relationship with you, he committed suicide by tying one end of his bed sheets to a bedpost, the other end around his neck and jumped out of his bedroom window. Do I have to go on? Yes, you can marry Rich if you want to. Frankly, I don't give a shit! But you better be in here at 8:00 a.m. sharp tomorrow, and the next day, and the next day, until I say it's over. Also, I don't mind sharing a little of your autobiography with him and a few bedroom pictures with his colleagues!"

Tears began to stream down Marinia's cheeks. In between sobs, she said, "Cintura, you make a very compelling argument. Isn't there something I can do to assist you, yet still be with him? I do love him, but I definitely don't want him to find out about my past. I admit I did a lot of foolish things, but I've changed, and he has helped change me."

"I didn't know that all it took was a little bit of passion to erase a lifetime of pain from your consciousness. Sure, we can make a deal. Marry him and have as many babies as you two would like. However, I still want to know what's going on in the Finance Committee. Tell him you like your job so much that you want to volunteer three days a week. I want useful information and his support on issues which I will share with you from time to time." Cintura moved a little closer as she pursed her lips and said, "If you cross me, you'll be the next Crystal Bunston!"

Marinia readily agreed and exhaled a big sigh of relief as she went out the door. However, she couldn't get Cintura's last words out of her mind. "If you cross me, you'll be the next Crystal Bunston!"

CRYSTAL

Crystal Bunston was a young lady who used to work as an intern. However, she was dismissed for disciplinary reasons and killed shortly after she lost her job. Her body was found in a Washington, D.C. drug-infested neighborhood. Crystal's face was beaten beyond recognition. Her jaw was broken in four places, and the coroner could not make a match using dental records. He had to use the results of DNA testing that took two weeks after the murder before he could confirm that the body was Crystal's.

Marinia got the message loud and clear. Passing on information was a small sacrifice she had to make to get the man of her dreams. She was honest with Senator Gallah about her family and most of her background. He took her by limousine to see his parents the following week on Valentine's Day. As they stood near the brook that led to their estate, Rich took out a large diamond ring he had hidden in his shirt pocket. He got down on one knee and proposed to her. Marinia immediately said yes as tears of joy flowed down her cheeks. She leaped into his arms after he put the ring on her finger.

After kissing for what seemed like hours, they made their way up to the main house and knocked on the door. The family butler escorted them to the sunroom where Rich's parents were sipping lemonade. Both of his parents were physicians. His dad was a neurosurgeon and his mother a physiatrist. Rich told them the good news and they were ecstatic. They approved of Marinia despite her lower, middle-class background.

"I've always wanted a daughter, but the only thing I was able to have was a hardheaded, spoiled boy. However, he has developed an excellent taste in women lately," his mother said with a smile. Marinia hugged and kissed her. Rich and his dad just stood looking at this instant bonding and shook their heads.

"When I told Mom on the phone I wanted to get married, I thought that she would give me a lot of grief. But I think she was almost as excited as I was."

"Son, your mom and I just want you to be happy. We're ecstatic that you fell in love with someone so nice."

After exchanging pleasantries for about forty-five minutes, Rich's mother ushered them into the dining room where dinner was served. The Ten-foot oak table with ivory figurines inlaid with gold in the center was perfectly complemented with matching napkins and holders. The paintings on the walls seemed to reflect the Victorian period. However, the blue paint on the walls seemed out of place considering the base and top of the walls had gold trim. The chef, Broderick, placed seven types of fresh bread and butter in the center of the large rectangular table. The oval bowls blended in well with the imported blue Italian china and stemware. After 20 minutes of eating and chatting, Broderick served roast duck and pheasant spinach salad. The very appetizing bite size chunks of fowl were deliciously perched atop the pieces of spinach leave and diced cucumbers. Rich commented that he hadn't had such a stupendous salad since he had visited London's restaurant, Le Roche.

"That's why we hired their chef." Rich's mother smiled and continued eating her salad. During the next few minutes, the clicking of forks on the china was the only sound to break the silence. Marinia could not believe the magnificence of this simple but elegant dish. Rich and his parents finished their salads slightly before Marinia and casually observed her smile broaden as she ate. Just as Marinia was chewing the last morsel of salad, the chef served Kobe steak.

"That's the largest steak I've ever seen," Marinia exclaimed.

"It's traditionally served in 16-ounce portion; however, you may not be able to eat it all. If you look closely at your portions, it is cut into three pieces," Rich explained.

Marinia sliced a small piece and put it in her mouth. "This is simply delicious; how was it prepared?"

As the chef was about to return to the kitchen, he heard her question, turned to her and said, "It's an old Chinese recipe that the English discovered about twenty-five years ago. Kobe steak is thoroughly trimmed of all fat. Then it is marinated with a mixture of thyme, salt, a dash of wild ginseng, saffron, red savina and two cups of 1985 Romantée-Conti wine. A large iron grill skillet is liberally covered with olive oil and set on medium heat. When the skillet is hot, the steak is placed inside and browned on both sides. Then 1~ chopped green onion, 1° cups chopped, green bell peppers, 5 cups Romantée-Conti wine and the steak are placed in a covered dish and baked for 30 minutes at 250 degrees. The covered dish has a grill rack in the bottom of the pan, so only the aroma of the pan's contents soaks into the steak. It is served hot as you can see with the wine well blended throughout the meat."

Everyone admired Broderick's love for cooking and they were momentarily speechless as he described this exquisite dish.

"Thank you," Marinia said, licking her lips. Broderick smiled and returned to the kitchen.

"I'll see that Broderick gives you the recipe," Rich's mother said.

Marinia nodded appreciably while chewing the delicious beef. After finishing her meal, she looked at Rich's parents and said, "I appreciate your hospitality. Rich told me that he had very sweet parents, but I did not realize how sweet you are. I very rarely get a home cooked meal or anything that comes close to this." Rich looked at his parents with pride.

"Dear, we are just glad that you were able to come. You must mean a lot to Rich for him to invite you," expressed Rich's father.

"And, I think it's about time," Rich's mother chimed in. Not knowing what to say, Marinia smiled cordially and finished eating her meal as Rich and his parents continued talking. No one had room for the sinful chocolate mousse cake; however, everyone enjoyed the 1985 Romantée-Conti wine.

After dinner, Marinia called her mother and told her the news. Marinia could hear her mother crying and asked, "Mom, are you all right?"

"Yes dear. I'm just so happy for you. He must be very special as much as you talk about him in your letters. You've never written this much about anyone."

"Can I say hello to my future mother-in-law?"

"Of course, honey," Marinia said in a sweet peppy voice.

"Mom, Rich wants to say hello."

Rich was excited and very cordial. He exclaimed that he was on top of the world because Marinia accepted his proposal and then said that his mother wanted to extend her greetings. Mrs. Gallah came to the phone, shooed away the happy couple and talked to Marinia's mother for about two hours. They agreed to meet the following week more informally at a picnic at Rich's home. Marinia couldn't believe it. It seemed like a fairy tale romance.

As they rode home, Marinia explained that she did not want a long engagement. She told Rich that she wanted a May wedding and that he could pick the date, time and place. He selected May 1st.

"Why May 1st?" she asked.

"It is an easy date to remember. When I was in elementary school, I remember all the fun I had at May Day celebrations. We used to dance, play Pin the Tail on the Donkey and burst Piñatas with a stick."

Marinia snuggled close to him and whispered in his ear, "May 1st it is honey." Then she kissed him on the right cheek and rubbed his chest. Unable to resist, Rich's lips met hers as they shared the passion of two lovers oblivious to the distractions of the world.

At the picnic, the mothers busily discussed wedding plans and every so often asked Rich and Marinia to check the food on the grill to see if everything was okay. The air was filled with an aroma of barbecue chicken and hamburgers. Marinia and Rich monitored the grill as their parents became better acquainted. After they ate, Marinia told Rich that she would get married in a hearse just as long as they got married. They settled on thirteen bridesmaids, and Marinia asked her sister to be her maid of honor.

Rich's friend, Roosevelt, agreed to be his best man. They have been friends since they were sophomores in college and even pledged as Sigma's together. Rich introduced Roosevelt as Rosie. He said they called him Rosie because of all the mischief he used to get into as a child. His butt was pretty "Rosie" from all of the spankings he used to receive.

Rich and Marinia sent out 1,.346 invitations. They got married at Saint Paul's Cathedral in Northwest Washington, D.C. All of the White House staff attended the wedding, even President Bob. As President Bob hugged Marinia in the receiving line, he handed her a bulky envelope and whispered, "Just a little something to remember me by." She took the envelope gracefully, thanked him, and continued to greet the other guests.

After the receiving line, the photographer took pictures of the wedding party outside on the cathedral grounds by the orchids. Later a limousine whisked the happy couple away to the Slatel-Tropicana International Catering Hall for the reception. The only people who had more fun than the bride and groom at the reception were Rosie, the best man, and Pam, Marinia's mother.

PAM

Pam was 53 but looked 40. She had black hair that came to her neck, jet-black eyes and a natural mysterious beauty. Pam was beautiful by most standards, but her personality was such that you wouldn't want to leave her presence. She was down to earth and sincere. Pam had two children of whom she was very proud. She was crazy about both sons-in-law and was looking forward to Rich and Marinia providing her with a few more grandchildren.

When it was time to throw the bouquet, Pam was already in the garden area talking about how lovely the ceremony was. Marinia spotted her and turned her back as the single women waited anxiously for the prize. Marinia tossed the bouquet long and hard. Out of the corner of her eye, Pam could see the bouquet was aiming straight for her head. In an effort to avoid it plopping down on her head, she put her hands up and caught it. The women chided Pam about being the next woman to go down the aisle.

After a few minutes, a chair was provided for Marinia, and the band played an old stripe tease tune as Rich removed the garter. He summoned the single men and said that he wished that each of them could find a woman that made him as happy as Marinia had made him. Rich faked tossing the garter twice as the men lunged for the toss. The third time he let it fly and Rosie made a swan dive and caught it. The men escorted him to where Pam was sitting, and he put the garter on her right thigh slightly above the knee. After the bride and groom had their first dance, Pam and Rosie danced the night away. They enjoyed dancing and having fun. Rosie was a show off, so he fit right in with Pam's personality.

As they were leaving that night, Rosie kissed Pam on the cheek and said, "Thank you for making my best friend very happy by having a daughter that is almost as beautiful as her mother. I have to go home in the morning, but I hope to see you again sometime."

Rich and Marinia honeymooned for two weeks on the French Riviera. Marinia opened President Bob's card while Rich was in the shower. It had a beautiful note which read, "Wishing both of you a world of happiness." There was also a smaller note inside that read, "Marinia, thanks for the office surprise; I think you need these." Inside the second envelope was a pair of lace, crotchless panties. Marinia tore up the second note and put the panties in her purse. They returned home suntanned, ecstatically happy and in love.

Marinia wanted to have children right away; however, after six months of trying nothing happened. Despondently, she went to see Dr. Samuel Argust, her gynecologist, to find out why she wasn't conceiving. Her red eyes, gloomy voice, and fretful disposition gave away her sleepless nights of tears. Dr. Argust listened attentively and nodded as she emptied her concerns onto his shoulders. In a low compassionate voice, he assured her that he would find out what was going on. The doctor took a urine sample and two vials of blood, explaining that he would run a few tests. He told her not to worry and would get back to her as soon as he received the test results.

Several days later, Dr. Argust called and asked her to come in with her husband. He would not give her any information over the telephone. Marinia immediately requested an appointment for the following day at 9:00 a.m., explaining that the curiosity was killing her. She wanted to know one way or the other. At 8:45 a.m. the next morning, Marinia showed up alone and walked into Dr. Argust's office clenching her hands so tightly that her nails were pricking her skin. The receptionist called the doctor, and he immediately came to the reception area. Dr. Argust invited

Marinia to follow him. They walked slowly to his office, and she sat in one of the two chairs in front of his large executive desk.

Dr. Argust said grimly, "The test revealed you have uterine cancer. The cancer is blocking your fallopian tubes, and you need to have surgery immediately. After surgery, you will need to have several months of radiation or chemotherapy treatment. However, either treatment would result in you becoming sterile. If we do not treat the cancer, you will die within six months." Dr. Argust's words hit Marinia like the atomic bomb on Hiroshima. Devastated by the thought of being barren, she began to cry uncontrollably. Then Dr. Argust summoned his nurse and gave Marinia a mild sedative. After twenty minutes, Marinia calmed down. Dr. Argust suggested that she call her husband or a close family member. Still sniffling and wiping her tears on a pale blue handkerchief, Marinia said that she would be okay and got up to leave. As she walked toward the door, she said she would discuss her condition with her husband and get back to him. Marinia was very somber, with tears still trickling down her cheeks, as she drove home.

Marinia didn't know how to break the news to Rich, so she called her mother for advice. Pam said, "Be honest with Rich. He will understand and see you through this ordeal. I will help in any way I can."

Later that night, Marinia told Rich everything she knew about her illness.

"Although I always wanted children, you are much more important to me than kids. We can get your cancer medically treated and always adopt."

"I love you very much and will follow your advice," responded Marinia, teary-eyed and despondent.

After seven grueling months, the chemotherapy worked, and the cancer went into remission. Although she lost all of her hair and eyebrows, Rich hung in there but started to drink excessively and became a little distant. Even after her treatment ended, he lost interest in sex.

Marinia concluded that if he wasn't doing anything with her, he must be fooling around with someone else. She was still reporting to Cintura several times a week. When Marinia couldn't make it into the office, she would call.

Out of frustration, Marinia told Cintura, "I want to save my marriage and want to know who the woman is that is stealing my husband."

"You really don't want to know. If you are patient, the affair might very well end on its own," responded Cintura.

"I demand to know, said Marinia forcefully.

Seeing her determined to get to the bottom of her husband's cavorting, Cintura said, "Go to room 226 in the Madison Conyers Hotel, a five star hotel in Dunmore Fairfax, Virginia, about 10 miles away."

Marinia got dressed and went to the hotel. She told the front desk that her room number was 226, and she had mistakenly locked herself out of her room. After verifying Marinia's identification, the clerk gave her a second key. She proceeded to take the elevator to the second floor. Marinia strutted hurriedly down the hallway, turned the key in the door and barged in to see her husband's naked body on top of a woman. However, she could not see the woman's face. The noise from their lovemaking initially made them blind to her presence. Marinia walked over to them as their bodies exploded with passion. Before their bodies separated, she was able to see the woman's face. The woman turned her head toward Marinia and as their eyes met, they simultaneously said, "Oh my God!" Marinia saw her mother making love to her own husband. Pam and Rich were naked as jaybirds.

"How could you bastards betray me like this?"

"Honey, I'm so sorry. We didn't mean for it to happen. When you were being treated for cancer, we were so scared that you wouldn't pull through, we found comfort in one another's arms. We didn't mean for it to happen, but it did," Pam explained.

"Now let me get this straight. Because I've got my ass in a hospital fighting for my life, you screwed my husband out of concern for me! You two are two sick puppies!"

Rich tried to butt in and said, "Honey, we didn't mean for it to happen."

"Just like on our wedding day, she didn't mean to steal away with President Bob to our honeymoon suite. While we were downstairs dancing and having fun, she and President Bob were rocking between the sheets."

Marinia looked at Rich with a chilling scowl. "When you and I finally got to bed that night, the sheets were still wet and smelled like fresh sex. You thought I had just gotten out of the shower." Marinia turned to her mom with a look of disdain and said sharply, "Oh Mom, what did you say that night? Oh yes, I remember, 'My new pair of white, bikini panties were snatched off my snatch between his teeth.'"

"Look Rich you can have her. Yeah, just stay over there and finish what you started. I want a divorce. I want the house, two of our three cars, and $25,000 a month. Both of you can kiss my ass! I'm out of here. I don't have a husband, and I don't need a mother!" Marinia stomped out of the room and slammed the door behind her so hard that it vibrated the room. Once Marinia got on the elevator, she could not hold back the tears. Marinia started to go home, but she needed someone to talk to. Marinia couldn't call her sister, so she called the only other person who knew her situation, Cintura. Cintura agreed to meet her at LaRouge Lounge. Marinia explained what happened, leaving out no details. Cintura listened attentively and after Marinia finished, Cintura told her that she had known what was going on for a while. Marinia said that she wanted to get even with both of them and wanted Cintura's help. Cintura told her that everything in life has a price. If you are willing to pay the price, anything can be done. Marinia agreed to return to work full time if Cintura ruined Rich without involving her. Cintura agreed.

Rich and Marinia obtained a quiet divorce by flying to Nevada the followng week. Rich signed over one half of his assets to completely sever his relationship with Marinia. He didn't want the anguish of her draining him every month and seeing the look of disgust on her face. Rich had $957,000 in the bank, owned 23 acres of beachfront property in Orlando, Florida, and 12 acres of beachfront property with a 2-bedroom home in San Diego. She took the property in San Diego.

Two months later, the police pulled Rich over for a routine traffic stop. He had downed a few drinks before hitting the road, and the police made him take a sobriety test. Rich failed the test, so his car was searched. They found one and a half pounds of cocaine in his spare tire. He was arrested and his home was also searched. There they found 180 packets of cocaine with a street value of $72,000. All of his assets were frozen. He was charged and convicted of drug trafficking, which carried an automatic penalty of fifteen years in prison without parole.

Pam tried to make peace with her daughter. However, Marinia did not return any of her phone calls but did return all of her letters unopened. One night Pam came and knocked on the door. Marinia called the police and got a restraining order. Pam was dejected and returned home to Pittsburgh hoping that someday Marinia would forgive her.

Two weeks had passed since the divorce and Cintura hadn't heard from Marinia. She called her and told her she had two weeks to get her act together. Cintura explained that love and hate are the two greatest emotions. "Love is hard to maintain because it is predicated on an unknown commodity, your lover. Whoever your lover is, you don't really know him; you only know a few things about him. You know that he makes your heart flutter and pussy jump, but you don't really know him. You give all of yourself to him hoping that he doesn't break your heart. On the other hand, hate is the best emotion. You can control it as long as you harness and focus it. Your problem is you have to focus your anger. Get even with him by reaching through the ally of success. You have money in the bank, invest it. So what if you can't have kids. Count it as a blessing. You can find love anywhere. Most men don't know what they have when they have it. If they did, they'd treasure it a little more."

It was hard for Marinia to digest what Cintura said; however, she knew that Cintura was right. Deep down, Marinia admired Cintura and wished she had her spunk. Two weeks later Marinia showed up for work. When she arrived, Cintura told her that she and Traci, a family friend, would attend a dinner party later that night. Traci would be dressed in a dark blue, sleeveless dress. She told Marinia to wear something that was conservatively sexy and enticingly revealing. Traci would steer two men her way. One was the new Senate Majority Leader, Carl Thomas, and the other was Chairman of the Federal Reserve Board, Smithian Kris. Traci would focus her attention on the Senate Majority Leader, and Marinia's assignment was to involve herself with Smithian. President Bob wanted him to lower interest rates to spur national spending and encourage business growth.

Marinia wore a hunter green, silk dress. It had an eight-inch sheer mesh material on the top front of the dress that revealed her size 38 breasts. Marinia's hair was pinned up stylishly, and she wore black frame reading glasses. She mingled cordially with guests and waited patiently for Traci to find her. After forty-five minutes, Traci came strolling along with Smithian and Carl. Carl and Smithian were quite a contrast. Carl was only 5 feet 9 inches tall but looked very athletic. This was a result from years of handball workouts three times weekly. Smithian looked like a nerdy accountant who was last laid at the turn of the century. He was only 38; however, he looked much older especially with his receding hairline. Smithian was all nuts and bolts and lived and breathed his job. He preferred to talk about finances because that was his comfort zone.

After being properly introduced, Smithian began discussing his job. Marinia talked about her work on the Hill and the fact she had some funds that she needed to invest to get a quality return. Smithian rattled off about twenty companies that had experienced a 40 to 80 percent rate of return for the last ten years. Marinia told him that she had neither pen nor pad but would love to discuss it over dinner at her home. Smithian smiled and agreed. Marinia complemented him for the excellent job he did keeping the economy in check. Smithian said that President Bob had given him the opportunity of a lifetime. This was the culmination of Smithian's lifelong dream. Even though the White House staff had not been pleased with all of his policies, Smithian believed he'd done a good job. Then Marinia inquired about the country's interest rates. Smithian said that now is the time to raise interest rates in order to encourage people to invest. The economy is stable, and he doesn't want to slow business growth or curb economic spending.

While Marinia and Smithian were engrossed in their financial discussion, Traci and Carl danced a few times and left after forty-five minutes. Carl found Traci quite charming and wanted to talk to her in a more subdued setting. They went to the 13th Floor Club at the Belvedere Hotel in Baltimore, Maryland. They had a quiet evening slow dancing and getting to know one another. Carl told her that he was married with a 4-year-old child. He enjoyed her company but didn't want to mislead her in any way.

Traci said that she had no desire to get married again but was looking for someone who wanted to have an exclusive long-term relationship. She could accept his marriage, but would not tolerate any other women. They kissed and spent the next few hours sipping wine and dancing. At 12:15 p.m., Carl drove Traci home. He walked her to the door and kissed her just before she went in.

Carl called her the next day and said, "I had a delightful time last night. I am a little nervous today because I am taking over the office previously held by Richard Gallah."

"I wish you well. Let's meet for cocktails after you get settled."

Without giving it a second thought, Carl said, "Yes."

Traci knew that Carl was well prepared for his new job as Senate Majority Leader. He was a Democrat just like President Bob, with no hidden agendas. Carl often said that he wasn't a "yes man" but liked President Bob's policies and was planning to stick to them. Traci and Carl became a regular item.

Marinia put out the catnip and Smithian followed like an old hound dog to a fox's scent. He set up 20 separate investment accounts for Marinia. Smithian told her that she would quadruple her money in five years while at the same time, she could spend one-third of her funds annually. She showed her appreciation by inviting him to be her permanent escort. Smithian was genuinely honest, telling her he had a few relationships in his life. The last one was with the shot put champion at his high school. On their sixth date, Marinia was invited to his apartment for dinner. She was casually dressed in a yellow sundress. After dinner, they sat on the couch and exchanged childhood mischief stories. He talked about a time when he did a science project in his mother's bedroom. Smithian was building a volcano, and it erupted on his mother's bedspread. Marinia told him about one day while she and her sister played make-up, her mother caught them wearing two of her newest dresses with rouge on their cheeks and red lipstick haphazardly smeared on their lips. The dresses were a little too long, so they found a pair of sewing shears and had shortened them. As they laughed, Marinia kissed Smithian. This unleashed the pent-up passion that had lain dormant for years. They made love on the couch, floor and coffee table. He kissed every area of her body and didn't miss a spot—spending more time in some areas than others.

As Smithian drove Marinia home, he talked about what a great time he had and admitted that she was the first woman that made him want to have a long term loving relationship. She kissed him goodnight after he walked her to the door.

Smithian sent Marinia four dozen roses a day for the next two weeks. She pleaded with him to stop because she ran out of places to put them. Marinia jokingly suggested that if he didn't have anything better to do with his money to send her a $400,000 Rolls Royce with vanity tags that said "MARINIA." The flowers stopped coming. However, to her surprise, the car showed up a week later fully loaded, with the vanity tags and a 13-inch, pop-out TV. They christened the hood of the car with their passion before they took it out of the garage for a test drive. Marinia let Smithian spend the night, and he was just like a little boy in bed with a new toy. They made love until he went to sleep. Smithian woke up early the next morning expecting Marinia to be in bed and she was.

Smithian proposed marriage twice a week after they first made love. Marinia told him that she could not accept the ring because she wasn't ready for marriage. She held Smithian's right-hand, placed the ring in his palm and said, "I'm not interested in seeing anyone else. I love you, but I'm just not ready for marriage."

Clearly moved and contented knowing that she loved him, Smithian made a passionate appeal. "You can have the ring. Keep it until you are ready. I waited this long to find you; I can wait just as long for you to tell me yes. Please don't say no."

Marinia took the ring and put it on a gold chain that was dangling from her neck with a heart-shaped pendant. She took off the pendant, gave it to Smithian and said, "Now you have my heart." Smithian's heart was now entangled in Marinia's web because she had followed Cintura's suggestions. He continued to shower her with gifts: a heart-shaped, four-inch diamond broach, a diamond-studded, gold charm bracelet with their names on it, a three-quarter length sable fur, and a summer home in Cape Cod.

On Capitol Hill, no one cares about relationships as long as you don't talk about them. However, once you discuss it, it's an unwritten rule that everyone else must condemn it. It's crazy, I know, but that's the political climate of our nation.

One weekend Smithian left Marinia in bed while he spoke before the Washington Chamber of Commerce at their monthly breakfast meeting. Marinia woke up and discovered he had left. She read the note he left on the nightstand. "Hi Moni, you looked so comfortable sleeping, I couldn't bear to wake you. I'll be back at noon. Love, Smithy." It was only 9:00 a.m., but she showered and got dressed. Marinia flitted around Smithian's home basking in her own glory. *Finally, I'm on top of the world,* she thought. As she was looking at Smithian's awards in his den, she noticed a high school yearbook sitting on a bookshelf. Marinia grabbed the book and flipped through the pages to see what her man had looked like in high school. To her surprise, he had long brown hair in his class picture. She kept thumbing through to see which clubs he belonged to. Marinia discovered he was on the debate team, investment team and was student government president. However, something was strange; there were no women in the pictures. She flipped back to the first page, and there it was in bold letters, **James Madison All Male Prep School**. Now Marinia felt dirty and used. Smithian had never told her that his high school date was another man.

Disgusting thoughts of Smithian making love to a man consumed her consciousness. She paced the floor until she heard him turn his key to open the door. Marinia waited until the door shut, and Smithian came in all smiles ready to share his morning activities with her. He could see by the look on her face that she was in no mood for pleasantries. Smithian asked Marinia what was wrong. She handed him the yearbook and asked him to point out his high school date. Smithian opened the book and pointed to a male student. "But we never actually had real sex. We only fooled around a few times, and that was a long time ago. I'm a different person now," he insisted.

"You certainly are a different person! I'd like you to take me home. I'll send for my things tomorrow."

Looking dejected, Smithian did as Marinia asked. They were both silent as he drove her home. The moment the car stopped at her home, she got out and did not bother saying good-bye. Marinia strutted to her front door and let herself in as Smithian drove away.

Marinia told Cintura what had transpired. Cintura listened attentively and then told her, "Go back to Smithian because it is important to President Bob that the Federal Reserve Board continues to keep interest rates low. Several Board members are trying to raise them and the President believes that if they are successful, it will result in reduced public confidence and an economic downturn. Make sure Smithian averts this by utilizing his clout as Board Chairman."

"I don't want to go back. Smithian is a closet homosexual and has not been honest with me," said Marinia disheartened and tearful.

Cintura lit into her like a cat on a piece of fish and said, "For someone so bright, you're pretty stupid. Here you are sleeping with a guy for months. He knows relatively nothing about your background, and you're condemning him for playing "hold the weenie" with a high school buddy. Give me a break!" She waited a minute to let her words sink in, lowered her voice and said, "Smithian's given you gifts, showed you ways to make money and maintain a high class of living, and I know the love making wasn't all that objectionable. Here's what you do. Don't answer the phone tonight. He'll call a few dozen times. When he calls in the morning, reluctantly make up."

"Okay, I'll make up with him. However, if he gives me AIDS, I'll kill him!"

Smithian called as Cintura predicted. The next day Marinia answered his sixth call. He was very apologetic, pleading with Marinia to forgive him for his deceit of silence. She finally agreed to meet him for lunch at Heritage Hunt Golf and Country Club. Smithian had arranged for Minard Carrington, a noted R&B singer, to sing "I Love You Lady." The words were so tender and sweet that Marinia began to cry as he got to the second stanza. She tried to mouth the words between sobs.

I love you lady, because you have given me,

The love I need to grow and the joy to set me free.

I love you lady, because I've seen in the mirror what dishonesty brings.

You've seen the beauty beneath a mask of shame.

I love you lady, because through pain and sorrow,

We have mastered our past, mapped out our future and you know.

I love you lady, from the first time we met,

You have tamed the storm in me, and the beast in me.

I love you lady and I'll always let you know

How much you mean to me, until the end of all time.

I love you lady for the rest of our lives,

I'll make you happy and won't criticize.

I love you. I love you. I love you lady.

As Minard ended the song, the other patrons gave him a standing ovation. Marinia hugged Smithian and told him that she loved him. She lost herself in the moment and said that she wanted to spend the rest of her life loving him, but there were so many things he needed to know about her. He said remorsefully, "All I need to know is that you love me. Anything that's past is past because 'I love you lady.'"

Cintura gave Marinia permission to marry Smithian with the understanding that she would report Smithian's activities weekly via e-mail with an untraceable forwarding chip. There is a new chip developed by Minicroft that allows transmissions from anywhere in the world, and the source cannot be traced. Most government agencies have them, yet few companies and private citizens can afford them.

They got married in a small ceremony in Washington. President Bob, Diane, Cintura, Traci and Carl were the only ones in attendance. Smithian had no living relatives; his parents had died in a rear-end collision caused by a drunk driver, Albee Swindel, about eight years ago.

Alberta and I

No, I didn't mean to do it. It happened shortly after Alberta and I had an argument. I had a few drinks before leaving our home to go to a bar, and I was still thinking about our fight. I was driving, and I didn't know the car in front of me was going to stop for a yellow light. I tried to hit my brakes, but it was too late. I slid into the rear of the car, and their gas tank exploded. The impact threw me from my car because I wasn't wearing a seat belt. However, Mr. and Mrs. Kris were killed because they could not dislodge their seat belts before their gas tank exploded. I had just gotten the job with President Bob and told Cintura what had happened. She fixed everything, and I didn't even have to go to court. Smithian received $3 million from a life insurance policy he didn't know his parents had.

I've paid my debt to Cintura many times over. Shortly after the crash, President Bob came to my apartment and told me not to worry; I still had a job. There were no points on my license, so everything was okay. I told him I'd make him proud of his confidence in me, and he said, "I know." He was sweet and seemed genuinely sincere. Being 22 years old and a little impressionable, I kissed him. I don't know what made me do it, but I did. Within a few seconds, the shorts set I had on was on the floor, and we were making our way to the bedroom leaving a trail of our undergarments behind. He spent the next hour satisfying my every erotic wish. I was glad it happened and lay in bed savoring the memories until Alberta dropped by to interrupt my reflections. Seeing the look of total satisfaction on my face, she asked me what had happened. I told her every detail but made her promise not to tell a soul.

The next day I showed up for work as usual at 7:30 a.m. President Bob showed no evidence of our encounter. Diane was with him, and he looked radiant and confident. I drove them to various destinations and dropped them back home at 7:00 p.m. Then I attended a play, *The Phantom of the Opera*, at the Warner Theater. When I got home, Alberta was in the shower. I asked her how her day was, and she said, "It was crummy until my late night visitor arrived. While I was taking a nap in the fetal position wearing my panties and bra, I felt a hot moist tongue sucking on my right breast. I opened my eyes and instantly recognized the President's face. I wanted to experience the joy you had experienced last night, so I urged him on. I did not stop until I drained every drop of love juice that he had to give."

I became angry and slapped Alberta. President Bob was not my man, but she tarnished my memory of him. We parted ways until I saw her again in the Hilton Ballroom. Sisters can share clothes, make-up, and shoes but not men.

To this day, I don't know if President Bob knew it was Alberta and not me. However, I know he kept both pair of panties after we made love. Mine was a pair of aqua, high leg panties and Alberta always wore a violet thong.

I was the enforcer, and Cintura and I were girlfriends. My sister's betrayal drove me into her arms. Everyone thinks President Bob is the one that runs the country; however, Cintura has total control. Behind every head of state is a good woman twisting his balls to keep him straight. Our Amazon sisters taught us to use the power of our superior sex to overcome our adversaries.

Cintura has accumulated over $475 million in assets. That's more than the gross national product of many third world nations. She admitted to screwing President Bob prior to me, but at least she was honest about it. Cintura had given birth to Traci Barbara Richmond and Arlen Richmond but never told anyone. However, President Bob should have suspected something. A woman doesn't take a six-month leave of absence to visit an ailing mother when it's clear in her personnel file that she was an orphan. After Diane gave birth and became hysterical, the doctor ordered President Bob out of the room while they gave her a sedative. He walked toward the elevators to the visitor's lounge for a cup of coffee. President Bob glanced in the rooms as he walked down the hall and saw other doting expectant fathers or new fathers standing at their significant other's bedside. However, Cintura was in the next to the last room he passed. A nurse was sitting her up in bed encouraging her to get up and walk. President Bob came in, and Cintura told him about the twins.

Cintura had graduated from the Sisterhood of Grace Orphanage Elementary School. Shortly after graduation, a childless couple adopted her. As she explained during our quiet time, she went from the poorhouse to the penthouse, and she'd be damned if she would ever go back.

Her early education was a lesson in humility. The orphanage taught her that if there was a God, he must have skipped visiting the poor and needy long ago. Cintura's winters were chock full of colds from the cracked walls, uncaulked windows, and drafty doors. Her first sexual experience was with a horny 47-year-old nun who had fallen in love with her breasts. Cintura didn't complain because of the extra privileges and money she received for her silence. President Bob and the nun had taught her life's most important lesson. It's better to receive than to give, just as long as no one sees you receive.

When Cintura was 13, the neighborhood bully was a large, very agile 15-year-old girl named Cheryl. She lived on a farm with her parents and older sister, Cherylene, about a quarter mile from Cintura's parents' farm. Cintura used to walk that old dirt road to school every day, and Cheryl used to beat her up and take her lunch. Cintura would run away, but Cheryl was faster and always caught her. The biggest problem was that Cherylene was meaner and leaner than Cheryl.

Cherylene was 23, and the word in the bushes was that she had served four and a half years in prison for killing her boyfriend, Billy Jones. One night Billy went out with the boys and had one beer too many. He came home, stumbling in the door singing a popular country tune, "I've Gotta

Git Some Good Lovin." As he went into the chorus, "I've gotta git some good lovin baby," Cherylene came into the room and said, "You ain't gittin nothin here but a couch." She tossed him a pillow and blanket, then walked angrily into the bedroom and slammed the door shut. Billy followed her like a bee to honey. He grabbed her arm and when she tried to protest, he slapped her several times across the face, knocking her into an ironing board in the corner of the room. The ironing board toppled over from the collision. Cherylene grabbed the iron with her right hand as it hit the floor and swung it at him, but her 5-foot-9-inch, 185-pound frame was no match for him. Billy snatched it away, punched her in the face and the stomach with his fist. Cherylene struggled to hold him to avoid his blows and in desperation, she grabbed his revolver out of his holster and pulled the trigger.

Her court appointed attorney, Bernard Stanley, instructed her to wear a conservative dress and look feminine each day of the trial. Cherylene pled not guilty due to self-defense. She wore a simple print dress but no make-up. Cherylene's hands had calluses and broken fingernails. Her boyfriend was 6 feet 2 inches tall, weighed 248 pounds, and was very muscular. She might not have been convicted if Billy hadn't been the county's deputy sheriff. Also, it was reported in the local newspaper that most jurors suspected she killed him out of anger instead of fear. She didn't just shoot him once or twice. Cherylene emptied the gun into his chest.

The jury found Cherylene guilty of second-degree murder. At the sentencing, the judge asked her if she had any remorse. Cherylene said, "No. If I hadn't killed him, he surely would have hurt me. I hope that SOB burns in hell!"

The judge sentenced her to twenty years in prison and then suspended all but five years. She was paroled a year early due to her good behavior.

Cherylene wrote Cheryl every day. Cheryl loved her sister. Four years of not being able to see her caused a deep-seated anger. Cheryl became hardened and came to despise men, as she blamed them for her sister's incarceration.

Since Cintura couldn't beat Cheryl in a fistfight, she decided to outsmart her. She knew Cherylene would be home soon and would endure the wrath of both sisters. Cintura tried to tell her parents, but they were good old Amish people, filled with notions about turning the other cheek. Earlier, she'd overheard Cheryl talking about how she took a bath twice a week, on Tuesday and Friday afternoons. Every time Cintura took out the bathtub to bathe, her mother made sure to escort her stepfather to the store to pick up something she conveniently forgot. One Friday morning while her parents were at the store, Cintura borrowed her father's hunting knife and slipped inside of Cheryl's house through an open rear window. She crept up to Cheryl from behind while she was scrubbing herself in a large washtub. Cintura put the knife to her throat. Realizing what was happening, Cheryl pleaded and begged Cintura not to hurt her, but all Cintura could see was the cruelty that she had suffered at Cheryl's hand. In the span of a few seconds, Cintura's anger turned to rage. She slit Cheryl's throat and stabbed her repeatedly as if experiencing a catharsis with each blow.

As Cheryl's body lay limp in the bloody water, Cintura retrieved a nearby kerosene lamp, poured its contents around the cabin, and lit it. She slipped out the same window she had entered and watched Cheryl's home burn as she scurried home.

The police found Cheryl's skeletal remains in the tub, as scalding hot water from the fire had boiled the flesh from her body. The detectives were baffled by the circumstances surrounding Cheryl's death. Then they found the lamp next to the tub on its side. A large thin piece of tin from the roof was also close to Cheryl's body. The police reported Cheryl's death as an accident.

Some people may have called it cruel, but Cintura called it justice. However, the contented feeling of knowing her nemesis was dead was short-lived.

For some reason, Cherylene suspected Cintura had something to do with her sister's untimely death. When she got out of prison, she found Cintura fishing by Salado's Creek. She told Cintura that she had killed once, and she'd kill again…once she found the person who had murdered her sister.

"I enjoy fried snake!" Cintura retorted.

"My sister was no goddamned snake!" She grabbed Cintura by the throat and tried to choke her to death with her bare hands. Cintura pulled a straight razor from her hair, slashed Cherylene's throat, and pushed her into the creek. She spat on Cherylene's body as the current took it downstream and under water.

Cintura went home and explained to her parents what had happened as soon as they walked in. They became very distraught and told her that the church elders would banish her because church doctrine under the Mosaic Law prohibited the taking of a life, and she had taken two. They gave her $250 saying that was all of the money they had. She would have to go away but made her promise to be good. Before the next sunset, Cintura was in a new home. Her parents sent her to live with some friends, Steven and Carla Gray. The Grays were a childless Catholic couple. Cintura missed her parents the first few months, but after that they became a distant memory because they never wrote or came to see her. To this day, Cintura believes living with the Grays was the first time she felt free from her fears.

I admire Cintura's record of no suspicion of wrongdoing after years of public service. With intimidation, persistence and intellectual visionary skill as tools, she has carved out a piece of the American pie for herself. Cintura has more politicians in her pocket than Old Mother Hubbard has children. It's amazingly simple how she "milks the cow." If Cintura doesn't have dirt on an adversary, she has it on the lover/spouse. Then Cintura squeezes them until needed information/cooperation comes out. The only exception is when the dirt doesn't materialize on its own or her competitors resist her coordinated remedies; then they are eliminated. In other words, "The best competition is no competition." The proof is in the meat loaf—assimilated—or eliminated.

DILLY

"Peaches and Cream—Changes of Hope" is the code name for the White House barbershop. It's located at Andrews Air Force Base. Master barbers Jonathan Peachtree and Miguel San Cream are typical barbers, self-proclaimed experts on everything from politics to sports, love and theater. Regardless of what time of day or evening you stop by, they'll give you their opinion whether you ask for it or not. It's hard to dispute them with a razor at your throat. The barbershop is one place where President Bob can let his hair down. Both barbers are civilian federal employees. They are contractually obligated not to divulge any military or governmental information and are subjected to a mandatory ten-year prison term and/or $50,000 fine.

Today as I sit at my station by the door, I hear Peaches greeting President Bob. Peaches is a 65-year-old codger who is always recounting tales of how life was back in his day. Most patrons determine that he wasn't much different back then from how he is now—always full of crap.

Cream was Peach's one man congregation. Whatever Peaches said, Cream affirmed, "That's right." Once they were discussing women's changing role in society. Peaches gave the opinion that if women spent more time rearing their children and instilling values in them, society would be better off. Then men wouldn't have to search so hard to find a decent job, and the women who had to work would be nurses or teachers.

Cream immediately said, "That's right. I remember the best teacher I ever had could make the most difficult subject simple. Male teachers tend to speak above their students' heads and expect everyone to understand Plato's Theory of Forms without understanding who Plato was or expect them to understand Einstein's Theory of Relativity without knowing mathematics or science."

Peaches then changed the subject to the problem at Mica Corporation. Two mid-level managers had been accused of harassing a female employee. She had come to work dressed in spandex pants and a halter-top. Had they told her that she was wearing inappropriate attire for the workplace and sent her home to change, there wouldn't have been a problem. However, they said, "Honey, you definitely are throwing the right curves today. If my wife had your body, I'd still be at home. If you need anything (while looking at her torso) just call and I'll come." The employee complained to upper management, and they performed a cursory investigation. The men admitted to making the comments. The employee and managers had worked together for several years, and they had made similar comments to one another on a routine basis.

Chief Judge Judy Van Sistern wrote the majority opinion for the court and explained that Mica Corporation was vicariously libel because they benefited from the manager's activity. Peaches adamantly opposed the court's decision and told President Bob, "Chief, I don't know much about the law, but if a female participated in this conduct on an ongoing basis with the two managers, I don't think she can accuse them of sexual harassment. It was probably her time of the month. You know what I mean; every man has been pinched on the butt now and then by a female. The female laughs and you laugh, even if you're embarrassed. No one ever complains. What's the difference?"

"That's right. I remember the time I was in church, and a girl pinched me. I yelled so loud that the congregation turned their attention from the minister in the pulpit and focused on me," Cream said.

"So you got caught fooling around?" asked Peaches.

"Hallelujah! Everyone thought I was caught up in the Pentecostal service."

Everyone in the barbershop howled. President Bob laughed so hard that tears flowed down his face. On our way home he said, "Peaches and Cream would have been excellent politicians as well as comedians. They enjoy their work, help others in the community, and put smiles on their customers' faces."

Peaches and Cream used to have a female barber, Dilly, six years ago. Dilly had soft hands, a big heart, and a foul mouth. She was an ex-marine who could out-cuss and bull jive any man. She was only 5 feet 3 inches tall and weighed about 125 pounds. Her motto was, "Good things come in small packages, but great things come together." When she uttered these words, her expressions made the listener perk up and conversations slant.

President Bob once told her, "You're just a little 'hot ass.'"

"You couldn't handle it if you had it."

"We'll see."

A few weeks later, he saw and she saw. I drove him to Dilly's home that was located near Taylor Avenue in Washington, D.C. It was 2:45 a.m. and the streets were relatively deserted. Dilly's split-level home was on a hill. They were only up there a few hours, but President Bob came down all smiles as I drove him home. He was humming some gaiety song from the 60's and kissing the "hot spot" of a pair of mint green panties.

Several days later, as I was about to take my shower, I noticed the car of the President's physician outside. Apparently, Dilly was a little too hot to trot. But good old Mr. Penicillin did the trick and solved his problem. The next time we went to the barbershop, we were told that Dilly had quit and moved away.

"You just can't keep a good woman because Dilly was a good woman," said Peaches.

"She sure was. But how do you know? I thought I was her only late night visitor," said Cream.

"Damn man. We'd done shared everything—this barbershop conversation and now my woman. We're strange bedfellows. But you're still my main man." Both laughed boisterously as President Bob masked his feelings beneath a tight grin of silence.

DIANE

Cintura and President Bob plotted Diane's demise but sealed their bodies through joint suffering. As his first term was waning, so was Diane's temperament for President Bob's propensity for satisfying other women. I thought she had made peace with herself long ago by enjoying frolicking with me while waiting for presidential summonses.

Diane shared with me that they hadn't made love in over a year, and she wished President Bob's adversaries would hasten his demise. She'd be well taken care of through existing insurance and pensions that were due her. As usual, I said nothing. Later that evening, I reported her desire to Cintura and was advised to do nothing other than to deliver a written message to Paul Comto. I did as she asked, but Mr. Comto told me to tell her no.

I told Cintura his reply. She said that the President was out of town and she would handle it. Cintura calmly reached into a White House office safe and handed me an envelope with strict instructions to deliver the envelope to Mr. Comto within the hour and wait for a reply. Cintura sent Paul Comto copies of pictures from his most recent Quintessential Studies Course. There was a sign superimposed over Tuesday Lawrence and Paul Comto's bodies that read, "If you don't do it, you will come up empty." Mr. Comto got the message loud and clear. His line item veto was reversed.

The next day Paul Comto stopped by to see Diane. He invited her to dinner at an exclusive restaurant in the Department of Quintessential Studies. Diane had no plans for the evening, so she agreed to meet him at 8:00 p.m. in the parking area. Paul arrived first and waited patiently in his sky blue Jaguar that was strategically parked, so he could see her arrive. As I pulled close to the building's entrance at 7:50 p.m., Paul walked over, opened the door, took Diane's hand, and helped her out of the car. Diane thanked him and took his arm as he escorted her inside. Her modest cream-colored, cocktail dress looked almost white as the moonlit night reflected off of its soft chiffon texture. Paul's silver-gray Almonti suit perfectly complemented his athletic build.

Curiosity and the pleasantness of the moment seemed to lure them inside. However, Diane came out thirty minutes later in a frenzy. She looked so pale as if she had seen a ghost. Later I learned that Mr. Comto had shown her two short videos. One was of President Bob's sexual exploits, and the other was of hers. Paul told her that all of her activities and conversations were recorded. If she attempted to follow through on harming President Bob, she'd be arrested, convicted, and would serve as someone's girlfriend in prison for a long, long time. About midnight, I heard an ambulance pull onto the White House grounds. Apparently, Diane had fallen off her bedroom balcony. It was hard to explain how she fell over a 5-foot wall. There were mumblings of suicide among the staff; however, no note was found.

The media noted that President Bob was grief stricken. His numerous friends and world leaders sent expressions of condolence. President Bob ordered the funeral home to prepare her body and dress Diane in her favorite blue evening gown and a blue diamond necklace with matching earrings. As a tear rolled down his cheeks, he remarked that she always looked so beautiful in them.

Emanuel Baptist Church in Washington, D.C., was selected to be the funeral site because it was the largest church in area. They had a membership of 10,000 and Vice President Leon and his wife were members. The church seating capacity was 4,200. They accommodated their large membership by having numerous activities throughout the week and Sunday

Services at 8:00 a.m., 10:30 a.m., and 4:00 p.m. The church's pastor, Reverend Winston Pride, Sr., DD, was a well-respected member of the community. He allowed the Secret Service full access. The church was checked from top to bottom, and the FBI did background checks on the church officials.

Three days later, the funeral director brought in Diane's body. A guard was stationed at the head and foot of the open casket. Her body was on display in a blue steel coffin cloaked in pink ribbons for two days. Visitors far and near came to pay their respects. Numerous mourners left bouquets of flowers and commented how beautiful and peaceful she looked. Around 7:30 p.m. each day the flowers were taken and donated to area hospitals. The cards were placed on a large display board in the rear of the church.

At the funeral, President Bob came in with the heads of state from Canada, England, France, Spain, Germany, Israel, Japan, and South Africa. Vice President Leon and his wife, Barton Craig and his family, a nanny, Jason, Denise, Cintura, and the other members of President Bob's cabinet followed the heads of state.

I don't know what the pastor said in his eulogy, but President Bob looked shaken when he came out of the church. Maybe it finally hit him that a woman he had loved for so long was gone. Whatever the reason, he was silent as we drove back to the White House. The Vice President entertained the visiting heads of states and their entourage at a repast in the Senate's ballroom. President Bob's grandchildren were taken back home to Texas on a private chartered plane.

The next day, President Bob told the press that he was taking an immediate two-week respite at Camp David, Maryland. Surprisingly, the press respected his privacy, and the traditional band of reporters stayed away. His only visitors were Vice President Leon, Barton Craig and Cintura, but I don't know how long they stayed. After I took him to Camp David, he told me to go back to the White House where my services would be better utilized. President Bob said to pick him up in two weeks, and I did as he requested.

Several months later, Rose made the mistake of telling President Bob that she'd give anything if she could have attended college after high school. She said, "I love you Bob and realize that I can't be the woman in your life that I want to be. My past would bring you shame."

Her bubbly personality had dissipated into anguish. I have always thought, "Once a whore always a whore." I guess the old adage is right, "Fifteen minutes of passion causes a lifetime of pain." Our choices aren't as simple as they seem.

President Bob paused for a moment and held her tenderly in his arms. He told her, "Contrary to popular Republican and media opinion, voters don't give a damn about a politician's past. What they care about is the same thing businesses have always cared about—the bottom line. They want to know how much green you are bringing to the table. Are you going to give them tax relief, better schools, lower crime rates, do something about the drug problem that is killing a generation of young people?" President Bob shook his head in affirmation of what he said and continued. "Voters don't really care if you are a priest or a whore. In fact, most politicians are whores. They may not sleep with 5, 10, 15 different people a day, but they will screw 5, 10, 15,000 people a day with nepotism and self-serving policies."

"We've had Presidents in the past that I think did a great job and I have a lot of respect for, such as President John F. Kennedy, Thomas Jefferson, and Ronald Reagan"

"Look at the so-called greatest leaders in history. Thomas Jefferson had more children by his slaves than by his wife. John F. Kennedy bedded more women than there are days in the month, but no one's ridiculing him because he did a good job while in office. Martin Luther King, as great as he was, accepted white and black folk's money to finance his agenda. There were some closest to him who talked about rumors of infidelity. True or false, no one gives a hoot whether you screwed me or the paperboy. The bottom line is what are you going to do with a degree if you earned it? Are you going to use it for toilet paper or as a stepping stone? If it's for toilet paper, then don't waste the money. If it's a stepping stone, I'll find you a job making double the amount you make now."

Well, Rose just about peed in her panties. She loved President Bob but never wanted to admit it to him. Rose didn't want to take a chance on rejection. It took all of her strength over the last year to hold onto the little pride and dignity she had left. Today, Rose finally was able to tell him how she felt. President Bob gave her a gift that had eluded her most of her adult life, confidence. Rose was 32 years old and had nothing to show for it. She cried briefly on his shoulder and told him thank you.

"Yes, you do have something. You have something that belongs to me." President Bob kissed her and patted her left breast.

Rose kissed him over and over as the tears flowed from her eyes, like an avalanche from the peaks of Mt. Everest. President Bob told me to drive him to his cabin in Hanover, Pennsylvania. It was only an hour away. I closed the inside window to respect their privacy, not that it mattered. They were caught in a moment of bliss, and their worlds stood still as they found relief from their daily grind.

The staff at the cabin consisted of a Secret Service agent who was stationed in a guard shack a hundred feet from the cabin. As the limousine approached, the guard came outside and bade me to stop. I drove slowly and stopped as directed. I flashed my ID and indicated the President was inside. The agent took my ID and scanned the bar code in a handheld computer that was slightly larger than a palm pilot. The computer cleared me within seconds, and the agent bade me to proceed to the cabin. When we arrived at the cabin, I let them out; then I parked the car in the garage attached to the rear of the cabin. I went to the kitchen and prepared myself a drink. Then I retired to my room in the basement of the cabin.

At 2:00 a.m., President Bob called and asked me to pick up his personal housekeeper and cook, Ruth Ryner, and have her there between 7:00 and 7:30 a.m. He had called Cintura and Barton earlier and had told them to cancel all of his appointments until Sunday. It was early Friday morning, and I had just enough time to go home and catch a few hours of sleep before I was expected back.

I arrived at the cabin at 7:15 a.m. with Mrs. Ryner. Mrs. Ryner wore my ears out with her constant chatter. She talked about being the mid-wife who had delivered President Bob. His father lived four miles from town and had totaled his car when he hit a deer the night before President Bob was born. His mother's water broke, and she didn't think she would make it to the hospital in time. The closest neighbor with a car was a half-mile away. Ruth was their young maid and had delivered her sister's baby six months earlier, so she was summoned to assist in the delivery. Ruth came in with a scarf on her head and a jean dress and looked weary from a day of housework. She asked President Bob's father to quickly boil water and sterilize some towels and scissors. President Bob had been a difficult delivery because he was a breech birth. Ruth said that President Bob's dad had exclaimed, "That boy's going to be special because he's coming out ass backwards." His dad was so happy he had a son that he kissed Ruth before he kissed his wife. She said that it was only on the cheek, but she beamed as if it had happened yesterday.

Mrs. Ryner was kept on as his personal nanny and to this day, he calls her Mother Ruth. Her pecan skin is a little wrinkled, but she is still a healthy and strong 77-year-old woman. Although I offered to carry her overnight bag, she insisted on carrying it herself.

By 9:00 a.m., the kitchen smelled of bacon, ham, eggs, pancakes and grits. President Bob and Rose were served breakfast in the master bedroom while we ate in the kitchen.

The Indian summer, autumn weekend typified the love and warmth inside the cabin. Warm breezes danced through your hair as you walked the grounds observing the leaves changing from their summer green to beautiful shades of red, orange, and yellow.

As we left the cabin early Sunday morning, President Bob, Mother Ruth, and Rose sat in the back discussing the beautiful day. I wondered if the leaves of time would be kind to President Bob. I guess they would bristle just as leaves do when they are trampled and winter approaches. They become brittle and used as fertilizer for flower beds. Events that are unique to the moment may not be appreciated tomorrow because values change, but their essence cannot be destroyed.

We took Rose home first. President Bob walked her to the door and kissed her gently before turning and observing us gazing at remnants of their love. When he returned to the car, he started to talk about politics, and Mother Ruth changed the subject to cats.

"I had this alley cat once. I cleaned that cat up and fed it well. It was the cutest little thing. Someone told me it was a Siamese. Well about four months later, I was in the park with my cat, and a young white fellow got out of a Bentley along with his cat. The strange thing was that his cat looked like mine, and they got along like two pearls on a string of beads. A long time ago, my mother told me the only difference between a poor cat and a rich cat was where he wagged his tail."

Who knows what that was all about? Was it wisdom or foolishness? President Bob seemed to listen, but I think the old gal had a few screws loose upstairs.

The next day, Chancellor Scroggings from American University called Rose and said that an anonymous benefactor donated a $40,000 three-year scholarship in her name. However, there was a prerequisite that she first attend a year at Prince George's Community College, in Largo, Maryland. The college tuition came with a four-year lease on a two-bedroom condominium in Georgetown, Washington, D.C.

Rose called President Bob and asked to meet him. Monday evening I picked up President Bob and Rose and took them to Watergate Towers where they ate dinner. President Bob admitted to being her anonymous benefactor. However, he told Rose that she would have to earn the degree on her own. He would not call, visit, or write to her while she was in school. But after Rose graduated, President Bob would see her as long as she wasn't committed to someone else.

President Bob monitored her progress over the years. Rose applied herself to her studies. The community college experience with its small class size and personalized attention bode well for her. She majored in nursing and her minor was political science. Rose stayed in the community college one and a half years, so she could complete her license for practical nursing. After graduation, she worked as a nurse's aide from 11:00 p.m. to 7:30 a.m. on weekends. Two months later, the hospital offered her a position as a Licensed Practical Nurse (LPN), and she accepted.

At American University, Rose majored in business administration and minored in political science. She was tempted to join Delta Sigma Theta Sorority but decided against it for fear it would distract her from her studies. Rose thoroughly enjoyed her college experience. The more she studied, the more of a catharsis she experienced. Through reading, Rose traveled the world and learned about other cultures. She found that many of her classmates were from privileged backgrounds but only had textbook knowledge. When the professors asked difficult questions regarding life issues, her classmates had no real life experience to draw upon. This was also evident in other students' reluctance to participate in class discussions and school debates. Rose found her past experiences were an excellent frame of reference to draw upon. She was often complimented as having extraordinary insight. Rose was elected by her peers as most likely to succeed and graduated magna cum laude. The college president was supposed to deliver the keynote address; however, he introduced President Bob as the guest speaker and allowed him to deliver it.

There was an enthusiastic applause from the audience as President Bob made his way to the lectern. The Secret Service took their places around the auditorium. President Bob looked over the audience and smiled. He began his presentation with a joke. "When I was in the third grade, a teacher asked the students in the class what they wanted to be when they grew up. Most of the students gave traditional answers such as a fireman, policeman, teacher, businessman or preacher. When it was my turn, I said that I wanted to be President of the United States. The teacher asked me why I wanted to be President of the United States. Why are you aiming so high? Mother Ruth always told me that life is like going hunting with a large rifle. If you aim for the moon, you may get a star. If you aim low, the kick from the rifle may knock you over. Not only will you miss your target, a dog may come along and pee in your face." The audience roared with laughter.

President Bob waited a few minutes for the laughter to die down and then continued. "As you know, I was recently elected to my second term." He received another enthusiastic applause. The President appeared moved by the cheers but kept his composure and lifted his right hand so the audience would quiet down a little. "Many of you began college several years ago after graduating from high school or working for a few years. The inner drive that motivated you to attend college is the energy each of you must harness in order to be successful in your life endeavors. I want to give each of you a personal gift to use daily. Your self-worth does not lie in what anyone thinks about you. Your self-worth lies in what you think of yourself. Mistakes—yes, we all make mistakes. I have made my fair share of them, and you will to. The challenge to each of you is how you will overcome your mistakes. Will you become a turtle and hide your head in your shell when trouble comes, or will you assess the situation and deal with it, utilizing everything at your disposal? I tend to follow the BOSS system of living.

Be the best that you can be.

Own a piece of the rock. Don't spend all of your hard-earned money on material things.

Stash something away or invest it, so you will be prepared for a rainy day.

Share the best of what you have with those that mean the most to you. Associate yourself with family members and friends who are there for you in the good times as well as the bad. They can be a buffer to life's problems and a sounding board to hash out possibilities. Thank you." The audience gave President Bob a standing ovation. Tears ran down Rose's cheeks as she and her classmates tossed their hats high into the air knowing that their lives were just beginning.

Later that night, President Bob went to Rose's home. He told her that he loved her, but he wasn't husband material. President Bob said that he would support her in any decision she made and would not stand in her way of achieving her life's goal. Rose told him that she'd always be there for him in any way he wanted her.

President Bob said, "Rose, if you really love me, remember the BOSS Principle and go for it. You are quite a woman and have a lot to offer. I've followed your life the last four years, and you've met every challenge and succeeded academically at one of the toughest universities in the United States. I'm very proud of you, and I've arranged an administrative position for you at the National Institute of Health in Bethesda, Maryland. Your job will be as a liaison to Atlanta's Center for Disease Control and the Surgeon General's Office. It only pays $75,000 annually; however, it comes with a larger condominium and a new Mercedes Benz biannually."

Rose started to protest, but President Bob kissed her before she could utter a word. Before leaving early the next morning, he told her that it would be a long time before he could share himself with a friend again.

TAMMY

Due to the numerous assassinations in the 1960's, top officials at the CIA, FBI, Pentagon and the Secretary of Health formed a coalition to accelerate the development of the cloning process. It had already been successfully performed in plants and animals. They allocated $750 million out of the U.S. special funds account to pay for its cost. The best genetic minds in the United States were selected to work on the project. Dr. Satren Molton, a geneticist and hematologist from the Centers for Disease Control in Atlanta, Georgia, was appointed director. They would work on this top secret cloning program at the National Institute of Specialized Health in Rockville, Maryland.

They used blood drives to obtain DNA and blood samples from unsuspecting military and governmental personnel. It was quite easy to get skin and blood samples since pre-employment HIV and drug testing is legal. People are quite gullible and will believe virtually anything the government says, particularly under the umbrella of the Food and Drug Administration, Surgeon General or military leadership.

Also, military gynecologists, who received patient complaints about having difficulty becoming pregnant, would transfuse their patient's nucleus into an artificially created egg, coated with an irritant and permit it to develop to a pre-embryonic stage. The women would subsequently come in complaining of nausea and digestive problems. The doctor would ask them questions such as, "What foods have you eaten the last few days?" "Have you been out of the country recently?" "How often do you and your spouse or significant other have sex?" "What is your sexual preference?" Once the heterosexual patient gave the appropriate affirmative answers, the doctor would inform her that he did not suspect anything significant was wrong but as a precautionary measure, he wanted to test her urine to rule out complications.

Usually, the patient would go to the restroom and provide the requested sample in a plastic cup. After taking a urine sample and dipping it in a multicolored strip of litmus paper, the doctor would inform the patient that she was pregnant and place her on a prenatal program with biweekly follow-up sessions. On the patient's first prenatal visit, the doctor would implant a pre-embryo in the patient's womb. Great care was done to match patients and embryos based on race and sex. If the woman changed her mind, the doctor would simply remove the pre-embryo and use the cells for transplants.

When the doctors were short on donors, they would implant embryos during routine GYN examinations. On a subsequent examination, the doctor would tell the patient that she had a small ovarian cyst. The patient would usually believe the doctor and consent to the surgery. Most people tend to hold doctors in high esteem and take them at their word; however, Jehovah's Witnesses and the Amish were excluded from the procedures due to their religious beliefs.

On May 5, 1986, the first successful clone survived outside of a lab environment. The clone passed the initial physical test; however, she was slated to be terminated when she was three years old because it was discovered during psychological testing that she had no conscience. The coalition did not want to take the chance that she would become psychotic and uncontrollable, so they gave the order to terminate her. Dr. Molton, not wanting to be a party to a murder, faked her death and secretly got her out of the facility in a medical wastebasket. He took her home and told his wife Hilda that a colleague was having marital problems and feared for his child's safety. Since they had been childless for 17 years of marriage, Hilda was ecstatic. Hilda asked what the child's name was, and Dr. Molton looked around, spotted The Common Hunter Magazine, and said "T.C. Hunter."

Hilda asked, "What does T.C. stand for?

"Tammy Cornelia."

They agreed to affectionately call her "T.C.," and she received home tutoring by his wife, a former fashion designer.

T.C. developed normally but tended to be a loner and was standoffish with people outside of her immediate family. She never laughed and found little humor in the concept of laughter. One Saturday, shortly before her eighteenth birthday, Hilda tried to teach T.C. how to make a dress. She laid out material on an eight-foot table and placed a pattern on top. Hilda demonstrated how to properly cut the material utilizing her pattern as a guide. Then she handed T.C. the shears, asked her to continue cutting and to inform her when she was done. T.C. did not cut the material correctly, and Hilda jokingly told her that she would look like a lop-sided fool wearing a dress like that. Instinctively, T.C. picked up the sewing shears and stabbed Hilda with one thrust, as the shears imbedded deep into her chest cavity. Hilda fell forward and landed hard on the wooden floor. Her body quivered for a few seconds and then became motionless. T.C. rolled Hilda's body on its side, wiped off the shears and put Hilda's right hand over them.

Then T.C. called Dr. Molton at work and told him that Hilda was accidentally injured while cutting cloth. He said that he would come home right away and to keep Hilda calm. Dr. Molton hung up the phone, then called 911 and told the operator that there had been an accident at his home. The operators asked Dr. Molton for his address, telephone number and if his wife was still breathing.

Dr. Molton said he did not know if she was breathing or not. He gave the operator his home address and phone number before hanging up and dashing out the door. Dr. Molton arrived at home seconds before the ambulance, hugged T.C. and told her that everything would be all right. When the paramedics arrived, Dr. Molton told them that Hilda had slipped and fallen with shears in her hand. T.C. tried to catch her mother and brace her fall; however, she was unsuccessful. The paramedics felt for

Hilda's pulse and checked her vital signs. Then they told Dr. Molton that Hilda was dead and their procedure was to notify the police when someone died as a result of an accident.

By the time the police arrived ten minutes later, the enormity of the situation finally sank in. Dr. Molton realized his wife and companion of twenty-six years was gone. As Dr. Molton sobbed in the living room with T.C. calmly at his side, the police asked him several questions. They saw that he was clearly shaken by the loss of his wife and cut their interrogation short. However, they asked him to come to the police station the following day, so they could complete their report. Dr. Molton agreed.

At the police station the following day, Dr. Molton repeated what he had told them the day before. They detained him for two hours until Cintura arrived with an attorney. Then he accompanied Cintura back to her office. She asked him what had happened, and he gave her the same story he gave the police. Cintura grabbed him by the tie with one hand, and by his genitals with the other. She began to squeeze and said, "I don't give a damn what story you spun for the police! I want the truth," as she tightened her grip. Dr. Molton confessed and told her that he didn't want anything to happen to T.C. She had been a good girl growing up and had not caused them any problems. He believed it was an accident. Dr. Molton was detained in a holding area while two burly men dragged T.C. into the room. They shackled her to a metal chair, so Cintura could interview her. Cintura had heard about T.C.'s history earlier in the day from Dr. Molton's colleagues. However, she hadn't seen a picture of her. To her surprise, T.C. was beautiful. She was 5 feet 11 inches tall with long red hair and deep brown eyes. Her bust was at least a 38 and looked firm in the halter-top she was wearing. T.C. gave direct answers to all questions but did not add any additional information.

Cintura asked one last question. "How do you feel about the murders?"

"I don't feel anything," T.C. replied stoically.

Cintura offered her a job on the spot as a business development specialist for Project Gray Wolf. Just as the gray wolf steals and eats cattle, her job responsibility would be to seek out prey to be used for President Bob. She would be on 24-hour duty daily, paid $250,000 annually and trained in self-defense and how to handle the latest weapons. Cintura told T.C. that her only choice was to accept her offer or be terminated. However, if she accepted the offer and crossed the line even once, she'd personally take her out.

"OK, I'll accept the job," T.C. agreed.

Cintura said, "Good." Then she ordered the guards to take off T.C.'s restraints and transport her to Andrews Air Force Base for initial training. The next few months T.C. received intensive training. She enjoyed the rigors of training, especially the intelligence apparatus she utilized. On the rifle and pistol ranges, she received perfect scores of 200/200. Participating at the Friend or Foe Obstacle Course Shooting Range was her most difficult activity because she had trouble differentiating between friend and foe. T.C. was born without a conscience and innately worked to eliminate all threats. She shot all obstacles through the heart or temple. The range instructors had to define the characters in terms of threat or no threat. After they did this, she had no further problems.

T.C.'s first assignment was to take out a Chinese ambassador, Zamin Chang, because he was adamantly opposed to civil rights activists in his country. He said that the pro-democracy protestors had gotten what they deserved in Tiananmen Square. Mr. Chang vowed to block any U.S. corporation's access to his country even if its presence would have a positive impact on their economy. T.C. posed as a U.S. exchange student. It was arranged for her to receive a citation from China for her volunteerism at churches and nursing homes. As T.C. accepted her award and shook Ambassador Chang's hand, she had a poisonous dart in her ring. As they shook hands, the dart dispensed its slow working poison. Two hours later, Ambassador Chang dropped dead due to an apparent heart attack. Since their customs prevent autopsies, his body was cremated and his ashes were spread over the fields outside of his hometown of Nayasac.

Cintura was pleased with T.C.'s work habits. She hadn't wasted time completing her duties. T.C. was swift, accurate and left no trace of evidence. Cintura discussed with PB various ways they could use her talents. PB invited Cintura and T.C. to the White House during the Labor Day Weekend. The White House journalists who were usually busily buzzing around and about town usually spent this time with their families. I drove her to the White House around 9:45 p.m. President Bob was in the Jefferson Room. He greeted Cintura with a hug and extended his hand to T.C. as we entered the room. President Bob described the historical significance of the White House and proceeded to give T.C. a grand tour. Cintura and I stayed behind. He ended the tour by allowing T.C. to experience joy and pain in his upstairs bedroom, the same that presidential wives and friends who had preceded her had experienced. Although President Bob wasn't quite up to his usual performance, T.C.'s youthful sensuality caused him to experience the rise and fall of harmonious bliss. Then they bathed in the sunken tub together and explored, discovered and experienced the sensuous nature of the human spirit.

Hours later, they returned to the Jefferson Room as cool as they were when they had exited: President Bob, handsome as ever and T.C. with her placid look of tranquillity. He told T.C. to wait while we accompanied him to the terrace garden.

President Bob told Cintura that T.C. had excellent qualifications; however, she was dangerous. Under her cool congenial exterior, she enjoyed extracting emotions only to satisfy her needs. T.C. took pleasure in pleasure but more pleasure in pain. He could still feel the grip of her nails in his side, back and torso long after their lovemaking was over and their passions had subsided. Her intellectual grip beckoned him to go back for more. However, his poignant self-control compelled him to use restraint.

"Then she's ready for work?" Cintura added.

President Bob responded, "Yes." Then he ordered me to drive T.C. and Cintura home. I did as he requested and then went home.

Six weeks later Marla Morrison announced her engagement to Sheik Ahmad Demur of Saudi Arabia. She needed his wealth in order to continue living an affluent lifestyle. Marla would not have access to all of her grandparents' money until her parents died, and they were only 47 years old. Her $14,000 monthly inheritance check was barely enough to maintain her homes in Carmel, California, and Fort Lauderdale, Florida. Sheik Ahmad found her youth and vibrancy intriguing and her political connections necessary. He wanted to purchase a massive amount of property in the United States. The Sheik had his eye on about 575 acres in Houston, Texas, and most of Kennebunkport, Maine. Immigration laws prohibit non-citizens from owning more than 100 acres of property in one location.

Sheik Ahmad rented The Starlit, a small luxury cruise ship, to take 350 of Marla's family and friends to Saudi Arabia for the wedding. Marla agreed to dress in the traditional Arabian wedding dress including a face covering. As the ship reached the shore, Sheik Ahmad was waiting for them, escorted by his armed guard. His armed soldiers had several tractor-trailers packed with luggage and gifts.

The President and his entourage arrived on Air Force One at 6:00 a.m. the next morning on an exclusive airstrip at King Khalid International Airport in Riyadh, Saudi Arabia. The ceremony didn't begin until 2:00 p.m., so Sheik Ahmad gave the President a brief tour of Riyadh, a bustling and vibrant modern city with commercial centers and industrial areas. We concluded our tour in Harhazelah, an exclusive and posh community of estates located 21 miles east of Riyadh. The Sheik's estate is analogous in size to the King Ranch in Texas. Its opulence engages the casual observer with the Sheik's enormous modern palace, acres of well-maintained botanical gardens, multiple swimming pools and massive security walls with guards patrolling diligently. The palace is elegantly crafted with Italian marble and Islamic inlay. The oak doors are trimmed with gold and remotely controlled by the guards.

As we departed the cars and walked toward the palace, we were escorted to the door by beautiful butterflies. President Bob commented, "They're cute Plain Tiger Danaus Chrysippus and Diadem Hypolimnas Misippuis butterflies."

"But I would rather find some milkweed and Calotropis Procera as a souvenir," Cintura commented in a muted tone that only I was close enough to hear. I never had a chance to ask her what she meant.

President Bob asked the Sheik where he learned to speak English so well. The Sheik confessed to receiving a traditional education in Saudi Arabia. After graduating from high school, he was sent to England's University of Windsor. The Sheik majored in economics and minored in political science. He told the President how much he loved his fiancée as well as the United States. The Sheik also offered to donate $2 million to President Bob's favorite charity.

"That isn't necessary. I'm sure we will be able to reap mutual benefits and conduct fund raisers for our constituents in the future," President Bob replied.

The women gave Marla a surprise wedding shower. Everyone dressed in bathing suits and pretended that they were going to swim in the hot spring that ran through the basement of the palace. As Marla neared the spring, the women yelled, "Surprise!" Marla was surprised and very pleased with the sexy teddies and negligees she received. Later that night, she was listening to Cubby Knight sing, "I Got What I Deserve." She had her headphones on with a mini CD player clipped to her shorts. Marla had her eyes closed and was oblivious to her surroundings.

> I got what I deserve baby, and I deserve you.
> You make my days and nights honey and so whatcha gonna do?
> You feel my every need baby, and I deserve you.
> All my lovin' is for you baby, so whatcha gonna do?
> I love you down to the bone baby, and I deserve you.
> You said you'd love me forever, uh huh and so whatcha gonna
>   do?
>
> I want to come to you baby, cause I deserve you.
> Come on let's rock it baby, so whatcha gonna do?
> Tell me whatcha gonna do? Tell me whatcha gonna do?
> Tell me whatcha gonna do?

President Bob and Sheik Ahmad were returning to their rooms when they heard Marla singing. She was near the pool outside her bedroom patio. As they walked toward her, Marla opened her eyes and became startled because she was still dressed in her nightgown. She turned to grab for a robe and slipped, falling into the swimming pool. Her neck hit a pool hook hanging on the side of the pool, and Marla's neck snapped like a twig. President Bob knelt down and grabbed the hook. The Sheik dove into the water and propped up Marla's limp body as President Bob pulled Marla from the water. They both appeared shocked.

The Sheik kept saying, "But we're supposed to be married tomorrow. This will be a national embarrassment. I'll be the laughing stock in my country."

President Bob tried to console the Sheik and said, "I'll assist you in any way I can. I understand how the public can misconstrue events." After pausing for a few minutes, President Bob explained that he had a member of his staff who was an expert at handling sensitive events. He would find her and instruct her to find a solution and resolve the situation diplomatically.

Then President Bob met with Cintura. He explained the situation, returned to the pool area with her and left her and the Sheik alone to discuss a plan. Cintura arranged for T.C. Hunter to disguise herself as Marla and marry the Sheik. At the ceremony, the veil always remained on the bride, and photographers were not allowed within 50 feet of the couple. Once T.C. put on a wig and colored contacts, not even her mother would be able to tell the difference. The couple honeymooned in Florida and bought several large parcels of land. On their way back to Saudi Arabia, his wife was reported kidnapped by international terrorists. The sheik agreed to pay a $5 million ransom; however, when he went to retrieve his wife, she was found dead.

T.C. became President Bob's most potent weapon. The Sheik paid dearly to euphemistically dissolve his marriage. He agreed to cut $2 per barrel from oil prices for two years and donate $10 million to President Bob's Election Campaign Fund. This would be his second term, and the Constitution prevents him from succeeding himself more than once. However, he is allowed to keep all monies in the fund after he leaves office.

T.C.'s salary increased as a result of her successful job performance. After Marla's termination, her salary was raised to $300,000 annually. This was a bargain considering each assignment she completed was worth 10 times that amount.

For example, Crystal Payne, an extreme right wing Republican and Chairperson of the House Finance Committee, had refused to let the President's bill on national health insurance come out of committee. The last two and a half years, she tried to hinder the President's agenda. It was common knowledge on Capitol Hill that she was a happily married woman of 32 years. Her husband was a successful political science professor at Georgetown University in Washington, D.C. Their four children were educators as well. Crystal's career began as a district attorney in New Hampshire. After five years of successful state service, the Republican Party urged her to run for a seat in the House of Representatives. They were courting woman voters and knew Crystal would be an attractive candidate. Her political views were consistent with the party's. She was a proponent of "right to life," a smaller federal government, big business performing traditional federal jobs and tax relief for big business. She easily won the election and has served faithfully for five consecutive terms.

It was difficult for the President's staff to get close to her because she was grounded in Southern Baptist values and Republican political views. It was decided that they would use T.C. to cultivate her. However, if her efforts proved unsuccessful, Crystal would be terminated. As Cintura, always says, "The best competition is no competition."

Crystal's birthday party was two weeks away, and Cintura arranged for T.C. to be invited. She called Crystal and told her that she had a bright young staff assistant who wanted to get into politics but was unsure of how to begin. Cintura explained that T.C. knew in theory how the executive and legislative governmental branches function, and T.C. desired to seek political office in order that she would better appreciate how the Congress functions. She endeavored to find someone such as Crystal, who had successfully conquered the "old boy network" and was recognized as a skillful politician. Crystal was flattered and told Cintura to make sure T.C. attend her birthday party and introduce herself. She would try to find time to talk to her about the nuances of congressional jobs on the Hill.

T.C. arrived in a plain after-five, hunter green, knee-length dress with matching purse and shoes. She wore very little make-up and lip-gloss. T.C. was very subdued and casually introduced herself to other attendees.

When she met Crystal, T.C. told her that she had followed her career and was interested in getting some career advice. Crystal was flattered and said that if T.C. had time before she left, she'd love to accommodate an aspiring young Republican.

Crystal had a propensity to slightly overindulge in alcohol. She enjoyed the party, mingled with her constituents and talked about items on the current political agenda. Near the end of the evening, she felt a little dizzy, excused herself and went into the ladies room. T.C. followed her inside. Crystal poured water on a paper towel and wiped the perspiration from her face. T.C. commented on how much she admired Crystal and wanted to follow in her footsteps. Crystal reached out to shake T.C.'s hand, slipped and fell forward. T.C. caught her in her arms and kissed Crystal gently on the lips. Crystal lost herself momentarily as their tongues greeted and parted tenderly. She quickly composed herself and said, "I'm not that way. It must not happen again. I'm married." T.C. told Crystal that she was sorry, and she understood. However, T.C. then handed her a business card and said that she still needed advice on how to proceed with her career. She would rather get direction from a woman who knew how to favorably utilize the political process to achieve her objectives. Crystal was speechless but took the card. T.C. smiled and returned to the party. T.C. stayed within eyesight of Crystal during the rest of the party but did not talk to her.

Several days later, Crystal invited T.C. to her home for dinner. Her husband was at a teacher's convention, so she had the weekend free. T.C. came dressed in a navy blue dress that was slightly above the knee. Crystal wore a fashionable pantsuit. She shook T.C.'s hand and offered her a drink. T.C. graciously said she'd have a Hairy Navel.

"I thought only men had those," Crystal said.

They both had a good chuckle.

They talked about fashion, children and politics. Crystal was very candid in her professional and political views. She said, "It's a thankless male dominated profession. You have to prove daily that you belong and are competent. Even though I have two masters' degrees in history and economics, and a doctorate of jurisprudence degree in law, I'm still tested. Why do you want to enter politics?"

T.C. moved within two feet of Crystal, touched her on the shoulder and said, "I have conservative political ideals, and I find myself sometimes moving into areas that are traditionally prohibited, and that excites me."

"I don't have any lesbian tendencies. I respect the fact that you aspire to political office, but sex isn't the way to get there. You have to be honest, trustworthy and stick to your political ideals. You can satisfy your sexual appetite discreetly. Then Crystal handed her a list of political strategists and told her they could be beneficial to her. Crystal said that it was getting late and escorted her to the door. They embraced and T.C. whispered, "Thank you very much for your advice. If you ever need something from me, don't hesitate to ask." T.C. paused, looked her in the eyes, turned and walked out the door.

Later that night, Crystal called T.C. and asked her to come by right away because there was something she wanted to ask her. T.C. was wearing a nightgown but agreed. She quickly slipped on a jacket and drove to Crystal's. When she arrived at Crystal's home, she rang the bell. Although it was a little cool, Crystal was surprised to see her in a three-quarter-length jacket. Crystal thanked her for coming and asked, "What attracted you to me?"

"I found you attractive and desirable." T.C. took off her coat exposing her naked body and kissed Crystal passionately. Whatever inhibitions Crystal had, they were lost in exploring, experimenting and satisfying. After an hour of ecstasy, they sat and sipped wine while sitting in bed. Crystal told her that she never felt as liberated as she did at that moment. The time they had just spent together was eye opening. Crystal said that she loved her husband and would never leave him; however, she wanted to explore their new friendship in more depth. She needed an administrative assistant and would be happy if T.C. accepted the job. It was a year and a half before the next national election, and she could mentor her in the political process. T.C. would be able to learn political survival techniques that are not taught in colleges and universities.

T.C. replied that she was looking for a position where she could have input and all of her intellectual attributes could be appreciated. Crystal pondered momentarily and said, "If you develop recommendations based on adequate research to show that something would be in the best interest of right wing politicians, I will seriously consider your recommendations and will follow many of them." After hearing that, T.C. readily accepted the job offer.

T.C. and Crystal met every other week, a different day of the week, at different locations. They were careful at work and only got close in the restroom. T.C. convinced Crystal that national healthcare had popular support and would not hurt big business if it was limited to people with incomes less than $25,000 annually. Also, she proposed that welfare recipients be barred from participating because they received healthcare through other federal programs. T.C. pointed out that census data revealed that 95 percent of people with incomes of $25,000 or more have adequate healthcare. The other five percent can afford to pay for it themselves but choose not to.

The bill had bipartisan support. The house voted for the bill; however, the Republican-led Senate Committee on Social Security and Health Care defeated the bill and was very critical of Crystal. They thought her stance was too liberal and scolded her harshly during hearings. Stanley Morgan, the committee chairperson said that his committee would never approve such a bill.

It was close to summer recess. Crystal, who never gives up a fight easily, decided to use the recess to court Senator Morgan and garner his support. She invited him to a meeting with her in Morea, French Polynesia. Crystal told him that she was invited to meet with island officials to discuss tourism and trade. Senator Morgan agreed, and she arranged for him to be part of her entourage. They stayed at the Ritz-Simmons Hotel. It was a five-star hotel and the most exclusive 280-room hotel on the island. Senator Morgan was given the presidential suite. The rest of the entourage had regular suites.

T.C. met Senator Morgan at the hotel registration desk when he arrived at 9:30 a.m. She informed him that Congresswoman Payne would meet him in the hotel boardroom at noon.

The Senator noticed T.C.'s shapely figure, pleasant personality and professionalism, and then asked, "What are you doing the next few hours?"

"I'm not doing anything other than reviewing my notes for the noon meeting."

"T.C., how about showing me around this quaint little island after I check in?."

"I'd be delighted."

Senator Morgan summoned a bellhop to carry his bags to his room, as they followed close behind. After the bellhop finished unloading the cart, Senator Morgan gave him a $20 tip. He noticed that his balcony faced the beach, so he and T.C. walked arm in arm onto the balcony and felt the warm ocean breeze. "You may have over packed. All you need is a bathing suit," T.C. said.

"From where I come from honey, most of the time we didn't need that. I was born in San Diego, California, where skinny-dipping is a way of life. Seriously, I never wore a business suit until I was 18. I lived in shorts, tee shirts and sandals. I'd be a beach bum today if I hadn't received a break early in my political life."

They chatted for a few more minutes and left arm in arm to explore the island. T.C. and Senator Morgan admired the huts on the island but wondered how they ever withstood the periodic flooding and monsoons that occur annually. Other than five other smaller hotels, the island was free of Western influence. Vendors lined the streets close to the hotel to peddle their wares since they were prohibited from transacting any business along the beach.

At 11:45 a.m., they headed back to the hotel. They entered the boardroom, and Crystal was already there seated at the table. She saw that they were walking arm and arm, and her initial smile became a slight irritated frown. Crystal told Senator Morgan that she appreciated him taking time out of his busy schedule to discuss some vital issues with her. She explained the significance of her bill and indicated that the Speaker and

Senate Majority Leader supported it. Crystal said, "I don't want to pressure you, but if you looked at the situation objectively outside of Washington's beltway bureaucracy, you'd agree with me."

Senator Morgan looked at T.C. (who was seated at an angle between the Senator and Crystal) and said, "I intend to look at everything objectively, down to the bare essentials. I'll let you know my decision in a few days."

After he left the room, Crystal asked T.C. what she had done with the Senator the past few hours. "I was showing him the island and encouraging him to support your bill."

"Just don't support him too much," she said patting T.C.'s behind and kissing her before she left the room.

T.C. agreed to meet Senator Morgan for dinner at 7:00 p.m. She wore a short jump suit that looked more like a halter-top with hot pants attached. Senator Morgan was dressed in shorts and a colorful island shirt. They strolled along the beach after a delicious dinner of blackened salmon, steamed vegetables and peach cobbler.

Senator Morgan recalled his upbringing. His mother, Ursula Martinez, was pregnant at 16 by a sailor, but she refused to identify who the sailor was. Her pregnancy brought shame to her family, and they thought she was too young to raise a child. They wanted Ursula to have an abortion; however, despite her parent's objections, she decided to have her baby. When she was two months pregnant, Ursula's parents sent her to live with her grandmother who lived in a low-income housing development on the south side of the city. They sent her $200 monthly, and their health insurance covered her healthcare.

Ursula had sent numerous letters to Ensign Stanley Richardson, the baby's father; however, she did not receive any response. She surmised that he was not interested in being a responsible parent. Ursula decided to go on with her life without his support. After little Stanley was born, her grandmother insisted that she finish high school. Almost daily, her grandmother would say, "Ursula Martinez, it's no shame to raise a baby without the father; however, it would be a shame to raise a baby without a job. And you can't get a job without an education." Ursula eventually graduated from high school and got a job with Northeast Airlines as an airline stewardess. After 18 months on the job, she met and fell in love with a handsome young banker, James Toliver Morgan. They dated for six months and got married at John Paul Cathedral in San Diego, California. Soon after the wedding, James adopted little Stanley and gave him his surname.

Stanley was an average student. After high school he attended San Diego State. Stanley took general courses and didn't decide on a major until his junior year. He decided to major in political science with a minor in history. Stanley didn't want to teach school or enter politics; he was just taking the easiest route to get a degree. Stanley figured that his degree would open up doors for him in the job market. During the summers, his stepfather arranged jobs for him as a teller or customer service representative. He enjoyed meeting customers and hearing their concerns. During his last semester of college there was an opening on the Republican ticket for the city's court clerk, and it paid $37,000. However, he was a registered Democrat. He borrowed $50 from his stepfather and paid the registration fee to change party affiliation. After graduation, he stood on street corners, attended community events and handed out fliers. Several classmates assisted him by distributing leaflets. The Republican Mayor, Monaro Cairo, heard about the groundswell of support Stanley was receiving. Monaro agreed to endorse Stanley's candidacy and hoped that his gesture would attract youth votes for himself.

After winning the election, Stanley rode the coattails of Mayor Cairo and garnered political contacts and savvy. Four years later, Mayor Cairo ran for governor and supported Stanley for mayor. At the end of the next term, Stanley ran for a seat in the U.S. House of Representatives and supported Morgan for governor. At the end of his first congressional term, Cairo was content as Chairman of the House Armed Services Committee and supported Morgan for senator. Each election was a relatively easy win for Stanley.

Senator Stanley Morgan had been briefly married to a Hollywood diva, Melissa Rothchild Anderson. Although they were very much in love, the press never left them alone. They could not find time together so their marriage could flourish. Although they have been divorced for six years, they remain good friends.

Senator Morgan realized that he had been talking about himself for the last few hours. He lit a Cuban cigar and asked if she wanted a Tip. He explained that it was his pet name for his cigars. She declined, and then he asked T.C. to tell him a little about herself.

"I was born to two wonderful parents, a doctor and a seamstress. They loved one another and me. However, my mother had accidentally fallen and died as a result of her injuries."

"I'm sorry to hear that. She must have been a beautiful woman to have such a ravishing daughter. According to French folklore, 'The women on this island are so beautiful that a glimpse of their beauty melts the hearts of men and makes their passion explode.'"

T. C. smiled as he hugged and kissed her again and again.

After they walked back to the hotel, Senator Morgan escorted T.C. to her room and asked if he could see her for breakfast.

"I'm supposed to go over some information with Congresswoman Payne in the morning, and we will be evaluating other trade proposals tomorrow afternoon," T.C. replied.

"We've just met, and I'd love to see you again and get to know you better."

T.C. opened her door and asked, "I have a perfect view of the moonlight from my room; do you want to see it?"

Senator Morgan beamed with joy and followed T.C. inside. As they entered the dark room, the red message light on her phone was lit. T.C. turned on the light and asked Senator Morgan to make them a drink while she checked her messages. The Senator kissed her gently and said, "Sure honey," as he walked behind the bar. After scanning the various bottles of alcoholic beverages, he asked her what she wanted to drink.

"Use your imagination," T.C. whispered, then picked up the telephone and called the operator.

Senator Morgan took out two cocktail glasses, some ice and made two drinks while T.C. was on the telephone. The operator told her that she had one message. Crystal had called to say her husband was arriving tomorrow afternoon, and she wanted T.C. to spend the night with her.

As T.C. stood smiling and pondering what she would do, the Senator came back humming and carrying two Singapore Slings. As he handed T.C. her drink, she said coyly, "A Singapore Sling? I thought you wanted Sex on the Beach!"

A broad smile instantly appeared between his rosy cheeks, and he laughed heartily at her candor. She sipped her drink and walked deliberately to her window, as he followed her hips, unable to resist her charm and sensuousness.

Senator Morgan and T.C. gazed briefly at the moonlight before enjoying the sweetness of each other's lips. Their hands roamed freely while caressing one another. Eventually, they shed their clothing and made love well into the night going from the balcony, to the couch, to the floor and to the bed. About 1:15 a.m. while their bodies were still wet from their erotic romp, T.C. told Senator Morgan that she was tired and had to be up at 5:30 a.m. Then she suggested he take a shower but had to return to his room. The Senator was well satisfied with their interlude and complied. She also told him that if he could give in a little regarding Senator Payne's bill, she'd see if she could get Congresswoman Payne to cancel their luncheon.

"I'll give in on the bill if you promise to spend the next two days with me beginning tomorrow afternoon," Senator Morgan said.

T.C. agreed.

After Senator Morgan left, T.C. went to Crystal's room. She let herself in, saw that Crystal was asleep, got undressed and then snuggled close to her. Crystal felt the warmth of T.C.'s body and kissed her as they both fell asleep.

After eating breakfast in bed, T.C. returned to her room about 7:30 a.m. There was an amusing message from Senator Morgan that said, "Good morning T.C. I bet you didn't make it out of bed at 5:30 a.m. today. However, it's 6:30 a.m., and you still managed to shake it out of bed. So right now are you asking yourself, what is the 'it' that Stanley is talking about? Over the years you've heard people say shaking it, doing it, handling it, juggling it, judging it, holding it, loving it, and watching it—don't you get it? Now I can hear your sweet voice saying, it's too early to get into it, going over it, or finding the energy to nurture it, so beat it."

She took a shower and laughed in amusement, joking to herself that all Crystal and Stanley had needed was a little variety and spice, so they wouldn't be so cranky.

Cintura was pleased with T.C.'s progress. She had successfully cultivated Congresswoman Payne and Senator Stanley Morgan. Since T.C and Congresswoman Payne's rooms, bathrooms and balconies were under 24-hour video surveillance, Cintura had ample ammunition to turn the screws of influence as the need arose. She allowed both relationships to develop, that is until Senator Morgan became obsessed.

The Senator romanced T.C. in Morea for three days, and he wanted to extend their visit for another week. But she told him that she had a job to do. Although Congress was out of session until the day after Labor Day, it was Saturday and she was expected back at work at 7:30 a.m. on Monday morning. Her boss is a taskmaster and doesn't tolerate lateness or last minute leave requests. Senator Morgan reluctantly followed her wishes, but insisted on seeing her every day for lunch or dinner.

A week after returning to Washington, he flew in his parents to meet her. They liked her and were pleased that he had finally found a nice woman to settle down with. Senator Morgan asked her several times to marry him. However, she told him that even though she loved him, she wasn't ready for marriage. She enjoyed their relationship the way it was. They had a good friendship, relationship and love life. Why destroy a good thing with marriage?

Senator Morgan could not understand why T.C. did not feel as he did. He felt that any other woman would jump at the chance to marry him and felt insulted each time T.C. told him no. Senator Morgan began to linger around her neighborhood whenever he brought her home from dinner. He rented a home across the street from her and used an old telescope to monitor her comings and goings. T.C. noticed his car in her rearview mirror one day when she was leaving for a rendezvous with Crystal. She reported to Cintura what was happening and awaited instructions on how to proceed.

Cintura gave her two airplane tickets to Rangiroa in French Polynesia. She told T.C. to call Senator Morgan and invite him to join her on a quick romantic weekend. They would stay in a bungalow, have the entire weekend to themselves and she could contemplate his latest marriage proposal.

T.C. relayed the request to Senator Morgan. Grinning mischievously, he replied, "I'm scheduled to be the honored guest at a rodeo and air show in Salinas, California. However, I feel a cold coming on and think going to the islands with you would cure it in short order. I heard that the wine cellars in Rangiroa contained 25 to 50 vats of the most exquisite wine in the world."

They left the next morning and arrived in Rangiroa that afternoon. When they got to the baggage claim area, Senator Morgan noticed T.C. only had an overnight bag and asked her why she had packed so light. T.C. said, "Sweetheart, I don't think we'll have a need for a lot of clothes. God gave you the perfect suit when you were born. Do you mind showing it off a little for me?" She stroked his leg and torso, and he stood smiling yet speechless.

The warmth of the sun's rays was pale compared to their passionate back seat twenty-minute ride to their bungalow at the beach's resort. Perspiration had soaked through Senator Morgan's shirt and shorts. T.C.'s cherry lipstick had dissipated with their kisses, and her jumper was still unzipped to her midriff as a third of her breasts could easily be seen by passersby as they got out of the car. The driver quickly brought their bags inside their bungalow and thanked Senator Morgan as he slipped him a $50 bill before he walked out the door.

The Senator put the dead bolt on the door and reached for T.C.

She rubbed his chest and said, "Baby, let's get comfortable and take a shower. You go in first, and I'll join you in a minute after making a drink. I brought an excellent bottle of wine to celebrate our time together."

Senator Morgan, still stimulated from their romp, took off his clothes, tossed them on a chair and blew her a kiss as he glided into the bathroom. T.C. continued talking.

She took a pint bottle of Kenyan Chan Gaa. It's affectionately known in the Western world as the "two step" special. After drinking a sip of it, you are dead before you take two steps. Others call it Root or a Tornado Special. It's a mixture of formalin, excess car battery acid and methanol. The formalin is a poisonous substance used to preserve dead bodies.

After taking a shower, Senator Morgan made a toast to T.C. He said, "May the depth of your love for me be truly revealed, and may I always love you as much as you love me."

They touched glasses, and Senator Morgan drank a large sip of his wine before T.C.'s glass touched her lips. As the wine made its way down the Senator's throat, his face blushed in anguish as he fell dead onto the bed.

T.C. got dressed and emptied the flask of Kenyan Chan Gaa onto the bed. Then she lit a Cuban cigar, stuck it in the Senator's mouth and tossed a match onto the spilled substance. She grabbed her overnight bag and purse and walked out the door. As she left the room, she smiled at Senator Morgan's limp body and said, "Here's a tip honey. Smoking is hazardous to your health." Within thirty minutes the tiny bungalow was reduced to dust."

The next day, *The Washington Globe-Post's* headlines read, "Senator's Career Up in Smoke While Vacationing in French, Polynesia." There was no mention of T.C.

Meanwhile, in an effort to showcase the ongoing "Harmony of Change with Harmony in the Family" sponsored by federal employees throughout the country, President Bob declared Friday, August 20, 2009, as federal "Bring Your Baby to Work Day." The idea was for each employee to bring their significant other to work so their loved ones could see the employees' strong and vibrant sense of community, giving and sharing. The attendees were made aware of the selfless acts of service the employees had exhibited the preceding twelve months.

T.C. was recognized for her ability to mediate issues and negotiate legislative compromises. Her father was in attendance and told her how proud he was of her. Dr. Molton was retiring from government service and moving to Florida. He asked her to visit him when she had a vacation.

There were 31 other awardees. All were proud and graciously accepted the President's citation as the reporters milled around and snapped picture after picture.

One of the photographers, James Paska was escorted off the grounds because he was a political and financial pest. At one time, James had been the Comptroller of Camden, New Jersey. One day as he was driving from his office to the city's Board of Estimates meeting, he stopped at a light, reached in the back for his portfolio and felt a slight twinge in his back. He felt certain that he had sustained a serious injury and had his back examined by several doctors. The first five orthopedists examined and x-rayed his back and determined that there was nothing wrong. However, the sixth doctor he went to was an orthopedic surgeon by the name of Horace Julian, M.D., who shared a practice with a chiropractor, Chalton Byrd. They agreed to support his alleged illness of degenerative joint disease of the lumbar spine precipitated by acute lumbar strain.

Dr. Julian performed an MRI of his back that showed degenerative changes that could have been due to age. James then filed a workmen's compensation claim. The city's insurance division investigated his claim and found out that he was moonlighting at the Federal Reserve Bank and had filed the same claim with them. The bank paid him $175,000 on the claim. After his improprieties were discovered, he was tried, convicted of fraud and served eighteen months of a ten-year prison sentence. When he was released from prison, he couldn't find a job. Then he purchased a few cameras and started chasing celebrities and ambulances, so he could sell his stories and photos to newspapers and magazines.

President Bob and others on the Hill affectionately referred to him as "James Pissy." They stayed away from him because between the press and the law, he always ended up painting himself into a legal corner. However, this changed after the awards banquet. Before being tossed out of the White House grounds by the Secret Service, James had slipped Cintura a note offering her $50,000 if she gave him access to the White House. He wanted to catch President Bob in a compromising situation. Supermarket tabloids pay top dollar for stories about heads of states.

Cintura showed the note to President Bob. President Bob told her to make sure Paska received as shocking an answer to his shocking proposal. Cintura called T.C. and gave her instructions on how to dispose of him.

T.C. left the office, went home and changed her clothes. She wore a white halter-top, a hot red, micro mini-skirt, four-inch, red pump shoes, black fishnet stockings and a blond wig. T.C. painted a mole on her right cheek, red lipstick on her lips and black eyeliner on her eyelids. She grabbed her small red shoulder bag on her way out the door. Then she drove to the police station and paid Mr. Paska's bail of $4,500.

Looking perplexed, he muttered, "Why did you bail me out?"

She grinned slightly and replied, "I admire you for trying to gain access to the White House. President Bob is nothing but a womanizer and a cheat. He raped me a year ago while I was working a temporary job as a secretary, and President Bob paid me $20,000 to forget about it. I thought I could, but it's hard. That's why I'm working the streets, just trying to get the experience out of my mind. However, whomever I'm with, flashbacks of that experience just keep coming back. I'm off work until tonight; where can I drop you off."

"I live at 1784 Wisconsin Terrace. I'll pay you $25,000 for your story if you go back with me, so I can write it down on my computer."

"Okay, but I want cash. I don't take checks from any of my customers, and I'm not taking one from you."

"All right. Then stop at 1st District National Bank; it's only six blocks away."

T.C. drove her Mercedes Sports Coupe and parked it across the street from the bank. Mr. Paska got out and returned twenty minutes later with the money. He showed her the money and agreed to give her $12,500 right away and the other $12,500 when they got to his house. T.C. smiled and nodded in approval. After Mr. Paska gave her an envelope with 250 crisp $50 bills, she drove him home.

When they arrived at his home, T.C. asked for the rest of the money. He willingly gave it to her. T.C. then asked to use the restroom. Mr. Paska escorted her inside and told her that the powder room was down the hall to the left, adjacent to the living room. As she hurried to the restroom, he commented that he was going to fix some coffee while he waited for her. T.C. said that she did not want any, so he just fixed a cup for himself. Several minutes later, T.C. strolled into the kitchen and mentioned that when she had used the commode, the toilet would not flush. Mr. Paska was a little irritated; however, he hurried to the bathroom to flush the commode. As he pushed down on the toilet handle, he let out a loud yell. The jolt from the commode handle made him jump five feet against the bathroom wall; then he fell dead. T.C. put on a pair of plastic gloves from her purse. She then removed the 12-volt car battery from the commode's tank and the wire that led to the handle. T.C. plugged in a small electric radio and placed it in the sink.

T.C. left Mr. Paska's home and got inside the gray sedan that was waiting for her. When she arrived home, she took off her disguise and gave it to the driver. The car had untraceable tags. Everyone knew that the state used prison labor to make license plates. For a few dollars you could obtain a few plates under the table. Cintura had thought of everything. Not only were the car's tags untraceable, T.C.'s clothes were destroyed.

President Bob took pleasure in knowing that James "Pissy" Paska was no longer a threat. He mused that Paska's hair stood on end as he met his end. President Bob commented that he must have been an ugly sight, but he wasn't as ugly as some other things were, particularly laws.

There was an "Ugly" law in Chicago that allowed the state court to fine an ugly person from $1 to $50 daily for appearing in public. Illinois Governor George Wallin had anchored a six-month campaign to discourage disabled and disfigured people from appearing in public. He noted that their appearance weakened our nation because they made the U.S. appear weak and helpless in an ever-changing world. One day his mother, Mable Wallin, had injured herself while handling fireworks. However, she wasn't a candidate for plastic surgery because her burns were too severe. After coming home from the hospital following a month of comprehensive treatment, Governor Wallin discouraged her from going out.

However, one morning Mable went out grocery shopping at a major food market, so customers complained that her grotesque appearance made them sick. The store manager, Mr. Henry Parkson, asked her to leave the store, but she refused because she hadn't finished shopping. Mr. Parkson called the police, and Mable was arrested and charged with violating the "Ugly" law. She refused to pay the $50 fine or sign the citation. Sandy Collins, the court commissioner, cited Mable with contempt then set her bail at $500. Mable refused to post bail and was fingerprinted and jailed. Governor Wallin attempted to get his mother out of jail without going to the city jail. Later that same day, he sent his secretary with $500 to bail her out, but Mable refused to accept bail. At 2:30 a.m., the Governor went to convince her to come out. He told Mable that although he loved her, she was an embarrassment to him.

Mable reminded George that when she was pregnant with him, she had become disfigured for nine months. She could have had an abortion to retain her girlish figure, but instead, she suffered embarrassment for 36 weeks and had him. She often told him to think about the old boxing maxim that says, "It's the shape of your character and not your kisser that counts. If you can't remember that, then you're not worthy of being my son."

The first two weeks of this bizarre mother-son debacle was funny. However, as it dragged on, it proved to be the primary topic of local, state and national politics.

However, when President Bob went to China recently, Chinese Premier Mao-tai Tse-tung asked him, "What do an ugly duck and a doctor with chickenpox have in common."

"I don't know."

"Both are quacks, ugly enough to be arrested but can go out freely when their condition wears off," replied Premier Tse-tung.

President Bob smiled but didn't laugh. He ordered Cintura to resolve the Chicago problem immediately.

Cintura had Governor Mallin arrested late that night and transported him to the state psychiatric hospital. Upon his arrival, he was taken to the ground floor, stripped naked and beaten with wet towels with oranges wrapped inside. Next, he was injected with heroin and left in the cold basement tied with silk cords. The next day he was awakened at 6:00 a.m. and beaten again. He kept crying out, "Why are you doing this to me? I haven't done anything to you." The Governor was gagged and lost consciousness several times only to be awakened with buckets of cold urine tossed in his face.

Around noon the next day, Cintura arrived and spoke to the Governor. She said, "I'm going to say this one time and one time only. Firstly, by 3:30 p.m. today, you will have your mother home and allow her to go anywhere she pleases per a special gubernatorial order. Secondly, you will request a special session to repeal the "Ugly" law within two weeks. Thirdly, you will publicly declare that Illinois was wrong in enacting the law and doubly so for not removing it from the books years ago. If these three things aren't done within the time frames I just mentioned or you mention your ordeal to anyone, your life will terminate in two weeks and one day from today. There will be no discussion. The guards will blindfold you and return you near your home."

Two weeks later, everything that Cintura had told him to do was done. The Governor was now a changed man. He became an advocate for the poor and downtrodden. His mother couldn't understand the sudden change in her son, but she was quite pleased that he had become so protective and supportive of her.

Several months after the law was repealed, Governor Mallin was in a car accident. He was experiencing a flashback from his ordeal, suffered a heart attack and lost control of the car he was driving. The Governor was hospitalized for three weeks before being discharged with the following instructions:

- As tolerated, walk and climb stairs, but do not lift, push or pull anything heavier than ten pounds or drive for four to six weeks;

- Follow-up with Dr. Pin in four weeks, and schedule an appointment with home health; and

- Call Dr. Pin and report complaints of chest pain, shortness of breath, nausea, vomiting, or excessive fever.

His mother cared for him while his body healed, and he had to take a leave of absence from his job.

TAYLOR AND TEAL

There are always a few people you meet along the way whom you wished you had never met, yet once you meet them, they tend to become leeches. They suck all of the blood they can get out of you and then move on. If you don't keep your guard up, they'll be like the brown bomber and hit you with a nice short uppercut and knock you senseless before you can see it coming. Taylor Moriana and Teal Reynolds were both like leeches. No, they weren't sisters, but they had been friends since childhood. What unified them was their ability to play coattail politics. They'd ride anyone's coattail they thought would put them ahead. After I got my job with President Bob, they pressured me, insisting that I find them a position within the government. As Taylor puts it, "They wanted a cruising type of job, and they weren't cruising for a bruising."

When I told President Bob my dilemma, he pretended to be generally interested—and he was. The Fraternal Order of Police was having their national conference at the Washington Marriott. President Bob was invited to be the keynote speaker and asked me to bring Taylor and Teal to see him in the presidential suite prior to the meeting in the ballroom. They both wore short black dresses. Taylor's low V-neck cut exposed her well-endowed breasts and Teal's dress had a full collar; however, the right side of her dress had an 8-inch slit. When she sat down, the slit in her dress rose slightly below her panty line. President Bob asked both women how much they were willing to sacrifice for their country. Taylor and Teal said that they would be willing to do whatever it took. They did not have a great deal of work experience but were willing to learn. Taylor had an undergraduate degree from Dartmouth in computer science, and Teal had a bachelor's degree in English literature and a master's degree in sociology. Both brought resumes and letters of support. However, President Bob told them he had colleagues perform a little background check on them.

"I know that both of you are attempting to use your influence with Albee to obtain a prominent position. I respect people who are ambitious and want you to take a test that will give me sufficient information to properly evaluate your knowledge, skills and abilities. If each of you passes the test, I will arrange jobs so you can work in the same building but for different individuals. However, if only one of you passes the test, only that person will be given a job. The starting annual salary is $75,000, and the job may require occasional travel," said President Bob.

Taylor blurted out, "For $75,000 a year, I'd make love to you every day of the week and twice on Sundays."

"Then we have a deal?"

"I was only kidding. I wasn't serious."

Teal cut in and said, "Taylor, let's go powder our noses." She grabbed her by the hand and took her into the bathroom."

Once they closed the bathroom door, Teal told Taylor that $75,000 is three times as much as they made at their last job two years ago. For a little inconvenience, they'd be well compensated. Taylor nodded her head in affirmation. They returned from the restroom and told President Bob they accepted his offer. He told them that their test was to be his personal chaperones that night. President Bob was spending the night at the hotel in his suite and wanted them to attend to his every need. He then took off their panties and invited them to join him downstairs at the conference. President Bob told them they would be his inspiration as he delivered his speech. They were flattered and giggled as they left the room and joined the other guests downstairs in the ballroom.

President Bob entered the room moments later to a standing ovation. Reporters scrambled to get as close as they could to the podium as if they'd miss a major world development and hung on his every word. His speech had me in tears.

"My fellow law enforcement officers, I understand your situation. You are charged by your communities to enforce the law, and the very people you are sworn to protect constantly stab you in your back or place barriers in your way to hinder your progress. As President, I know firsthand how your opposition will try their damnedest to dig up enough dirt to tarnish your reputation. I will stand on my integrity and boldly articulate my vision for the United States of America today, tonight and as many times as necessary, so that all will know that we are committed to the ideals and principles that keep our nation strong and steadfast."

The audience applauded enthusiastically for ten minutes as President Bob left the podium and shook hands with attendees. Taylor and Teal followed him to his suite as he left the room. I took my station in the adjacent room. I know even the king-size presidential bed had difficulty accommodating their night activity from the bump and grinding noises that kept me awake most of the night.

Taylor was not a small woman, but she had a sweet smile and cute face. She stood 5 feet 6 inches tall and weighed about 210 pounds. Taylor had tried many diets, but none seemed to work out. She'd lose 30 to 40 pounds but always felt hungry. Exercise caused her to lose body fat; however, she became crabby and short-tempered. Taylor also felt as though her face looked like it was sunken in. After several years of dieting, Taylor concluded that she enjoyed being pleasingly plump. Any man who wanted her had to accept her just the way she was.

Teal was also quite chubby. She was 5 feet 8 inches tall, weighed about 230 pounds and was a happy-go-lucky person. Teal was adventurous and enjoyed meeting men although her size made most of them shy away. About seven years ago, Taylor and Teal tried losing weight at a dieting workshop. However, their propensity for enjoying strawberry shortcake and butter pecan ice cream overrode their desire to lose weight on a diet of tofu salad and baked eggplant. Teal always maintained a good attitude about her weight. She said, "Some men like a sheet and some men like a blanket. My man likes a blanket to keep him warm in the winter and something to think about in the summer. If you can't rock it, then don't knock it!"

President Bob was what some women call "a total pleaser." If a woman hadn't known all of the sensitive spots on her body prior to meeting President Bob, she did after she got to know him. That's why they always came back and were loyal to him. He never lied to them and didn't make any promises he couldn't fulfill. Occasionally, he requested that they use their talents to retrieve information; however, if they were hesitant to accept an assignment, he didn't pressure them. President Bob said that he'd rather have someone do a job confidently than a nervous person blow their cover trying.

LORI

That's similar to what Cintura said about recently hiring Carl Peters and Lori St. Paul as White House interns. She said, "Carl Peters was very appreciative because he finally landed a job after two years of diligent searching and sending out 260 resumes. So what that he graduated from the University of Virginia in the top one percent of his graduating class. He didn't have the essential qualifications the employers were looking for—fairer pigmentation and Republican values. No, I'm not saying all Republican values are wrong. However, most of their values are wrong because they're self-centered. It's easier to be a Republican than a Democrat.

"I should know because I'm a Republican. When our politicians voice their opinions about education, taxes, religion, etc., it's all self-centered gobbledygook. We always talk about vouchers for education and doing away with public education. What we are actually saying is the cost of public education taxes us (Republicans) too much. If we give the poor vouchers, they will be able to attend private school, pay a little more taxes or tuition and in the long run, we will pay a lot less taxes. So those who are least able to pay will pay more, and those who are better able to pay more will pay less. We do want prayer placed back in our schools; however, we don't care what the United States Constitution says about freedom of religion. Nor do we care about separation of church and state. Do people have a right to be atheists? Apparently not! We have the attitude, 'My child will be better if he could say a silent prayer before, during and after school.'

"What we want to do is to change students' behavior and instill positive values. In order for their behavior and values to improve, family values must be instilled in the child by the parent(s)/guardian(s). Once a child learns the nuances of appreciating basic values, this will serve as a foundation upon which learning can be built."

Cintura paused and smiled as if amused by a joke where she was the only one who knew the punch line. Then she continued, "I asked Lori St. Paul why she wanted the job. She initially gave me the typical bullshit that they teach you in college—to improve herself and seek better employment opportunities. I let her recount her repertoire of answers and asked her again why she wanted to work for the White House staff. I wanted to know her thinking process and what in her background made her worthy of such a prestigious and sensitive job. There were plenty of honest hardworking daughters and sons of senators and representatives. Lori's smile turned to a confident air of arrogance. She said that she was a poor black woman who was fortunate enough to pull herself up by her bootstraps and escape her family's pattern of welfare dependence.

Contrary to popular belief, not everyone on welfare is lazy, uneducated and a product of drug abuse and sexual promiscuity by their parents. Lori's mother had been very studious and had a high school education. However, during her mother's senior year, she met and fell in love with a young man. They got married shortly after graduating and agreed that she would work until they had children. After they had children, she would stay at home and raise them. Her mother got a job in the cafeteria at the University of Texas at Austin. She worked there as a cashier for a year and a half until she was six months pregnant with their first child. When she began to have kidney and gland problems, her doctor put her on bed rest for the final three months of her pregnancy. Eight weeks later she gave birth to Lori's elder siblings, triplets—John, Jim and Jason. They were better known at the time as Triple Trouble and required a lot of individual attention. She tried the nurturing mother bit and made a futile attempt at breast-feeding. However, it proved to be impossible with three infants, so she put them on formula. Her grandmother, Genevieve Slater, came and stayed with the family until the infants were six months old because Harriet could not handle them alone."

I told Cintura that I couldn't imagine anyone raising kids in such an environment. An 18-or-19-year-old mother with triplets, a young husband and a limited income was sure to have been constantly frustrating.

Cintura continued on as if oblivious to my remarks but wanted to finish retelling the tale. "The real fun began once Triple Trouble became toddlers. They pulled out pots and pans and pretended to be the latest band, they played hide and go seek and locked themselves in the attic.

Then Lori was born a couple of years later. Her dad worked two jobs at that time. Her grandmother called him at work and told him that Lori had just been born. He was so excited that he took the rest of the day off. On his way to the hospital, a police vehicle hit his car broadside. By the time the paramedics arrived at the scene, he was dead. His body was taken to the morgue in the same hospital where Lori was born. Lori's mother's dilemma was a life-changing question. What does a 21-year-old mother of four do when she has a very limited work history? The $5,000 life insurance policy was barely enough to cover funeral expenses. Regardless of Lori's tragic upbringing, they always had love."

Cintura had a look of momentary bewilderment and said, "Have you ever tried to eat love when you were hungry or drink love when you were thirsty? In spite of all of that she went through, Lori and her brothers completed college with 3.5+ grade point averages and graduated in the top five percent of traditionally white, Division I universities. Lori is a loyal employee and would give her best effort daily to do a quality job.

"I told Lori that her cathartic approach was much better and offered her the job. I told her that success is not measured by the enormity of the obstacles you overcome; however, each obstacle you overcome is a success. She thanked me, and tears of joy welled up in her eyes while in her exuberance she exclaimed, 'I never dreamt that I'd ever get a job like this.'"

Evidently, Carl and Lori worked out well. However, their initial meeting was quite confrontational. The first day at work Carl had a 5" x 7" picture of his girlfriend, a petite, blue-eyed blond.

Lori was pleasant but didn't say anything about the picture. However, at lunch she asked, "Why do black men always choose to date out of their race, when there are plenty of nice black females available? Do you see Chinese or Russian men doing that? No, only low down, good-for-nothing black men like you!"

"Look Lori, I don't know about most men. But I do know about this man! The woman in the picture is not just any woman! Her name is Samantha Petralski. Seven years ago, she was a new student at my high school who had just arrived from Poland. She didn't know anyone, and I befriended her. We found out that we had similar interests and goals in life. Samantha and I were practically inseparable, fell in love and have been together ever since. I didn't set out looking for a little white girl as a trophy. I was raised in a diverse neighborhood and although there were plenty of narrow-minded people who didn't hesitate in expressing their views, my parents taught me to make decisions based on morals and integrity. So, I really don't give a damn what you or anyone else thinks about who I chose to love! I put her picture on my desk because she's someone special in my life. So you can take your narrow minded self and narrow-minded ideas and kiss off."

Lori walked quickly away and went into the ladies room angry and embarrassed. After a few minutes, the stream of tears stopped. She went back to the lunch area and apologized to Carl. He accepted her apology and calmly told her that he would never forget who he was. Carl said soberly, "I have 260 reminders. The same companies that turned me down after my first interview hired my white and Asian classmates. It didn't matter that I had superior grades or qualifications. A good resume may get you an interview but when you don't receive any job offers after 30 interviews, it's not hard to read between the lines."

Carl was sent to shadow a bill through the House Subcommittee on Social Security, and he was ordered to report all congressional opposition. The bill would allow disabled Americans to retain their full health benefits if they received computer training and found a job in the workforce that paid $20,000 or more annually. The President did not want to reduce disability benefits. Instead, of the 23 million Americans who received them, he wanted to encourage those who could perform some type of competitive work activity to find employment. However, he realized the loss of health benefits is the most significant deterrent that keeps disabled people from trying. A few years ago some organizations tried to come up with a more politically correct phrase to describe the disabled population, and they decided on "physically and mentally challenged." However, the phrase didn't change people's perception. People still viewed them as a group of people that could not function normally in society, had little value and had to be coddled. Hopefully, the President's bill will change this perception.

The second day on the job, Carl reported to Cintura that he overheard Thomas Jefferson O'Malley, the Republican Representative from Mississippi, in the restroom trying to get the committee chairman, Cheswolde Greene, to table all discussion on the President's bill. However, Congressman Greene said the public wants a debate on this issue, and he's determined to have one. He told Representative O'Malley that he could voice his concerns in the committee hearings and meetings. In response, Representative O'Malley threatened to use his political allies to pressure him into being more conciliatory.

The next day Carl gave Representative O'Malley a yellow envelope from Cintura. It contained a picture of Representative O'Malley at a strip club sitting on the bar kissing a stripper's sweaty hot thong as he slipped a $50 bill into her garter. On the back of the picture was written, "Either the bill passes or start collecting your Social Security checks!"

It's amazing how a little friendly persuasion influences people's agenda on the Hill. Lori had a similar experience with Matthew Solomon, a Cable Network Masters (CNM) reporter. He had invited her to dinner and since he was a very nice, well-groomed, articulate, black male, she accepted his invitation. During their conversation, he asked her questions euphemistically about the President and his ideas on various issues. While they were eating, Lori excused herself from the table indicating she had to go to the ladies room. She called Cintura from a courtesy phone.

Cintura gave her the following instructions: "Finish your meal and pretend as though nothing has happened. If he asks any additional questions, tell him that you are not privy to the information he is seeking. But, you can secure it for him. If he asks when he can see you, just tell him tomorrow."

Lori did as she was told. Cintura had placed a microphone in one of Lori's hairpins and told her to play along. After discussing their workday, Matthew asked her what it was like working for President Bob. What type of people did the President ally himself with? How could he gain the President's ear? Matthew explained that he had valuable information and mentioned that the President would probably like to purchase it. Lori said that she was a loyal employee and, as far as she knew, President Bob was an honorable man. She wasn't going to be used as a wedge to divide the White House staff. Lori told Matthew that she would take a cab home.

Matthew was ashamed of what he had done and tried to apologize, but Lori just stalked out. The next morning MZT TV reported possessing videotape with a news reporter attempting to bribe a federal official. CNM fired him and put out a statement in the national newspapers apologizing for the reporter's conduct.

Carl received a promotion to White House Legislative Monitor of Transportation, and Lori received a promotion to White House Volunteer Coordinator. Carl celebrated with Samantha, his girlfriend, at Club Sixteen in College Park. Lori was supposed to meet them for drinks at 5:30 p.m. but got caught in the Washington D.C. traffic on U.S Interstate 395. As Lori neared the club, she could see an ambulance outside. The police would not let her park on the block where the club was. She had to park two blocks away. As Lori walked back to the club, she was quietly praying that nothing had happened to her colleague. Lori had never met Carl's girlfriend, and their first heated conversation just kept playing over and over in her mind. When Lori arrived at the club, she could see police sheets covering two bodies. She pushed her way through the crowd and saw Samantha sitting at a table alone looking sad. Lori suspected the worst and blurted out that she was so sorry for being late; but before she could say anything else, Carl came walking in from the restroom.

He explained, "A driver lost control of his car, hit a telephone pole and ended up killing himself, his wife and 2-year-old son." Lori responded that it was tragic to hear about the family; however, for a split second she thought something had happened to the two of them. She hugged them both and told Samantha how much fun it was working with Carl. Lori also said that she was going to miss Carl and wished him the best. They had a few drinks before going dancing at the Four-Play Nightclub. Since it was Friday and no one had to go to work on Saturday, they partied at the club until it closed at 4:00 a.m.

Saturday morning, Cintura came to Lori's home unannounced. She said that the FBI had just cleared 45 people to work as White House volunteers, but two of them were communist agents. Cintura gave Lori their pictures and told her to keep an eye on them but not to be too obvious. They wanted to follow the agents' paper trail to see where it led before they deported or terminated them.

Lori played along and gave Cintura weekly reports of agents Mukuto Chironu and Milinu Kateruo's activities. After three weeks, Cintura told Lori that the two agents would be terminated over the weekend. Lori was happy because it was a little nerve-wracking keeping track of two men when she was supervising a staff of 82. She assumed that since the two men were being fired, she'd eventually get replacements for them.

The following Monday, *The Washington Gazette* had the two agents' pictures on the front page with the headline, "Two Chinese Men Found Dead in Garage with Engine Running After a Night Out on the Town."

Lori asked, "Cintura, how could two people fall asleep in a garage?"

Cintura educated her on the finer areas of politics: "The two Chinese men were terminated with my assistance. The White House staff's main job is to remain loyal and to protect the integrity of the executive branch of government by all necessary means. The Chinese had resisted the idea of deportation, and the Gazette's article would be more palatable to the American people than knowing that spies in the White House had been taken out in handcuffs."

Cintura also told her that President Bob wanted to be personally briefed on the remaining volunteers and wanted a list of talking points, so he could prepare a speech for their welcome luncheon later that week.

Lori spent the rest of the weekend gathering the information. She had never talked to the President at a meeting or one on one. Lori admired him because of his principles and wanted to make a good impression. Her meeting wasn't until 9:30 a.m.; however, she was at his office at 9:00 a.m. dressed in a navy blue suit. President Bob arrived at 9:10 a.m. and noticed that she was already there. He told her to come into his office and broke the ice.

"I am aware of what happened to the two Chinese agents. Thank you for your act of valor in the interest of national security. The American People and I appreciate your bravery and assistance in insuring their freedom. I have followed your brief employment at the White House. If you remain diligent and work hard, you will not only go far under my administration, I will encourage the Vice President to find a place for you in the next administration."

In her exuberance, she stood up, gave him a hug and then said, "I'm sorry and thank you, Mr. President."

President Bob embraced her, kissed her gently and said "You're welcome, and you may go."

Lori was startled, smiled and returned to her work area. After she returned to her desk, she became rattled by a number of emotions. She felt ashamed for hugging the President, weird because he kissed her out of compassion and surprised by his gentleness. But what scared her most of all was the passion he unlocked inside of her. She wanted more than the kiss but thought it was an impractical whim in response to a moment of kindness. Her life was full with work, but somehow it wasn't fulfilling. She had gotten lost somewhere inside the pages of her work. And, in order to find her way out, she needed to come out of the pages and live.

President Bob smiled as Lori left the room. Her caring attitude and reaction was genuine and amusing. He felt drawn to her but knew better than to pursue it. Lori's nice soft body and cute innocence was refreshing. Honesty isn't the norm on the Hill; it's usually the exception. He sent her an E-mail message to meet him in the Oval Office Thursday morning, two hours before the volunteer luncheon. This time she went in with a more defined outline. Lori had a seating chart and a list of all the invited guests.

As she started to give her report, she felt President Bob's eyes looking longingly at her. The more Lori tried to explain her report, the slower her speech became. President Bob embraced her as she had done to him a few days earlier. Her body could not resist him, and his credenza and executive chair became their paradise for the next hour. Then they showered in the President's washroom and got dressed. Lori left for the meeting, and President Bob followed five minutes later with a pair of dainty, bikini, lime green panties in the right pocket of his jacket.

Lori and President Bob made eye contact and smiled at one another as they entered the room. Cintura spotted their sensuous gaze but acted as though nothing had happened. President Bob gave an impressive presentation and complimented the volunteers on their willingness to give of themselves to others. After pausing momentarily and scanning the room, he said compassionately, "The nation is indebted to you for your passion and the things you've done to positively affect the lives of others."

Cintura accompanied Lori back to her office. She told Lori that the luncheon went well. Cintura closed the door, then turned to Lori and said, "I hope you and the President had a good time because that's the last piece of him you're going to get. Honey, if your panties are that hot, take them off. Go back to John Plimpton who you humped in high school or Eduardo Covington who you fell for in college. But you keep your horny little skirt off of President Bob. He may be the President, but he's like every other man. You dropped your drawers, and he'll drop his. However, he has much more to lose than a few minutes in the sack with two balls and a catcher's mitt. He's not getting married again, and politically he can't afford a mistress, so if you're hot and care for him, get your ass in a cold shower and get over it. You're being transferred to the Washington, D.C. oversight committee. Beginning tomorrow you will report to the City Hall building. You will receive a 20 percent salary increase and a new Lincoln Town Car. However, I expect a comprehensive report on my desk every Friday by 9:00 a.m.

Embarrassed and dejected, Lori stumbled to her desk and cleaned it out. Then she muttered, "How could I be so stupid." Then she left. Cintura was crass but probably right. It had taken her a lifetime to get a job at the White House but only an hour to lose it.

SHAMANDA

John Caliparia, the former New York State Attorney General, was appointed by the Justice Department as special prosecutor to investigate President Bob's alleged impropriety. He had made a name for himself by obtaining convictions on Mafia kingpins with a 92 percent conviction rate and the average sentence was fifteen years without a chance of parole. President Bob came to power with $320,000 in the bank and currently has $3.5 million spread over several accounts. It's impossible to trace the money because the money was deposited in amounts of less than $9,750 over the last three years. His attorney and business accountant, Shamanda Bradley, spent the last four months in prison for refusing to give the court the President's books. She claims the court's request violates attorney-client privilege. Shamanda is married and has grown children and two grandchildren whom she misses terribly. However, she remained loyal to the President, so he always looked out for her. When hurricane Betsy came blistering in with 24 inches of snow in three hours last winter and cut off her heat and electricity, President Bob took in Shemanda and her husband Whitney. He had the National Guard pick them up in four-wheel drive vehicles. While the President and Shamanda stayed up late discussing his books, Whitney said he was tired and went to bed. The next day, President Bob was happy as a lark and mentioned that her lacy orange panties were very sexy.

I discovered today that the Justice Department decided to scrap the investigation. Shamanda had refused the latest offer by Mr. Caliparia, which was full immunity from prosecution, a clear record and the ability to limit her testimony to accounting matters. Also, Cintura found John Caliparia had a weakness for kinky sex. She sent T.C. to bait him into the Hilton one evening after work. T.C. tailed him for a week to observe his habits. The following Monday morning she got off the elevator, carrying a cup of coffee. As Mr. Capilaria was entering, T.C. stepped into his path, so he ran into her and scalded her with the coffee. She pretended to be startled, and he took his handkerchief and tried to soak up some of the coffee. He asked her to come into his office and use the private bathroom to see if she could get some of the coffee out. She reluctantly agreed as she pulled her buttoned blouse away from her skin. T.C. went into the bathroom, closed the door and took off her blouse and bra. She rinsed them out with soap and warm water, so they wouldn't stain.

Then T.C. opened the door slightly and asked, "Can you assist me?" Before she could finish the sentence, Mr. Caliparia walked in.

She proceeded to say, "Call my boss, (202) 789-1213, and tell him I'll be a little late."

Mr. Caliparia became very apologetic saying, "I'm sorry I thought you needed me to undo something." T.C. placed her blouse in front of her and told him she'd accept his apology. Blushing bashfully with beads of sweat on his brow, Mr. Caliparia scooted out of the door, made the call as she had asked and sat patiently while T.C. got dressed. After she got dressed, he begged her to have dinner with him, so he could make it up to her. T.C. said that she was staying in room 417 at the Hilton Hotel and had planned to have dinner in her room, but he could join her at 6:00 p.m.

Mr. Caliparia found T.C. attractive and charming. When he came to her room that evening, she offered him a drink. He asked for Scotch and water. She mixed the drink and gave it to him. He sipped it as his eyes admired her figure and his mind reflected on their earlier encounter. They began to discuss how they met. Mr. Caliparia felt a little faint and then passed out on the couch.

Taylor, Teal and Teal's cousin, Jermaine, came out of the bedroom and helped take Mr. Caliparia's clothes off. They put a male thong bikini on him. On one butt cheek, Jermaine tattooed a naked woman holding her breast with her right hand; on the other cheek, he tattooed a naked man holding his penis in his right hand. Across his back, he tattooed "the rights of passage." Taylor and Teal got naked and posed as Jermaine took some revealing shots of the three of them on the floor, on the couch and on the bed.

Mr. Caliparia woke up the next day and found the pictures and one of his hands handcuffed to the bed. The first picture he saw showed him on the bed between Taylor and Teal. The three of them were naked as jaybirds, and his head was buried in Teal's chest. As he flipped through the pictures, his face flushed with embarrassment and anger. Each picture was more graphic than the last. A note on the back of the last picture read, *A little cooperation could prevent the media from knowing the naked truth.* The next day, the case was closed. Shamanda was released, and President Bob went to pick her up. They celebrated her release by christening the seats as tinted windows hid their pleasure from me, and I did my job.

It's amazing what the art of persuasion can do. Taylor and Teal really enjoyed their jobs. President Bob was honest with them and didn't ask them to do anything they weren't comfortable doing. Although he often placed them in compromising situations, they never had to make love to anyone. The only one I've seen them satisfy is him. He has made them feel special and good about themselves. President Bob genuinely cared about the people with whom he came into contact. He assisted them in fulfilling their hopes, dreams, aspirations, and...

MICHELLE

President Bob's charm worked well on everyone except Michelle. Michelle was an ex CIA operative. He was born Michael Constantine. Michelle was 5 feet 4 inches tall, weighed 110 pounds, had naturally wavy blond hair and blue eyes. He had worked as a reporter for ten years in Russia posing as a woman. Michelle had become comfortable with his feminine role and often fantasized what it'd be like to be a woman. On one of his visits to Moscow, Michelle was assigned to cover the President's visit. Michelle was quite attractive. After the President addressed the media, he noticed Michelle's smile and interest in him. President Bob was flattered. As he walked down from the podium, he mingled with the media, shaking hands and expressing how much he was enjoying his visit. President Bob shook Michelle's hand and gently patted him on the butt as he passed by.

Later that evening, as President Bob was putting on his bathrobe after taking his shower, he heard some commotion outside of his door. A security guard was informing a female reporter that the presidential quarters were off limits. President Bob opened the door and invited Michelle in. The guard scanned him with a metal detector before permitting him to enter the suite. Once inside, President Bob threw Michelle face down on the floor and with one swift tug on the snap, removed his bronze thong panties, leaving his buttocks fully exposed to President Bob's lustful desires. Michelle screamed in protest; however, the plush carpet muffled his voice. Michelle struggled to free himself but was no match for President Bob's strength. His hot breath and forceful entry caused Michelle's body to cringe. After President Bob was done, Michelle cursed him. Michelle told President Bob that he was an undercover CIA agent, and he would file formal charges against him for assault and battery. President Bob called the guard, had Michelle taken to the American Embassy and detained. Then he called Cintura and explained what had happened. President Bob asked her to come and take care of the situation, as he could ill afford a public scandal.

Cintura arrived the next day with $50,000 in cash. She read the FBI file on Michael Constantine and discovered that he had been bisexual. His first gay experience had transpired when he was twelve. A young Catholic priest found him attractive, bought him gifts and developed a friendship with him. Michael was an altar boy, and on Saturday afternoons he helped to prepare the altar for Sunday communion services. One day, after he finished, the priest hugged him in gratitude. Michael responded by kissing the priest and then became entangled in a two-year love affair that ended when his parents discovered stains in his underwear and questioned him about it. The priest was reported to the Bishop and defrocked. Michael was then sent to a military college where the upper classmen appreciated his orientation.

Armed with this knowledge, Cintura walked into Michelle's holding area and introduced herself. She had her hand-picked presidential guards accompany her. Two guards held Michelle down in a chair while Cintura took out a 38 revolver with a silencer, put it in Michelle's mouth and said, "Look you slimy piece of crap. I have a question to ask you, but first I want to explain something to you, and don't you say one damned word until I'm done! I've read your file and know what happened."

Cintura put the gun on a nearby table, pulled out his file and flipped through pages and pictures. As Cintura continued to talk, Michelle's voice was muffled by the fear of his impending death and embarrassment of an uncovered past. Her voice sounded like a stoic judge-pronouncing sentence, "Screwed a priest at the age of 12, eight boys by the age of 13, plus a high school science teacher and his daughter by the time you were 15. You

Presidential Indiscretions

enlisted in the Air Force after graduating from nursing school. After serving four years at the hospital on Lackland Air Force Base in San Antonio, Texas, you left the military for a better opportunity with the CIA. They were looking for Russian-speaking train agents. Oh, yes, (pointing at a paragraph on one of the pages) here it says you learned Russian in high school and took a few courses in college. However, you lived with a Russian immigrant the four years you were in the Air Force. I'm sorry; it says here you lived with a Russian couple for four years while you were in the Air Force. You were screwing your Russian female high school teacher. She followed you to Texas after finding out she was pregnant with your child. Her husband tried to win her back but settled for a lovely triangle arrangement you suggested.

"Shall I go on Michelle or Michael or whoever the hell you want to be today? I'm going to tell you what you're going to do. You're going to call your editor and request an immediate two-week vacation to care for a sick relative. Then you're going to take this $50,000, get as much alcohol and love that it can buy and forget about the President and what transpired today. You will be monitored from a distance 24 hours a day. If you attempt to betray this President in any manner, our marksman will sniff you out quicker than you can get it up." Cintura retrieved the revolver from the table and asked Michelle, "What's your answer, Hawaii or some daisies?"

"Hawaii," Michelle said nervously. Cintura put the $50,000 in Michelle's purse, turned and walked swiftly out of the room. The guards escorted Michelle back to his home.

Cintura reported to President Bob how she disposed of the matter and then assured him that there would be tight monitoring of Michelle's activities. President Bob continued his visit without further complications and returned to the United States three days later.

Michelle took the Hawaiian vacation and tried to put the President Bob incident out of his mind. He was a realist and knew that he was no match for the President's powerful connections. When he returned to work, he was rejuvenated and absorbed himself with work. He did an excellent investigative report about the Siberian family of Canciel Chambergov, a man accused of incest and fathering his daughter's child.

When Canciel was 16 years old, he had fallen in love with a 15-year-old neighbor. Their parents didn't approve of the relationship, but their love became stronger than the parents' attempt to keep them apart. One night while their parents and siblings were fast asleep, they slipped out of their homes carrying a few possessions in two tattered suitcases and an overnight bag. They hitched a ride to a town 19 miles away and convinced a circuit preacher that they were both 18 years old, so he married them. Six months later, they had a daughter. Unfortunately, his wife had a complicated delivery and died giving birth to their daughter, Candi. He couldn't find a job to sustain himself and a newborn, so he contacted his parents, and they allowed him to come home until he could get on his feet. Canciel returned to school and finished high school and college. His mother took care of his daughter while he was in school, and the daughter started to call his mother, Mom and his father, Dad. He felt that it was okay and after a few years started dating again. By the time Canciel graduated from college, he no longer looked at his daughter as his daughter because he had not spent much time with her while she was growing up. To Canciel, Candi seemed like she was another member of the family. He got a job at the Siberian Oil Company and moved out of his parents' house. His parents were attached to Candi, so Canciel did not take her with him.

By the time Candi was 14, she had developed into quite a young lady. She was 5 feet 4 inches tall, had size 36" breasts, brown hair and hazel eyes. She always greeted him with a kiss when he came over. He seemed more like a good buddy to her than a father. One day he came by after having been at a pub for a few hours drinking beer. His parents were still in town shopping. Candi kissed him and he got carried away. Her youthful exuberance, hormones and curiosity caused her to give in to his overtures. They ended up in her bed with a trail of clothes following them. His parents came home and found them still embracing under the covers of shame. His mother began crying and his father pulled the covers off of them and yanked him out of bed. His father had been a coalminer, and the hard callus from his hand felt like sheets of steel. His father beat him up, threw him out of the house and made Candi take a bath in lye soap. After that, father and daughter were banned from seeing each other.

Later that night, Canciel sneaked into his parents' home and took his daughter. The next day they discovered the daughter missing and called him. He admitted that he had come for his daughter. They told him that if he didn't return Candi to them, they never wanted to see him again. After Canciel discovered Candi was carrying his child, he became very rueful. He stayed away from the pubs and became very attentive to her. He made sure she went to school every day until it was time to have the baby. His parents refused to take any of his calls, so he sent them a letter apologizing for his actions and informing them that Candi was pregnant. In anger, his father reported Canciel to the police, and Canciel was arrested.

Canciel willingly admitted to the consensual statutory rape. In Russia, statutory rape carried a fine of $500, but incest carried a mandatory prison sentence of ten years. Although Canciel pled guilty, his attorney insisted that the required blood test be done to confirm paternity. The test was done and came back negative. All these years, Canciel had carried a burden that wasn't his. Candi was sitting behind him as the results were read. She leaped from her seat and kissed him passionately as the judge dismissed the case. Canciel was summarily released. Canciel's parents were seated in the rear of the courtroom, and his mother was crying.

His father embraced him and apologized, "I love you, but my anger at what you did caused an unfortunate void between us."

Eventually, they both forgave one another and vowed to allow their family wounds to heal. Canciel and Candi got married weeks after she graduated from high school, and he encouraged her to attend college. She majored in education and became an elementary school teacher. By the time she graduated from college and landed her first job, she was pregnant with their fourth child.

Michelle's article about Canciel and his family received rave reviews and was nominated for a Pulitzer Prize. He received invitations from colleges, universities and political parties. Michelle accepted most of the invitations and reported his activities to CIA officials. He also gained access to the Kremlin.

Things went well for him until a friend tipped him off that he was about to be discovered by the Russian secret police. Michelle realized that if he were found out, he would be tortured and killed. He sent word through CIA intermediaries that he wanted the sex-altering surgery. However, his superiors denied his request because he had never received the psychological counseling that is usually given weekly for two years prior to the operation. Before they could pull him in for counseling, he had contacted a surgeon and had sex altering surgery performed. After the operation, he identified himself as a woman to everyone. Michelle's mind went haywire and she was unable to focus on her job. Also, she became forgetful and preoccupied with sexual fantasies. The United States Ambassador to Russia arranged for her to be transferred to Washington, where she was debriefed and evaluated by a Pentagon psychologist. The following report was given to Cintura and Barton Jr., while Michelle was retained under guard in the Mental Health Unit at Walter Reed Army Hospital.

MENTAL STATUS EXAMINATION: The patient arrived 40 minutes late for her appointment. Her hair was matted, and she looked as if she hadn't bathed in weeks. She appeared to be malnourished, but she was alert and able to relate to me reasonably well. Patient's mood appeared withdrawn with a flat affect. She expressed that she feels down and depressed about her condition. Patient's speech is irrelevant and incoherent although her IQ is above average. I have noticed pressured speech during the last six months of her biweekly visits; however, there's no evidence of retardation. Patient's thought process appeared to be abnormal. She has a history of hallucinations and said she currently receives messages from the TV set and subliminal messages in radio commercials. The messages tell her that everyone is looking at her and is out to get her. She appeared to be confused. When I asked the patient to interpret the common quote, "Don't cry over spilled milk," she responded by saying, "If something goes wrong, don't cry about it. You should get even." When I asked the patient to interpret the quote, "Every cloud has a silver lining," she responded, "It means if someone messes with you, you should take them out. You'll have your chance later." When she's not hallucinatory, which appears to be about sixty percent of the time, her memory appears to be fair for both past and recent events. Patient has some insight into her current difficulties. When I asked the patient to name four of the last seven Presidents, she said, "Kennedy, Nixon, Clinton, and Nelson. I don't pay attention to them. They're just a bunch of crooks anyway."

Cintura told Barton Jr. that she'd handle Michelle's disposition. She instructed T.C. to disguise herself as a nurse. T.C. did as she was instructed, went into Michelle's room and checked her pulse and temperature. Michelle was wearing a hospital gown and was lying down handcuffed to the bed.

Michelle asked, "T.C., how long are they going to keep me here?"

"I don't know but believe that it might be just a day or so."

Michelle whispered, "I don't like being confined and have broken no laws. I am being held against my will. I will pay you $5,000 if you assist me in getting out of the hospital."

T.C. said "No."

Michelle responded with an offer of $15,000.

"I'd be fired on the spot if you got caught, and it could take me six months to a year to find another job."

"Okay, I'll pay you one year's salary."

"You mean you will pay me $41,000 just to get you out of the hospital? What did you, kill the President? On second thought don't answer that, I don't want to know."

"All you have to do is get me out of the hospital. I have a key to a safety deposit box in the heel of my shoe. I'll give you the key and the box number if you get me out of here;" Michelle said, sounding more reassuring.

T.C. paused for a moment, and in a concerned voice responded, "Okay I'll do it. In an hour and a half, I'll come and get you. You should be receiving your dinner in a few minutes. When I return, I'll tell the guard I'm taking you to have an electroencephalogram (EEG). If he accompanies us, I'll take you into the room and get you out the back door." T.C. pulled the patient's chart, and wrote, "Perform EEG test one hour after dinner." Michelle nodded in agreement and then reclined in bed feeling a little more relaxed.

An hour and a half later, T.C. returned as promised. She told the guard she had to move the patient to Radiology for an EEG and showed the guard in the chart where the doctor had ordered it. The guard said okay; however, he'd have to go with her to the room where the test would be performed. T.C. appeared to be a little annoyed by all of the security precautions, but reluctantly agreed. As T.C. wheeled Michelle's bed into the Neurology Department's EEG Center, the guard positioned himself outside the door. T.C. wheeled Michelle inside; then she removed the hospital rail to allow Michelle to slip her hands outside of the rail while her hands were still cuffed. T.C. pointed to a window in the corner. She told Michelle to meet her in the red Ford Contour, tag number MPT276, which was parked on the street. There was a raincoat outside the window behind a bush that she could put over her shoulders to cover her gown.

Michelle quickly did as she was told. T.C. told the guard that the doctor was with the patient and should be out in about twenty minutes. She then walked away as if she were going to see another patient.

When T.C. got to her car, Michelle was waiting anxiously in the passenger's seat. T.C. got in and asked her where the bank was. Michelle gave her directions to the bank and slid down in her seat, so no one looking into the car could see her face. As T.C. pulled off, she passed a flask of Vodka to Michelle and told her that she understood what she was going through. She had been in a mind-boggling situation not too long ago, and it took her a while to get over it. As they began to talk, Michelle began to drink more and more from the flask to calm her nerves.

About five minutes later, Michelle was feeling a little woozy. T.C. drove Michelle to the rear entrance of the Washington Zoo. As they got near the zoo, it was getting dark. There was a sign that said closed at dusk, but T.C. entered anyway. As they went into the zoo, T.C. said that they were meeting someone near the fish tanks. She led Michelle to the tanks and they waited patiently. While they were waiting, T.C. lifted the top off one of the large tanks. Michelle commented about the beauty of a red fish in the tank. As she bent over to see the fish, T.C. pushed her in. The tank was filled with piranha. They immediately devoured the flesh from Michelle's bones as she screamed in agony. However, there was no one near or far to hear her cries.

After the fish had their fill, T.C. took a hook, removed Michelle's bones, shoes and clothes from the tank and put them in three separate bags. She took the bones and ground them up with a wood-chipping machine that was used to grind up old Christmas trees. T.C. cut the lining and heels of Michelle's shoes with a utility knife but did not find a key. She sorted through the clothes for identification. T.C. shredded all the pictures and cut up the credit cards. The $827 in cash she kept. As she put it, "Michelle will not be spending it where she's going." All remaining evidence was dried and incinerated.

T.C. had experienced quite an eventful day and was ready to relax. She drove home to take a bath and prepare dinner. After arriving home, she quickly got undressed, placed all of her clothes in the fireplace and lit them along with a few logs. After taking a nice hot shower, she dried her hair, wrapped a towel around herself and went into the bedroom to put on a lounging dress. As she entered the room, two men grabbed her and tied her to the bedpost. A copper wire was placed between her legs, and an electric switch contraption connected to a car battery was placed on the bed. T.C.'s eyes became large as she trembled with fear. Although she had no problem taking someone out, she feared her own demise. Cintura had a large steel hunting knife and held it close to T.C.'s throat and said, "Didn't I tell you a long time ago that you only had one time to cross me? I've paid you well, and this is the respect that you give me? Keeping $827! Is that all that you think you are worth? Bitch, I've made $32 million off of you."

T.C.'s eyes pleaded with Cintura to give her a second chance. However, her body would not move for fear of Cintura's blade.

Cintura raged on. "I'm disappointed in you. Don't you know a piranha has a distinct scent, and all money has a scent on it? The money you stole contained new bills Michelle had gotten earlier in the day from an ATM machine. I don't leave traces, and I had you trained not to leave any, but you failed me. You think you are a hot dog, but you're nothing but a weenie. I'm going to let you experience the pain your victims felt from time to time." At that moment she threw the switch that sent 24 volts of electricity coursing chillingly through her body. Then Cintura decapitated and dismembered her. Her body was carried to D.C. Meatpacking Plant and was ground up in the sausage machine.

All of T.C.'s accounts were electronically transferred to her father. He was paid a visit that night and told that his daughter was killed in the line of duty. He was then informed that she left him all of her assets totaling $1.75 million. Dr. Molton was also given a book entitled "Silence is Golden."

This was a bittersweet ending to a long bittersweet saga for Dr. Molton. The two people he had loved most in the world met their demise because of him. He had loved them until death, through death and despite death. Their golden memories were locked in a treasury of silence.

If J. Edgar Hoover invented the "Spin Machine," then Cintura perfected it. The major newspapers said all of the appropriate things after a "reliable source" provided them with (FBI) photos of the tragic motor vehicle accident that had taken T.C.'s life. Reportedly, two teenage boys had borrowed their parents' car while they were asleep and went to a classmate's party. They smoked a few marijuana joints and drank about a fifth of tequila. On their way home, at about 2:45 a.m., their car crossed the solid yellow line and hit T.C.'s car that was coming in the opposite direction on a one-lane stretch of road. Both boys' blood alcohol levels were 1.5. There wasn't any alcohol found in T.C.'s blood. Apparently, both kids and T.C. Hunter died as the cars caught fire and exploded shortly after impact. All of the bodies were burned beyond recognition and had to be identified by utilizing dental records.

Nevertheless, Dr. Molton held a memorial service for T.C. White House and congressional staff came dressed with somber faces, sad stories and crocodile tears. If it weren't for the solemnity of the occasion, the funeral could be viewed as a shadowy reflection of a shell and not a meaningful reflection into a life once lived.

President Bob preceded the eulogy with words of comfort extended to Dr. Molton. He said, "The hardest thing for a parent to experience is to have a child predecease you. I know that you loved T.C., but God loved her best, and now she's in a better place. We will miss Ms. Hunter because her smile lit a spark in all of us. She was a valued employee whose work ethic was an example for her peers to follow. Her diligence and integrity were uncompromising. We will always hold her in high esteem. She was vital as a business development specialist in facilitating business endeavors between foreign and domestic businesses, the Department of Commerce, Department of the Interior, the White House and congressional committees. I've ordered all federal offices next week to observe a moment of silence in T.C.'s honor each day at 12 noon."

Preacher John came to the podium, and said, "About ten years ago, I stood before this sacred desk and was asked by an honored guest on the podium, 'What's all the commotion? Is it because the choir sang, "Precious Lord?" I smiled and said, 'No.' They realized something that most people discover too late. What goes around comes around. That will be the theme of my sermon today, 'You Shall Reap What You Sow.' Not many are willing to pay the cost to be the boss. One may ask, 'What is the cost?' If you don't know the answer, then it's okay to ask the question. Laws keep our society from chaos. Those who break the law must pay a price; and some have not counted up the cost. The Bible says, 'You shall reap what you sow.'" As President Bob, Cintura and I sat still and nodded at the appropriate moments, others squirmed in their seats as if uneasy in their respective positions.

Midway through his sermon, Preacher John slipped in another verse, "Be not afraid, only believe."

It came from Mark 5:36 in the Bible. I never got around to reading it. How can the dead be afraid of anything or believe in anything? Preacher John's message was short, sobering and sweet. I doubt that he ever met T.C.

He said, "There's nothing I can say that can bring this delightful young lady back. Tammy Cornelia Hunter was struck down by that demon that torments each of us, the one that urges us to do wrong when our integrity motivates us to do right."

He began to pace and flail his arms while making his point with each phrase as beads of sweat ran down his cheeks. He continued. "Two kids sought to find tranquillity in drug infested cigarettes and alcoholic beverages. I'm sure as the children's parents rested comfortably in their beds, they thought their loving children were asleep in their rooms. They may have been the best of parents. They may have attended PTA meetings, softball games, basketball games, modeling classes, school activities and church. However, something went wrong to cause the children to go astray. Perhaps they listened to a demon that's locked inside us all: the demon that, once is allowed to roam freely, causes us to lose all sight of reason.

"T.C. Hunter's remains lay before us. She hadn't even reached the prime of adulthood, and her life was snuffed out (snapping his fingers) just like that. In a twinkling of an eye, her life as we know it on this earth was gone. As innocent as she was, as talented as she was, as dutiful as she was, as gracious as she was, as giving as she was, as steadfast as she was—she's now gone.

"We can not mourn her loss because she is in a better place. I don't know if she ever made peace with her Creator, but this much I do know. We have a God that loves us in spite of us. He provides for us in spite of us. Although we are weak, He is strong. Although we have shortcomings, He will bridge the gap. God provides hope to those that are hopeless. He provides comfort for those who are comfortless. When we are down, it is His love and mercy that picks us up. When we go astray, it is His compassion that tugs mightily at our heartstrings and conscience to bring us back within the fold. I say to you today, that there's nothing we can do to bring T.C. or those two young people back. But we can use the legacy that they have left behind to remind us daily that each of us has to make a choice. The choice is very simple. Are you going to choose right or wrong? We all will die, but where will you spend eternity. Will you spend it in heaven with our maker or in hell? The choice is yours."

The joyful "Amen" response to admonitions by the preacher was only matched by the sincerity of the message. Whether it was a concerted show of devout believers or an expected response to a carefully crafted speech is not my concern. The warmth or chill of those sitting in judgment bothered neither the deceased nor me.

As the eulogy was delivered, the tears flowed from T.C.'s colleagues. Cintura's onion-scented handkerchief held its usual magic. Other faces around the room were stoic and concerned as the media huddled outside the church trying to peer through the stained-glass windows.

As I sat in an all too familiar spot, witnessing this exercise of futility, I couldn't help but reflect on life's boomerang. Most people believe that there are three distinct parts of one's life: birth, daily life and death. The first and last parts don't matter. It's what's done in between the two points of destiny that etches meaning into our existence. Of all the things T.C. felt, she never could grasp the tenderness of emotion. The loneliness she must have felt can't be quantified with words.

On the following Monday, Dr. Molton contacted his attorney and had him prepare a will leaving the $1.75 million to the T.C. Hunter Scholarship Fund. The money was designated for deserving young students desiring careers in clonal research.

President Bob's administration had floundered slightly during his second term. The press had noted that he was a lame duck and hadn't accomplished much. He did; however, handle the economy, and it was more robust than it had been in the previous four Republican administrations. His approval rating was at an all time high of 82 percent. However, he wanted history to remember him well. He had sought opportunities where he would be seen as a positive political strategist and statesman.

Kerry Kisner, Drug Enforcement Administration (DEA) Director, came to the Oval Office six months ago under the cloak of darkness to obtain the President's approval to investigate the FBI. He came armed with proof that Clint Hoffman, the Director of the FBI, planned to kill Vice President Spencer Leon. Mr. Kisner gave President Bob a note asking him to walk with him in the White House garden for fear the White House was bugged. President Bob wrote in response that his staff has the White House and the grounds swept weekly because he doesn't like surprises. However, he accompanied him to the garden.

After entering the garden, Mr. Kisner disclosed that Mr. Hoffman was convinced that if Spencer Leon were elected President, he would have too liberal an agenda and planned to comprise his cabinet with African Americans and Hispanics. Mr. Hoffman feared that traditionally American values would be further compromised if the FBI and CIA directors were replaced with minorities. Mr. Hoffman attempted to use Mr. Kisner's cooperation in carrying out his scheme. The FBI had two kilos of cocaine to plant in the Vice President's home and $640,000 to place in his savings account records (with $5,000 to $25,000 deposits over the two years). They also had a recently arrested South American drug lord, Julio Santino, who was willing to turn state's evidence for a reduced sentence. However, they needed the DEA to corroborate their story. Mr. Kisner played along with them to discover the names of everyone who was involved in the scheme.

After reviewing the documents that contained Mr. Hoffman's signature, President Bob said that he would bring Mr. Hoffman to justice swiftly and sternly. He directed Mr. Kisner to inform the Justice Department and seek court authority before any search and seizures. President Bob obtained the support of Chief Supreme Court Justice Byron Nelson and U.S. Attorney General Halsey Fox to advise the DEA regarding when to seek subpoenas prior to arresting corrupted FBI staff.

As usual, President Bob consulted with Cintura. She cautioned President Bob that the FBI's key to success lay in their ability to control information. They have thousands of documents on 247 million American citizens. All transactions made via computer are reported to the federal government. Also, 98 percent of all citizens have Social Security cards. Within a keystroke, the government has detailed access to all aspects of your life. Bank accounts, mortgages and retail purchases are all subject to its scrutiny and manipulation.

It's well known that the FBI has an unlimited budget as well as an unlimited amount of arms and spies worldwide. Last year they spent $1.46 billion, and I haven't heard one newspaper or TV reporter ask, where did all of that money go? No one asked why they planted spies in the Black Panther Party, National Organization of Women, National Association for the Advancement of Colored People, Ku Klux Klan, National Rifle Association, etc. They've made more hits on governmental officials than the CIA, Mafia and South American drug lords combined.

The DEA had given the President the ammunition he needed to dismantle the FBI, and he had the balls to do it. However, he and Cintura decided to let the beat of public opinion create an atmosphere for change. As the DEA and Attorney General made arrests, the media had their cameras poised to deliver the venom that would change a man who had everything, to a man who had nothing. Newspapers across the nation contained headlines quoting portions of past presidential speeches. The one that aired the most was Ramon Mousil Dixon's quote which said, "When caught in a web of deceit and shame, why cry? It's time to celebrate and try again."

Mr. Hoffman won't be doing any celebrating in the near future. *The U.S. Express Newspaper* just reported that Mr. Hoffman was indicted by the Grand Jury on treason for attempting to assassinate the President, wire fraud for intercepting state and federal transmissions electronically without court approval and lying on his employment application 29 years ago. Apparently, he had checked the block indicating that his race was white. He was born in Louisiana and his great-great-grandfather was white; however, he had taken a liking to one of his female slaves, Karsi. She was a large woman with light tan complexion and beautiful Ethiopian features. Karsi was always given the best jobs in the home. When Karsi told him she was pregnant, he said he could not promise her that she could keep the child. However, he ordered her to be silent until the child was born. Karsi gave birth to a boy in the master's house.

Mr. Hoffman's great-great-grandfather told Mary, his white wife of twelve years about his dilemma. She tacitly agreed to support whatever decision he made. No one knew about his paternity other than the house servants. They feared their master's whip, so they kept silent. Karsi's child was very fair with dark blue eyes, so his father and his wife kept and raised the child as their son. To this day, Louisiana law states that any person having one thirty-second of Negro blood is a Negro, so he was guilty of being Negro. The punishment on record for passing is a mandatory 10-year prison term and/or $25,000 fine. A conviction for treason carries a mandatory sentence of death by a firing squad. This is the only conviction for which the President cannot grant a pardon, and he can delay the execution for no longer than one month after the sentence.

Not wanting to undergo a lengthy public trial, Mr. Hoffman and his 237 codefendants opted to plead guilty. He figured that Congress would pass legislation and save him from the firing squad. There hadn't been an execution by firing squad since the 1800's.

Unfortunately, Mr. Hoffman underestimated "mob mentality and the power of the press." Everyone jumped on the "get Hoffman bandwagon." His wife and six children all of a sudden appeared on front covers of newspapers with slogans such as, *We don't want to be black*. Photographs of Mr. Hoffman with a remorseful look on his face and head tilted downward with a slogan that said, *What you do in the dark will come to the light* were also freely displayed. His family began to receive phantom deliveries of watermelons and fried chicken. The first day they took it all in stride as a joke that would blow over. However, they lost their fortitude after the KKK sent them a watermelon filled with cyanide and a note attached that said, *We love you to death. Here's how you can take a bite out of crime*.

Mr. Hoffman, his wife Sarah Lea Hoffman and Deputy Director Anthony Williams were indicted for misuse of government property since they had used an FBI jet to go to the 1998 Super Bowl. Mr. and Mrs. Hoffman and Mr. Williams were charged with accepting illegal gratuities. The alleged gratuities were $3,500 worth of Super Bowl tickets, which were given to them by John Hampton of Sealtex Weapons, Inc.

Mr. Hampton was subsequently charged for making an illegal gift. Prosecutors contended that Sealtex Weapons was trying to win Mr. Hoffman's support in future weaponry purchases for the FBI. They said that John Hampton acted in a way that benefited his company. The law prohibits the giving of gifts and favors to government officials if they are meant as a reward for past or future actions.

Mr. Hoffman's staunch Republican comrades quickly disappeared. The Senate Majority Leader expressed outrage at Mr. Hoffman's conduct and led the Senate in passing a resolution to condemn his conduct and wanton abuse of power. He and the Speaker of the House appointed a bipartisan committee to dismantle the FBI and divide its duties among the ATF,

CIA and DEA. The Justice Department obtained a court order to continue paying all workers their salaries. However, they were all given thirty days administrative leave to allow their books, computers and facilities to be audited.

The audited results were staggering. The most striking portion of the report was the amount of drugs, real estate and weaponry. The drugs found had a street value of $1.1 billion dollars. This included $275 million of crack cocaine, $328 million of powdered cocaine, $180 million of heroin, $275 million of marijuana and $46 million of miscellaneous drugs. The FBI owned 47 Mercedes Benzes, 14 Rolls Royces, 22 chateaux in Italy, 11 homes in Mexico, 16 houses in Spain, 18 homes in Germany, 45 homes spread across the former Soviet Union and 62 homes spread across the United States. The average home-assessed value was $575,000. Each home was fully equipped with small arms and surveillance equipment, and most had two or three floors built underground. The FBI also owned 282 planes, 57 helicopters, 1800 sedans and 53 office buildings in the United States. They had more weaponry than Iran, Iraq, West Germany and Israel combined.

When the President saw the report from the committee, he immediately summoned the Speaker and Senate Majority Leader to the Oval Office. They arrived within two hours. He had Vice President Spencer Leon, Barton Craig and Cintura with him.

The six of them discussed the report and agreed that the public deserved to know the results of their investigation. However, for the good of the country, they had to package the information, so it would be palatable for the electorate. They asked Cintura to write a statement for the press. She agreed to do it immediately, fax them a copy that night and then disseminate it to the major news organizations across the country. It read as follows:

"After a thorough audit of FBI computer files and records, we have proof that the 238 people in custody abused their position for financial gain. Since many of our loyal citizens are serving around the world in sensitive positions, the details of our investigation are sealed via court order. All parties have pled guilty and have accepted full responsibility for their crimes. Congress and I will work in concert to orchestrate a smooth dismantling of the FBI. Their duties will be distributed among several agencies to include the CIA, ATF, DEA and the Department of Interior. Due to the diligence and tenacity of a few concerned citizens who reported corrupt governmental employees, we have been able to punish the guilty and restore confidence in a federal government that our forefathers shed their blood to protect and preserve. As the preamble to our Constitution states, 'We the people...form a more perfect union.' It takes all of us working in concert to keep our tenets safe from the potential tyrants within our union and the fanatics around the world."

After it was published, Cintura's strokes soothed the readers' fears and restored confidence in the federal government. The President's approval rating shot up to 96 percent, and Vice President Leon led in the polls at a ratio of four to one in 38 states, but only had 68 percent of the voters. Cintura was guiding Leon throughout his campaign with tacit advice and political influence. However, it was evident that he was content to ride to the White House on the coattails of President Bob.

President Bob called Vice President Spencer Leon and said, "Get the lead out of your behind. I've built the Presidency for you, and you are walking around like the last black martyr. Sure we had a few setbacks, but don't be walking around as if it's doomsday. When you do, that someone will come along and squat in your face. You have to be proactive. If you lead in the polls by 70 percent, try harder and make it 80 percent. Don't settle for appearing on top or the status quo. Your job as President is to make it appear that the country is moving forward as a world power economically, educationally and in the in areas of human rights and military might. I don't care if you're the last of Shaka Zulu's descendants or the last guy to disco on the moon, to be presidential you must appear presidential. You still have a year before the election, so get moving!"

"Why the hell do you care so much? You'll be out of office in a year."

"I care because I give a damn! We've come a long way since you were a paperboy spending half your check on Caedie."

"How did you know about Caedie? We come from two totally different backgrounds."

"Yes, Leon, we come from two different backgrounds, but we were cut from the same damn cloth. Some people were cut from the BS cloth, and BS does not stand for boy scouts. Those people spin knowledge from the tongue and not from the head. Then there are the FA's. Yes they are the 'fat asses.' They spin knowledge from the head and not the heart. Then there are the 'don't give a shits.' They don't know anything, don't want to know nothing and do absolutely nothing. And lastly there are the BA's, yes bad asses. That's you and me. We spin knowledge from the head as well as the heart. However, we know how to maintain the balance between what we have to do and what we want to do and then do what we believe is right. We stay a step ahead of the competition, give them just enough rope to hang themselves and stay close enough to mourn them and benefit from their demise. I give a damn because I don't have room to tolerate complacency.

"You are sitting where you're sitting because I took a chance. Everyone told me in my first presidential campaign to choose a white, Southern, moderate Democrat as my running mate. But I chose you because you were the best candidate available. You were a Lieutenant Colonel in the United States Air Force. You flew more combat missions in Desert Storm than any other American pilot. I could have cared less if you were green with purple polka dots. You come to work and do the best job possible. I care what the opposition has to say as well as every man and woman who took time out of their busy schedule and voted for me. I didn't get out there and lie or play the peasant game, I'm better than you. The American people are like babies; they can spot a phony a mile away. I gave the American people hope. That's all any of us can give. Hope that their tomorrow will be better than their today."

President Bob hesitated to digress for a minute then said, "Now as for your Caedie, upon taking office, I had you, the White House staff and cabinet investigated by the FBI. As you know, they had already obtained background information on me. We took an oath to govern this country to the best of our abilities and within the framework of the law. With our jobs came a responsibility to subject ourselves to public and political scrutiny. We always want to be able to lift our heads high and say to the world,

'Look all you want, the only thing you'll find is a man of integrity, honesty and loyalty.' I know Caedie was 29 and you were 17 when you two met. You delivered more than papers to her on those cold New York nights. By the time you graduated from high school at 18, she had your twin boys. You joined the armed forces and sent half of your check to her for seven years until one day you came home and found out she was married, and the children weren't even yours. You're walking around here like a swollen peacock and have tried to bury the past. But you don't understand that you must use the past to forge your future. Sure the FBI found out and don't think any reporter worth his salt won't dig for dirt. You have an obligation to turn the mound of dirt into a puddle of clear water. In your acceptance speech just say, 'I made some mistakes in the past, but I always did what I thought was right.' Then let the reporters dig. You'll get compassion from your constituents and win the respect of your opposition.

You know 'the game.' The higher the office the more you have to play 'the game.' Being at political gatherings, hugging and kissing babies and their mothers, aunts or grandmothers is all part of the game. Getting in bed with opposing foes in order to circumvent a common interest is part of the game. Obtaining financing among the politically connected and business elite is part of the game. Staying two steps ahead of your opposition, while walking beside him, is part of the game. Shouldering others' responsibilities when it's to your advantage and shedding it when it isn't is part of the game. Wearing tuxedoes to parties when you'd rather hang out in jeans with your old army buddies is part of the game. Attending late night parties alone, when your wife is tired of all of the phoniness, is part of the game. Coming home after an exhausting day at the office looking to someone for affection and understanding who had said years prior 'For better or for worse' is not part of the game but part of the problem."

Vice President Leon had learned more about political strategy in the last few years under President Bob's tutelage than in his 15 political science classes in college. As the President talked, his defensive demeanor softened to a savvy sponge.

President Bob paused, put his hand on Vice President Leon's shoulders and said, "I care because I believe I made a difference; I believe you can too. When everything is said and done, that's the only thing that counts. Remember, it was just a flicker and not a flame that caused the Great Chicago Fire, and so it is with politics."

Vice President Leon thanked the President for his advice and friendship. He then excused himself, so he could go home and reflect on their conversation and chart his political future.

JESSIE

As Vice President Leon strolled out of the door, President Bob thought about how he first met Vice President Leon and his wife Stella.

President Bob met Stella while she was practicing for the "Up With People" talent competition at the University of Texas at Austin. At that time, he was a young senator and contest judge. The day before the actual competition, the three-judge panel was given a tour of the university's theater and trained on the contest rules and scoring procedures, while the contestants were practicing their routines. Most of the contestants saw the judges, made eye contact and flirted.

Desiree Washington conveniently bent at the waist to tie her shoes, so her voluptuous breasts dangled for the judges to see. Her auburn hair and hazel eyes accented her 5-foot-8-inch frame and long shapely legs. Stephanie Portals performed provocative dance routines after slowly stroking her pelvic and pubic areas. Her jet-black hair followed her every movement like a horse's tail in a close race. Stephanie's smooth Filipino skin made her appear like well-tanned beach goers in Manila. Jessie Thompson's lips became suddenly dry, and she massaged them with her tongue. Her pageboy cut caused her sandy hair to accent her youthful innocence. At 5 feet 9 inches tall and 120 pounds, she appeared too tall to perform her contortionist routine. However, once she spread her legs, her joints became as flexible as a maestro in the midst of a Mozart concerto. Stella patiently waited her turn. She was dressed in blue jean shorts and a halter-top. Stella had slender legs, a small waistline and large breasts. Her large 38D breasts looked like two oranges glued onto a Coca-Cola bottle. She did not notice that Senator Bob was gazing at her but thought it odd that the judges were allowed to see them prior to their performances.

After Senator Bob, Josephine Siplica, owner of Universal Model, Inc., and Patricia Rameal, President and CEO of Georgia de La Hoya's Fashions, concluded their tour and training, they went to the restrooms near the lobby entrance. When Senator Bob came out of the restroom, Jessie was standing outside. She told Senator Bob his fly was open. As he looked down to see, she said "Gotcha! I'm just kidding. However, I'm glad you're interested in seeing how we perform prior to tomorrow's competition. I may be practicing something new later if you care to stop by." Senator Bob smiled and thanked her for the offer. She leaned forward, hugged him and stroked him with her right hand as she slipped her room key into his pocket. As they separated, Stella walked toward the restroom and saw their embrace. Senator Bob blushed and told Stella she was very talented and if he could ever be of assistance to her, not to hesitate to call.

She said, "Okay, but I always rely on my Christian upbringing. My mother used to say that between the sheets of time we all meet our destiny." She then excused herself and walked into the restroom smiling.

Later on, Senator Bob wished Jessie luck and told her, "I am only one of three judges and have to be impartial because the most talented performer should win. All of the contestants are winners and will receive their awards in due time. I'm attending a dinner party at the Seven Doves Hotel next week, would you like to go with me?"

The Seven Doves Hotel is a five-star hotel that recently hosted the first Emmy Awards held outside of Hollywood, California. Rooms generally were $350 a night. And the presidential suite, which was a mere $1,100 a night, came complete with a full kitchen, Jacuzzi, 50" television, a separate den complete with office materials, a fax machine, personal computer, 6' x 6' balcony, a living room, a dining room and two king size bedrooms.

"Senator Bob, will there be dancing?" asked Jessie.

"It will just be a formal dinner party with after-five attire. However, we will have ample time to let our hearts dance with joy over time in my suite following dinner."

"Okay." Jessie retrieved the key from his pocket, smiled coyly, turned and strolled away. Her hips swayed like firm Jell-O, rocking ever so slightly each time Jessie moved.

The night of the contest, Senator Bob stood in awe as Stella's sultry voice and stage presence held the audience on a string as she sang "Nothing's Between Us But Love." Her stage presence and voice were similar to Billie Holiday, and she had the beauty of Lena Horne. Stella was dressed in a black sequined evening gown with a thigh high split on the left side. Her shiny black hair was combed back resting comfortably on her shoulders. Stella's ears were accented with onyx earrings inlaid with a one-carat diamond. During the judge's deliberations, Senator Bob told the other two judges that all of the contestants were polished, but Stella was a star and had more talent than her competitors. They agreed with him and awarded Stella first place prizes of $10,000 and a record contract with UStar Records.

While the other contestants hugged and congratulated her, Senator Bob's thoughts were about an incident that occurred the day before the competition. Stella was a starlet, and Jessie was a "milker." Jessie was the typical "wannabee." She was the type of woman who had no problem trading sex for position or wealth. Jessie would use her seductive powers to milk people in position for all they were worth and then move on. Senator Bob knew this the night of the dinner party, so he ignored her all night. She was dressed in a modest evening gown with a low neckline. Jessie tried to make eye contact with him several times; however, he always looked in another direction as if to ignore her invitation. She became frustrated, so she mingled with the other guests. Near the end of the evening when Jessie was alone, he walked over to her and said, "Meet me in the presidential suite in thirty minutes." Senator Bob then made his parting remarks to influential guests and retired to his suite.

Jessie waited five minutes after he left and then went to his suite. She knocked on the door, and Senator Bob opened the door and invited her in. He closed the door and pulled her close. Senator Bob kissed her hard and pulled her torso to his. She offered no resistance but rubbed him with a cat-like pull as he squeezed and caressed her breast with one hand and felt his way up her sleek long legs along her stockings to her auburn crotchless panties. They made love on the carpet until their bodies were soaked with perspiration and love juices. Then they took a shower and bathed in the Jacuzzi. As the jets soothed their private areas, Jessie turned her back to him and snuggled close in his arms. Senator Bob rose to the occasion and another lovemaking interlude ensued.

Early the next morning, Senator Bob told me to drive her home. Sometime during the night he had made Jessie his Austin, Texas office manager. She was to receive an annual $65,000 salary, and her duties were to satisfy his political needs in Austin. The Senator was building coalitions for future political ambitions and made it clear that his team would benefit as he rose in politics. Jessie currently serves as his national poll consultant in Washington, D.C.

Stella never called until many years later when Vice President Leon had expressed interest in running for Vice President. She called President Bob while he was considering a number of running mates. He did not recognize her name at first; however, when she reminded him of how they met, he instantly recalled their relationship. While she talked about the positive attributes Vice President Leon would bring, particularly a significant number of black votes, he agreed to float his name around to see if the voters would support a black Vice President or Chief of Staff. The polls showed an 85 percent chance that President Bob would be elected with a black Vice President and 25 percent if he had a black Chief of Staff. So, Leon's vice presidential election was easy.

President Bob knew that Barton Craig coveted the Secretary of State position but did not have any international governmental experience. He did not have the heart to tell Barton no, so PB summoned him to the office and told him that he had two positions to fill, the Chief of Staff and Secretary of State. President Bob described the position of Chief of Staff as requiring someone that's media friendly, extremely organized, wouldn't mind traveling periodically and able to supervise a 250 member White

House staff. He indicated that the Secretary of State position required worldwide travel to resolve issues regarding national security. President Bob gave Barton two weeks to make his decision. Barton called the next day and accepted the Chief of Staff position.

Now it's six years later, well into President Bob's second term, and politics have changed very little. Most politicians talk without having anything to say. They have a classic case of "me-itis." The world revolves around them, and they are the center of their own universe. The sad thing is that they realize it yet do nothing about it. However, society is the worst culprit because it placates the self-centered, not with a blanket of silence, but with the fear of not saying anything that would prolong the politician's monologue. The good politicians are viewed as an enigma. They come across cocky, confident and intelligent. They listen to their constituents and articulate their constituents' concerns before legislative bodies and decision-makers.

All one has to do is to look at the shakiness of the Russian empire which is due to poor leadership. Their economy is in shambles due to decades of catering to the state run colleges, businesses and healthcare institutions. The lack of assistance from the business community has resulted in community resentment and hostility. Businesses have closed and boarded up their doors in anticipation of riots.

While the United States economy is robust and unemployment is low, Russia wallows in despair with no apparent solution. President Bob sent Carmon Bridges, Chairman of the Federal Reserve, to chair the Big Nine Economic Summit. The countries in attendance included Japan, England, France, Spain, Great Britain, Russia, Germany and China. Royal Simonsenov, Russia's Economic Minister, came with an open mind and a willingness to learn from his counterparts. After fourteen days of intense deliberations, these economic leaders drafted a document that included a $1.54 billion loan from the International Monetary Fund. They also executed an agreement that would protect the United States policy of International Hold from any adverse criticism.

Originally, International Hold was a process to confine and quarantine military personnel stationed in Thailand, the Philippines and South Korea who had contracted incurable strains of venereal diseases. They were coerced into signing documents allowing military scientists and hospitals to treat them with unapproved experimental medications. Their families would be notified that they had been killed in the line of duty by car bombs or terrorist attacks involving explosions, which hadn't left any body parts.

Today, International Hold is the federal government's process of incarcerating immigrants for unspecified time limits after securing secret incriminating evidence on them. The evidence is usually derived from a "reliable source" that would accuse someone of Arab or Muslim descent of associating with known terrorists. It's not unusual for a defendant to spend three years incarcerated before he/she is allowed to talk to an attorney or is deported. Defendants rarely confess; however, by the time they get out of jail, their perceived threat to national security has dissipated, and they are deported.

President Bob believes it's in the interest of national security that this process be left intact. He has explained on numerous occasions that although the United States is the world's largest superpower, it has the responsibility of being prudent in its tactical approaches to potential terrorism. The House and Senate Republicans threatened to play the "intimidation card." They have threatened to leak to the press that President Bob's administration has supported an evil and illegal International Hold process while simultaneously accusing China, Russia, Serbia, Bosnia, Iran, Iraq and Cuba of human rights violations. They are hoping this maneuver will weaken Vice President Leon's candidacy and embarrass the administration.

President Bob called Cintura and directed her to immediately coordinate a media information campaign to teach the public about the International Hold process and obtain their support in retaining it. This tactical maneuver would placate the voters and keep Vice President Leon's momentum going. Nothing kills a campaign quicker than negative publicity. So, Cintura arranged a fireside chat for President Bob from the Oval Office with the American People. By 7:00 p.m. that evening, President Bob was on all of the networks. A wife and mother of two victims of the

Oklahoma bombing incident accompanied him. He introduced one of them as the parent of three children and the other as a widow with two children. President Bob told both of their stories as the camera focused on their faces. He explained how their loved ones had gone to work on the day of the bombing as they had done so many times before. They were dedicated to their families, churches and jobs. However, due to unscrupulous terrorists, their lives were taken away. President Bob hesitated for a moment because both women began to sob uncontrollably.

After they composed themselves, he discussed the history of International Hold. He stated that it had been created under the leadership of President Dwight D. Eisenhower. President Eisenhower had instructed his presidential police to handle what he perceived as a threat to the American people. President Bob paused for a moment, and said, "That's why I'm here today." I don't want the press or my congressional or judicial colleagues to misunderstand our history. We are a people that must stand united to thwart threats aggressively. We have always sought world peace; however, we are willing to defend what is inherently ours and that which is in our national interest. So I ask for your continued support as the Congress and I continue our dialogue." A fifteen-minute film showing the criminal history of 24 men who had been detained for the last two years followed his speech.

The next day Jessie reported that the President's speech got a 90 percent approval rating in the polls. Cintura told him that congressional phone calls and faxes had poured in through the night pledging their support for the current International Hold process. President Bob informed Vice President Leon of the good news and urged him to always stay one step ahead of his Republican opponent, Peter Pekins, and never underestimate the intelligence of the American people.

Vice President Leon was ready to leave because he was scheduled to meet his wife for dinner at Casey's, an upscale restaurant in the heart of the city. President Bob asked Leon to escort Cintura to her car while he and Jessie retired to his office to review the poll data again. Vice President Leon readily agreed and got up to walk her to the parking lot. He smiled to himself as he and Cintura made their way out the door.

Jessie was quite a chameleon. She played the part of the devoted staff member; she dressed conservatively in the office and wore her hair up and donned stylish black-framed glasses. Jessie dated well-to-do, older professional men and graciously accepted their tokens of affection that included two sable coats, four mink coats, a Mercedes sports car, several diamond rings and necklaces and a Japanese Spitz. Jessie confided in President Bob that she was a showpiece for most of the men who were either too old to get it up or needed a "showpiece" to mask their homosexual activity.

President Bob knew her resume yet didn't mind her excursions because she was loyal. The Secret Service agents were always close, so those closest to him knew how to be discreet. Jessie and the President entered his office discussing charts, figures and demographics. As he shut the door behind them, Jessie dropped the folders she was carrying on the floor.

She said coyly, "I'm so sorry, Mr. President. I'll pick them up." As she bent over to pick up the folders, her butt rubbed against his zipper. President Bob gave in to the moment, reached up her skirt finding her silver crotchless panties, a narrow passage to temporal paradise. His presidential couch a rocking horse of pleasure.

An hour later, Jessie came out of the office looking relieved from the warm shower she and President Bob had shared after their erotic exercise. She told him that his office had all the amenities of home, and every woman needed a full bathroom adjacent to her office. As he stuffed her panties into his right pants pocket, he commented that she could use his facilities whenever the urge arose. Since it was late, President Bob ordered me to drive Jessie to her car about a half-mile away in the White House staff parking lot.

President Bob returned to the Oval Office to review his calendar and prepared for the next day's events. His itinerary noted that he was scheduled to meet with JR Pecker, a long time friend.

JR Pecker was the son of the deceased Houston, Texas billionaire and restaurateur Milton Pecker. As most people know, Houston, Texas, has more restaurants than any other city in the United States. It's so hot in Houston that the average family eats out four days a week. Although they have a huge Italian and Mexican presence, beef restaurants represent 65 percent of all sales. There were six Pecker restaurants in Houston. The average cost of lunch was $10.95 and dinner was $15.95. Day or night, the Pecker Restaurants were always full with customers.

President Bob's favorite two Pecker entrees were Pecker Barbeque and Pecker Killer Steak. Both burned hotter than a jug of year old corn whisky. The barbeque had a house blend of seasonings with a special ground pepper called a skit.

Milton Pecker had initially pursued a degree in agriculture because he was interested in farming. However, in his third year of college, he changed his major to culinary arts. He saw Houston changing and realized the community needed more restaurants. The average daily temperature in Houston was 96 degrees, and he suspected families would prefer to dine out if they could find a good restaurant with reasonable prices which was located in a safe section of town.

Old man Pecker graduated from college with bachelors degrees in business administration and culinary arts. He couldn't afford to open a restaurant on the main street, so he opened it on the second floor of his cousin's barbershop. Old man Pecker asked Millie, his college sweetheart, to work with him until she found a better paying job. He offered to pay her ten percent of his income from Pecker's.

In order to get customers, he convinced some schoolmates to print leaflets and hand them out at local schools, colleges, universities and businesses. The leaflets read, "Opening Day Sale. Taste the best barbeque in Texas for 25 cents. We have three kinds—measly mild, hot and spicy or shake your bottom. We also will have a steak tasting contest between our Killer Steak Sauce and Sweet-N-Sassy Sauce. It only costs 50 cents per plate, but all the contestants will get their name with a group picture in the local paper."

People arrived two hours early on opening day. Milton made 25 gallons of lemonade the night before. He explained to the people outside that he was not quite ready to feed them, but they were more than welcome to come in, sit down and have a glass of lemonade on the house. Well you've never seen people move so fast. Customers continuously came out of curiosity and others to taste food prepared a little differently. Milton's little restaurant could only seat 35 people, but they didn't mind waiting. After they ate their meals, most customers commented that the food was quite tasty, and they would be back. They also left tips on the table for the waitress. By the end of the day, Milton's one-week supply of food was gone. He had made $253 at a time when you could buy a side of beef for $50. Millie decided to keep her good paying job and married Milton two months later. Through *The Houston Chronicle* and the neighborhood grapevine, word spread far and wide about Pecker's activities, and the community responded with support.

After their first six months in business, the Peckers invested 30 percent of their money in Houston Oil, a start up company. Their investment turned into a gold mine. Within a year, they realized an annual income of $20,000. They were philanthropic and donated funds to community projects, college scholarships and mentoring programs.

President Bob's father had attended junior and senior high school with Milton and Millie. His father was the high school's quarterback, and Milton was a wide receiver. President Bob's father had dated Millie in high school. At their senior class barn dance, she caught him necking with a hot senior cheerleader and broke off their relationship. He tried to explain that the girl was only giving him a good-bye kiss.

Millie retorted, "Just make that two smacks on the lips; Miss Hot Pants gave you one and here's another." She balled up her fist, hit him in the mouth and strutted away.

President Bob's father didn't bother to pursue her. He got up, dusted himself off and returned to the dance.

President Bob's parents took him to Pecker's when he was 5 years old, two years after Pecker's restaurants opened. When President Bob's father walked into Pecker's Restaurant, he introduced his wife and son and congratulated them on having an excellent restaurant. President Bob's father told Milton that he had the second best girl in Texas. He winked at Millie as he shook Milton's hand. Millie gave him a hug and in that brief moment, he knew he was forgiven. President Bob never told Millie that the girl he had been caught kissing was Milton's girlfriend.

Millie was pregnant with Milton Jr. at the same time President Bob's mother was pregnant with him. The babies were born two weeks and two days apart. Their parents remained close friends until they died several years ago in a train crash. They were taking a cross-country trip together when the engineer of an oncoming train fell asleep and failed to change tracks. The collision crushed the first five train cars. Unfortunately, they were in the second car. Milton Jr., known as JR Pecker now, heads the National Democratic Committee and oversees the Pecker Restaurant empire.

During a recent Presidential visit to Italy, JR Pecker was part of President Bob's entourage. While sipping cocktails on Air Force One, they reminisced about the three weeks they had spent in Italy and Spain between their sophomore and junior year in college. JR ribbed President Bob about being the first one to make love in the Sistine Chapel. President Bob chided back and reminded him of the time they were observing the beautiful architecture in one of Barcelona's many Gothic cathedrals, and a very attractive Spanish woman caught his eye. They had started talking and twenty minutes later were making love in the women's restroom only to be interrupted by a cleaning lady, who must have been a devout Catholic.

She exclaimed in a typical European tone as she clutched her rosary beads, "Oh my God, Great St. Francis of Assisi. You kids stop that right now! You should be ashamed of yourselves!"

Her small 5-foot-3-inch stature and gray hair did not cause JR to move from his comfortable position. However, when she shoved the beads in her smock pocket, took the broom stick out of its head and held it high ready to wield with her callused hands, he pulled up his pants. The girl pulled down her dress, grabbed her panties and ran out the door. She made it out the door unscathed. However, JR received several licks before he got past the cleaning lady. President Bob and JR had a good chuckle. Later they talked about how they traveled from Barcelona by boat to Capri. This charming little island was located in the Gulf of Naples. The cave-like summerhouses called grottoes were not air-conditioned but were surprisingly cool. The islanders were very friendly, and they enjoyed nightly parties during the summer.

JR told President Bob that he was ready to settle down. He never had any problems meeting women or satisfying his sexual desires, but he had never found a woman he could trust. They all either loved his money or his lust. He said he wished he could meet someone down to earth. President Bob thought for a moment and told him about Jessie.

"I know a young lady that you may be interested in. She's quiet and a little shy, but she is a very nice person. This woman worked for me in Texas as well as in Washington. She's dated but has never been married. I usually don't believe in matchmaking; however, she will be in the White House for a meeting when I get back."

"So what does she look like? She's probably freckled, 4 feet 8 inches tall and weighs 210 pounds."

"Why don't you stop by the White House and see for yourself? If you get a date, I'll even lend you my driver."

"Maybe I will."

The rest of the trip went well. JR found a nice area where he could open his first restaurant outside of the United States. Continental International Hotel, Incorporated had recently built a small 200-room hotel on Capri. They tunneled out part of the mountain and built the hotel so it protruded into the mountain. The owners allowed JR to place his restaurant at the front of the hotel, so patrons would have a good view of the island. In gratitude for President Bob's assistance, JR told him he would give him a permanent room in the hotel.

After a week of discussions and touring several textile and automobile plants, President Bob and Italian President Santos signed a free trade agreement. This would mean $2 billion in additional exports for the United States and millions of jobs for the Italian people. US businesses would be able to purchase cars and textile products at a low price and use them for manufacturing other products and automobiles to be sold around the world.

When they returned home, the media gave a positive spin to their trip but did not mention that JR was there. Newspaper articles and broadcasts stated, "President Bob was accompanied by US business leaders who wanted to develop additional markets for their businesses. They paid for their own expenses…"

President Bob told Jessie about JR and what he said about being ready to settle down. President Bob said that he did not want Jessie to get involved with JR if she couldn't be true to him. He respected her loyalty, but he would not force her to do anything she wasn't comfortable with.

Jessie said she would consider it. However, if she didn't like JR, she wanted the option of continuing their relationship as time permitted. However, she wouldn't become involved with anyone else. President Bob agreed and informed Cintura of this agreement after Jessie left. He asked Cintura to keep an eye on their relationship and report to him anything that happened out of the ordinary.

Cintura met with her security team and ordered them to activate the listening devices in area restaurants and cafeterias. She admonished them to keep a low profile while providing 24-hour surveillance on both JR and Jessie.

The next day JR came to the White House. Jessie was dressed in a gray suit, her skirt was slightly below the knee and her hair was pinned up. She was waiting outside of the Oval Office. Cintura introduced JR to Jessie and asked him to wait with her because President Bob was in consultation with Vice President Leon and Barton Craig, Chief of Staff.

As JR shook Jessie's hand, he couldn't help notice her beautiful smile. Her slightly brown, tinted wire-framed glasses made her hazel eyes appear mysterious. She had full lips and wore a light but sensuous perfume. He asked her what the name of the perfume was.

"It's called Nightly Magic."

"As sweet as you smell, it should be called Daytime Delight." They both laughed.

"Thank you very much for the compliment."

"I'm sure you receive compliments all of the time. You are pretty and must have a good head on your shoulders because you either work for or bring work to the White House."

They began sharing impersonal background information as President Bob, Vice President Leon and Barton Craig came strolling out of the President's office. President Bob told JR and Jessie he was sorry that he could not meet with them today. He had a pressing meeting with congressional leaders in thirty minutes and asked if they could reschedule their meeting for later in the week.

JR said, "Only if this pretty little lady will join me for lunch."

"Of course I will," said Jessie.

Jessie looked at JR and heard something she hadn't heard from her other suitors—honesty. He was like a country Georgian boy sent north from the family farm to a big city like Chicago. JR was ready to tell his whole life story to the first person who was really interested in hearing it. Jessie was fascinated with his upbringing, but she was more impressed because he took a family empire that was passed on to him and did something positive with it. JR had increased the value of the company by 25 percent during the seven years he had full control. He also was involved in a great deal of philanthropic activities. JR had created a breast cancer research facility, built shelters for the homeless and battered women and created welfare-to-work-programs in Houston.

However, his welfare-to-work programs got the most political acclaim. Less than a year ago, the Texas legislature passed a law that terminated people from the welfare rolls who were healthy and had less than three children. JR spearheaded an effort to hire and train the first 200 single women that had been terminated. He bought an all-suite hotel and allowed the women to stay there rent-free with the stipulation that they give a 100 percent effort daily. JR provided free day care services for children less than 5 years of age, after school programs for children age 5 and over and daily six-hour free educational classes in preparation for the GED examination. He also provided scholarships for gifted and talented programs.

Jessie noticed that JR was not as handsome as President Bob; however, he was attractive. His eyes lit up as he discussed seeing the look on the children's faces as they received scholarships; he viewed these scholarships as a chance for a better life. When JR talked, he was very expressive with his hands. He had gotten too carried away, caught himself and asked Jessie to describe her background.

She talked about meeting President Bob at a beauty pageant, obtaining her first job from him and respecting him for giving her a chance to prove herself. Jessie came from a middle class background. Her mother had been a business education teacher for thirty years, and her father was a Baptist minister. She had spent her childhood attending church several times weekly. Monday was Baptist Training Union where the young people learned about the tenets of the church; Wednesday night at 7:30 p.m. was Bible Study; Thursday night was choir rehearsal; and, Sunday school was at 9:30 a.m. and morning service at 11:00 a.m. Jessie said, "By the time I was 18, I was prayed out, sung out and churched out, so I got out. I went to the beauty pageant against my parents' wishes, and they never forgave me.

"I have two sisters who are happily married. One has three kids, and the other has four. They are both teachers and raise their children according to church doctrine. They feel the church helps their kids develop the moral integrity they need to survive in this world. As Pastor Miligan says, (pausing and standing stalwartly with an authoritarian look of humility on his face) 'God gives man rules of ethics to govern his conduct, and man in turn has historically given God a hard time. Even as kids, you're taught to say thank you sometimes.' My parents are still there praising their God and expected me to do the same. I just couldn't take it anymore. I've always had the "bootstrap mentality." You pull yourself up by your bootstraps and make it in life the best way you can. I still visit them on holidays and birthdays, but our worlds are totally different. They know I love them, and that's all that really matters."

JR told her that she was fortunate to be reared with two siblings she could confide in. He had grown up as the only child and since his parents were deceased, God was the only one he could talk to. JR never talked to God or maintained a personal relationship with God as many Christians claim; however, most of the time God had to listen in to find out what was going on with him.

JR asked her why she didn't have a man in her life.

Jessie said, "The same reason you probably don't have a woman in yours. Most people are not honest and faithful. They'll sleep with anyone, anytime and any way. That's a sad commentary on the greatest nation in the world. But the hell we're in now, you just make the best of a bad situation and say to yourself, 'He or she isn't worth my time if he or she isn't true to me.'"

"I told you that you were an astute woman," JR proclaimed.

They ate at Poor Timmy's and had salads and Maryland crab cake platters.

He told her, "The crab cakes are nice, but you haven't done any good eating until you have tasted a good Pecker steak. Why don't you come to Houston, Texas, and have one on me?"

"My job keeps me in Washington twelve months a year, but I wouldn't mind having another meal with you locally."

"How about having dinner at a nice cozy restaurant?"

"Yes, honey. That would be lovely"

"Jessie, what's your address?"

Jessie took a pen and paper from her purse and wrote her name, address and telephone number down and gave it to him. "I'll be ready at 7:30 p.m.," she said. Jessie extended her hand, and they shook hands as they left the restaurant. Since she was only across the street from her office, he walked her to the door and said goodbye.

JR arrived at Jesse's home at 7:15 p.m. Her four-bedroom home was in the north end of Takoma Park, Maryland, where most well-to-do Washington socialites live. Jessie answered the door dressed in a conservative pantsuit, small diamond studded earrings and matching diamond pin on the left upper chest portion of her jacket. JR handed her a dozen red roses and a box of Godiva chocolates. She thanked him as she put the flowers in a vase with water. He asked to use the restroom, so she escorted him to a large half bathroom next to the powder room on the first floor. It had pink hand towels and artificial floral arrangements.

"Your home is beautiful and a perfect reflection of your tender and caring spirit."

"That's a sweet thing to say," Jessie said blushing. She closed the door behind him, carried her candy to the kitchen and put it away.

While he was in the restroom, she remembered the last time that she received flowers was from President Bob. It was a dozen pink roses with a card that said, "The fragrance of their beauty is nothing compared to the nectar of your love." Her heart melted with the thought about one of their last pleasure-filled nights making love in her Jacuzzi.

JR came into the kitchen and watched her as she smiled and appeared to be deep in thought. He suspected that his gesture had lit a candle in her heart. After a few seconds he said, "Beautiful lady, are you ready to go to dinner?"

She composed herself and said, "Yes."

Jessie picked up her purse and followed JR out the door. I held the limousine's door while they got into the rear seat. We drove off as the car CD player played a series of love ballads, "You're Too Special and You're Mine," "I Was Searching Until You" and "Let's Take a Chance on Romance." As the music played softly they talked about their likes, dislikes and politics. JR took Jessie to David Gregory's in Washington, D.C. It was a casual elegant restaurant that serves exquisite, contemporary American cuisine about twenty-five minutes away.

When we arrived, I let them off in front of the restaurant, followed the valet's directions and parked the presidential limousine in the valet parking lot. Carlos, the maitre d', introduced himself to JR and Jessie as they walked inside the restaurant. He said the restaurant was a little crowded but since they had reservations, their table was ready.

JR slipped him a $100 bill as the maitre d' said, "This table in the back is perfect for such a charming couple."

The maitre d' escorted them to a table in the rear of the restaurant on the outside veranda. It was enclosed, and you could see the brightly-lit moon and stars. They both ordered medium-rare filet mignon served with Caesar salad, asparagus and oven-roasted potatoes. JR asked the waiter for a bottle of his best champagne and five minutes later he was being served from a bottle of Paul Mason, 1968. JR and Jessie continued to talk about politics, while enjoying the seductive and charming flavor of the restaurant's cuisine and décor. They both felt that politics was a necessary evil.

"The institution is good, but it is inherently flawed," chimed in JR. "The founding fathers assumed that politicians would be elected by the people to work for the ultimate good and would be kept in line by the other branches of government. However, all too often, Congress becomes a forum where personal agendas are espoused at the cost of constituents not receiving desired and deserved services. That's why Washington, D.C., is known as the land of compromise."

"Yes, compromise your principles, politics, and puss—I mean position."

JR was startled for a second and said, "You don't pull any punches, Jessie. I like you, and I think you know that. We can take it as slow as you want. I don't have anyone in my life right now. Do you have someone in yours?"

"Yes."

"Well, he is a lucky man," JR said, looking despondent.

"I was just kidding. No, there's no one in my life. However, long distant relationships very rarely work. I can't go flying off to Texas every week, but we'll see how it goes. Let's try friendship and see where it takes us."

"To friendship," JR said, as he picked up his glass.

"To friendship," Jessie raised her glass also and touched his. "So why don't you tell me about your last relationship."

"What exactly do you want to know?"

"I want to know about her and what went wrong. You seem to be a pretty nice guy. I don't understand how she let you get away."

JR hesitated momentarily, squirmed in his seat, and looked stoically as he collected his thoughts and said in a low sincere tone, "I was engaged once. Her name was Amanda Marlin. We met at a chamber of commerce meeting. She was vice-chairperson and moderated the meeting. Amanda was bright and very attractive. We dated for about six months, became very close and discovered a lot of things about one another. The only problem was that everything I told her was true, and everything she told me was a lie. Amanda told me that she was born in Houston and was the daughter of a tailor. She also said she worked her way through college as a waitress, saved her money and majored in business administration. My parents adored her but without my knowledge, they hired a private investigator to check her out. They found out that she was head of an underground organization called The Sisters of the Confederacy (SOC). Each member of this sisterhood pursued men of means or position and used them to finance or support their cause. They had evidence that revealed an instance where she embezzled $8 million from a bank president, one of her suitors. She got the money, skipped town and left the banker holding the bag. All of the money had been funneled through accounts in his name. He was tried, found guilty and sentenced to fifteen years in a medium security prison."

"I've never heard of The Sisters of the Confederacy. What is their agenda, JR?"

"Their agenda is to prevent Hispanics and black Americans from becoming the majority. The SOC fears that they will become the majority race and will control the political, social and financial climate of America. They also cling to the Old Dixie proposition that minorities' access and usage of education would change the Confederacy forever. I think that the SOC members are little Hitlers in skirts!"

Jessie saw that the conversation was getting a little too distasteful for her palate so she said, "Well my last love interest was a lot less exciting. Toliver was an epidemiologist, a Nobel Prize winner and a fascinating man. Once he started talking about work, I just couldn't understand a damn thing. I was a liberal arts major, okay. I had one year of biology, lots of English, mathematics, and technological courses but no science courses. Our relationship was over after the first date. He took me to his office at Johns Hopkins Hospital in Baltimore, Maryland. Toliver spent an hour and a half discussing the intricacies of the Ebola virus. To this day, I don't know what the hell he was talking about! To top it off, we had lunch in the cafeteria, Dutch!"

They both laughed. Then Jessie began discussing things she liked to do in her spare time. She said, "I enjoy walking through the park, hiking and horseback riding."

"I owned a 250-acre ranch and had 10 racehorses. One of my mares recently had a foal, but I haven't named it yet. I'll name it Jessie."

"No, Jessie is not a horse's name. A horse's name should be memorable like the flowers you gave me. I know, Thorny. Name the horse Thorny. No relationship is smooth all of the time. Successful relationships happen when two people discover how to deal with the thorny problems."

"Thorny it is."

After dinner JR took Jessie home; I watched as he walked her to the door and opened it for her. Jessie said, "It's late, JR. Thank you for a wonderful evening. I had a very nice time, and we should do it again soon."

JR leaned forward to kiss her, but Jessie extended her hand and said, "I don't kiss on the first date."

"Then what do you do on the second date?"

Jessie shook his hand, kissed him on the cheek and said, "I guess you're just going to have to wait and see." She said goodnight and turned to go inside. His eyes followed her hips as she glided like an angel through the door.

JR called Jessie later that night and thanked her for a lovely evening. Jessie said that she also had a good time. He mentioned that he was only going to be in town three more days and wanted to see her the next evening. Jessie agreed, and they ended up spending all three evenings together. JR did not get a kiss until the last evening, on Saturday night, when Jessie had invited him for dinner. She had never learned how to cook, so she had their meal catered. The caterers prepared grilled orange roughy stuffed with crabmeat in a wine sauce, cheese mashed potatoes, steamed broccoli, fresh rolls and champagne on ice. They left instructions for her to serve the meal within twenty minutes of her guest's arrival, so the fish would not taste dry.

As JR walked up to Jessie's door, he could see in the front bay window that there were no lights on inside. He rang the bell. Jessie greeted him at the door smiling warmly and wearing a short black, silk chemise. Her thick hair was laying beautifully 3 inches below her shoulders. Jessie had contacts on instead of her usual glasses. White candles were burning in the living room and the dining room, and two red candles were flickering on the dining room table beckoning JR to Jessie's lair. She escorted him to a seat at the dining room table and told him she wanted him to have a special meal before he returned home.

JR bubbled with joy like a kid in a candy store and said, "You didn't have to go through so much trouble for me."

"Yes I did because I think you're worth it and much more."

They ate their candlelit dinner savoring every moment and losing themselves in a sea of romance. Each compliment he paid her resulted in a kiss. He said that the candles were lovely and the ambiance was very romantic; then she kissed his right ear. JR commented that she looked radiant in candlelight; then she kissed his right cheek. He said softly that she was the sweetest woman he had ever met; then she kissed him on the eyebrow. Jessie then fed JR a piece of the orange roughy with his fork. JR chewed slowly as if savoring the tiny morsel and said that the fish was almost as tender as her compassion; then she kissed him on the nose. He said that she had become a significant part of his life. Finally, Jessie kissed JR on his lips ever so sweetly and sat down beside him at the table. They finished their meal gazing at one another with panting hearts and the silliness that make new love discoveries passionate. Their minds raced with the frivolities of love.

Jessie served strawberry shortcake for dessert. JR took one bite and said that it was delicious. However, he had the cream from the cake all over his mustache. She took a napkin and wiped it off, so he thanked her for her thoughtfulness.

"I wanted to do something special for you. You've been very sweet to me every since we met. I just want you to know that you are special to me. This is my way of saying thank you."

JR appeared speechless for a moment then looked her in the eyes and said, "I am the one who needs to thank you for putting a spark back in my life. I want to make a toast." They both lifted their glasses as JR said, "To Jessie, the most beautiful and wonderful woman in my life."

"No." She lifted her glass in a lively spirit-filled fashion, while meeting his eyes with a mesmerizing gaze and said, "To us—a relationship that is blossoming into something special." They touched glasses, sipped a little champagne, rose and slowly walked toward one another. Jessie and JR ended up embracing and kissing. One kiss led to several more and one caress led to a night of passion.

The next morning Jessie was awakened by the smell of frying bacon. She went into the bathroom, brushed her teeth and washed her face and hands. Then she put on a robe and walked into the kitchen. The table was set with fresh orange juice and two glasses. A half-pound of bacon was perfectly cooked and resting comfortably on a plate. Buttered toast was on another plate, and scrambled eggs with cheddar and American cheese was ready to come out of the skillet. She thought that JR looked kind of cute with his bikini shorts and apron on. After he emptied the contents of the frying ban into a bowl on the table and placed the skillet in the sink, Jessie hugged and kissed him. JR joked that she can't kiss the cook before breakfast and sat her down as she protested modestly. They both ate heartily and joked back and forth about their spontaneity the night before as well as the special lunch and dinners they had shared throughout the week.

"JR you're the first guy to ever fix me a meal. I think that was very sweet of you, and I wish you didn't have to go."

JR put one finger to Jessie's mouth and said, "Shhh. I'm not saying good-bye because we will see one another soon. I have to go home and take care of some business, but I'll be back soon; I promise."

"Just make sure it's no other woman's business you're taking care of, and hurry back." She kissed him as he put his arms around her waist and pulled her close.

Soon the plush carpet became their bed, and Jessie's robe became their pillow. After an hour of frolicking, JR spotted a clock on the wall that was chiming. He looked up and saw it was 10:00 a.m. JR informed Jessie that his flight was at noon, and President Bob's car was supposed to take him to the airport at 10:30 a.m. Jessie immediately noted that she was going with him to the airport, and he didn't protest. They showered together like two high school kids playing grown-up for the first time. Bubbles and

laughter became hot discovery zones. They were dressed and ready by
10:25 a.m. Other than JR's zipper being spotted down by the driver, they
were presentable.

They walked arm in arm all of the way to the airport. When it was time
to board the plane, JR kissed Jessie for what seemed to be an eternity to
the airline clerk. He was a first-class passenger, and all other passengers
were on board. The clerk started clearing his throat and finally interrupted
this passionate couple. Jessie blew a kiss good-bye to JR as he boarded the
plane.

As JR's plane taxied to the runway, Jessie walked back through the airport's parking lot feeling as though her heart was being torn from its
chamber. Anyone within earshot could hear her muttering to herself, "JR
my love, please don't forget me."

The swirling winds of doubt encompassed Jessie's every thought. She
spent the twenty-minute ride home doing the balancing act that all lovers
engage in. Battling juxtaposed thoughts aloud, in one breath, she
described JR as the greatest man in the world; however, in the next breath,
she talked about how unfaithful men were. Jessie concluded that she cared
for JR and joked that if he jilted her, she'd cut his balls off. She smiled and
pretended to be holding a knife in her right hand and cupped her left
hand, ready to receive JR's jewels upon completing the act. Her fantasy
was masked by a worrisome smile as she muttered, "I don't care either
way."

At the same time JR was whispering to a stewardess, "Once you have
tasted a Pecker, it's hard to let your lips and palate taste anything else." He
handed her a business card and invited her to visit one of his restaurants
the next time she was in Houston.

She asked, "Why?"

"Turn the card over Jessie."

She read it in a low voice, "Complimentary dinner for two."

"Yes for two."

"Thank you so much, but I don't know a soul in Houston."

"You do now."

The stewardess was very attentive to the passengers in first class and made an extra effort to insure JR was comfortable. While she was serving the other passengers snacks, she slipped him a small piece of paper with her name, address and telephone number. JR grasped the stewardess's hand gently as his index finger stroked the inside of her palm. She blushed, turned and quickly walked away; then she served the other passengers.

JR watched this hot little stewardess experience what President Bob calls a two-second orgasm. He believed that if two people found one another attractive, each could experience an orgasm without having intercourse by lightly touching sensitive spots on their love interest's hands or pelvis. Although JR was flattered by the stewardess's attention, he realized he had something special in his relationship with Jessie. He closed his eyes and dozed off, thinking about their last night together of total surrender to passion and love. The plane hit some turbulence, and the sudden 100-foot drop woke JR. He sat up, noticed a rise in his pants, took an airline magazine and put it over his pants. JR was embarrassed that Jessie had such a profound impact on him and stayed awake the remainder of the flight.

Instead of going home, Jessie called President Bob on her mobile phone to discuss her relationship with JR Pecker. President Bob told her to come by the Oval Office because he would be working there late and would make time to see her. Jessie readily agreed, closed her flip phone and proceeded to the White House. She arrived twenty minutes later, parked her car in the VIP lot, retrieved her purse and briefcase from the passenger seat and was escorted to the Oval Office. Jessie confidently greeted the President with a sturdy handshake as the Secret Service agent closed the office door. President Bob took her hand and put it around his waist, while gently kissing her lips. Jessie blushed, composed herself and told President Bob that she was in love with JR.

"Do you love him or his pecker?"

"There's only one pecker that I truly love—but JR's the one that's available!"

President Bob reached under her skirt and removed her pantyhose and dark-brown lace panties. He took the crotch of the panties and kissed them gently before slipping them into his left pants pocket. President Bob told her that after tonight she could follow her heart to Texas, but she should keep in touch. Jessie was so happy that she kissed President Bob on the lips, neck, nipples, navel and…They made love as two lovers saying good-bye before going off to war.

After the pulsating beat of their pleasure-filled escapade reached its crescendo and then dissipated, Jessie and President Bob hugged gently; then he kissed her softly. President Bob got up and allowed Jessie to retrieve her clothes that were strewn around the office. She was so excited that she could almost taste her freedom. Her cloak of embarrassment was finally being lifted a little so she could breathe. However, she knew that Cintura and President Bob had the keys to her happiness or destruction. Jessie's fate was in their hands, and she was prepared to make the necessary sacrifices to preserve her relationship with JR.

President Bob watched Jessie dress nervously without comment until she reached behind his desk where she thought her panties had been tossed. Seeing her search vigorously in vain, he smirked and said, "I kept a little final keepsake. I hope you don't mind"

"No, I don't mind as long as it's final." She then turned and walked toward the door.

Before she reached the door, President Bob grabbed the doorknob, looked at her intently and said sternly, "It's final as long as your loyalty is final." Then he opened the door and said, "Keep in touch." He watched Jessie scurry away.

ANDREA

Russ Scarboro, JR's driver, met him at the airport in his baby blue limousine. Russ told him that his daughter Andrea was at home in a tizzy because she had expected him to be home earlier in the week. JR told him that Andrea was always upset about something. If her love life wasn't going according to her script, she would come home, get in the Jacuzzi and pout for hours, as if brooding would solve her problems.

A few weeks earlier, Andrea had come home and announced that she found the man of her dreams, Donald Cameron. He was a recently hired, TV anchorman who had been recruited away from a popular station in Nashville, Tennessee. Donald had all of the essential elements she required. He was young, tall, handsome and made a very nice salary. His boyish charm, sense of humor and polished gentlemanly demeanor were his most attractive features. Andrea had met him in the parking lot his first day on the job when Donald asked for directions to the station's general manager's office. She said it would be easier to escort him to the office than to tell him how to navigate the station's 27-story mega-complex. After his two-hour orientation, the station manager gave him the rest of the day off, so he could find a house or an apartment. Donald found Andrea and told her that he was going to scout around for a place to live. She volunteered to show him around town. He accepted her offer and agreed to drive. Andrea directed him to various places in the suburbs where homes were nice, new and reasonably priced.

The ride in his Jaguar convertible was like a genie's carpet ride, swift and smooth. Andrea's sandy brown, shoulder length hair flowed in the wind, and the sun had been kind to her easily tanned skin. Her most distinguishing features were her deep black eyes and cute black mole on her right cheek.

Donald found her irresistible and charming. Despite looking at seven or eight places, he didn't find an apartment, condominium or house he liked. As the beautiful orange-red sunset adorned the skyline, Donald said to Andrea, "It's getting late, let me take you to dinner."

"All right, just take it slow around the curves," responded Andrea.

As they drove to the restaurant, Donald was relaxed and began to open up a little: "I'm excited about my new job but I'll never forget my humble beginnings in the TV industry." His voice perked up as he explained why he had been reluctant to leave his job in Nashville. "Prior to coming here, I was in Nashville since graduating from high school nine years ago and intended to work there just for the summer before going to college. I was hired as a runner to carry *Associated Press* stories from the wire service area to the TV anchors and reporters. On my days off, I used to fool around the station's set and pretend to be a weatherman. One day, unbeknownst to me, one of the station's cameramen had taped me. When the station's weatherman put in his two-week resignation on August 15, the cameraman gave the tape to the station's general manager. The manager liked my impromptu performance, called me in and offered me the job provided I serve a six-month probation. I was so excited, and asked, 'How soon can I start?' That same day, I was given a standard weather script, told to review it and report for work the following Monday."

Donald beamed with excitement as he continued. "Throughout the weekend, I practiced various approaches to delivering the script. I settled on using various types of pointers to get the audience's attention. I started out with a traditional aluminum pointer, then an alligator pointer and after that an umbrella pointer. After about a week, members of the audience began mailing me pointers. I would mention each person's name in the telecast and thank him or her for their originality. Within six weeks of my initial broadcast, the television station's news ratings had gone from third place to first."

"That was quite an accomplishment. I bet the women loved you!"

"Thank you. They did, but it nearly cost me my girlfriend. She didn't approve of women approaching me. Frequently, they would come to me with a pen and paper and ask for an autograph, while at the same time they would slip me their phone number or hotel room key. At first I took it as a compliment. However, my girlfriend became irritated, so I politely declined giving autographs."

"So what did you tell your fans?"

"I just told them the truth. I appreciated their interest, but my girlfriend was uncomfortable with me giving autographs, and the only bedroom I felt comfortable frequenting was hers. They usually respected my comments."

"So what did your family think of the family celebrity?"

"Family has a way of not letting you get a big head. My dad was a custodian at the Grand Old Opry for 37 years. He didn't think the television job would last, but he encouraged me. Dad said, 'Son you can always go back to college. Heck, they're offering you more money to start, than I got when I retired three years ago.' Thirty-six thousand five hundred dollars isn't chicken feed. There aren't many recent college graduates making that kind of money. My mom was just happy that I had a job. My younger brother who was 17 thought it was great to have a brother with media exposure. It got him a lot of dates because girls would go out with him in order to meet me or in the hope he would follow in my footsteps. I explained to him the dangers of dating around. You know how young people are. They think AIDS only affects the gay guy down the street and never rears its ugly little head in the straight community."

"So where's your wife or girlfriend?"

Donald looking dejected and responded, "I just broke up with my girlfriend. She didn't want me to leave Nashville. I wanted her to come with me, but she refused. She's a legal secretary. I offered to find her a job at a comparable or higher salary in Texas. However, she said that if I couldn't put a ring on her finger before leaving Nashville, she wanted me to leave and not come back."

"What did you do?"

"I left and I haven't seen her in four weeks."

"Do you miss her?"

"I'm not going to lie. Yes, I miss her. However, I am too young to get married. She doesn't understand that. I didn't want her to move from her parents' home to our home. I wanted her to live on her own just like I need to. We both need to experience our independence first before we can appreciate the nuances of a committed relationship."

Donald threw his hands up as if exacerbated by the thought and said, "I don't know if I did the right thing or not, but I told her the truth about how I felt."

"She probably realizes you were right. She'll come around; you'll see. You're a good catch, and she may have been foolish. She isn't a fool or you two would have never gotten together. She'll be back."

As Andrea made her last comment, Donald pulled his car in front of the hotel. He handed the valet his keys and strolled hand in hand with Andrea into the hotel.

They walked inside to the restaurant. The hostess seated them in a cozy little booth in the rear. The subdued lighting, modern décor and soft jazz emanating from ceiling speakers were perfect. It was loud enough to be soothing to the ears yet soft enough to allow patrons to talk and clearly hear one another.

Donald realized that he had done most of the talking and asked Andrea, "Why don't you have a hot date tonight?"

Andrea pretended to be stunned and said, "Didn't I tell you? He was arrested last week for stealing my heart and skipping town!"

They both chuckled.

"Seriously Andrea, don't you have a love interest?"

Andrea replied in a sincere, coy, mimicking tone, "Seriously Donald, I'm interested in love, but I do not have a love interest. Most guys aren't like you. They are not serious about a relationship or anything else. Our parents lived though the sexual revolution of the sixties, but most young men during their era had a work ethic. Today, we're living in the 'do nothing' cultural revolution of the 21st century. Twenty percent of eligible male workers are unemployed, another 30 percent are in jail and the remaining 40 percent are usually high on drugs or alcohol. So in other words, no matter how bright and intelligent I am, if sufficient guys aren't available, they aren't available."

Donald saw the conversation digressing, so he said, "I'll tell you what; I'll go out with you for dinner, a movie or dancing until you find someone more compatible, and you can go out with me until Jane comes back. That's her name, Jane Sue Montgomery. This way I can screen your suitors." Donald grinned mischievously and said, "I know your parents don't want you running off with a stranger."

"I like that idea, especially the dinner and dancing. The only man in my life is a father who's never home. My mother died from uterine cancer when I was 7 years old. They weren't married, but he came and got me when she passed away. He made sure I attended school and sent me to Oberlin College where I obtained a bachelor of arts in journalism. The station hired me as a result of my having worked as a summer intern after college. Unlike you, my starting salary was $22,000, but I've received annual bonuses and raises."

Donald, feeling impressed by her work ethic, leaned back in his seat, uncrossed his legs and smiled. He wanted to know more about this interesting young lady. "Your dad must have loved you and your mom very much to come get you."

Andrea looked a little startled by his comment and, as if pondering the thought she said, "I don't know. He never talks about her. When I ask him, he just looks off in the distance and has a serious look on his face. I don't know. Half the time I think he loves me; the rest of the time I think he wishes that I had never been born. Don't get me wrong; he's been there for recitals, graduations, bad times and good times. However, he just won't tell me what happened between my mother and him."

"Maybe he asked your mom to marry him, and she said no. He probably will tell you someday. Parents tend to think their children will never grow up and are not emotionally mature enough to handle certain information, even when the child is 42 and the parent is 62."

"You're definitely right about that," Andrea said, and then she laughed.

They paused long enough for the waiter to take their order and bring their food. Then they ate and continued to talk for the next two hours. After the waiter cleared the dessert dishes from the table, Donald told Andrea that it was getting late, and he should take her home. "Tomorrow will be my first full day on the job, and I want to be well rested and ready for the rigors of the day."

"All right Donald, I understand."

After settling the bill with a credit card, Donald escorted Andrea to the car. They walked arm in arm as they discussed the excellent ambiance, cuisine, and décor and how much they enjoyed one another's company.

Donald drove Andrea home and walked her to the door. He asked for her keys and opened the door, but he did not go in. He grinned modestly and told her they must do it again soon, and she said that she'd like that.

As Andrea turned to go inside, Donald said her name softly, "Andrea." The slow sweet way her name rolled off his lips pricked her heart. In one brief moment, she turned to find he had stepped forward to have his face in a perfect position, so she could taste and feel his tongue and lips kiss her with unabashed affection. Although she was surprised, she did not resist. "We have to get together again real soon. I'll call you," he said.

"That would be nice," she said, then turned and went inside.

Andrea wanted to tell her father all about Donald, but he wasn't home. JR had left a note a week ago that said he would be out of town for a week or two but did not indicate when he'd be back nor did he provide a phone number where he could be reached. Andrea called JR's secretary to get a phone number to call her father.

The night before he was due to come home, JR called Andrea and told her that he would be home soon. She started to tell him that she was angry because he hadn't told her that he was going out of town. However, after hearing his voice and realizing he was okay, she told him to hurry home because there was something she wanted to discuss with him. JR was non specific when she asked him what time he'd be home.

"It will be sometime in the afternoon."

However, he didn't get home until 4:00 p.m. Andrea was in as frenzy because she had been waiting for him at home since 12:30 p.m.

JR's driver took him home and updated JR on Andrea's new friend and coworker. So when they arrived, JR was prepared for Andrea's tantrum. He had barely walked in the door when Andrea started in on him.

"Daddy, I don't appreciate you going half way around the world without telling anyone. What would I do if something happened to you? Suppose I was seriously injured. I had no way of contacting you. Do you hate me that much? I know you may think I cramp your style because you didn't plan on raising a bitchy daughter like me." She threw up her hands in frustration and began crying.

JR put his arms around her and said, "Honey, I love you. You're my daughter. Yes, you can be a bitch at times, but you're my daughter. And you're right. Sometimes I get caught up in business and forget to let you know where I am, and I'm sorry. You don't cramp my style. In fact, you are the one thing that I've done right."

Andrea, began to perk up a little and said "Daddy, there's something I want to discuss with you. I met this guy, and I think I blew it. I like him. I mean I really like him, but he's still in love with his old girlfriend even though they haven't spoken in weeks. We have been going out almost every night. The odd thing about him is he has told me the truth about everything. He told me about his family, friends, girlfriend and job. I have tried to be honest with him, but I don't know how to be. Talking to him so honestly and openly made me think about our relationship, Daddy. You have held back information that I think I should know. I'm an adult, yet I don't even know how you and my mother met. Did you really love her, or was it just a fling? I need to know. I think that's why I was scared to death to date in high school and didn't know how to go about it in college."

JR clasped his hands as if a deep-seated secret had been pried from the surface of his subconscious. After several minutes of soul-searching, he said, "What went on between your mother and me is really none of your business. However, we loved one another. There's nothing I wouldn't do for her, and she knew that. I wanted to marry her, but she had other life aspirations, so she followed her dreams. There wasn't a day that I didn't pray and ask God to keep both of you safe. However, there was nothing I could do. After you were born, she didn't want me to see you at all. Then shortly before she died, she contacted me and allowed me to know my daughter, my left-handed wonder child. When I first saw you, you were a thin little seven-year-old tigress; you were angry because a little league coach told you that you couldn't pitch for a boy's team. I said then, "You have your dad's tenacity."

"I have your appetite too. Let me fix you something to eat. I don't know if I should ask you this because you always tell me no. But I'll ask anyway. Did you meet any women while you were away?"

"As a matter of fact, I did."

"Well hot damn." She sat down beside her father on the brown leather couch in the living room and said, "Now tell me all about her."

JR smiled, told her how he and Jessie had met, and that they had spent the last week getting to know one another.

Andrea listened patiently. After JR stopped talking, she asked, "Do you love Jessie?"

"What kind of question is that to ask your father?"

Andrea cackled, composed herself and then said with an elitist air, "A question that any concerned loving daughter would ask a father whom she adores, respects and looks up to."

"Cut the bull. Yes, I love her. We are getting to know one another and will be seeing a lot of each other. I want you two to meet, and I want you to be nice to her."

Andrea egging him on, said, "Well if she's going to be my new mom, I can't wait to meet her. Is she pretty? How old is she? Can she cook?"

JR was amused, yet a little agitated by her inquisitiveness. He responded, "Andrea, you'll get those answers in time; however, not today. But I will talk to her tonight and ask her to come down and spend next weekend, okay?"

Andrea smiled and said in a cute satirical whiney voice, "Okay, Daddy dear, whatever you say. But if she hurt you, I'll scratch her eyes out!" Not wanting to let the subject go, Andrea asked probingly, "Is she a good woman according to today's standards?"

"What do you mean by today's standards? Today's standards are the same as yesterday's standards. The only difference is fewer people follow them."

Realizing she finally got her father to open up Andrea said, "Way back in ancient history, when you were growing up, women expected men to be the breadwinner and bring home the bacon. Men expected women to be married, barefoot, and pregnant by the time they were 18 years old. Today, most women define a good man as someone who is trustworthy, friendly, has a good sense of humor, treats her with respect and has integrity. Most men define a good woman as someone who is faithful, friendly, affectionate and passionate yet not too inquisitive."

"Honey, today's definition is the same as back in my day. That barefoot and pregnant business was just the way life was. There was little work to go around. Most of the available jobs involved heavy lifting, and men were more suited for those jobs. College education was more of a luxury than a necessity. The well-to-do people attended college because they were the ones who could afford to. Women usually had the time, but wealthy people had time and money. If you were poor and female, your options were limited. So it was important for you to find a man with a job, income and home, who treated you well."

"That hasn't changed. I think I've found the right man for me. I want you to meet him, and I want to meet the woman who stole my daddy's heart."

"As I said, I'm going to ask her to fly up next weekend. Will you be available?"

Andrea, feeling cautiously happy, smiled and asked, "Then is it okay if I invite Donald to have dinner with us?"

Realizing his daughter's subtle manipulation, he couldn't help but chuckle and answer yes.

Fifteen minutes later, JR was on the telephone leaving the following message on Jessie's answering service: "Honey, I made it in okay. Please call me when you get in. I miss you, and I love you very much. Bye." JR hung up the phone, took his bags to his bedroom, got undressed and took a shower. As the showerhead sprayed his body with warm water, he sang the few stanzas he knew of "Tales of Love."

While JR was in the shower, Andrea called Donald and invited him to dinner. However, he said that he had a previous engagement. He was supposed to go with some male coworkers to a rodeo that was in town. Donald then commented, "I could go out with those guys anytime. I'd rather be with you."

Andrea's heart just melted. You could have sold her for 25 cents. Donald was the sweetest person she had ever met, and he constantly showed how much he cared for her. Her lips could not form the words that were in her heart. She just said "Thank you, honey. I'll talk to you later. Bye." However, instead of just saying good-bye, Donald softly said the three words that cut to the core of any love relationship, "I love you."

As Andrea hung up the phone, she thought about how strange life was. The minute she gave up and said to herself that there's no Mr. Right out there for me is when he came bumbling and stumbling along.

At that moment, JR came downstairs and saw Andrea staring into space with a large smile and tears welling up in her eyes and streaming down her cheeks. "Well, slap me silly, I believe my daughter's in love," JR blurted.

Andrea retreated to the kitchen and said, "Daddy quit teasing me. I never said anything to you about love."

"So you don't love him?"

"Daddy, I didn't say that I loved him, but I do. But before you get started, promise me that you won't give him the fifth degree. He's a nice guy, and I know you'll like him, but I don't want you to intimidate him and scare him away."

"Now, have I ever scared off one of your boyfriends? I have always been polite to them. Even that nerdy guy; you remember. He was two inches shorter than you, thin, with thick black-framed bifocals."

"Daddy, Bartholomew was a computer engineer!"

JR just kept egging her on, smiling and said, "Yeah that's because he couldn't stand to be around people. He treats people meticulously the same way that he works on computer circuit boards to correct their flaws."

"Daddy! He wasn't that bad."

JR realized he had won this round of mental gymnastics and retreated from his assault. He said, "I remember when you invited him to come over for the first time. While you were in your room getting dressed, he rang the doorbell. I opened the door, extended my hand and he shook it. I introduced myself as your father, and he nervously shook my hand again and said his name was Bartholomew. In the next breath, Bartholomew asked if I had any antibacterial soap. I really wanted to stomp his head into the ground, but I kept my temper for my little buttercup." Grinning, JR looked into her eyes and explained that he had always bent over backwards to insure that her friends felt comfortable when they visited her.

"Okay, Daddy. Please make an extra special effort to be pleasant to Donald. He's cute and quite bright."

"Sensing that Andrea was going a little overboard on her little fling, JR said, "Okay, enough already about Donald. The way you talk, he's the best thing since the Taj Mahal."

"Well, to me he is. Don't you feel the same way about, what's her name?"

"Jessie!"

Amusingly, Andrea retorted, "Yeah! That's it, Jessie. Just make sure she's not like Jesse James and robs you blind the minute you pull your pants down!"

"Now, who's the parent and who's the child?"

They both laughed and spent the next few hours playing, "I remember when."

"I remember when I was a little girl, Mom would hold your picture for hours and close her eyes and smile. Once I asked her what she was smiling about, and she said that love is like an unquenchable flame. Trials may test your faith, struggles test your courage and love tests your commitment. Your commitments to those you love transcend temporal things and fill the space in the heart's chamber."

Later that evening, JR sat on the right side of the bed rereading Stephanie's last letter. The following are the last few lines that drives home a nail that haunts him to this day, "I never wanted the money, power or position. I wanted you, but you rejected me. Our daughter holds the key to true happiness. She is all that I have in this world, so please take care of her. She loves you very much."

The memory of what was and what might have been caused JR's eyes to well up with tears. They slowly rolled down his cheeks like heavy maple syrup. Pride kept him from crying out for forgiveness from a woman who had caused him no harm yet he had killed with crude heartlessness. At the pinnacle of his relationship and maturation into adulthood, he forgot that a man is not measured by his losses. His assets measure him.

STEPHANIE

Andrea's mother's name was Stephanie, and she and JR had been madly in love. He had given her a key to his home, and periodically she would spend the night. JR had been out of town for a few days, and called her about 9:30 a.m. one Sunday morning to say he was coming back that night. Stephanie said, "JR, you know I'm off on Mondays. I have to run some errands and visit my parents, but I will meet you at your home later this evening."

"Great baby, so we can spend some time together. I miss waking up with you in my arms."

Stephanie beamed with the wonderful joy of being appreciated and loved. She repeated what he knew to be true and blushed each time she said it. "JR you make my days brighter, my heart lighter and my life over-flow with love. I love you so much."

JR's macho persona that the world now knew changed to the humble-ness of a lamb. His heavy voice became a whisper as he said, "I love you too, baby."

As Stephanie was running her errands, she passed the "To Love To Lin-ger Lingerie Boutique. She decided to stop in for a minute, just to see if they had a little something JR would like her to wear. Within a few min-utes, a cute cream colored teddy-gown with matching panties caught her eye. Stephanie looked at it over and over and then decided to purchase it.

She handed the sales clerk $50, and he gave her $3.25 change. Stephanie stuffed the gown and panties into her purse.

After Stephanie finished her errands and spent some time with her parents, she went to JR's house. He lived about six miles away in a three-bedroom tri-level home. When she arrived at his home, she opened the door, crept up the spiral stairs and looked for JR in the master bedroom. Not finding him there, Stephanie quietly looked in the smaller bedrooms and two bathrooms, but JR was nowhere to be found upstairs. She crept downstairs and checked the den, kitchen, dining room and family room. Stephanie spotted him in the family room stretched out fast asleep on the couch under a blanket. He was sleeping peacefully curled up in the fetal position facing the back of the couch. Stephanie didn't have the heart to turn the lights on to awaken him. She slipped into the teddy-gown, snuggled close to him and smiled as she felt his silk bikini briefs. He felt the warmth from her body and kissed her. Their hands and bodies explored, caressed and found themselves in numerous pleasurable positions.

After they had exhausted themselves from the lustful experience, Stephanie snuggled in Senator Bob's arms on the couch under the spider lamp, looked up at and let out a scream. "No! No! I thought, I thought you were JR!" she wailed and cried out.

"I thought we were part of a wonderful dream."

"Who are you? And what are you doing on JR's couch?"

"I slipped into town to see my best friend but surprisingly found out that JR was out of town. His secretary told me that he would be back sometime tonight or tomorrow morning. I tried to wait for JR to arrive, but fell asleep. I'm sorry for the mix-up, but it isn't exactly my fault since you came on to me. I don't think we should say anything to JR."

Although JR was his best friend, Senator Bob knew that even friends wouldn't understand such an indiscretion.

Sobbing and shaking, Stephanie said, "I feel dirty and used. I haven't been with anyone since I met JR, and you have violated the trust we've built. I have to get out of here to think."

She didn't see her panties on the couch. She searched the crevices but could not find them. Out of frustration, she snatched her coat off of a chair nearby, put it on and left. Her cream fishnet panties were safely in Senator Bob's hip pocket. He wondered if he would see Stephanie again and why JR hadn't mentioned her. This incident had occurred on Saturday morning, and JR did not get home until 2:40 p.m. When JR arrived, he was delighted to see Senator Bob.

"Hi Bob, it's good to see you. Did anyone call or stop by?"

"No, I've been here all night, and the only thing that stirred was my imagination."

"Bob, I met this beautiful and wonderful down-to-earth woman. We hit it off well."

"What's her name?

"Stephanie. And you know what, I bought Stephanie a wedding ring and will give it to her on Valentines Day."

"JR, why haven't you mentioned this girl before?"

"Because she is different than the fast women I've dated in the past. Stephanie owns, Perfectly Lovely Salons, a chain of four beauty salons. Her business income is comparable to one third of mine. I will call her and ask her to come over."

"I don't think that's necessary. I can meet her some other time." Senator Bob felt his pants pocket to make sure those panties were safely tucked away.

"If you're going to be the best man at my wedding, you had better meet my bride." JR grabbed the telephone off the coffee table and called Stephanie. Stephanie tried to force an upbeat conversation. However, JR could sense something was wrong. "What's wrong?" JR asked.

"I just received news that my uncle died, so I'm a little upset. Baby, I'm in no mood to meet strangers, but there are some things I have to take care of."

"Take your time honey. I love you and I miss you."

"JR, I love you too."

Senator Bob pretended not to hear JR's pillow talk. However, when JR hung up the phone, Senator Bob pretended to have a female voice and said, "Oh JR, I love you too." They both laughed.

Stephanie could not handle the thought of lying to JR and having slept with Senator Bob. She managed to get out of going over there that weekend, but Stephanie knew if she saw Senator Bob, her facial expression would give her away. She loved JR but knew that his knowledge of their tryst would hurt him, and she couldn't bear the thought of that. Stephanie wrestled all weekend with the horrid thought of making love to the wrong man and decided that Monday she would tell JR the truth. She had a good Catholic upbringing and knew the penalty of telling lies. They were like boomerangs. Regardless what direction you throw them, they always come back.

Monday evening when she arrived, JR hugged and kissed her affectionately. Stephanie asked JR to fix them both a double shot of vodka with lime. He had never seen her so down, so he tried to say something to lift her spirits. As he prepared their drinks, he started to tell her about the time he and his best friend got caught reading girlie magazines. After taking out a wooden paddle that looked like it was half the size of an oak tree, the teacher made them both bend over. They got fifteen licks each. The teacher called both sets of parents and told them what had happened. JR's parents didn't discipline him that day because he was already sore from the paddling he had received at school. So the next night, after his bath, his father was waiting for him with an old barber's strap. JR amusingly commented, "I had more moves than Fred Astaire that night."

Stephanie looked grim and tried to force a smile. She said, "JR I have to be honest with you. I slept with someone by mistake."

JR's face turned red in anguish. It was as if someone was repeatedly stabbing him in the back; he was powerless to stop him or her. The woman he was planning to marry had betrayed him. The look of shock and disgust showed on his face like speckles of pepper in a bowl of salt. JR didn't ask whom, what, where, when or how. The only question he asked was "Why? Why didn't you tell me you were attracted to someone else? Why did you deceive me? Why did you tell me you loved me, when obviously you didn't? Why didn't you come and meet Senator Bob? Did you feel guilty for betraying me by sleeping with someone else? Why don't you take your coat, and get the hell out of here? Why don't you go back to your mistake because you've destroyed what we had!"

Dejected and rejected, Stephanie started to interrupt JR's tirade several times only to be cut off with his constant questions. In frustration, Stephanie retrieved her coat and left. JR was angry; he did not want to lose Stephanie, but he had too much pride to tell her not to go. He didn't call her for a week and when he did, it was too late. She was in a non-forgiving mood. Instead of giving her an opportunity to explain, he had readily concluded that she had done something intentionally that was unforgivably wrong.

JR tried to call her at her salons, but she refused to take his calls. He sent flowers and gifts, but they were returned as she refused to accept them. After six weeks, JR finally gave up. He had heard through friends that Stephanie was pregnant and assumed it was her lover's child. JR told himself that he didn't care, but he did. He knew he loved her in spite of the child she was carrying. JR just didn't know how to make it right— make them right. Stephanie sold her businesses after the child was born and moved away. She had instructed her parents not to divulge her whereabouts, so they didn't. JR begged and pleaded with them but they told him, they had to respect their daughter's wishes. She hadn't told them what went wrong in their relationship. They knew their daughter but had never seen her this solemn and despondent. Despite being a new mother, her natural bubbly personality was trapped in a storm of despair. Stephanie's parents assumed that JR must have done or said something to hurt her deeply. And although they suspected JR was the father, they were puzzled that Stephanie did not allow him to be part of the child's life.

In her frustration, Stephanie contacted Senator Bob and requested financial assistance. She told him that he had cost her a totally committed and loving relationship with JR. Finally, she realized she'd never win him back.

"I understand why you are angry at me, but I don't understand why you haven't mended fences with JR. Regardless of what he says, he still loves you. If I could turn back the hands of time and correct our indiscretion, I would."

"I no longer blame you. I was stupid for jumping into bed with someone before verifying who it was. If anyone is to blame, it's me."

"We both are to blame. I could have stopped, but I didn't." He attempted to reach out, hug and console her but caught himself. He clasped his hands and commented, "I heard you were pregnant. Am I the father?"

Stephanie became so quiet that the echo of silence was almost deafening. Only two minutes had passed, but it seemed like hours. Her facial expression went from casual concern to shame as she said, "I don't know."

Senator Bob told her that he would help her financially in any way he could. However, he was in love with another woman and could not provide her with the love and support that was readily available from JR.

"I don't want your pity, but I'll accept your financial assistance. I have to take care of this child and get on with my life. You can then go on with your life without fear of reprisals from me. I'm not vindictive, but I don't want to see you again. I'm going away for a while." She reached in her purse and took out a pen and a note pad. Stephanie wrote down an address, handed it to Senator Bob and said, "You can mail a check to me at this address. Raising children is expensive. I'll let your conscience determine how much you should give." Stephanie turned and walked away quickly before Senator Bob could see the tears behind her facade of strength.

Senator Bob looked dumbfounded realizing he had ruined the life of a wonderful woman. Stephanie could have ruined his political career, but instead she chose to suffer the public humiliation of raising a child alone. In time, both he and JR would be safe under the cloak of marriage to other women.

While JR was reminiscing upstairs, Andrea was on the speakerphone in the family room making dinner plans with Donald and wishing Jessie and JR were experiencing the same kind of love that they shared. Andrea advised Donald not to discuss politics or religion. She raised her right hand and rattled on sarcastically, "If you do, my dad will talk for hours non-stop trying to get you to agree with his point of view. Most people give in because they'd rather admit that he's right than hear his redundant arm-twisting speech."

"I may tell him that I want to marry his beautiful daughter."

"While you are at it; tell him to give us the Hope Diamond as a wedding gift," Andrea said giggling.

Both laughed and after a few minutes, Andrea composed herself and said, "Seriously Donald, I want you to make a good impression on my dad. It means a lot to me."

"Well it means a lot to me too. I'll get there at least an hour early, okay?"

"Okay, honey, I'll talk to you later. Bye."

The weekend seemed to take forever to arrive. Andrea and Donald had lunch and dinner together daily, and they became more nervous as the week wore on. They wanted to make a positive impression on JR and Jessie who seemed to be a twosome now. Andrea told Donald that although her father was always his own man, He had never talked about any of the women he dated as much as he now talked positively about Jessie.

Donald was madly in love with Andrea, but her obsession with pleasing her father wore on him. She wanted him to be prepared with pat answers to any questions JR might ask. Donald tried to follow her script but by the second day, he told her that if he responded to JR's questions as she suggested, he would appear pretentious and superficial. He explained that he had to be himself.

Andrea, realizing that Donald was right, sighed and shook her head in agreement. Then she whispered, "Donald, honey, just let him see the man I see and am crazy about, and we'll be okay."

Donald made the mistake of asking, "Andrea, what are you going to wear?"

Andrea gasped, clutched her chest and yelped, "Oh my God, I have got to go shopping! I have to get a dress or pantsuit. I'm sure she's going to be perfect. Daddy will want me to be presentable, and I don't have a thing that's appropriate to wear!" She began to pace frantically as she rambled on and on.

Donald chuckled at her sudden hysteria and was bedazzled by her seemingly low self-worth. He reached out and held her hand to halt her cadence and make her understand that her worries were unfounded. "What do you mean? I saw those two walk-in closets filled with clothes. I'm certain you will look ravishing in anything you decide to wear."

Andrea slipped out of his grasp and continued to pace as she considered Donald's last statement. "You are so right. I'm going to look ravishing in the new outfit I'm getting from Macy's designer section. My slogan for shopping is 'when in doubt, buy it out.' Don't you want to go shopping with me? I need a man's opinion, and I promise that I won't be long."

The pleading look Andrea gave Donald caused him to give in. He disliked shopping but loved being with her, so he reluctantly agreed. It was Wednesday evening, and they had just finished eating dinner. She said, "Okay, then let's go. It's only 5:30, and the store will be open until 9:00." Donald grabbed their coats, assisted Andrea with putting hers on and then put on his coat.

This was the first time Donald had accompanied Andrea shopping. Little did he know that when Andrea said that she would not be long, she meant that she would not be as long as it usually took her. She failed to explain that shopping for her was usually an all-day experience. It wasn't unusual for her to try on 20 to 30 outfits before settling on one or two. They finally walked out of the Versace Boutique at 9:15 p.m. with two dresses, a pantsuit and two pairs of shoes.

As Donald drove Andrea home, he was amused and tired. Andrea was content and drifted off to sleep while Donald hummed as the radio disc jockey played the tune, "I'm Not Your Pearl, I'm Your Baby." Donald could only remember the chorus, so he hummed the solo part with the artist and sung the chorus. Donald's tenor, slightly off-key voice bellowed:

> I'm not your pearl. I'm your baby.
> Don't treat me shabby or I just maybe
> Leave you and find some lovin' and huggin'
> Cause I'm not your pearl.

Andrea was awakened by her sweetie's singing but kept her eyes closed and was content to enjoy the concert. Thirty minutes later they pulled into her driveway. Donald carried the bags inside but explained that he was tired and was going home. She was tired too so did not encourage him to stay. Andrea said, "Thanks for a wonderful evening honey. I don't know what I'd do without you." They kissed briefly before he made his way out the door and promised to call her the following day. The rest of the week passed quickly as Andrea, Donald and JR immersed themselves in their work.

JR contracted his chief chef, Deuce Chauser, to prepare the food for dinner. Deuce arrived at JR's home at about 1:15 p.m. although the meal was not going to be served until 7:00 p.m. The meal included Pecker steaks, rice with gravy, steamed peas, key lime pie, a fruit cup, wine and beer.

JR left work early to pick up Jessie from the airport. She was due to arrive at 3:45 p.m., and it was only 2:00 p.m., but his anxiousness got the best of him. He knew that by arriving early, he would see Jessie disembark from the plane.

JR ordered his driver, Russ Scarboro, to stop by a florist on the way to the airport, and Russ complied. JR purchased two dozen long-stem, red roses arranged in a vase. His driver then got him to the airport in twenty minutes. JR took his time walking through the huge airport and after fifteen minutes, he found the gate where Jessie's plane was to arrive. Just as he arrived at the airport's security gate, a message came over the intercom system that Jessie's plane, Flight 696, was delayed due to engine problems. Her arrival gate was being changed to the far end of the airport, which was about a ten-minute walk. JR didn't bother conferring with the airline counter's attendant; he turned and walked to the new arrival location. Usually JR would scan the airport for attractive females; however, this time he did not. He was determined to make sure Jessie arrived safely. Nevertheless, he knew that even with all of his wealth, he was powerless to change either of their destinies. The huge arrangement of flowers caught the eye of everyone he passed. JR didn't notice that many of the women nudged their boyfriend or husband as they pointed at the huge flower arrangement he was carrying and commented that their so-called soul mate did not think enough of them to buy flowers anymore. JR arrived at the gate five minutes before her plane touched down and taxied in. Jessie was the second woman and the sixth passenger to get off the plane. Their eyes met simultaneously; they ran toward each other and embraced. For a brief moment, they forgot there were other people in the area.

As they separated, JR asked, "Jessie, how many bags did you bring?"

"I only brought an overnight bag for my toiletries, two pairs of shoes and a garment bag with three dresses, a jeans outfit, a lounger and two pantsuits. I traveled light, so we don't have to waste time in baggage claim when we can find far more pleasurable things to do." Then Jessie glanced at his torso up to his lips.

JR, with a broad smile, said, "I don't know what I'm going to do with you."

"I have a few ideas."

They laughed and walked hand in hand as they strolled out of the airport. Jessie carried the overnight case, and JR carried the garment bag. JR handed them to Russ when they arrived at the car. JR introduced Jessie to Russ and assisted her into the limousine.

When they arrived at JR's home, Andrea greeted her father with a tight hug and extended her right hand to Jessie and said, "I'm glad to meet you. Daddy has talked so much about you, and you are more attractive than he ever let on."

Jessie's friendly response equaled Andrea's greeting. "Your dad told me that he loves you more than anyone in the world, and I can see why. You have a lot of his qualities, and you are a very refreshing young lady. I'm so glad that we are finally able to meet. You are the first member of his family that I've met. Also, I understand we have something in common: There's a certain special young man in your life."

"Yes, his name is Donald, and he's a great guy."

"I guess that's another thing we have in common." They giggled as JR just shook his head.

"Well, I'll be darn. It didn't take you two very long to bond. I'll take the bags to my room while you two talk," said JR.

Once JR was out of sight, Andrea looked at Jessie and asked, "I know you like my dad a lot. What are your intentions toward him? Are you guys seriously talking about getting married?"

Andrea's frankness and questions caught Jessie a little off guard, but she didn't shy away from them. After thinking about it momentarily, Jessie recited everything she loved about JR. "Do I love your father? Yes. I have loved him since the first day we met. He's handsome, considerate, loveable, caring and giving. I can go on forever. JR's everything I want in a lover and friend. Yes. If he proposed to me, I would marry him. He has not asked me, and I don't know if he ever will. I'm content to take our relationship one day at a time and see where it leads. I can see in your eyes that you love Donald. The way you talk about him is the way I feel about your dad. I've been praying every since your dad told me about you that you'd like me and that we could be friends. I may not be what you expected, but I do sincerely care about him."

Andrea's defense mechanism clearly had backfired, and she could not help but say, "I'm glad you two met because he needs a woman such as you. You're almost as feisty as I am."

On that note, JR came into the room finding them giggling. He started to ask what was so funny but thought better of it. JR went into the kitchen and asked the chef when dinner would be served. He was told that it would be served on time at 7:00 p.m. JR looked at his watch and noticed that it was already 6:15 p.m. The doorbell rang as he left the kitchen.

"That must be Donald. He's always on time," said Andrea. She scurried away to answer the door. JR returned to the living room, walked over to where Jessie was sitting, bent down and kissed her. However, he quickly stood up as he could hear Andrea and Donald walking toward the room.

As they entered the room, JR walked over to Donald and shook his hand. He introduced Jessie as his girlfriend and Donald as Andrea's boyfriend.

Andrea sat with Donald on the loveseat, and JR joined Jessie on the couch. They all discussed how they met, and the interesting things they had done together. While they were exchanging pleasantries, Deuce came and announced, "Dinner is served." JR escorted Jessie to the bathroom in his bedroom, so she could wash her hands and freshen up. Andrea took Donald to the first floor powder room.

"So what do you think about my little girl now?

"Your little girl is quite a woman, and I like her already. I bet she keeps you in check."

"She does."

They entered the dining area and looked at the massive table with six matching chairs. Jessie said jokingly, "Somebody was planning on having a large family."

"No. I had planned on doing a lot of entertaining. It just hasn't worked out yet."

The couples sat opposite each other in the middle chairs at the table. Deuce served large portions of the scrumptious meal with a semi-sweet dinner wine from a winery in Wisconsin. It was so tasty that they polished off two large bottles. Their conversation went from sharing information about their personal backgrounds and views on politics and religion to where to go on vacation.

"Donald, Jessie and I are considering vacationing in Trinidad. Neither of us has ever been there. Andrea tells me that you've gone there recently with a relative. How was it?" JR asked.

"I initially went to accompany my grandfather on a two-week vacation in January. He had sustained a severe spinal injury eight years ago when he was 62. He had gone horseback riding with some of his grandchildren. The horse became spooked by a squirrel and threw my grandfather about ten feet. He landed on the base of his neck. By the time the paramedics arrived, he'd lost all feeling in his upper body. His speech was slurred but still understandable.

"Within a few months, my granddad had become depressed by his day-to-day struggle with the constant pain. He has found no relief despite enduring 17 nerve blocks in ten years. Even picking up his three-week-old great grandson, my nephew, became a struggle.

He saw an article in a travel magazine about Trinidad's warm climate, tranquil beaches and relaxed atmosphere and asked me to go with him. I had never been to this West Indian Island. We discovered that the island's inhabitants were celebrating Carnival, their annual week-long day and night party in the streets. This party supersedes all regular activity on the island and serves as a combination of a catharsis and a community bonding experience.

However, their beaches are not as pretty as the ones in the Bahamas, but they do have beautiful hills and majestic mountains. On a clear day, from the top of their mountains, one can see ten miles away to the island of Tobago. The native women there are beautiful. There are six times as many women as there are men, and the women are extremely sensitive about their men. However, the men enjoy the women's attention and periodically fight for it. Although my grandfather and I found Trinidad and its inhabitants fascinating, we like the good old USA better. Besides, the woman I love and adore is not in Trinidad; she's in America."

Andrea blushed at the compliment while stroking Donald's foot under the table. Not letting that comment slip by unnoticed, JR said, "If at any point you two have an inclination to get married, I had better be the first to know. My little girl is not eloping or having a two-bit wedding. She's my heartstring and will have the best wedding Texas has ever seen."

"Don't worry sir; I'm sure you will be the first to know. We've talked about that already." Andrea kicked him hard under the table. Donald wanted to let out a loud howl but for fear she'd kick him again, he gritted his teeth and held in the pain. Andrea sat with a forced smile and a stoic glare.

To break the sudden silence Jessie said, "JR, please tell me again about the place you call the pride of Texas"

"Oh yes, the South Padre Island. A friend of mine and I go there annually for a tasty serving of the red drum and atmosphere. It's a pretty 34-mile stretch of beach and coastal dunes. I'll take you there one day soon, honey."

Jessie's eyebrows rose, and she inquired pretentiously, "And who is this friend? What's her name?"

"Now hold your horses; my friend is President Bob. We've been friends since we were teenagers."

The rest of the evening went well. However, by 10:30 p.m. Donald and Andrea had excused themselves because they were going dancing at a local club. JR and Jessie were pleased because they wanted a little time alone. Deuce cleaned up after dinner, carried his equipment to his van and stored the leftovers in the refrigerator. JR thanked Deuce for preparing a delicious mea, and gave him his weekly salary, a $1,500 check.

"Thank you, sir." Deuce folded the check and put it in his wallet before he headed for home in his Grand-Am.

Jessie and JR took a bubble bath in the 8-foot Jacuzzi in JR's bathroom. They had fun relaxing and frolicking in the water. That night the water became their bed, and their bed became their sanctuary.

Both couples continued to date and saw each other as time permitted. After four months, both couples agreed to a short engagement, which culminated in a double ceremony in St. Paul's Cathedral, the largest church in San Antonio, Texas. Everyone who was anyone in Texas attended the wedding. Even President Bob made time in his busy schedule to attend and serve as best man at his best friend's wedding.

The wedding reception was held at the San Antonio, Texas Convention Center. As both bride and groom went from table to table thanking their guests for making their wedding day special, President Bob slipped Jessie a note that said, "As long as the information flows, you can keep your panties to yourself."

After reading the note, Jessie said, "Thanks, JR. Thank you very much."

Joyce

President Bob never watched a lot of television. However, there was one show that he enjoyed, "It's My Court." The show depicted people at their jobs, and a reporter would come in and ask them questions concerning their jobs or discuss issues related to their jobs. One day I delivered information to President Bob while he was watching a taped episode. He said it was his favorite show and invited me to watch it with him.

I reluctantly agreed and sat in a chair opposite his desk. The VCR and 46" TV screen were built into two sections of wooden wall paneling. President Bob operated the VCR, TV and wall movement via remote control on his desk. He had the first few buttons of his shirt undone, and the hair from his chest could easily be seen. President Bob was leaning back in his executive chair with his feet resting on a soft leather hassock.

This episode was about a fictitious U.S. President and reporter. I sat down and watched what was left of it. The reporter was a young 30-something, starry-eyed petite brunette who looked like she should have been in high school studying biology. The President was sitting at his desk in the Oval Office. He appeared to be about 50 years old, 6 feet 1 inch tall, and slender, with dimples when he laughed and a cleft chin. Most of the time, he had a serious but relaxed demeanor.

The reporter, Joyce Gibson, was busily asking him questions as he gave candid answers in his typical presidential controlled style. I heard and observed the following:

President Thompson said in a sincere subdued tone, "Judge Manard Steamer will always be remembered as the guy who destroyed the Republican machine. He was a good jurist but a lousy politician. Judge Steamer was appointed to be independent counsel to investigate the President, but he let partisan politics extend his investigation even when he knew it was time to end it."

Ms. Gibson shook her head affirmatively and asked, "What do you think happened?"

"Everybody knows what happened."

"Everybody?"

President Thompson snapped back, "Yes, everybody! Everyone in the media, in politics and around this country knows what happened."

Ms. Gibson appeared perturbed by his remark and said, "Then enlighten me."

President Thompson leaned back in his chair, paused for a moment as if trying to digest a greasy meal and then said, "There was a meeting just like the Malcolm X/Martin Luther King meeting and the Nixon/Ford meeting. Judge Steamer was ending his investigation after two years of evidence and $30 million that proved the President didn't do anything wrong. He was ready to accept an academic appointment to a posh college, and two of the worst things that could possibly happen, happened. The President's staff told the truth as noted above. Then the Speaker of the House who basked daily in the knowledge that a fellow Republican would do what was right for the party, turned over every rock, pillow or bed sheet until he obtained something substantial to bring before Congress."

"So you're saying it was personal?"

"Why would an independent counsel appointed by Congress to head an impartial inquiry into the conduct of the President spend countless hours worrying about his or her office image. Judge Steamer had an old pompous attitude cloaked in meaningless words of impartiality that said, 'I want the people to know I'm a man of integrity, and my staff is impartial.' If this were the case, then why did he make numerous commercial appearances to discuss facets of the impeachment inquiry? How many prosecutors try cases on television?"

"So, are you saying he had a personal vendetta against the President that blurred his vision and caused him not to end his investigation more timely?"

"Yes, I'm saying that. But I'm also saying there's a price one pays when doing that. Judge Steamer was appointed to be an impartial fact finder, and he did not do that. If the Reform Party has said anything in the last few years that I totally agree with, this may be it. If you are an elected or appointed government official, it's incumbent upon you to remember that you represent the people. When Judge Steamer lost his focus, that's when the American people lost faith in him. Yes, he'll make millions of dollars in speaker fees and will still get his posh appointment to a top university, if he still wants it, but he'll always be remembered as the guy who caused the Republican Party to lose their majority."

"So, why didn't members of the Republican Party distance themselves from Judge Steamer?"

President Thompson said snidely, "He was their boy. Clean cut, family man, morally above reproach, an excellent jurist and Republican. They polished his speech through intermediaries and presented him to the American people with two consecutive hours of prepared fiction."

"Are you saying he lied to the American people and Congress?" She then turned and looked at the President and awaited his response.

"I'm saying Judge Steamer lied to himself. He spent over $30 million of public funds using national police and FBI techniques to gather evidence and came up with nothing. He got into the gutter. Judge Steamer paid a witness who previously lied to tell what he believes is the truth. He proceeded to rifle through the President's office, bedroom and locker room to see if there were panties tucked away that didn't belong to his wife."

"Sir, those are serious accusations."

"History will prove it to be true. Ask Judge Steamer why he told the Speaker he was ending the investigation at the cost of $30 million and two days later he changed his mind to pursue sex, lies and partisan treachery."

It was getting late, so I told President Bob I had to go home. He chuckled to himself, appearing to be amused by the actors' interplay. As I grabbed my purse and walked out the door, he turned the TV and VCR off and walked me to the door. He told me, "Thanks again for dropping off the material."

I didn't mind but suspected the tape haunts him. President Bob was one of the few people I would get out of bed in the middle of the night for if he needed me. He has always treated me with respect and is a good listener.

Maggie

The political philosophy of Peter Pekins Willow IV, the Republican presidential candidate, was shaped by his great-grandfather and by growing up on T3C Plantation in Selma, Alabama. The 260-acre farmland was known for tobacco, corn, cotton and collard greens. At the height of antebellum, the plantation was host to several governors' balls and cotillions and employed 12 farm hands and 89 slaves. The White House, as the majestic 17-room mansion was called, sat on a hill on the northwest corner of the property. Its oak-lined walls and marble steps were the envy of the community. The bunkhouse, barn and silo were located in the center of the property. Twelve 9 x 9 feet slave shacks were conveniently built near the woods at the southeast end of the property. Their thatched walls and roofs could easily be seen from 50 feet away through the thin layer of rotted plywood and rusted nails that clung together like pussy willows on a branch. They were once home to 80 field slaves. The whipping block was 20 feet in front of the fifth house. Its corroded dried, blood-stained surface was agitated with the overseer's marks. Nine slaves had the privilege of sleeping in the 10 x 20 foot basement of their master's house.

Growing up, Peter had spent his leisure time frequenting the Bluespit Cafe. The Bluespit Cafe was a combination of an old west saloon and a red-necked bikers' haven. Peter and his friends rode Harley Davidson motorcycles and parked them outside the cafe. They had no need for chains although the faint-hearted hitched them to outside posts. Inside, the patrons would retell stories of Peter's great-grandfather's exploits. He was a well respected Confederate general who criticized the arrogance of President Abraham Lincoln for taking away the white Southerner's livelihood with one stroke of his pen, and illegally using the Union Army to impose its will on the sovereign state of Alabama. The citizens in the pro-slavery Southern states believed that the Constitution authorized the federal militia to defend the United States from outside forces; however, it had no authority to attack the citizens within the union. Therefore, once a state decided to secede from the United States, they believed that the U.S. government had no authority to compel the citizens of that state to comply with its mandates.

Peter IV retained the mores of his great-grandfather. At the age of 17, he had the baddest Harley around, the brashness of Andrew Jackson and the charisma of George Wallace. He made his enemies his friends, and he made his friends his bosom buddies. Women found his wealth and cockiness intriguing. His philosophy was that in order to catch a fly, you had to get close enough to observe it. Once you observed it and etched its flight pattern into your consciousness, you must grab and control it. If it was injured in the process, you needn't worry because that's the price one pays for being vulnerable.

He attended the Citadel because it was one of the few military institutions that encouraged Southern cadets to take pride in their Confederate heritage. After graduating with honors, he served 21 years and retired at the rank of major. However, his retirement was short lived because four months later his party pleaded with him to run for governor. Being restless and eager for a new challenge, he accepted and won easily.

Currently, Peter Pekins Willow IV is in his final year of his first term as the Governor of Alabama. He gained the respect of his party because he successfully used his conservative views to cut the income tax by 10 percent, attract new businesses with tax incentives, reduce the unemployment rate by 15 percent and reduce the homeless population by 40 percent. His significant reduction of the homeless population got the most media attention. It was called "Project Send Home." Homeless individuals were encouraged to go home and live with relatives or loved ones. Each participant was given a one-way ticket to his or her desired destination in the United States after signing an affidavit agreeing not to return to Alabama for a minimum of three years.

For all intents and purposes, Peter IV's reduction of unemployment occurred overnight. He bullied a measure through his state legislature whereby his state stopped counting unemployed workers after they had received unemployment checks for three months. In the black and Hispanic communities, the slogan went like this, "Last hired, first fired three months later on the dole, now out in the cold."

Governor Willow hated Vice President Leon and considered him an arrogant black male who forgot his proper place in society. He found black Americans morally, intellectually and economically inferior to their white counterparts and a race that continually sought to upset the natural balance.

Governor Willow often said, "The only person lower than a black person is a Hispanic. Both are vagabonds by nature and problematic by design." Governor Willow proved to be an astute foe of Vice President Leon, who used the media to foster his ideas throughout his presidential campaign.

Quoting his "I Have a Conscience" speech can best summarize Vice President Leon's view. "Some of those who call themselves Republicans and moderate Democrats have lost themselves in a monologue of racial hatred, wrapped in a so-called dialog seeking debate. They do not want to discuss issues such as unemployment, education, healthcare, Social Security or crime. Instead, they want to fan the flames of racism until those who were once shackled and stripped, regain their chattel status. These spineless politicians never seek to embrace African or Hispanic Americans. They invest millions of dollars in affluent neighborhood schools compared to only a few thousand dollars in depressed neighborhoods. Yet when standardized tests are taken and results are tabulated, they claim ignorance as to the reason why there is great disparity in the results. As my grandmother used to say, 'You only can pour out of the pot as much as you pour into the pot.' How can a student learn to navigate the Internet and research data without access to computers? How can students study, when they have no books? How can one learn biology and science without talented instructors? We've been depriving the most helpless among us in the name of racial injustice. My problem is that I have a conscience.

"Those irresponsible Republicans in power have the audacity to criticize some of my constituents and describe them as shiftless and lazy. My constituents were not the ones who opted to move 80 percent of the manufacturing jobs and 40 percent of the labor jobs to Mexico and Asia. The U.S. Census data over the last 100 years clearly show that Americans will work if they have access to employment. It doesn't matter whether they are black, white, red, blue or brown; people will work if there is work available at a fair wage. I have a conscience.

"It turns my stomach when I look around and see those with corporate authority neglect to train their workforce as technology changes. Japan and Taiwan have invested in their people and it is paying off. Their economy is robust. A few years ago they had a few problems, but they pulled together to snatch themselves out of a mini-recession. It takes some sacrifice on everyone's part in order for the wheels of change to turn smoothly.

"I have a conscience when Americans adopt five times as many children from China, Korea, Japan and Russia, as from the United States. America has turned its back on its children, and I think it's disgraceful.

"We can no longer chase the carrot that some bigots use to divide the races. They cite polls that show black parents place school quality over diversity. This is no great revelation. All black, Japanese, Korean, Hispanic, Indian and white parents want a quality education for their child. I've never heard a racist cite the objective data that's available through a bipartisan national educational think-tank, the Carnegie-Mellon Institute of Learning. The results of their ten-year study revealed that children who are raised in a culturally diverse environment and are challenged educationally perform comparable to upper white class students with a quality education.

"The problem with an education in a sterile environment is you create culturally brain dead citizens. I had the option of sending my children to a predominantly black public school or a predominantly white private school. However, I discovered I had a better third choice. I sent my children to an academically sound culturally diverse public school in Alexandria, Virginia. I realized that after high school graduation, my child would work and live in a culturally diverse world. It's okay for him to learn the three R's (reading, writing and arithmetic) as well as to be computer literate. However, if he cannot properly socially interact and respect the customs of others, I've failed as a parent. History has taught us that people tend to align themselves with people they are comfortable with. It's incumbent upon all of us to give our children the opportunity to be comfortable.

"I challenge each of you to have a conscience and make our children's tomorrow better than their today, and their future a future of hope, opportunity and progressive thinking."

The audience, clearly moved by his passionate pleas, applauded for what seemed like hours, while smiling and shaking their heads affirmatively, as Vice President Leon waved to the crowd. Cameramen and reporters moved feverishly trying to capture the moment on film and paper but knew they could not replicate the crowd's exuberance. For a brief moment, Vice President Leon was able to replicate the charismatic persona that President Bob always exhibited to audiences. Even his adversaries found themselves applauding.

Vice President Leon proved that a person could come from meager means yet use education as a vehicle to make his life meaningful and productive. He attended gala affairs dressed in tuxedoes or three-piece suits and became the pride of the black community. When he addressed audiences in the neighborhoods, his oratory skills dazzled them. He was a man who could articulate their problems and identify with their pain. His wit and confidence was tempered with realistic optimism. The Vice President left audiences encouraged by his ability to make a positive difference in their lives.

However, Vice President Leon realized that he needed to carry the middle class white and black voter in order to defeat Peter Willow IV. He addressed the National Teacher's Association National Conference in Chicago, Illinois. The Vice President told them, "Every invention known to modern man was discovered because someone was curious and assertive enough not to settle for the status quo. Some of my opponents would have voters believe that white Americans created all inventions. Instead of recognizing minority achievements in manufacturing, medicine, economics, science and education, they tend to lower the barometer of achievement according to race. I respect Jesse Owens and Jackie Robinson, but I also respect Benjamin Banneker, Eli Whitney, Charles Drew, Frederick Douglass, William Edward Burghardt Du Bois, Thurgood Marshall and Martin Luther King, Jr. No, I'm not saying that education should be minority focused. I'm saying that every child should receive a quality education. Children should be taught American history and not American fiction. It took many cultures to pull together to make the United States a national power. Darkened places can be illuminated if each American allows light to shine from the torch of freedom.

He reminded them of a Republican television commercial showing blacks in North Carolina with jobs as ticket takers at a train station, and stewardesses, airline fuel attendants, waiters and hospital custodians. Each black had their patented "Aunt Lucy's" grin with a do-rag on their head. He noted that the National Association for the Advancement of Colored People (NAACP), Southern Christian Leadership Conference (SCLC) and Rainbow Coalition condemned attack-oriented campaigning as unethical and immoral. Also, negative attacks make people less likely to go out and vote. As long as the "no show" voters were Democrats, his opponent could care less. Vice President Leon stated authoritatively, "Governor Willow's mission to raise the flag of states' rights vs. federal mandates point out his serious character flaws and limited national vision. Here is a first term, right wing popular governor that recent polls show would have a lopsided margin of victory if he chose to run for a second term, but would receive a minuscule number of votes if he sought national office. However, the future of the South is analogous to the future of the nation. If one bigot can control the political activity in one state, he will spend four years putting the blinders of racism on his constituents and converting others to share his views."

The Leon vs. Willow political battle proved to be perfect ammunition for national news services. Numerous reporters were sent to cover the daily friction. Southern politics hadn't seen this much excitement since the Harvey Gantt vs. Jessie Helms Campaign of 1996 when North Carolina voters were forced to choose between an extreme right wing Republican and a moderate Democrat. The fall campaign was projected to have record voter turnout spurred on by the negative campaigning.

Everybody was buzzing about the race. Conversations from barbershop and beauty shop experts to corporate executives were filled with opinions about affirmative action, racial bias in sentencing and imprisonment, to "not my dollars in their community, let the churches take care of the aged, depressed and homeless, and let government handle the rest." At each end of the spectrum, people were divided by racial and socioeconomic status.

Even Maggie Goodnight, a madam in the red light district of Selma, was quoted in *The Alabama Banner Press*. "If the world didn't discriminate against people like me and my girls, then the economy could rock toward improvement and not roll toward disaster. I've made millions by giving my clients what they needed, and the government should follow suit. Listen to their gripes, stroke their egos and place them in a position to relieve their tension harmlessly. A little TLC (tender loving care) can go a long way."

The very next issue of *The Alabama Banner Press* contained numerous letters to the editor from the schoolmarm type. One letter stated, "Ms. Goodnight should spend her days working a real job instead of working Mandingo all night."

Another reader wrote, "What is the world coming to when a whore can utilize a regional newspaper to tout her soiled profession as if she's Joan of Arc?"

A third reader used sarcasm to get his point across by stating, "When a Goodnight woman finds a man on a good night and has a good night with her man, can a Goodnight woman compare her man to a good man. Hell no! Goodnight woman!"

A fourth wrote, "We live in the information age when the frenzied media spins stories like a 7-year-old used to spin a spinning-top—carefree and reckless." Whether someone is mourned or affectionately mocked, narrow-minded people become vicious. Maggie's message was lost because many readers saw Maggie but refused to hear her.

MELISSA

Maggie is no different than Melissa Shane, a conservative pundit at *The South Star Conservative Journal*. Melissa wrote a scathing editorial about the unnecessary negative criticism Maggie received. She noted, "Maggie's view of the world is 20/20 while most of her critics walk around blind by bias and refuse to see, feel, smell or touch what really matters."

Melissa prided herself on being a self-made woman. She was raised in the Southern Baptist town of Austin, Texas. She was fortunate to be born to Dr. Paul and Dr. Juliet Shane. Paul was a pediatrician, and Juliet was an obstetrician. As they affectionately chided each other, God made kids for the world: Juliet brought them in, and Paul carried them through. Melissa's parents raised her to follow in their footsteps. They took great care in selecting all of her courses. She took advanced English, math, history and biology classes throughout her high school career. On birthdays and special holidays, they gave her medical books or novels about medical issues. Melissa read the books to appease them but became drawn to journalism, and she was editor of her high school newspaper, *The Critic's Lair*, and captain of the debate team. Melissa graduated salutatorian, accepted an academic scholarship to Smith College in Massachusetts and followed her calling by majoring in journalism. Her parents were not thrilled with the idea; however, they supported her decision.

Melissa was 5 feet 7 inches, 110 pounds and flat as a board. Her ankle tugging dresses, black-frame glasses, pinned up black hair and dislike for wearing make-up caused potential suitors to find more attractive ground in which to sow their wild oats. However, in her junior year, she met a woman that had a profound impact on her life, Professor Janet Roentin. She was a brilliant feminist writer who recognized tremendous potential in Melissa. Melissa's drive for report writing and command of journalistic prose won Janet's heart and respect. Although they spent numerous hours discussing Melissa's career choices and her outstanding editorship of the school's newspaper, Janet was careful to respect their teacher/student relationship. Janet urged Melissa to attend her alma mater, Johns Hopkins University in Baltimore, Maryland. This prestigious world-renown university is known primarily for its medical school; however, it has an excellent journalism department. Four of the top ten national newscasters are Hopkins graduates. Melissa applied to Harvard, Yale, George Washington, Georgetown, Princeton, Notre Dame, St. Johns, Johns Hopkins, University of Southern California, Florida State and Howard University.

Every school except for St. Johns offered her a full graduate scholarship. Melissa was tempted to go to Harvard because of its prestige and the fact that many of her friends were going there. However, she was never one to back down from an academic challenge, so she chose to attend Johns Hopkins.

Professor Roentin was thrilled with Melissa's choice and attended the commencement ceremonies. After graduation, the school had a reception for all the graduates, family and friends in the school's cafeteria. Melissa's parents and 24 well-wishers waited for her in the cafeteria. When Melissa arrived, they took pictures with her and asked questions about her long-term career goals. Many of her instructors came over and talked at length with her parents telling them how bright and conscientious their daughter was. Her parents beamed with satisfaction hearing how their child had garnered the respect and admiration of the faculty. Professor Roentin spotted Melissa alone and presented her with an envelope. Melissa tore open the envelope, read the card and found a $1,500 check inside. She hugged and thanked Professor Roentin for her generosity. As they embraced, Professor Roentin's hands and arms quickly slid from Melissa's waist to her hips, and their torsos touched for a split second that seemed like hours. Melissa didn't resist; instead she gave into the moment. Professor Roentin leaned forward to kiss her, but she caught herself, smiled, told her to keep in touch and scurried away down the corridor.

As her parents drove their rental car back to her dorm room to pick up her suitcases, Melissa began to question her sexuality. She had never dated in high school or college. Her second cousin was her prom date in high school. She had always blamed a lack of a social life on her dedication to pursuing her education, studying for classes and trying to get her career started before venturing off into an unknown territory. Melissa suspected that she was the only virgin in her graduating class, and now she wondered if it was because she gave off lesbian vibes that caused guys to stay away. She had just graduated from the most prestigious all girls' college on the East Coast and never had a lesbian encounter until now.

However, her worries quickly dissipated the minute she and her parents dropped the rental car off and boarded the cruise ship for a two week cruise to the French Riviera. This was Melissa's first time traveling outside of the United States. She was a typical tourist and took pictures of everything. The cathedrals, buildings, sunrise, sunset, peaceful waterways and free-flowing fashions did not escape her photographic eye.

She thought one of the ship's stewards was handsome. The only problem was that other women on the ship found him attractive as well and vied for his attention. So she did not even try to entice him. Melissa's mother noticed her attraction to the steward and asked her about it when her father was outside on deck participating in the aerobics class.

"Mom, the other women on the ship are more attractive than I am, and I can't compete with them to win his affection."

"Honey, when you go fishing you have to have three things—a rod, a line with a hook on it and some bait. Now let's work backwards. In order to be bait, you have to feel attractive and look the way you feel. For the last ten years your wardrobe has been full of tee shirts and jeans, your hair has been pinned-up in a bun and your conversation has been school, school and more school. You have to dress to impress. God gave you a 5 foot 8 inch frame, beautiful legs, a beautiful smile and a wonderful personality. Let's go shopping at the ship's store, get you a few dresses and then visit the beauty parlor, so they can do something with your hair. I'll tell you like my mom told me, 'When you're trying to get someone's attention, think about what it's like going shopping for a can of tomatoes. You don't have to open the can to buy the product. Melissa, just package it in a fashion to entice the shopper to read the label.' We need to let your hair down, wash and style it." Melissa respected and envied her mother because of her usual frankness. She accepted her mother's tips on style; however, she chose not to pursue the steward.

Melissa thought the French Riviera was the closest thing to heaven she could imagine. The warm breezy nights, sweet romantic music, sunny beaches and friendly people made her trip very enjoyable. When they returned to their home in Texas, Melissa began preparing for her fall semester. She called *The Baltimore Star* to get a job as a freelance writer. The editor, Terri Mills, asked her to fax copies of some articles she had written as an undergraduate along with her resume. Melissa did, and two weeks later she was offered $250 per article. She accepted, and her life as a journalist began.

Things went well until her second semester when Professor Mark Everett, her journalism instructor, was assigned to be her mentor. This third-year black professor's wavy brown hair, silky smooth tanned skin and light brown eyes caused Melissa's stomach to flutter and her speech to stammer when they talked. His slender 6-foot frame was more fit for the cover of *GM Magazine* than the classroom. He could sense her attraction and made a point of always talking to her in the classroom or his office. Professor Everett knew that perception in most business environments carries just as much, if not more, weight when it comes to personal relationships with subordinates.

Professor Everett was a former assistant editor of *The Washington Probe*. Three years ago he had tired of the deadlines, lack of creative talent and political gamesmanship the newspaper exhibited. When the opportunity arose allowing him to shape and encourage unbridled talent, he immediately accepted it.

Professor Everett required each student to submit a 25-page research paper on a political figure and reveal little known facts about these individuals. Melissa indicated her research paper would be titled, "The Tyranny of the Presidency." He liked Melissa's topic because she was bold enough to challenge the political establishment and willing to do the legwork every good reporter must do: develop, analyze and synthesize evidence that can be fashioned into a credible story. Melissa decided to use President Bob's presidency as a model for her topic and began research by surfing the Internet for information regarding his journey to the White House. However, files on his friends, White House staff and cabinet members were inaccessible. She contacted the President's family and friends and offered to keep their names out of her final paper if they would give her useful information to complete her project. Melissa also attempted to use the Library of Congress files to access the White House historical files that are sent on a monthly basis. However, they were sealed in a category titled <u>Top Secret and Confidential</u>, followed by a stern warning that improper access would result in a $50,000 fine and up to fifteen years in prison.

Melissa solicited Professor Everett's advice regarding the propriety of surfing the net to access the governmental files she needed. He told her to utilize other tools at her disposal to get the desired information. Professor Everett recounted stories of how he had won his first two Pulitzer Prizes by going underground as a Jamaican Weed Lord (marijuana kingpin) and uncovered a multi-million dollar drug distribution operation.

Melissa obtained a job as a reporter for *The South Star Conservative Journal.* She knew she would have access to the *Associated Press* reports and media information that was inaccessible to most college students. Melissa was also a fan of *The Journal* since it was a conservative publication grounded in Christian values and created to reach a diverse audience.

Melissa used the Washington Probe Library to research President Bob's background. She began with his 10th, 11th and 12th grade classmates. The President had 84 classmates; however, 12 had died as a result of drug abuse, diseases and automobile accidents. Melissa sent the remaining 72, fact-finding letters. She used Ideal Computer Match Center (ICMC) to locate their current addresses. ICMC produced the software that allows law enforcement agencies to locate relatives of accident victims when they have their relatives' names but no addresses.

Usually a 5-percent response to a survey is considered good. However, Melissa received letters from 92 percent. Each response recounted a different positive story about President Bob. However, five letters were from former girlfriends, and two of these were a little edgy.

One said, "Bob was a great guy, lots of fun and the best lover I ever had. I should have followed his advice and kept in touch. He may have prevented me from making poor choices in life."

The other letter said, "Bob and I will always have a special bond. We met as strangers and parted as little more than friends. I went into our relationship with my eyes wide open and came out of it with a greater appreciation for life."

Both women lived only a few hours' drive from Baltimore. Joyce Notion lives in Newark, New Jersey, and is owner/manager of Imaging Model Agency, and Susan Bunting owns New York's avant-garde newspaper, *Point Break*.

Melissa thought that it was peculiar that President Bob would have five girlfriends in three years. For years, the newspapers had portrayed him as having only one love interest growing up and that was his deceased wife, Diane. Melissa decided to take the next two weekends and drive to visit Joyce and Susan. She hoped by observing their expressions as they described their relationships with President Bob, she would gain a better insight into his desire for political office. So far, it was clear that he had some type of charisma because he had positively affected so many of his classmates.

Melissa first went to visit Joyce. They met in O'Shea's Restaurant in downtown Newark. Joyce was a very spirited and cordial woman. Her petite, 5-foot-5-inch, 100-pound frame made her look years younger than her age. She was a natural blond with hazel eyes. Her make-up was applied very lightly and complemented her warm complexion. She wore small diamond earrings that nearly matched the one on her ring finger. Joyce wore a short, pink jump suit with matching sandals. She talked about how President Bob had inspired her to do something positive with her life. Joyce had been a high school cheerleader with a passion to marry the first nice young man who had a job and asked her. However, President Bob talked constantly about the importance of small business ownership, utilizing one's talents to maximize potential and channeling one's passion to make a difference in the world. Joyce mentioned the only regret she had was that she wasn't able to come to President Bob's first inaugural ball and plant a nice juicy kiss on his lips.

However, the visit with Susan was very strange. They met for lunch at an outdoor cafe located near Central Park and a quarter mile from Grenwich Village. Susan was casually dressed in blue jeans and a Grateful Dead tee-shirt. She appeared a little nervous, fidgeting with the belt loops on her jeans. Due to the thick hot humid air, she used a tissue several times to wipe beads of perspiration from her forehead and mascara that was running down her cheeks. Her hair was jet black with streaks of red in it, and she was soft-spoken. When Melissa asked her to discuss her relationship with President Bob, she froze up to the point that she began talking about other issues. After a little prodding, Susan said that they had met when she interviewed him during her sophomore year.

President Bob was the first player ever to make the baseball and debate team his sophomore year. He was always well prepared and knew his opponents' weaknesses. President Bob studied film for hours after a game to learn his opponents' tendencies. One time the opposing team had the bases loaded in the ninth inning. He was playing shortstop, and the opposing batter hit a ball to left field and the ball fell in fair territory. The left fielder picked up the ball and failed to throw it to the cutoff man. Instead, he threw wildly, and the ball ended up at third base. Two runs scored and President Bob's team lost 4 to 3.

President Bob did not yell at the guy who botched the play although his other teammates were giving him grief about his error. When they got in the locker room, President Bob invited him to come over on Saturday to practice his throws. So even as a youth, President Bob was able to mediate problems. Melissa asked her how President Bob was romantically.

"He was the combination of Don Juan, Rudolph Valentino, Humphrey Bogart, Yul Brenner, Spencer Tracy, Omar Shariff and Sean Connery.

President Bob made everyone feel special. He dated around and would admit to having more than one intimate friend. He was very special to me, and I would never do anything to hurt him. Although we have not spoken in over twenty years, I still consider him a close friend."

Melissa didn't see a ring on Susan's hand, so she asked her candidly if she had ever married. Susan smiled and said, "I never married because my first and only love deserted me for higher office." She said that President Bob encouraged her to pursue her education. Susan came from a background that some might call "poor white trash." Her mother was an unemployed Polish immigrant, and her father was a displaced, tenant potato-farmer from Ireland. Education and founding a business was her ticket out of poverty. Susan had attended New York University on scholarship after graduating from high school. She worked for the *New York Tempest* newspaper but left after four years and founded *Point Break Publications*. This newspaper had a circulation of 156,000 readers. Susan never found time to stop and smell the roses. Her personal life suffered as her personal ambitions soared.

Melissa thanked Susan for her time and willingness to share information. Susan wished her well on her research paper and graduate degree. Melissa mulled over Susan's comments while driving back. A week earlier Joyce had explained, how and why she still held a puppy love romance in her heart for President Bob. However, Susan never described the attributes President Bob displayed that caused her to feel that she could not find that quality in another man, and it had been at least thirty years since they were in high school. Certainly she knew that President Bob was married. Even when questioned directly about their relationship, Susan's rose-colored view of what could have been clouded what was or is. Melissa knew that she had to do a little more digging.

In her research, Melissa came across a college paper Susan had written and just didn't know what to make of it. It was titled, "Bobbie, the Male Turandot." Turandot is an opera, based on a Chinese fairy tale about an icy princess who poses three riddles to each of her suitors. When they can't answer correctly, they die. Puccini, the composer, was dying when he wrote the opera, and it was rumored that one of his students wrote the finale. The story is about how love can overcome hate. Susan's paper notes, "Bobbie's conduct was filled with riddles, and the riddles answers were in the echoes of his suitors whose voices grew faint with their demise."

Melissa sent a letter to Palmer Reese, a noted presidential historian, informing him about her project and requested a meeting. A week later, she received a call from Mr. Reese's secretary, Peggy Martin. Ms. Martin said that Mr. Reese was agreeable to a meeting with her in two hours at the presidential retreat in Camp David, Maryland. He was doing research there but would only be there until noon the next day. Ms. Martin insisted that Melissa's visit be confidential because of the tendency of the press to be belligerent and misconstrue things. Melissa, excited at the opportunity to meet someone of Mr. Reese's ilk, readily agreed. She showered, dressed and drove the short forty-five minute drive to Camp David. When Melissa arrived, the guard let her drive into the grounds. A Secret Service agent met her in the parking lot and escorted her inside. Once inside, several men in dark khaki garb grabbed and strip-searched her. She protested, kicking one of the men in the groin and slapping another violently across the face as they wrestled her to the floor. Melissa was handcuffed, gagged and blindfolded; then she was taken to an upstairs bedroom and tied to a four-poster bed. For four days she was injected with heroin and allowed to go to the bathroom every four hours. Melissa was dressed and taken back to her apartment and tossed to the kitchen floor. The men extinguished the pilot light in the oven of her gas stove and rigged the top burners to trigger an explosive devise that left no residue when they were turned on. They put powdered cocaine in Melissa's nostrils and 1/4 ounce in her pockets along with two marijuana cigarettes. They put a cigarette in one of her hands, a cigarette lighter in the other, shook her until she woke up and then walked out the door. Melissa was groggy and could not see anything due to the darkness of the room. She staggered to her feet and realized that she was near the stove. Then she turned it on so she could see. As Melissa did, she smelled gas. However, before she could turn the stove off, it set off an explosion that could be heard six blocks away.

Professor Everett's body was found the following morning due to an apparent suicide. He had hung himself with a picture of Melissa in his hand. The newspaper read, "Deadly love triangle…black man, white woman and drugs."

The Baltimore City Police Department tried to call Melissa's parents around 1:00 a.m. However, they got no answer. They called the police department in Austin, Texas, and explained the situation. They asked the Austin police to contact the parents and notify them of Melissa's death. The community relations' officer on duty, Marty Bell, was dispatched to the Shane's home with another officer. They rang the bell, but there was no answer. So, they waited in their patrol car until the doctors returned home.

One of Juliet Shane's patients had gone into labor at 11:45 p.m. the previous night and had called her prior to going to the hospital. Dr. Shane told her to proceed to the hospital, and she would meet her there. Since it was late, Paul drove her to the hospital and waited in the lounge for her. The patient had an easy delivery and by 3:15 a.m., the new father and mother were taking turns holding their baby girl. Dr. Shane washed up, woke up her husband who was fast asleep in the visitor's lounge and they went home.

When they pulled into their driveway, to their surprise two policemen were sitting in a police vehicle. They asked the officers what was wrong. Officer Bell identified himself and asked if he and his partner could come inside for a moment to explain. The Shanes suspected something was drastically wrong but tried to maintain their composure. Once inside, Officer Bell notified them that their child and Professor Everett had died and informed them of the facts surrounding the case. Melissa's parents listened attentively while Officer Bell talked. They could not hold back the tears.

"Professor Everett had ample to money to buy drugs. The police in Baltimore, Maryland suspect that he had fallen in love with Melissa, who was one of his brightest students. They were seen often after school and on several lunch breaks together. The police said activities such as this occur quite often on college campuses but usually don't get this serious. Most of the time, when the school's administration gets wind of a student teacher relationship, it gives the instructor an ultimatum to end it or find another job. Usually the teacher chooses to end the relationship rather than have his personnel record blemished. However, traces of drugs found in the torched apartment and the professor's apparent suicide made this an open and shut case."

"Officers, your information is hard to believe because we are a close Christian family, and Melissa would never use drugs. This would go against everything she believed in," said Melissa's father.

"Melissa had written to us weekly regarding the exciting project she was working on with her professor's assistance. She never mentioned that they were romantically involved," said Melissa's mother.

Officer Bell told them that he could understand their grief and their need to know everything surrounding their daughter's demise. He gave them the name, address and telephone number of the community relations' officer in Baltimore who was assigned to the case. Officer Bell also gave them the number of a local parent-grief counseling and support group. The Shanes thanked the officers for coming by and saw them out.

The Shanes spent the next few hours crying and wondering what they could have done to prevent this tragedy. Maybe they should have protested when Melissa had expressed an interest in going so far away to college. Maybe they should have visited her more often in Baltimore. Maybe she became lonely and depressed while away from home and got caught up with the wrong people. Maybe the professor used his influence to take advantage of her. Nothing made sense to them, but they needed to get some answers. After agonizing several days, they decided to take a leave of absence from their jobs to investigate the circumstances surrounding Melissa's death. They had ample money in the bank to sustain them for years. They packed and left the next day for Baltimore.

The flight seemed like an eternity. They loved Texas and every few years would venture outside the state and travel with their church or medical society to an island resort. Paul Shane told his wife that he knew about the Baltimore Orioles baseball team and about Johns Hopkins and University Hospitals. Both hospitals are world-renowned facilities. Juliet Shane said the only thing she knew about the city was that someone killed their daughter and should be caught, prosecuted and punished. She then began to cry. Melissa's father hugged his wife and tried to comfort her, but he too was overcome with grief and cried along with her.

The stewardess assigned to the first class section noticed their grief. She asked politely if there was anything she could do or get for them. Melissa's father said that they were en route to Baltimore to bury their only child. Then he asked for some spring water. The stewardess left and quickly returned with two cold bottles of spring water and two cups. He thanked her.

"My name is Traci, and I'm going to Baltimore on a two week vacation. If you need assistance in making funeral arrangements or have difficulty getting around town, I know quite a few people there and will be glad to assist." Traci handed them a card with her name and phone number on it.

Melissa's parents thanked Traci, and Juliet put the paper in her purse.

When the plane landed, Traci smiled, shook hands with the Shanes and wished them Godspeed. After retrieving their bags from baggage claim, they hailed a red and blue cab to take them from Baltimore Washington International Airport to the Renaissance Hotel in downtown Baltimore. The driver pulled as close as he could to the curb and got out. He opened the trunk and loaded the suitcases and garment bags. The driver was a typical Baltimorean who was very helpful and loved the city. Kevin asked the Shanes if they liked sports.

Dr. Paul Shane, grasping the much-needed distraction to take his mind off of Melissa's death momentarily, said, "I enjoy watching baseball and football games on television but rarely get to see one live."

The cab driver talked first about the plight of the Baltimore Orioles. "They have fallen on hard times due to lack of depth in their minor league and marginal records the last few seasons. However, for better or for worse I have been a die-hard fan since the 1966 World Series win over the Los Angeles Dodgers.

"When you say Frank, Boog, Brooks and Belanger, you've said something. Frank Robinson was the only professional major league baseball player to be Most Valuable Player in the American and National Leagues. He could turn on a fastball quicker than most politicians can lie. Boog

Powell had the softest hands at first base and could hit for average and power. Eddie Murray was the consummate professional switch-hitter. He hit more home runs from both sides of the plate than any other hitter. One day Eddie had hit a ball so hard that as it was sailing over the center field wall, the fielder managed to get a glove on it. The impact of the ball broke the fielder's hand, tore off the fielder's glove and became a souvenir item of an adoring fan. Brooks Robinson, the human vacuum cleaner, was at third. You hit it his way, it was scooped up and you were out before you tagged the bag at first. He also was known as Mr. Clutch because of his prowess at the plate and his knack for getting hits at critical junctures in a game. Now Mark Belanger was known as the Blade. He was tall, thin, fast and more graceful on the field than Fred Astaire was on stage. The Blade could go twenty feet in the hole near the outfield grass to field a ground ball and throw out the league's fastest runner."

"That's remarkable," responded Dr. Paul Shane.

"As good as our hitters and fielders were, our pitchers were just as awesome. We had Mike Cuellar, Jim Palmer, Dave McNally and Tom Phoebus—four twenty-game winners. Do you remember Nick Nicolas?"

"No."

"He's the only professional baseball player I know who could hit just like me. Nick couldn't hit a ball with a paddle thrown at ten miles an hour." The driver laughed with a high humorous chuckle, and Mr. Shane couldn't help but laugh as well. "Seriously, he had two good years as a hitter. But mostly couldn't hit his last name. However, as a glove man, there was none better."

Dr. Paul Shane was a little tired of hearing about the Orioles and told the cabby, "I know the Orioles have a rich history, but I didn't know they were in such a sports-minded town."

Dr. Juliet Shane, visibly upset with her husband's sudden cavalier attitude, considering their only child just died, glared with disgust at her husband and tightly squeezed his right hand.

The cab driver took Dr. Paul Shane's comment to mean that he wanted to hear more about Baltimore's sports' history. He then went on to discuss the plight of the Baltimore Colts.

"I still love that team. The best quarterback ever was Johnny Unitas. He played at a time when quarterbacks didn't play like sissies with sissy rules. Football is a contact sport. If an offensive player such as a running back or wide receiver has the ball and is running, then the defense's job is to always separate the ball from the ball carrier. I remember times when Johnny would get creamed by a linebacker, but he didn't get up and jump around like he wanted to fight. Johnny just got up and threw a 15-yard pass to the tight end, John Mackey, or a wide receiver. Before you knew it, my buddies in the end-zone stands would be yelling 'touchdown.'"

The cab stopped in front of the Renaissance Hotel, and the cabby assisted Dr. Paul Shane with unloading the bags. The fare was $22.50. The valets immediately took the doctors' bags and put them on a cart while the Shanes checked in. Once they were registered and had the bags dropped off at their suite, Melissa's father called Baltimore Community Relations Officer, Calvin Mooney. Officer Mooney agreed to meet the Shanes at 2:30 p.m. It was only 12:37 p.m., so they decided to walk across the street to the Inner Harbor for lunch. The harbor was lined with pavilions, an aquarium, science center, recreational boats, cruise ships and plenty of eateries. They wanted to get a good steak. However, they quickly discovered this was a seafood town first, Italian cuisine second, Soul food third and everything else followed.

They ended up eating at Morris's Crab Shanty. Morris was a petite, black man who may have weighed 90 pounds soaking wet. As they entered the restaurant, they noticed three young waitresses with fair pecan unblemished skin. Even the small drops of perspiration on their foreheads could not overshadow their beauty and hospitable personalities. They were attired in black shorts and red Morris Crab Shanty tee shirts. Two cooks in the kitchen busily prepared customer orders, taking great care to ensure each dish was as appealing to the eye as the palate. There were chairs and tables to accommodate about 80 customers. The harbor could be seen from anywhere you sat.

After Shantil, the waitress, gave the Shanes the menu, they were surprised to see that many dishes were made from crabs. Shantil said, "Didn't anybody tell you, Baltimore is Crab-Cake City? The state is known for its crabs, and Baltimore is known for its fantastic crab cakes." The menu included crab cakes, crab soup, steamed crabs and entrees stuffed with crabmeat. Dr. Paul Shane ordered a broiled crab cake platter, and Dr. Juliet Shane ordered orange roughy stuffed with crabmeat. The restaurant had the smell of fresh fish, and customers were buzzing talking about how good the food was.

While they waited for their food, Dr. Juliet Shane said, "I never thought the cab driver would shut up. He really loves this town. That cab driver must be getting a kickback from the tourism bureau."

"If he doesn't, he should," said Dr. Paul Shane jovially. "He painted a picture so vividly about Johnny Unitas; I almost gave him a standing ovation myself."

They laughed; but after a few seconds, their smiles turned to frowns.

After eating, they went to their hotel room and waited for Officer Mooney to arrive. He arrived at exactly 2:30 p.m. and called them from the courtesy phone in the hotel lobby. Mrs. Shane answered the phone, told him their room number and to come up. Within minutes he tapped on their door. Mr. Shane opened the door, extended his right hand and said, "I'm Dr. Paul Shane and this is my wife Dr. Juliet Shane."

"I'm Officer Mooney, and I'm sorry about your loss." He opened his portfolio and asked them, "Do either of you have any questions before I take you to view your daughter's remains?"

"Yes, we do. Thank you for coming. Come in and have a seat on the couch," said Melissa's father.

"Please explain the circumstances surrounding our daughter's death. We are not quite clear on certain aspects of what has been told to us secondhand by the police in Austin, Texas," said Melissa's mother.

Officer Mooney told them the same information that Officer Bell had relayed. He also said, "The city's coroner will be giving a preliminary report today regarding blood samples that were taken from Melissa. The coroner should have it done by the time we get there."

As they got up to leave, Officer Bell inquired, "How long do you expect to be in town? Do you want me to assist you in finding a funeral home or clergy?"

"We will be here as long as it takes to do what needs to be done for our daughter," said Melissa's father.

"We will find our own funeral home and clergy, but thank you for asking," added Melissa's mother.

The Shanes got up and followed the officer through the hotel to the parking garage. Officer Mooney was driving an unmarked red Ford Caprice. He gave them as many details as he could in regards to his department's investigation of their child's death. When they got to the coroner's office, the coroner warned them that the body was severely damaged by the fire. However, he had identified Melissa by using her dental records. The Shanes said they were both physicians and were well aware of the significant body damage that fire could cause but insisted on seeing Melissa's body anyway.

The coroner pulled out the slab with Melissa's body draped with a thick white covering. He lowered the sheet from over her head to her waist as both parents shrieked in horror.

Melissa's mother screamed "My poor baby!"

Melissa's father fainted, and had to be carried out on a stretcher.

They both were taken to Johns Hopkins Hospital and treated for shock. Then the Shanes were referred to Ms. Brooks, a grief counselor. The counselor asked them if they knew anyone in town who they could stay with. They should have other family members' support in such a trying time.

They both answered, "No." The only one they knew was a stewardess they had met briefly on their way to Baltimore. She was nice, but they could not impose on her. The Shanes were registered at the hotel and would be there only for a few days. They admitted that Melissa was the only family they had. They had her late in life and both sets of their parents were deceased.

Ms. Brooks listened attentively but deduced that they should not be left alone. She pushed the telephone to Melissa's mother and asked her to call the stewardess and accept her offer to assist with the funeral arrangements. Reluctantly, Melissa's mother pulled out the telephone number and called. Traci answered on the second ring and told them that she would assist in any way she could. Traci said that she lived in a two-bedroom condominium, and they were more than welcome to stay with her. It was in a nice neighborhood. If they felt uneasy about doing it, they could always give her half as much as they would have paid to stay at a hotel.

"Thank you very much for the offer, but we can't. However, we would like your assistance in making funeral arrangements," said Melissa's mother.

"I have a friend who owns a funeral parlor. He is very reasonable and could come to the hotel and explain everything. I have another friend that's a pastor of a local church. He could do the funeral if you provide him some background information on your daughter."

Melissa's mother thanked Traci again for being so sweet and helpful. She agreed to have the funeral director come by the hotel the next morning at 9:00 a.m. and the pastor to come at 10:00 a.m. Melissa's mother indicated that after Melissa's funeral in Baltimore, her remains would be transported to Texas by train. A memorial service would be held for Melissa in Texas, attended by their close friends and colleagues and would be followed by an interment.

Ms. Brooks gave them a 24-hour hotline to call if they had any questions or concerns. She also gave them her pager number. Officer Mooney was sitting outside of Ms. Brook's office. Following their counseling session, Officer Mooney drove them back to the hotel. They were tired, so they decided to have dinner in their room before going to bed.

At 8:00 a.m., Traci called to suggest that they have breakfast at Windows, one of the hotel's restaurants. Melissa's parents agreed. They met by the first floor elevators and walked to the restaurant where they had a breakfast buffet.

Traci told them that she had explained their plight to a local funeral home director and pastor, and both were eager to help.

Dr. Juliet Shane said, "We need to have these arrangements completed by noon because we want to go to Melissa's school and apartment."

"What do you expect to find?"

"I guess we need to know what went wrong in our little girl's life and how it went wrong. We should have been there for her but obviously we weren't."

"My car is parked in the garage. I'll be more than happy to take you. I don't have anything to do anyway. I understand the loss since I lost my dad before I could get to know him. At least you were able to know and love your daughter."

By the time they finished breakfast, it was time to return to their room. Mr. Charles Parsons, the mortician, knocked at the door within minutes of their return. He had a portfolio with various funeral plans including the state plan where the local universities give the donor's family $1,500 for their loved one's cadaver. They told him that due to the severity of their daughter's body, they would have a closed casket funeral, and they were not donating their daughter's body to science.

"You can either have the funeral in the church or at the funeral home. The chapel at the funeral home may be more conducive to your needs because the church seats 2500 people, and the chapel in the funeral home seats 80," Mr. Parsons said.

The Shanes said they knew that due to the limited number of expected attendees, a service in the funeral home's chapel might seem more appropriate. However, they were Christians and wanted a traditional funeral in a church.

Reverend Winston Pride, Sr. came at 10:00 a.m., but Mr. Parsons had not finalized the funeral arrangements. After Reverend Pride was introduced, Mr. Parsons mentioned that he had been the mortician at several funerals where Reverend Pride had officiated. Reverend Pride pastors a church in nearby Washington, D.C., which has an excellent outreach ministry. He was elected two years before as National President of the National Baptist Council. All of the Council's affiliate pastors would allow him the courtesy of preaching in their churches, as well as utilizing their sanctuary for services. Mr. Parsons then praised Reverend Pride for his hard work in the community.

The Shanes carefully looked through Mr. Parsons' casket catalog and selected a purple casket for Melissa's remains. Melissa's father commented that purple was her favorite color. One Easter, she tried to use a pail of purple food coloring in water to dye her white cat, Morris. As she picked Morris up to dip him in the colored water, the cat darted away tipping over the bowl of dye-colored water and splashed it all over Melissa. It took about a month for the dye to wear out of her hair. She was teased at school for being the first nerd punk rocker.

When Mr. Parsons gave the Shanes the price list for the cost of limousines traditionally used by families to follow the hearse with their daughter's remains, they immediately said the limousine wasn't necessary. They could drive their rental car. They also gave Mr. Parsons a poem to put in the program that Melissa had written when she was in the sixth grade.

Mr. Parsons unfolded the yellow-lined notebook paper and read the poem aloud slowly.

> The grass is always greener than I had imagined
>
> As I look across life's boundaries.
>
> When I got up and heard the robins chatter
>
> I did not leap, but crept to see what was the matter.
>
> They were welcoming in today, saying good riddance to the past
>
> Facing new challenges and content in knowing they wouldn't last.
>
> As the sun set on their day and my similar state,
>
> I found contentment appreciating what God gave us,
>
> Before and beyond this date.

Mr. Parsons just shook his head as his usual somber look mellowed as he repeated the last line in a slower and lower tone. He held onto each word as if discovering a sacred treasure.

As he folded the poem and placed it gently in his portfolio, he said, "Most obituaries contain poems from excellent well-known writers such as Robert Frost, Edgar Allen Poe, Charles Dickens or Maya Angelou. All of them started writing as adults. However, Melissa's poem is beautiful and profound. Her insight is above average. She found in her youth, a truth that many adults have yet to learn.

Since the funeral would be a closed casket ceremony, Mr. Parsons agreed to make a digital enlargement of a wallet-size photo of Melissa to a

16 x 20 photo. The enlargement would be framed, matted and placed on an easel next to her casket.

The funeral was scheduled to take place at Salem Baptist Temple. It was in the heart of the city and easily accessible to major highways. The Shanes told Reverend Pride that they wanted Melissa's funeral to be on Thursday. Since it was Monday, it would give Melissa's friends, family, classmates and colleagues several days to arrange to be in attendance.

Reverend Pride listened closely to Melissa's parents' concerns and request. He empathized with the loss of their daughter stating that his daughter had been killed at the tender age of 17 when she was walking home from the bus stop. Rival gangs decided to settle a turf dispute with guns. He said that the sad thing about it was the White House is less than ten minutes away from where she died. The Shanes asked Reverend Pride how much he charged for funerals, and he replied that he has never charged anyone for a funeral or a sermon. He accepts whatever donation is given to him.

"It's nice to meet a man of integrity and one who practices what he preaches," Melissa's mother said. Since she handles their family's finances, she took out her checkbook and wrote the mortician a check for $12,000, Reverend Pride a check for $500 and Salem Baptist Church a check for $500.

By 11:30 a.m., Mr. Parsons and Reverend Pride were pulling out of the hotel's parking lot to see the next client while Traci chattered about the excellent choices they had made.

Melissa's dad said he wanted to visit Johns Hopkins University. The dean of students, Menard Hatleman, had called them the day after Melissa died to express his condolences and requested that he be notified as soon as funeral arrangements were made. There were numerous students and faculty members who were grieving and held Melissa in high regard.

Traci said, "I know this city very well. I understand your need to retrieve Melissa's personal effects and notify her loved ones and friends. So, I don't mind driving you to the places you need to go. This will save you time and allow you to accomplish the things you need to get done."

The Shanes thanked Traci for being so understanding and sweet. They accepted her proposal with the stipulation that she would allow them to treat her to lunch and reimburse her for money she spent on gas.

Traci pretended to pay little attention to their monetary offer and said, "Then it's settled. I'll show you around town and save you a little grief."

They piled into Traci's car and started off for Johns Hopkins University. Traci continued talking because the Shanes were becoming very quiet, as if in the lead car of a funeral procession.

"Did you two know Levi Watkins and Benjamin Carson are famous African-American Johns Hopkins Hospital physicians? Dr. Watkins has done pioneering work as a cardiologist involving heart monitoring and Dr. Carson's prowess in carving new avenues in treatment of severe neurological abnormalities are mind-boggling.

"What makes these men so great is that they dared to delve into areas of medical science their colleagues were reluctant to," commented Melissa's mother. "I guess their medical curiosity fueled by their creative genius prevailed, resulting in significant advances in medical research."

"I never thought about it that way," said Traci, unimpressed.

Melissa's father joined in and told Traci that many people don't have her insight. They view people in the medical profession as someone who knows everything there is to know about medical science, when in fact the opposite is true. Most doctors can be general practitioners because that's what they are trained to be before they choose to specialize in a particular course of study. However, all doctors cannot be specialists because they don't have the inclination, money or talent to pursue additional specialties. They are more apt to return to school and obtain an MBA in accounting, so they are better able to monitor their finances. On that note, Traci pulled into the university's visitor parking lot.

Dr. Paul Shane thanked Traci and told her not to wait for them because they might be awhile and would take a taxi back to the hotel. Traci started to protest by saying she didn't mind waiting but thought better of it, let them out and said, "I'll catch up with you guys later." As they were waving goodbye, the Shanes noticed a campus directory about 30 feet away with a layout of all buildings and offices on campus. They quickly found the dean's office that was only about 1,000 yards away in a six-story marble building.

As they walked inside, two males appearing to be students were leaving the building and talking.

"I needed to get a class waiver in order to graduate. All students are required to take at least one writing course in order to graduate. I had taken a course titled, 'Checkmate: a history, a game and an idea.' I was required to do two research papers as well as take two written examinations. Although this was a history course, I was allowed to substitute it because the essential element of the class was a mastery of the English language in written form. I didn't know the dean was a very voluptuous female. When I went to the registrar and told her what I wanted, instead of saying checkmate I kept making a Freudian slip and said, 'chest mate.'"

They both laughed historically as they went to their car.

Drs. Paul and Juliet Shane proceeded to the dean's office. The dean's secretary was quite cordial.

"The dean is expecting both of you; however, he is in a meeting with a student. The meeting should be over momentarily. Do either of you want a cup of coffee or something to drink while you wait?"

"No, thank you," replied the Shanes.

"Okay. Please have a seat outside of his office doorway."

The Shanes walked over to the chairs; however, before they could sit down and get comfortable, Dean Hatleman came strolling out of his office laughing with a male student. He was surprisingly short of stature. The dean was only 5 feet 4 inches, plump and had a hearty laugh. As the student walked away, apparently going to his next class, Dean Hatleman turned his attention to his two visitors. He extended his hand to Melissa's father and said, "I apologize for keeping you waiting; please come into my office."

They followed him into his office, and they all sat at a small, round conference table. The arm-back chairs were very comfortable. Dean Hatleman made small talk as they sat down.

"Did you have a problem finding my office? Up the stairs to the right, beneath a mountain of paperwork."

The Shanes smiled somberly. Realizing that the ice was broken, the dean said, "I'm really sorry about the loss of Melissa. She was one of our brightest students." The dean reached inside his desk drawer and pulled out a check for $4,500. He handed it to Melissa's father and said, "The students wanted to do something for Melissa and her family. They felt that this could defray the costs of some of her funeral expenses."

Melissa's father thanked him and accepted the check. "That was nice of her classmates and instructors. Melissa had a heart of gold, and we will miss her. Please tell me about this professor she supposedly had an affair with?"

Dean Hatleman, with a look of remorseful concern, said, "Dr. Shane, that's the most puzzling part of all of this. None of the teachers or students who knew Melissa or Professor Everett ever saw them together outside of the classroom. Also, both of them never hinted at having abused drugs or being involved in a relationship. I know what the police have concluded; however, I haven't seen any proof that would lead to that conclusion."

"Tell me about this professor," Melissa's dad instructed.

"I know this is a tremendously difficult time for the Shane family; however, I am ethically prohibited from disclosing any information about a faculty member's education, personal data and work history. What I can tell you is that Professor Everett did not miss a day of work due to illness nor was he ever accused of sexual misconduct. He had been nominated as 'Professor of the Year.' Professor Everett had earned the faculty and students' respect because of his congenial but professional and demanding teaching style, which required students to achieve academic excellence. He was an excellent communicator and academician."

Paul Shane could not compose himself any longer and blurted out, "If this professor was so damned conscientious, and my baby girl was bright, sensible and ethically unencumbered, how could this tragedy happen?"

Dean Hatleman, looking exasperated and speechless, extended his hands parallel to his waist and said, "I don't know."

The Shanes solemn and remorseful facial expressions revealed the anguish they struggled with. Juliet Shane said, "This has been the toughest week of our lives. We never thought that our daughter would precede us in death. Burying a child! I had the good fortune of not only raising and nurturing Melissa but also knowing her from birth through adulthood as a daughter and as a good friend. That makes it that much more difficult to bear."

The dean's heart was torn because he reflected on his own two healthy daughters and how helpless he'd be in a similar situation. He fought back tears, and said, "I'm sorry folks. I wish there was something else I could say or do to comfort you, but there isn't. I'm going to have to explain the same thing to Professor Everett's family in less than an hour."

Dean Hatleman knew he had made a faux pas as soon as he said it. He did not want the families to combine their efforts and attempt to do what the police were doing—determine the actual circumstances that led to their children's demise.

"Well, the police concluded that it was a murder-suicide. I just don't know."

Dr. Juliet Shane fired back, "Look, Dean Hatleman, I don't care what the police concluded. My daughter would never cross the ethical line and date a teacher. This girl was a stickler for details and following the rules. She complained if her dad or I drove 5 or 10 miles over the speed limit."

Melissa's mother explained the funeral arrangements to the dean. He said he would post the information in the student lounge and on the student government bulletin board. Dean Hatleman also agreed to immediately send a memorandum to all faculty members.

As the Shanes got up to leave, Dean Hatleman shook their hands and escorted them to the door. As he opened the door, the Everetts were sitting in the waiting area near his secretary. Juliet Shane's eyes met Mrs. Everett's for a brief moment. Before the Shanes passed, Mrs. Everett stood and asked, "Are you Melissa Shane's mother?"

"Yes, I am, and this is my husband Paul." The Shanes extended their hands and shook Mrs. Everett's hand, and the hand of the gentleman accompanying her.

Mrs. Elvira Everett said, "This is my brother Thomas. My husband was killed years ago by a sniper in Vietnam. I'm sorry about your daughter, but we still don't understand any of this. No one knows anything, and all we want are a few answers. Everybody says, 'I'm sorry about your loss.' That doesn't mean much when you don't know them, and they don't know you. Everyone says how good they were, but all I want to know is if both of these young people were so good, what happened?"

Juliet Shane said that she shared her frustration. Before Dean Hatleman could come between their bonding, she jotted down their hotel address and room number and handed it to Mrs. Everett. Juliet Shane whispered, "Please call me later, so we can talk a little more freely."

Mrs. Everett tucked the note in her purse as she nodded in agreement, and the Shanes continued past Dean Hatleman and made their way down the hall to exit the building.

Dean Hatleman breathed a sigh of relief as the Shanes left him in a strange predicament. He expressed his sympathy to the Everetts as he had done with the Shanes. However, the Everetts were not as receptive to his comments after losing their only son. The scant information they received regarding their boy's death was problematic. The activities he allegedly had participated in within his last two months of life were inconsistent with his past behavior.

Mr. Thomas Everett pointedly told Dean Hatleman, "We appreciate your encouraging words, but we are frustrated and disheartened. The limited background information that you gave us regarding this tragic situation provides us little solace, and we are determined to get to the bottom of the actual events that led to Mark's death."

Mr. Everett's deep bass voice caused his words to reverberate in the dean's ear like an echo in a deserted hall. "We are determined to get to the bottom of the actual events that led to Mark's death."

Dean Hatleman suspected the school would never be the same again. He struggled to his feet and extended his right hand as he reiterated his condolences.

Mr. Everett grasped the dean's hand first with a strong handshake. The dean's hand dwarfed inside of Mr. Everett's, as he forced a smile and looked into Mr. Everett's piercing eyes. Mrs. Everett, suspecting her brother's 6 feet 4 inch, 275 pound muscular frame intimidated the dean, also rose and shook his hand. She handed him her phone number at the hotel and urged him to call if he had any additional information. Mr. Everett said that he was confident that the final police report, after their investigation, would allow everyone to better understand all the events that had led to the tragic deaths of Professor Everett and Melissa.

Dean Hatleman shook his head slightly as he watched the Everetts walk determinedly out of the building. He could clearly see where Professor Everett got his spunk. Mr. Hatleman sat down in his office chair, muttering to himself, "They said report everything." He called the Baltimore City Police homicide division and asked for Lieutenant Michael St. John. A few seconds later Lieutenant St. John came to the phone and said, "This is Lieutenant St. John. How may I help you?"

The dean identified himself and reported that the Shanes and Everetts were in town inquiring about the circumstances leading up to their children's deaths. He also gave the lieutenant their telephone numbers. Lieutenant St. John thanked him for the information and hung up.

As usual, Cintura's tactical intuitiveness paid off. She had the dean's office and home phones bugged and a video camera placed in the hallway leading to his office, as well as inside of his office. Her men parked a surveillance van outside of the school. Traci doubled-back after dropping off the Shanes and watched and listened to everything that transpired. She called Cintura and updated her on all events and asked for guidance.

Cintura calmly yet firmly said, "Play the concerned friend and encourage the families to meet and jointly seek 'the truth.' Once they receive a satisfactory explanation, they'll be able to return to their homes and put this tragedy behind them. As for the police, I've planned a little something special for them. The FBI will take over the investigation since we will have evidence that the professor has been under investigation for the last few years for obtaining classified information without official approval. We will put a muzzle on them in the name of national security, and their inquiry will die. As Confucius said, 'You can't have troubled seas on still waters.'"

When the Shanes arrived at their hotel room, their telephone message button was on. Juliet Shane checked the message, and it was from Traci. She smiled as she listened to Traci say, "Hi, I hope everything turned out well for you two with the dean. I have a few things to do now; however, if you need me, I should be in later tonight. I suggest that you contact Professor Everett's family. They may have some information that may help you get the details you want. As they say, two heads are better than one. I'll talk to you both later."

Juliet Shane turned to her husband, held him tightly and commented in a low tone, "Traci is quite a girl, and Melissa probably would have liked her. Traci said we should contact the Everetts and compare notes. She's right. I gave Mrs. Everett our phone number; I hope she calls."

Paul Shane, trying to be confident and supportive said, "I love you Juliet. We had a wonderful little girl, and I just want to know what happened. I agree; we need to talk to the Everetts, but I get the feeling that they won't know anything either. We will see."

They held each other tenderly and kissed gently on the lips. Each kiss followed another while their hands undressed the other to the rhythmic beat of lovers in heat. Their all-giving moment of bliss ended with a crescendo of passion that they previously thought was lost in time. They fell asleep clinging to their lover and best friend.

About 7:30 p.m., Mrs. Everett called the Shanes. Juliet Shane rolled over and answered the telephone. Mrs. Everett asked if they wanted to meet for coffee in the hotel's lounge. Juliet Shane answered yes. They'd be down in a few minutes.

Hearing the gist of Juliet Shane's conversation, Paul Shane got up from the bed he had been resting on so comfortably the last few hours, went into the bathroom and took a shower. Juliet Shane put on her silk robe lying at the foot of the bed and took out some clothes for her and her husband. She neatly placed undergarments, blouse, sky blue pantsuit, sky blue V-neck polo shirt and khaki slacks on the bed and then joined her husband in the shower. They both quickly showered. Paul Shane started to shave but thought better of it and just combed his short, sandy brown hair and dressed. Juliet Shane slipped on her clothes, combed her hair and put on some lipstick and make-up before accompanying her husband to the lounge.

When they arrived at the lounge, the Everetts were sipping coffee and reminiscing about Professor Everett's childhood. They cordially greeted the Shanes as they approached their table. Mrs. Everett said candidly, "We were sitting here thinking about how blessed we were to have had Mark. He was a good man. We don't believe the baloney we read in the papers and are interested in finding the truth. We think Mark and Melissa was murdered, but we don't know why. Do you know if they were working on anything? Mark never talked about his work. As reported, everything was kept secret or close to the vest as he would often say."

Juliet Shane lamented, "Melissa was just as elusive. She was excited about some research she was doing for a class, but she never said which class or anything else. She just said that it was fascinating and something about putting together survey results to complete a class project. Melissa always talked about school. She never talked about drugs or finding a new boyfriend or anything like that."

Paul Shane said, "Maybe her classmates know what they were working on. I'm sure the police have questioned them. Juliet, has Melissa ever mentioned a classmate's name to you? I don't remember her indicating anyone that she was close to."

The look of concern on Juliet Shane's face changed from a frown to smile as if a bell had gone off in her brain. "Wait a minute! There was one girl. A graduate student named Victoria Krinacki. They had been roommates for a while but were still friends."

The Everetts said that they had never heard about this friend or Melissa in their conversations with Mark.

Juliet Shane hurried to her feet and exclaimed, "I'm calling Shriver Hall from a pay phone in the lobby." She grabbed her purse and walked swiftly away. She called Shriver Hall and was told by a clerk that Victoria was not in but would be in tomorrow. Juliet Shane asked, "What time is Victoria expected in." The clerk asked her to hold on while she checked the schedule. Juliet Shane was irritated that she was being put off, but forced a smile and through her pursed lips said, "Okay." The clerk left to check the schedule and came back to the phone within a few minutes.

"Vicki works Monday through Friday from 7:30 a.m. to 3:30 p.m.

Juliet Shane thanked the clerk for the information and hung up the phone. She repeated to the Everetts and Paul what the clerk told her. They agreed to get a good night's rest and go to Shriver Hall at 8:00 a.m. to talk with Victoria.

As they slowly strolled to the elevator, the Shane's commented that their struggle to find answers might soon be alleviated. Unbeknownst to them, Traci had put a listening device on Paul's belt buckle, in Juliet's purse and on the desk lamp and phone in their hotel room. As they entered their hotel room, Paul Shane turned on the little clock radio and an old Tom Jones tune was playing. He held Juliet's hand close to his heart.

After the song, they called home to check their answering machines. Relatives, patients and friends had left numerous messages of condolences. Though well meaning, each one felt like a dagger of remembrance of what once was and will never be again. As the old adage goes, "A treasure lost is a gift unwrapped." The mournful expressions of despair appeared on their faces, and they talked about Melissa the remainder of the evening.

About 7:15 a.m., the Shane's phone rang shaking them from a peaceful sleep, Juliet Shane answered by saying, "Hello, may I help you?"

It was Traci. She asked, "So, how did it go yesterday? Were you able to contact the Everetts?"

Mrs. Shane recounted what had happened the evening before and said she and her husband had to hurry and get dressed because they were gong to meet Victoria in an hour. Traci insisted on driving them to see Vicki. However, Juliet Shane said that it wouldn't be necessary because the bellman told her Shriver Hall was only a short cab ride away.

Traci said, "Okay let's compromise and have lunch at Windows."

Juliet Shane agreed and indicated she would invite the Everetts to join them.

The Shanes and Everetts met as planned. The gentleman working at the concierge desk provided them with a Johns Hopkins University campus map and asked the bellman to hail a taxi. The bellman blew his whistle, and a taxi immediately pulled up. By the time they got in, told the driver where they were going, buckled their seat belts and got comfortable the cab was pulling into Johns Hopkins University's campus parking lot.

They walked nervously to Shriver Hall and at the first desk they came to Juliet asked, "Where does Victoria work?" The young lady directed them to the east of the building where Victoria was putting away materials.

Victoria introduced herself but told them they could call her Vicki. The Shanes and Everetts introduced themselves and discussed their relationship to Professor Everett and Melissa. After greeting them cordially, Vicki asked her supervisor if she could take a short break and talk to her deceased ex-roommate's parents and friends. The supervisor told her to take them to the conference room a few feet away. Vicki did as she was advised as she reflected on how she met Melissa. When they got inside the conference room, she asked them to sit down. Not knowing what to say to break the ice, Vicki commented that Melissa was very studious and ambitious but not arrogant. The Shanes and Everetts realizing that Vicki was more nervous than they were, smiled politely and allowed her to elaborate on Melissa's activities. They leaned forward in their chairs as Vicki continued. "Melissa never hung out, and her total focus was always on her schoolwork."

"Do you know any projects Melissa and Professor Everett were jointly working on?" asked Juliet Shane.

Vicki shook her head negatively and said, "We never talked about what Melissa did in her classes. We talked about general subjects, such as things that we wanted to do after graduation."

"Did she ever talk about being romantically involved with Professor Everett?" asked Mr. Thomas Everett.

Vicki smirked while explaining, "Every girl at school would have liked to be romantically involved with Professor Everett. He was handsome, bright, very intelligent and treated everyone, particularly women, with respect. Professor Everett didn't tell any off-colored jokes or disrespect others in any way. However, Melissa was a little shy when it came to men and would never have initiated or been involved in anything like that."

"Why didn't you tell the police that?" asked Mr. Everett.

"I did!" Vicki said defensively.

"So you don't know what projects she was doing in his class? If you don't know, are there any other girls at school whom she was close to or friends she would write?" asked Paul Shane.

As if deep in thought, Vicki paused a moment and said, "I don't know any projects she was working on. All I know is like most students she spent a lot of time in the library researching information for school assignments. As for friends, I don't think she had any other than me."

"Was the Professor seen with any female, teacher or student alone?" Elvira Everett asked inquiringly.

"He met periodically one-on-one with all of his students, discussing evaluations, projects, etc. Professor Everett had an open door policy. He wanted to insure that students had no excuse for failing. Professor Everett would find the time to meet with any student as long as they were trying their best to learn the material."

"Were there any students or faculty that did not like Melissa or Professor Everett?" Mrs. Everett asked.

"There may have been a short list of people, but they were jealous more than anything else. Professor Everett had a unique way of making everyone feel appreciated."

Mrs. Everett pulled out a small writing tablet from her purse and asked Vicki for the "short list."

Vicki explained that Peter Wormsley, Mathew Michaelsbee, Gardenia McNamera, Carthenia Blue and Miguel Canodo were the only ones that she could think of.

"What was their relationship with Professor Everett or Melissa?" Juliet Shane asked.

"Peter Wormsley was a student athlete who was dropped from the rolls for not attending class. Mathew Michaelsbee, the football coach, was furious because Professor Everett's action made Peter ineligible to play the rest of the year. Being dropped from Professor Everett's class caused him to go from being a full time student (12 credit hours) to part time status (9 credit hours), and the NCAA prohibits part time students from participating in sports."

Gardenia McNamera, is Chair of the Daughters of the Arian Nation, a community-based hate group. She was a senior and needed Professor Everett's class to complete her degree since there wasn't a similar class taught by a non-minority. She candidly expressed her biased views, and Professor Everett allowed it as long as she expressed her views within the context of the overall class topic or discussion.

During one class period, he told the story about one of his college professors who had been fired many times while working for other people. "When you work for other people, particularly the pundits that support the lazy shiftless people in today's American big cities, you have to know where their tolerance line is. Their line is cemented in political correctness. When you work for yourself, you draw the line based on your own credibility and integrity. The real dilemma is do you say to yourself, 'I'm going to stretch that line, but I'm not going to cross it, or do you espouse what you believe to be true and are willing to suffer the consequences?' Now, Ms. McNamara didn't agree with my professor's political views just like I do not agree with yours; however, you know what the boundaries are in my class. You may flirt with the edges as much as you want; however, when you cross the boundaries, be willing to suffer the consequences!"

Carthenia Blue was the vixen of Johns Hopkins University. The length of her skirt was only matched by the shortness of her IQ. She flirted with every man in pants including Professor Everett. The first time she did it in class, he ignored her. The second time, he scolded her for inappropriate behavior and threatened to report it to the dean if it occurred again. She was furious that he rebuffed her. She put her hands on her hips, tossed her head northward and pointedly stated with a sneer, "Who does he think he is to turn down what men really want deep down?"

Miguel Canodo was chastised by Melissa for making a joke of his presentation in English entitled "Man, Woman or Beast." He blurted out, "I bet you don't know what you are, man woman or beast! She told him with an air of sarcasm, "Obviously, you weren't breast-fed as a baby because you're used to having any old thing stuck in your mouth, such as your foot!"

The class laughed heartily but Miguel was beside himself with anger. His normal smiling face was wrenched in a scowl, and he vowed to pay her back for her comments.

The Shanes and Everetts began firing questions at Vicki without giving her an opportunity to respond. "Did the police question you about this? Did you tell them what you told us? How many different times did Miguel express his thoughts? Describe Carthenia? What does she look like? Do you think they were veiled idle threats or had she said things in the past and followed them with action?"

Vicki tried to be patient, but there were too many questions coming at her for her to form an intelligent answer, so she raised her voice and said, "Hold it one damn minute! I'm only one person."

They became silent, and Vicki answered their questions. She explained that the police had questioned her for two and a half hours the day after Melissa and Professor Everett were found dead. She told the police everything that she had just told them, but the police had not been back. Initially, the FBI was involved because there was some question about terrorist involvement; however, the police ruled this out. That's all I know, and now I have to get back to work.

As they all rose to leave, Mrs. Everett said, "Thank you so much for meeting with us and giving us information. I hope you understand our concerns. We will be going now, so you don't get into any trouble with your manager." The women hugged Vicki, and the men shook her hand. Mrs. Everett and Juliet Shane explained the funeral arrangements to Vicki, and she promised to attend.

After they left Shriver Hall, they walked to Professor Everett's classroom. Police tape still cut off the room from aggressive spectators and reporters, and there was a note on the door directing all students who had classes in this room to go to other classrooms. As they peered through the small 12 x 6 inch glass opening in the door, they saw an open classroom with chairs and desks but no back room or doors leading to other rooms. They did not want to interfere with Professor Everett's students during class but agreed to ask the dean to arrange for them to question some students after school. They called Dean Hatleman from a conference phone in the Student Union office. He was reluctant to honor their request and indicated that they might be interfering in the police investigation. After agreeing to have the police present while they questioned the students, Dean Hatleman consented. He stipulated that the meeting had to occur during the workday between 8:30 a.m. and 5:30 p.m. The Shanes and Everetts insisted that the students be interviewed individually.

The dean said, "We'll do it tomorrow in fifteen-minute intervals between 3:45 p.m. and 5:00 p.m. in my office. This will allow you to interview all five students and then leave thirty minutes for a group discussion with the police officer and me."

They did not want to have this type of meeting the day before they were scheduled to have a funeral and bury their loved ones but realized it was necessary in order to provide some illumination on the facts and closure to grief. They thanked the dean for agreeing to arrange the meeting at such short notice. He said, "It's my job. We try to assist families in any way we can when we lose a member of the Hopkins family."

As they left the Student Union office, they noticed Gardenia McNamera's picture and slogan on a flyer. "Support the Daughters of the Arian Nation and Get Your Voice Heard in Congress, Courts, and the Streets of America. Let this political action committee represent you." They shook their heads and kept walking, perhaps realizing that some things are not worth acknowledging.

Their last stop was at the campus post office. They left a letter in the Delta, Zeta, AKA, Kappa, Sigma and Omega mail slots requesting that they ask their membership to call them at their hotel if they remembered seeing anything unusual in the areas where Professor Everett and Melissa were seen on the night of their murders. They discussed offering a monetary reward but could not decide on a figure. The Everetts had no money available to commit because they had limited incomes and had just paid Professor Everett's funeral expenses and bills. Professor Everett left $15,000 in a bank account he shared jointly with his mother and a $250,000 insurance benefit that had not been paid. The insurance company was doing a separate investigation while waiting to receive the final police report. Professor Everett's policy would be "null and void" if his death was determined to be a suicide or if he died as a result of criminal wrongdoing that he initiated or knowingly participated in. The Shanes had a seven-figure income but did not want to attract scam artists and degenerates. The Everetts and Shanes felt a low-key approach would best assist the police in doing a thorough investigation. They decided if they did not receive answers within a week, they would rewrite the flyers and offer a $25,000 reward for any information leading to the capture of the culprits who had caused the demise of their loved ones.

Mr. Everett spotted a pay phone a few feet away by the restrooms and called Sunbeam Taxi. The dispatcher promised to have a driver there within ten minutes. They walked slowly to the front of the building and discussed what had just transpired during their encounter with the students. They thought it strange that all of the people they talked to had information regarding the circumstances surrounding their family members' deaths; however, the police or press had yet to mention most of it. However, they agreed not to pass judgment until the police finished their investigation and issued a final report.

The taxi came within minutes as promised, and they curtailed their conversation until they got back to the hotel. Chucky Martin, the cab driver, was very friendly and joked that he didn't know the school was hiring senior citizens.

As the others smiled, Mrs. Everett fired back snidely. "We were just shopping. A pint of knowledge is always worth more than a pound of foolishness."

Chucky, not moved but motivated to have some fun, asked, "So what do you want to know? I've been driving cabs since me and my tenth grade teachers couldn't see eye to eye."

Mrs. Everett asked, "What do you mean?"

Still smiling, Chucky said, "I mean I wanted to attend school two days a week without homework or tests. They wanted me to come to school every day and do homework as well as class assignments. One day I got fed up and told them, I had better things to do than waste my time learning a lot of material that I wasn't excited about, and I couldn't see how it could help me in the future. Since I had my driver's license, I worked part-time selling newspapers for two years and purchased my own second-hand car. I thought that I was big stuff. I thought I was on top of the world because I had $179 in the bank and a steady girlfriend. They told me that sooner or later all that I valued would be gone, and I would not have the knowledge behind a high school diploma to fall back on. I told them that I was my own man and fully capable of doing my own thing. They said to me, 'If I was my own man, why was I still living at home with my parents?' I got mad and walked to my car, and I've been riding ever since."

Mrs. Everett said compassionately, "Young man, I can see you enjoy your current job. However, your teachers believed that you had potential to do much more. Although I believe your teachers were correct, I commend you for making a choice and being willing to be honest with yourself as well as with others about it." Pausing for a moment and composing herself, she continued on. "That's why we are here. Two of our children died tragically, and we just want people to be honest with us. Evidently you have learned something in school or in life's school of hard knocks that convinced you that honest reflection leads to positive learning and growth. Unfortunately, other people don't share the philosophy of exercising truthfulness of thought and purpose."

"So, who are the kids?" Chucky asked.

"My son, Mark Everett and their daughter, Melissa Shane," answered Mrs. Everett, as she pointed to the Shanes.

"Oh, I heard about that. The papers say it was a love triangle. I think it was just a set-up. The media has a soap opera mentality. They think everybody is screwing everybody else, and no one can be honest anymore. I don't care if he was purple and she was green; she was a student, and he was a teacher. No one has proven that he messed around with any other student. I saw your daughter's picture, and she was an average looking girl. You just came from the campus. Did you see all of the good-looking beauties on that campus? That professor could have had the pick of the litter. Why would he fool around with someone in his class? It smells fishy to me."

Chucky was just getting wound up as the taxi pulled in front of the hotel. Paul Everett interrupted him and said, "Thanks so much young man. If you hear anything that has not been reported about the events that led up to these two deaths, please call me. I'm in room 249."

Chucky didn't know what to make of these four people. He said yes and took the $20 dollar bill Dr. Shane gave him. Chucky, thinking Paul Shane had made a mistake by giving him a $20 bill instead of a $10 bill, reached in his wallet to give Dr. Shane the $14.90 change. Dr. Shane said, "Keep the change son." Chucky wished them luck, darted back into the car and drove off swiftly down the road.

Juliet Shane made a comment as they walked through the hotel's revolving doors, "That's a most interesting young man. It's a shame he didn't finish high school, but he has found his niche."

"Thomas and I have to make some final arrangements for Mark's body to be shipped home to South Carolina. We'll see you both later."

Juliet Shane said, "I thought he was from Washington, D.C. I know his students and colleagues would love to see him and pay their respects. Salem Baptist Church, where we are holding Melissa's funeral at 11:30 a.m. on Thursday, is quite large. Would you consider allowing Mark's body to lie beside Melissa's at the church? I can ask the Reverend Pride, the presiding minister, to incorporate both of them in his sermon.

Mrs. Everett looked at Thomas and he nodded affirmatively. She then turned to Juliet Shane, and said, "Mark was born in my hometown of Darlington, South Carolina. We moved to the Washington, D.C. area when he was 7 years old. He has always worked in the Maryland-Washington, D.C. area. Mark's funeral is not until Saturday afternoon. The Mitchell-Josey funeral home in Darlington, South Carolina, was expecting his body to be shipped by train on Friday. If the church is able to accommodate another body, we will allow Mark's body to lie in state at the church."

The elevators opened, and they went upstairs to their rooms, both families trying to figure out whether a bridge of hope or hopelessness bound them together. Whatever the connection, their conduct left the casual observers bewildered.

After Paul Shane closed the door to their room, he called Reverend Pride and informed him that Mark Everett's body would be at the church also, and they wanted him to preach a joint funeral. Before Reverend Pride could respond, Dr. Shane said, "Of course, we will double your salary since we're asking you to do double the work."

"That won't be necessary. I will insure that space is made available at the church's altar to accommodate both caskets."

"Thanks again for all your assistance." Then he hung up. He asked Juliet Shane to call Traci and see if she would agree to meet them for dinner instead of lunch.

Juliet Shane smiled and said, "Of course I will, honey. I think we need to talk." She had kicked off her shoes and was lying across the bed. Juliet rolled over and sat on the side of the bed next to the nightstand while she made the call. Her right foot had fallen asleep, so she massaged it gently with her right hand while she waited for Traci to answer the telephone. Traci's answering machine came on and said, "Hi, this is Traci. I've just stepped out for a minute, but don't fret or fidget. After the tone, please leave your name, number and a brief message with a smile. Thanks for calling, and I'll return your call in a little while."

Juliet giggled at Traci's cute message then left a short message after the tone. She asked Traci to meet them in the hotel lobby at 6:30 p.m. They were going to have a nice quiet lunch alone in their hotel room but would have dinner with her.

"Juliet, why did you laugh after you found out that Traci was not home," Paul Shane asked.

"Traci may be 20-something, but she is still a kid at heart. She has the cutest message on her answering machine." Juliet then repeated what the message said. "A poet she's not. However, she gets an A for originality. Now what did you want to talk about dear?"

Juliet Shane's facial expression changed to a concerned grimace. She paused as if the words she wanted to express were buried too deep in her subconscious to retrieve. As Juliet began to speak, she reached out to her husband to come close. Paul Shane responded lovingly, taking her hands, arms and then embracing her. He held her and looked into her eyes as she explained that she had difficulty believing that Melissa was gone, yet no one had given them any believable answers. The behavior the dean and the police described was not Melissa's. She knew Melissa wasn't perfect but she was a very principled young woman. Juliet Shane exclaimed, "I have to know what happened to our baby. I just have to!"

Not knowing what to say to comfort his wife, Paul Shane just held her tightly in his arms. As Juliet began to cry, he did likewise. Paul tried to be strong for her, but seeing his wife's pain and remembering how sweet and innocent his daughter was crumpled his heart like a broken arrow. The ring of the telephone broke their sobbing five minutes later.

Paul Shane quickly but tenderly released his wife's grasp and sat her on the bed, composed himself and answered on the third ring. He spoke in a moderate tone and said, "This is Dr. Paul Shane. May I help you?" He felt a little embarrassed because it was Traci.

"I understand that this is a tough time for both of you. Something came up and I will not be able to have lunch with you today; however, I still can meet you later as you requested."

"Thanks so much, Traci. Dinner will be on us. You have been a godsend."

After she thanked him, he hung up and sat on the bed next to his wife. They silently hugged, and one kiss led to another. Before long, erotically they released pent-up frustration that few couples after 27 years of marriage are comfortable doing. Their catharsis passed quickly, and they realized it was time to get dressed.

While Juliet Shane was in the bathroom putting on the finishing touches of her make-up, the telephone rang. Knowing Paul was in the room dressing, she said, "Honey, please answer that. It's probably Traci. She's so prompt."

"Okay, dear." He lumbered over to the phone and the voice on the other end of the phone said in a bass voice, "This is Special Agent Tate Jackson. May I speak to Paul or Juliet Shane please?"

Startled, Paul Shane said hesitantly, "This is Paul Shane. What agency are you with Special Agent Jackson? Do you have any information about my daughter?"

There was a brief pause, then the agent said, "I'm with the FBI. And yes, I have new information about your daughter and would like to talk to you and your wife about it. Is it okay if I come to your room, or is there somewhere else where we can talk privately?"

"Please come to our room," replied Paul Shane. "It's room 569."

"I'm calling from my cell phone and will be right up."

Paul Shane told Juliet what was going on, and they both reserved the urge of speculating until the detective rapped on the door.

Paul Shane answered the door and asked, "May I see your badge?"

After Agent Jackson displayed his FBI badge, Paul Shane bade the agent to come in. The Shanes sat on the couch as the detective sat on the hard wooden chair that was under the desk.

Special Agent Jackson was a fair skinned black man with a thin mustache and short well-groomed, curly, dark, brown hair. He explained, "The FBI is assisting the Baltimore City Police Department with your daughter's case."

"What does the FBI have to do with a murder case or as the police department explained earlier, a love affair gone awry?" asked Paul Shane.

"Apparently your daughter and Professor Everett were murdered by some drug dealers. Melissa and Professor Everett may have been working late on a school project. Realizing it was late, the professor walked Melissa to her car. They observed a drug transaction in the parking lot. Once the professor and Melissa got to Melissa's car, he pulled out his cell phone to call school security. Unbeknownst to him, the drug dealers followed them to her car. Once they saw Professor Everett with the phone, they feared they had been found out, so they kidnapped and killed both of them and made it appear as if it was a murder/suicide."

Stunned and shocked by this tale, Juliet Shane gasped, "Oh my God".

Paul Shane looked horrified, but asked, "How did you find out all of this?"

Agent Jackson pondered a moment and explained in a controlled solemn voice, "The professor was reported walking Melissa to her car. The professor's cell phone was found in the student parking lot, and the first six numbers to the school's security office was still on the phone. Professor Everett's car was still parked in the faculty parking lot. Both bodies were found at separate locations away from the campus. Some prints on Melissa's car matched a well-known drug lord, Marvin Greene. We have him in custody and enough evidence to put him away for a long, long time."

Juliet Shane added, "And you have enough evidence to clear the professor and Melissa's name? They were innocent victims of being in the right place at the wrong time."

The agent nodded in agreement. After answering a few more questions, Agent Jackson said he had to go talk to the Everetts because they didn't know anything yet. The Shanes thanked the agent again for the information and escorted him to the door. As they closed the door behind Agent Jackson, they breathed sighs of relief because a millstone had just been released from around their necks. The knowledge the Shanes had just received brought them comfort but not joy. They discussed the detective's comments and concluded that they still had to pull themselves together and get through Melissa's funeral. It was close to the time that they agreed to meet Traci, so Juliet went into the bathroom and freshened up her make-up while Paul changed his shirt because Juliet's bronze lip print was on his collar and chest.

They met Traci in the lobby as planned. They asked Traci to take them to Mo's Seafood Factory in Glen Burnie, Maryland because the concierge had informed them that this restaurant served the world's best crab cakes. Traci readily commented that she agreed. They walked to her car, which was double-parked in front of the hotel lobby entrance. As Traci drove the short seven-mile trip to Glen Burnie, Maryland, she noticed the change in the Shanes' demeanor. Traci commented that they both seemed a little different and upbeat. She asked, "Did anything happen this afternoon. You two are sure in a better mood."

The Shanes looked at one another, and tacitly agreed to tell Traci of their good news. Juliet Shane said they would discuss it over dinner.

Traci, acting surprised and cordial, grinned and nodded in agreement and turned on the radio to a pop station. Fifteen minutes later, they pulled up in front of the restaurant. It looked like a large one-story house from the outside; however, once inside, one could tell that it was very spacious. It had two levels, a first floor and a ground level. The first floor was a bar with a lounge that could accommodate 150 people at the bar booths and tables. Downstairs could accommodate 80 people with cozier booths and tables. The hostess escorted them downstairs and sat them at one of the tables. A few minutes later, a waitress, introducing herself as Lydia, gave them menus, filled three water glasses and said she would be back in a few minutes.

Feeling thirsty, Paul Shane took several large gulps from his glass as Traci squirmed in her seat and asked, "So what's going on?"

Juliet Shane stated confidently, "Traci, we finally know what really happened to Melissa and Professor Everett, and we were right. They were murdered. The police even captured the one that was behind it all. We can finally be at peace with that."

Traci asked, "What happened?"

Juliet Shane recounted what Agent Jackson had explained to them. Traci listened attentively and appeared taken aback by the magnitude of this horrific event.

"At least now everyone else will realize that you were right all along. You had a very good daughter, and she must have been quite a young woman."

Paul and Juliet Shane said almost simultaneously, "Yes, she was."

"I'm happy for you both."

The Shanes' conversation turned to Melissa and Professor Everett's funeral arrangements. They compared notes to insure everything was in place. The Shanes hoped that a number of Melissa's fellow students and faculty would be able to come.

Traci said encouragingly, "I'm sure everyone who cared about Melissa will be there."

The waitress returned and took their orders. The Shanes ordered ice tea and crab cakes, and Traci ordered orange roughy stuffed with imperial crab. Lydia thanked them for their orders and scurried to the kitchen area. She returned moments later carrying a tray with a large basket of fresh baked bread, beverages and a few lemon wedges on a saucer.

Lydia's short skirt and low neckline caught the eye of Paul Shane. As she reached over to refill his glass with water, her size 40D breasts dangled like two oranges suspended on a string. Juliet Shane noticed his momentary gaze and nudged his foot under the table. Paul Shane whispered, "She was right in front of me. What am I supposed to do, cover my eyes?"

Traci said teasingly, "You tell him. That's what's wrong with most men today; they have a good wife or girlfriend, and the first little hotsy totsy woman that comes along, they're gazing at her as if they see something good to eat."

Paul Shane fired back, "Well, I may occasionally look, but I don't sample the soup. Juliet is the only woman I want and need."

Juliet Shane smiled with pride and squeezed Paul's hand gently.

They spent the rest of the evening discussing the excellent seafood they were eating and the aroma from spices and seafood that filled the air and watered their palates.

On their way home, the Shanes speculated about how the Everetts had taken the news. They found it strange that they were linked by fate. With nothing in common other than their children's tragic happenstance, they stood forever bound.

Traci turned on the radio to listen to her favorite station 1090 AM; however, the news was on. A station reporter was commenting on the close presidential race between Peter Willow IV and Vice President Leon. Traci quickly changed the station to 105.9 FM, a soft popular top 40 music station. She began rocking slowly in her seat and singing to the tune "No One Loves You Baby Like I Do." After hearing the lyrics of the first stanza, the Shanes began to rock to the beat, and hum as well.

> You and I have been through hell.
> What's the matter, most of the time I can't tell.
> You're caught in a world of make believe,
> Oblivious to life on its tempestuous seas.

Just as the song ended, they were pulling up in front of the hotel lobby entrance. The Shanes thanked Traci again for her help and told her that they would see her at the funeral. Paul Shane tried to give her a $20 bill for gas, but Traci would not hear of it. She told him that it was her pleasure to help, and she knew how it was to travel to another state or country and not know anyone.

The Everetts reacted differently to the new evidence. After Agent Jackson explained the circumstances that led to her son's death, Mrs. Everett's voice sounded like a piercing tremor as she exclaimed, "Lord, have mercy. These godless people of today just don't value life at all. For a few ounces or vials of dope, they killed my boy and his student. It's just shameful, simply shameful!"

Thomas Everett put his arms around Elvira Everett as she sobbed on his shoulder. Trying to hold back his own tears, he knew his sister-in-law finally had enough information to feel that her son would be vindicated and was comfortable enough to grieve. As the family's matriarch and Rock of Gibraltar, she knew her tears, pain and sorrow could not temper the family's void created by her son's death.

Thomas Everett thanked Agent Jackson for the good news and stated that he didn't know what the world was coming to. People commit crimes with no fear of accountability. They view the threat of being imprisoned as a consequence for their crimes as someone else's penalty.

Agent Jackson acknowledged that the country has a moral decay that is eating away at the core of its structure. He commented, "It was festering like a locust, lying low until it's prepared to prance on its prey and feast on the flesh of its victims. But that's why we have agencies like police departments, the FBI and the CIA to insure that crime doesn't pay."

Agent Jackson got up to leave and proceeded slowly toward the door. He shook Mr. Everett's hand, glanced at Mrs. Everett and continued out the door.

The next day, the Shanes and Everetts were seated at the funeral, amazed at the hordes of faculty, students, family and friends who came to pay their last respects. Even area politicians stopped by to pay their respect. The funeral had to be delayed an hour and a half so that everyone in attendance could view the bodies. The families consented to allow only one TV camera in the church and ten members of the press because they did not want the funeral to turn into a circus. Traci and six of her agents were strategically seated throughout the church to observe the Everetts and Shanes.

One of Cintura's guards, accompanied by a cameraman, was posing as a member of the press. I had the best seat in the house from one of the presidential limousines that received information from security cameras.

The funeral proceeded quietly until the eulogies were ready. Upon hearing the details of their deceased loved ones' lives, sniffles and cries could be heard throughout the sanctuary. Then Reverend Pride's sermon, "Have You Counted the Cost," caused the whimpering to continue. He began his sermon by quoting the first four words in the bible, "In the beginning, God…"

The most effective portion was when he asked, "Have you counted the cost? How many of you forgot that God was and is in the beginning, middle and end? How many of you live your lives as if you are your own god? I don't expect anyone to admit it, but at times, we all forget who was in the beginning. The Bible says that it was God that has made us and not we ourselves. We are the sheep of his pasture. Just like a flock of dumb sheep, we tend to go astray: Walk in circles where we want to walk, be identified with the 'in crowd' and forget about our past Christian upbringing. But I want to remind you one and all, that God is not marked. He knows when you are shucking and jiving and always conniving. God knows when you are sincere and when you are not. He also knows when you are resting on his promises versus marking time and participating in meaningless events or meaningless activities. I have only one question to ask. Have you counted the cost?"

Reverend Pride looked around the sanctuary with a piercing stare that made everyone in attendance feel as though he was talking to him or her. After giving everyone a moment to digest what he had just said, he repeated his theme. "Have you counted the cost? God never promised that it would be easy to follow him and his work. Have you counted the cost? Have you counted the cost of your deeds? Have you counted the cost of your misdeeds? Someone asked me just the other day, 'Pastor, which is worse, doing something wrong or failing to do what is right?' I told him, 'The sin of commission is just as bad as the sin of omission. The key is knowledge. Did you knowingly do something wrong or fail to do what you should have done?' The Bible says that God is faithful to forgive us for our sins. But the problem is we are not faithful in admitting guilt and asking for forgiveness." Reverend Pride continued on and discussed the lives of Professor Everett and Melissa Shane. Surprisingly, he ended his sermon by stating, "Melissa and Mark were Christians, and I am confident that they are in a better place, where peace abounds and there is joy forevermore."

After Reverend Pride gave the benediction, he led the funeral party from both families, quoting biblical passages unfamiliar to me. The audience seemed moved by his oratory skill and Biblical selections: "I am the way, the truth and the light..."

As the Everett and Shane families left the auditorium, well-wishers handed them envelopes containing cards and letters. Even Professor Janet Roentin pressed her way through the crowd to give each family an envelope.

The Everetts and Shanes graciously accepted the envelopes, shook hands and thanked as many people as they could. Once they got inside the black limousines, they placed the envelopes in two plastic bags the funeral home had provided them with.

After the funeral procession arrived at the cemetery, Traci walked with them to the gravesite. One of the agents took the plastic bags containing the cards and letters and left a note explaining that they had received a call that indicated one of the envelopes contained a bomb. Each envelope would be x-rayed and returned later that evening, if everything checked out okay.

Most of the envelopes contained cards; however, Professor's Roentin's envelope contained copies of Melissa's letters detailing her project with Professor Everett, a sympathy card and a small yellow sticky note containing Professor Roentin's hotel and room number.

Traci called Cintura and reported everything that was found. Cintura instructed her to take out Professor Roentin, then sweep her hotel room and home for the original material and destroy it. Traci agreed and then hung up the phone. She ordered Agent Jackson to return all of the non-threatening material to the Shanes and Everetts. The other five agents accompanied her in a Lincoln Town Car. Traci posed as a hotel employee delivering room service on a cart. Professor Roentin opened the door and said that she didn't order room service. Traci grinned slightly and replied, "A bottle of champagne or apple cider is complementary to all hotel guests on this floor. This is the concierge level." Professor Roentin observed that Traci looked sweet and innocent and wore a hotel employee's name tag, so she invited her in.

Traci asked Professor Roentin if she wanted champagne or apple cider. She said, "Champagne, thank you."

"Do you have a cork screw? If not, I can leave one with you."

Professor Roentin looked in one of the drawers with her back to Traci and said, "I don't have one."

Traci came up to her from behind with a rag soaked with chloroform, and put it under her nose. Within seconds, Professor Roentin was sprawled out on the floor. Then Traci pulled out her cell phone, dialed a phone number and instructed two of the agents to come up to Professor Roentin's room. While waiting for the agents to come, she undressed Professor Roentin and ran warm water in the bathtub. She also went through the professor's luggage and found Melissa's original letters and a sealed letter, with copies of Melissa's letters, that was addressed to the U.S. Attorney General's Office. The gist of the letter was articulated in the first paragraph, which stated:

Honorable Attorney General Beth Renos:

I am currently the Chair of the English department at Smith College in Massachusetts. Melissa Shane, one of my former students, was murdered recently, and I have evidence that suggests that members of our executive branch may have played a role in orchestrating her death. I respectfully request that you review the enclosed letters and call me, so we can discuss this matter in confidence.

I have only given Melissa's parents and you a copy of Melissa's letters. Please respond to this letter at your earliest convenience. You may reach me...

Traci placed the letters in the hotel's plastic laundry bags. She took the professor's laptop computer and radio/cassette player and set them to the side. There was a knock on the door, and Traci looked through the small peephole in the door and saw that it was the agents. She let them in and told them to put Professor Roentin's body in the bathtub. Traci took the radio cassette player and put in the professor's tape entitled, "Journalism, the Creative Approach for the New Millennium." She then plugged it into an AC outlet and tossed it into the bathtub. As the water sizzled, Professor Roentin woke up for a brief moment. Realizing her predicament, she reached for the radio before succumbing to the waves bolting through her body. Traci was smiling as they used terry cloth to remove fingerprints from the room. After they were done, Traci took the letters and computer to the car. They drove to an old school incinerator on Garrison Boulevard and burned the letters. She turned on the computer and inserted an obliterating virus (OV) disc. In forty-five seconds, the memory of the computer was blank and the computer disabled. Traci called Cintura and reported that her mission was complete but said the professor might have a computer at home.

Cintura replied, "Her computer has been replaced."

Traci called the Shanes and told them that she was glad to have met them but wished that it had been under better circumstances. The Shanes gave her their home address and told her if she was ever in the area, to look them up.

"I definitely will. I'll keep in touch." After hanging up, Traci took out the complimentary local morning paper and flipped through it until an article on the back page of the Maryland section caught her eye. It was titled, "Professor Dies in Tub, Listening to Lecture." Traci smiled and muttered under her breath, "That was an appropriate shocking end for a long nosed, fermented old hen."

Cintura then dispatched all the agents except Jackson to other parts of the country. She ordered Traci and Jackson to return to Washington, D.C. Cintura needed them to covertly assist Vice President Leon with his campaign.

Vice President Leon's major test came when he addressed the US Major Automobile Conference. The owners, manufacturers, engineers and labor leaders were discussing how the US could improve its marketing techniques to attract more US consumers. Jake Devlin, U.S. Steel Consortia's CEO, had just made a passionate speech with a protectionism nationalistic theme. He urged the audience to focus their energies on the US manufacturers' quality procedures and not on the few poor performers.

Vice President Leon listened attentively as Mr. Devlin stated his ideas. Next Carmon Smith, the conference coordinator, thanked Mr. Devlin for his comments, and the audience gave an enthusiastic applause. Then Mr. Smith introduced Vice President Leon. While he was being introduced, he reached inside his breast pocket for his prepared speech, but it was not there. He suddenly remembered he had left the speech on a table in his White House office.

Vice President Leon gathered himself, smiled and boldly declared, "There is no great secret as to why this country is lagging behind Japanese auto makers. In the 80's and early 90's, the big three American auto makers were viewed as producing inefficient cars and having a lackadaisical attitude when it came to making quality automobile repairs. However, Japanese automobile manufacturers not only say that the customer is always right, their daily work ethic proves it. If a dealership repairs a car, the customer is given a rental vehicle until the car is repaired. The customer is given a twelve-month warranty against defective workmanship and a lifetime warranty on all parts. Automobile company employees fail to realize that the customer is the one who pays their salaries. The customer buys a product based on good faith that the company has produced a quality product and is willing to stand behind it. If this were the case, there would be no conflict. However, such is not the case. The customer is put on the offensive to prove to the company that the car failed before the company is willing to evaluate the car for malfunctions. A positive attitude equals quality customer response. If we want people to buy American, they have to have something worthwhile to buy."

The audience clapped respectfully as Vice President Leon descended the podium to go to his next appointment. As I drove him to the American

Federation of Labor Unions rally, he turned on the TV to listen to Barton's speech. Vice President Leon was doing poorly in the Midwest and Southeast. Barton was sent to encourage farmers and cattlemen in the Great Plains and Southeast regions to support Vice President Leon's agenda. Today Barton was in Iowa City, addressing the Midwestern Farmers Association. Barton's speech was short, but effective.

Barton approached the podium smiling at the audience and tightly holding Nudyi's hand. He looked out into the audience and felt the cheers of satisfaction. He began by saying the following confidently into the microphone. "I have a prepared speech in my pocket that I crafted over the last few days. It contains my thoughts and vision for our wonderful country. However, I feel moved to speak to you from my heart. When Vice President Leon asked me to run as his Vice President, I felt honored. Here is a man that rose from humble beginnings to the pinnacle of an executive elected office. Our Vice President has reached out to colleagues who have come from similar backgrounds and successfully left the world better than they found it. I'm not going to give you the speech that we sometimes tell our kids to get them to respect the advantages that they have today. You know the type of story, 'I remember when I used to walk eight miles in the snow in sub-zero degree weather to get to a cold, one room schoolhouse.' That story worked fine on you. But what happens today when you tell your kids a similar tale? They go to their first family reunion, and Uncle Ned tells them you grew up in orange orchard country in Eutis, Florida." The audience laughed heartily.

"I've had the opportunity to meet hard working people all across this great nation. They have told me things that we need to do to make this nation even greater. We need to encourage economic development and renewal in our urban areas. We need to insure that farmers and cattlemen receive fair prices for crops and livestock. We need to insure that America's youth have a good education. We have to ensure that family values are taught. I am a realist. Statistics show that our children are beginning parenthood at a younger age. We must begin to teach planned parenthood in addition to encouraging abstinence. Children did not invent sex. There were just as many promiscuous and pregnant teenagers when we were kids.

However, we didn't have instant world news and daily national polls. We have to reach out and let our young people know that they don't have to seek love in all the wrong places. They can and should be able to discuss their problems with their parents, not their peers. They should realize life is more than an affectionate interlude.

"We must open the lines of communication, so we can allow our children to develop their minds and pursue their career choices after properly preparing themselves academically and emotionally. The cost of waiting is to risk losing a generation of bright, vibrant young people. That's a risk I'm not willing to take. We owe them an opportunity to be involved in an atmosphere that is conducive to learning, not partisan politics bent on fashioning road blocks for one-upmanship, and not on resolving issues such as inadequate healthcare, Social Security reform, IRS reform, homelessness and strategies to improve public and private education. If we join together in a concerted effort to make effective changes, the next few years will be very productive. Thank you for your attentiveness, consideration and continued support."

NUDYI

The audience cheered and gave him a three-minute standing ovation. As Barton stood smiling and basking in the thunderous approval of his ideas, Nudyi was at home reading a very disturbing letter from an old mentor.

It read as follows:

Dear Nudyi,

I don't know if you remember me, but about 35 years ago I was your summer camp leader. Apparently, you were young, impressionable and crazy about a young man your age, but your parents wanted to curtail your relationship. They felt you were just too young and had a bright future. However, as I learned from our experience at camp, you were quite focused and intent on pursuing your relationship. From the letters you sent me, your relationship lasted two years. I'm happy that you attended college, met and married your college beau and have several children.

I'm writing you because I believe you have a lot of integrity and cannot be compromised. Recently, one of my students and her professor were killed, and I believe there was government involvement. Enclosed are copies of letters that were sent to me by my student, Melissa Shane. As you will discover, she was utilizing her contacts at various Washington, D.C. newspapers, to obtain information about the President. I sent a copy to the U.S. Attorney General. However, due to his loyalty to the President, I do not believe he will respond positively to my concern.

Please read all of the enclosed letters prior to sharing it with your husband. Although I have never been married, I believe couples should not keep secrets. Due to your husband's close involvement with President Bob, his life may be in danger if you share my letter with him. Please help me find my student's killer(s).

Respectfully,

Professor Janet Roentin

Professor Roentin's words tugged at Nudyi's heartstrings. She suddenly flung the letters aside exclaiming, "Why now! When I first met you, you were 20-something, and I was a teenager discovering what it was like to be away from home for the first time without my parents. Now my mentor is reaching out to me for direction and assistance!" After a few seconds, she picked up the letters and reread them.

Nudyi spent the next hour agonizing how she was going to tell Barton. They had agreed long ago not to have any secrets and to be 100 percent honest with one another. Barton wasn't expected home for another few hours. Nudyi thought about it, and she did not want to put Barton in a compromising situation. She did not want him to be disloyal to a President who had allowed him to piggyback off of his success. Nudyi remembered that one of her colleagues, Lori St. Paul, a fellow member of the American Alliance of Woman (AAW), was also Chair of the Washington D.C. Oversight Committee and went to the White House regularly. Nudyi called Lori and asked her questions about President Bob's recent activities. She was careful not to mention anything about the letters. Nudyi told Lori that she was contemplating having a Halloween party and inviting the White House staff and some members of the House, Senate and Judiciary.

"It is inappropriate etiquette on the Hill. Halloween festivities offend certain religious groups, and it is politically incorrect to offend them. Voters are voters regardless of their religious preferences. But politicians have to exude religious neutrality."

Nudyi, appearing at a loss for ideas, paused and commented. "I just want to plan some social activities that will allow the country and Barton's colleagues to appreciate all of the integrity and intellectual prowess he brings to government."

Lori, sensing Nudyi's sincerity, softened and said, "I'm not that far away from your home, and my schedule is light the rest of the afternoon. How about I come by in an hour or so, and we can toss a few ideas around, okay?"

Nudyi smiled, and then said sheepishly, "Thanks Lori. That is why I enjoy working with you for the AAW. You are always willing to assist the committee members, and you come with fresh innovative ideas."

Surprised and flattered, Lori replied, "It's because of nice women like you that I enjoy our monthly meeting. We accomplish a lot because everyone appreciates that each of us at the table has something meaningful to contribute. I'll see you shortly."

They both hung up looking forward to their meeting and amused at their commonality of purpose. An hour later, Lori rang the Craigs' doorbell and Maime Leatherwood, their maid, opened the door. Lori identified herself, and Maime escorted Lori to the garden parlor where Nudyi was sitting under an umbrella, sipping lemonade, in front of finger sandwiches on a tray and a small fruit display.

Nudyi was dressed in a white pantsuit with her hair neatly combed and flowing down her back, resting just above her buttocks. Her warm cheery smile instantly put Lori at ease. Lori wore a gray business suit. Her hair was pulled back in a bun, and the long office hours were evident in the slight bags under her eyes. As they approached one another, they shook hands and sat down after exchanging pleasantries.

Lori got right to the point and said that she was considering arranging a pre-election dinner party in hopes of winning over some Republicans and voters.

Nudyi stated that she wanted to get the local newspapers to endorse her husband's candidacy. Traditionally, *The Washington Probe* and *The Capital News* endorsed the Democratic ticket. Perhaps due to the recent death of a former professor, Mark Everett, they had not yet come forward with an endorsement.

"I don't know, but I will inquire informally. *The Washington Probe* is extremely loyal to their employees and gets defensive regarding their First Amendment free speech rights when any formal inquiry is made regarding their staff. However, they are more loyal to their bottom line. If a story will cost them a substantial amount of money to run it, they will not run it. If the President would threaten to eliminate any news agency from accessing the White House if they ran a negative story, the news agency or newspaper wouldn't run the story. Do you honestly think that the media would come to the aid of a snooping dead young reporter? Please!"

Nudyi appeared flabbergasted. "Are you telling me that these newspapers and other media are just tools the President and his staff utilized to convey their information to the American Public? What about the daily briefings the White House gives?"

"Nudyi, Washington is entirely superficial. No one is really open and honest about anything. The press is told what the White House wants them to report. However, they believe that they have an innate right to discover 'their truth.' Their truth is not necessarily 'the truth.' Their truth is whatever they purport it to be. They all have a set of facts, but the frame in which those facts are hung portrays to the reader what the truth is. It's what we on the Hill call the 'floating truth.' People in office tend to spend the majority of their time ensuring that the printed truth run in concert with their version of the truth."

"Well, I guess that's why Barton is in politics, and I'm not. I'd much rather know what's really going on, rather than going through life in a clouded existence."

"Nudyi, that's an honorable stance that many would find foolish, but I respect you for having it. I will share any information I find with you if you give me your word that you will not divulge the source of any information you receive."

Nudyi nodded in agreement, but asked Lori, "What got you to this point in your life where you view Washington's political lifestyle so cynically?"

"The only thing that got me to this point is my conscience and credibility. To be truthful, that's the only thing that any of us have that is worth a damn. Everything else is just temporal."

"You are right. I appreciate any assistance you can provide. Please let me know as soon as you find out anything. Barton should be home shortly; please keep in touch."

Lori stretched out her right hand, and after Nudyi shook it, she looked into her eyes and said, "I will. When we meet again, let's select a non-sensitive political place."

Nudyi said that would be splendid and walked her to the door. As Lori drove off in her sky blue 1999 Jaguar, Nudyi wondered how frugal she must be to maintain such a car.

Barton arrived home ten minutes later. Maime told him that Nudyi was resting in their bedroom. He said thanks and carried his two bags upstairs. As he ascended the stairs, Nudyi greeted him at the top in a black lounger with slits on the sides that came just above the knee. Her sleek, size 8 shapely figure looked adorable and, as usual, made his heart melt. Barton left the bags at the top of the stairs and took Nudyi's hand and kissed it. He then grabbed her gently and pulled her body close to his. As he hugged her, he explained that although they had only been apart a few days, he missed her terribly. Barton picked her up in his arms while their lips found one another for a kiss that seemed to last an hour. He carried her to the bedroom and lay her in the center of their large heart-shaped, king-sized bed. Within minutes, she had taken off his clothes, and he had reached beneath her lounger and revealed what he suspected on first sight, that it was all that concealed her beautiful body from the world. They spent the next hour remembering, recapturing and reveling in their love and splendor.

Maime left them to their private moment for an hour and a half; then, she called their room on the intercom and inquired if they were ready for dinner to be served. Nudyi said that they would like to have dinner in their room. Maime replied that she would be up shortly with their meal.

Maime shook her head, smiled and took out a serving tray with silverware. She then put stuffed pheasant with steamed broccoli and carrots on two plates and two bowls of cream of crab soup on the tray. Maime made two trips. She brought the soup, silverware and napkins first. Then a few moments later, she arrived with the main dish and a bottle of Cerise, a semi-sweet cherry dessert wine from Galena Cellars in Galena, Illinois. As they ate the delicious meal, Barton shared the highlights of his trip. He proudly boasted of his last speech and the audience's reaction. Nudyi told him that she was proud of him, not only for his accomplishments, but also for his willingness to work to improve the quality of life for all Americans. Barton asked her what she had been doing with herself.

"I've been networking with members of the American Writers Association. I also have been thinking about different things that I can do to assist you in accomplishing your goals."

"Honey, with you in my corner, I feel as though I'm able to accomplish anything. My life would be nothing without you. I love our kids, but you are my love and my life."

They spent the rest of their evening just as they did any other evening when they were alone, in one another's arms, lost in a sea of bliss.

The next day, while Barton was at the White House, Lori called and asked Nudyi to meet her on the second level at Landover Mall in Landover, Maryland, by the food court. Nudyi said, How about 1:15 p.m.?"

"Fine."

When Nudyi got to the mall about 1:05 p.m., Lori was already there. Lori spotted Nudyi approaching her, made eye contact and began to walk towards her. Nudyi extended both arms as they got within five feet of one another. Lori responded in kind. As they embraced, Nudyi asked Lori to accompany her to the ladies room, which was less than 1500 yards away. They walked into the ladies room, and Lori explained in a voice slightly above a whisper, "I heard that *The Washington Probe* was doing an investigation surrounding the circumstances of Professor Everett's death. Evidently one of his students was doing a research paper involving President Bob's background. She hadn't found any concrete proof of presidential criminal wrongdoing. However, each time she scratched beneath the surface, there was a trail of tears and death. The word at the copydesk was that President Bob had cut a deal with the *Probe's* editor. His first term of office was about to expire, and the editor agreed to kill the story if the White House agreed to be more cooperative next term and give them an exclusive on breaking stories. Everyone knows that dirt sells; except when it involves a popular President. Readers will rebel with cancellations. Money is power, and newspapers won't do anything that will cut off its power source."

"Is Barton or Cintura involved?"

"Barton's name didn't come up, but I'm sure Cintura is ankle deep in it. She's a dangerous woman. Don't cross her. I made that mistake once, and it nearly cost me everything. I can't do or say anymore, or I will be found out."

Nudyi hugged her and said, "Thanks, I can handle it from here."

"I have to go now. I'll see you at the next meeting."

She darted out of the restroom, scurried down the escalator and did not look back for fear she'd bring attention to herself.

Nudyi waited a few minutes then walked slowly to her car. She talked to herself as she drove home. Nudyi did not want to cross paths with Cintura because she didn't want to blemish Barton's career. Everyone in President Bob's circle of friends and enemies knew that President Bob was a flirt and suspected he had a sordid past; however, no one could conceive that he would stoop to murder to avoid facing his past misdeeds or improprieties. Nudyi's dilemma was how to give Professor Roentin solace and not harm Barton. She concluded that she still needed additional information. Although Nudyi and President Bob were friends, she could not go to him and accuse him of committing murder or other misdeeds.

Nudyi arrived home shortly before Barton. President Bob caused her to feel dirty. She took a quick shower and changed into a sky blue, V-neck pantsuit. Barton came in as she was walking down the spiral stairs in her fresh attire. He looked at her and said, "You are a vision of loveliness."

"And you, darling, are a big flirt. I bet you say that to all the girls."

"There's only one woman that can put the wind in my sails, and her name is sweet Nudyi Sorienson Craig."

They kissed until Maime came in several minutes later and cleared her throat. Maime said, "I've worked for you two for over twenty-five years, and every day, those lovey dovey sparks just keep on flying."

Nudyi and Barton told Maime that love was the glue that held them together. They hadn't always had it easy, but as long as they've been together, it's been easy to scrimp, save and sacrifice to assure that their family and country are safe.

Barton, smelling the aroma emanating from the kitchen said, "Maime, "I don't know about Nudyi, but I'm famished. I'm going to wash my hands and then eat." He then walked into the powder room and closed the door.

Nudyi noticed Barton's newspaper was open on the coffee table. The headline read, "Prestigious Professor Roentin Accidentally Electrocutes Herself." Nudyi said, "I don't believe it. I don't believe it."

Barton came running into the room drying his hands on a hand towel saying, "Honey, what's the matter? What is it that you don't believe?"

"This poor woman died accidentally while listening to music. That's just awful."

Barton, knowing how sensitive his wife was, hugged her in consolation, and he then asked to see the article. Nudyi, still holding the paper, gave it to him and sat in a chair nearby. Barton scanned the article and noted, "She was an 80-year-old prestigious professor. Evidently she had a full life and left behind numerous students that will make a difference, and some may even follow in her footsteps. My mother used to say, "Teachers are like sugar in lemonade. The lemons are the students—some sour and some innocent. The teachers are sweet enough to cover the pitcher from side to side and top to bottom with knowledge, not caring where the essence of them will go. The sugar's only duty is to make a positive difference in the lives of the lemons. Let them know that they are more than tart little fruits."

Nudyi, holding back a few tears, forced a smile and said, "Evidently, your mother was a bright woman." Barton kissed her, and then they walked into the dining room arm in arm.

Nudyi knew then that Professor Roentin's grave would hold and preserve the things she couldn't handle in life.

ALBEE AND CINTURA

On election night, President Bob, Vice President Leon and Stella waited in the presidential suite while the rest of the campaign delegation, volunteers, well-wishers and members of the press were in the main ballroom. After the polls closed at 8:00 p.m., tallies began coming in from around the United States. Initially, Vice President Leon garnered votes two to one over his closest opponent, Governor Willow. A few hours later, his lead increased to three to one.

At 11:17 p.m. eastern standard time, Governor Willow gave his concession speech from his campaign headquarters less than a mile away. With a solemn face in a bittersweet statesman's tone, he said, "My fellow Americans, I would like to take this opportunity to thank the fine staff that supported me from New Hampshire to California and made my grassroots candidacy possible. However, my vision for what America can and should be for the next four years was not reflected in the voting today. I concede the election to my worthy opponent but not my views. I will return to the Governor's House in the great state of Alabama to serve the remainder of my term and exercise the faith and continued support you have given me."

After hearing the concession speech, President Bob and Vice President Leon shook hands enthusiastically and walked to the window of the 13th floor suite. Upon seeing the clear sky and bright lights across the city that made it appear as a reflection of a great mosaic painting, President Bob's stately piercing gaze and comments rocked Vice President Leon's soul as he said, "Tonight I entrust my country to you. Treat it as you treat Stella, with the utmost respect, passion and dignity. Never waiver on principle, falter on demand or cross her. The rewards will be great if you succeed, and the penalty will be just as harsh if you fail. Hold your head high with pride, but don't let pride prevent you from keeping your head."

Vice President Leon, visibly startled by President Bob's candor, replied, "Thank you, Mr. President. I believe it's time for us to face the nation." Without further discussion, Vice President Leon bade Stella to accompany them to the ballroom. Stella immediately took her husband's arm as he escorted her and President Bob to the elevator.

Their brief moment of solitude and pride was broken after they got off of the elevator greeted by dozens of reporters poised with questions and listening and looking for fodder for their next story. Flashbulbs and TV cameras hovered around them as honeybees move to honeysuckle. They asked streams of questions, but President Bob responded, "We have no comment until after Vice President Leon's victory speech in a few minutes from the rostrum in the ballroom." The reporters flowed into the ballroom and pressed their way near the podium as the presidential entourage made their way to the platform.

President Bob and Vice President Leon received a standing ovation as they approached the platform. They made eye contact and shook hands with as many people in the audience as they could before taking their seats, and I sat in the rear of the auditorium. Pristen Walker, the Democratic Party Chair, walked from the podium and greeted them with a hearty handshake. Vice President Leon and Stella sat to the right of President Bob, and President Bob sat to the right of Pristen Walker.

While Chairman Walker was introducing President Bob, Vice President Leon and President Bob were scanning the audience.

"It is my esteemed pleasure to introduce a man who has changed the course of history. His excellent leadership, superb vision and unique ability to build cohesive political coalitions to enact and enforce laws allow our great nation to be the measurement by which all other democratic nations' success is measured. He is the first man of the United States, President Robert Jordan Nelson."

President Bob strolled confidently to the podium and paused while the audience embraced him again with their applause. After a few minutes he held up one hand, silenced the crowd and politely said, "I came not only to thank the American people for the eight years you have allowed me to serve as your President but also for a committed, intelligent, resourceful, unselfish and diligent Vice President. I respect him because he has always been willing to do what's right for America. Even his staunchest opponent respects his willingness to listen to opposing points of view. He's a great father and excellent public servant, and I am proud to say he's my friend. He will be your next President. I give you the next President of the United States, Spencer Leon."

Vice President Leon was very gracious in his acceptance speech that Cintura had written for him. He had given her an outline of his thoughts, and she made it politically palatable. The five feet from his seat to the podium seemed like a mile. His feet seemed anchored by a heavy weight. However, as the roar and applause from the audience grew more enthusiastic with each pace, the burden of his gait was lifted. Speaking into the podium microphone, he spoke firmly and compassionately.

"My fellow Americans, this is the second proudest day of my life. The first proudest day of my life was when I asked Stella Estavan to marry me, and she said yes. She made a commitment to me that will last a lifetime, and this is the type of commitment I make to you tonight. No, I'm not perfect. I've made mistakes, and undoubtedly I'll make more. However, the mistakes I make will be made while giving my best effort daily to make our nation a better place to live, work and raise families.

"I realize there are some who are driven by greed. There's nothing wrong with aspiring for wealth. Wealth as a result of one's labor is the American way. What I want is for all political parties to work together, so that everyone can have the opportunity to share in that dream. I believe if businesses create jobs with decent wages and training, they will not have difficulties finding labor. If teachers are not paid competitive wages and given appropriate resources to teach our children, then our children will graduate not knowing why Jefferson said in the Declaration of Independence, 'We hold these truths to be self evident that all men are created equal with certain inalienable rights.' I truly believe if President Jefferson were standing at this podium today, he would say that our kids have a right to a decent education. Some people around the country want to resurrect 'Ugly' laws and force the weakest among us to hide their impairments as if in shame.

We're in the 21st century and need every American that is able, to work. Social Security is not a crutch. It was initially meant to supplement retirement income for the aged and totally disabled. However, Americans with minor ailments are bleeding the system unnecessarily. We need these individuals to avail themselves of training programs. I've obtained a commitment from 50 major corporations to insure that 10 percent of new hires will be physically or mentally challenged high school graduates. These individuals will be trained for competitive employment next year. SAT scores have been pitiful the last decade. I am appointing Crimson Thomas as head of the Department of Education. He will be coordinating with major corporations across this country to match schools with businesses. We want businesses to instill work ethics and values to those among us who need them. How can you tell a dropout in South Central Los Angeles about work ethics, when his environment is composed of homelessness, broken promises, poor employment opportunities and no role models?"

The audience clapped enthusiastically. After several minutes, President Leon continued, "According to the Bible, there was a young man who walked the earth doing good deeds. People criticized him, chastised and even murdered him for his beliefs. I stand humbly before you, for you. Whether you support my platform or not, I extend to you my hand in friendship with a steadfast commitment to make your world a better place." President Leon stretched forth his hand toward the audience, and this gesture was followed by applause. As most of the audience showed their approval, he smiled and made eye contact with prominent Republicans who were seated nearby. Then they begrudgingly clapped.

President-elect Leon followed their applause with a request. "I'm also standing here seeking a commitment from all of you. Business leaders, I can't keep the economy moving forward without your commitment to continue positive research and development initiatives and maintain a well-informed and educated workforce. Parents, I need you to commit yourselves to ensure your children attend school daily and to drop by the school unannounced a minimum of five times a semester. Teachers can only be as effective as the discipline you instill in your children. They must come to school daily with the attitude to learn. Children, you must be committed to doing your best daily. Doing your best does not mean never failing. You must do your best with the attitude that says, 'If I fail, I'll pick myself up, learn from my failure and try again.'

"We are the strongest nation in the world, militarily. We have a commitment to defend our borders and assist our allies to defend theirs. We are not the world's bullies but neither will we be their punching bags. Some nations seek to use guerrilla tactics to poke holes in our faith. However, we will weed out and severely punish anyone that threatens our security. I believe our forefathers did not make those sacrifices, so we could squander what they left us. We must join hands in unity to make what they left us a better place. Thank you."

There was a fifteen-minute standing ovation. President Bob beamed with pride as President-elect Leon delivered his speech, and then he shook his hand. Cintura had the other members of the ticket lined up to give speeches. Each one complimented the preceding one as if etched by the same pen. Stella, with tears of joy streaming down her cheeks, held Spencer's hand as if it was a prized jewel.

While President Bob said his good-byes, I got the limousine and waited for him outside. It did not take him long to slip away from this joyous celebration. After most of the celebrants and press had left, President Bob said to me, "It's President-elect Leon's baby now. I want you to drive me to St. Michael's."

Then I drove President Bob to his summer home in St. Michael's, Maryland.

As all presidents before him, he had his executive chair and hassock moved to his private residence. Unlike them, it housed 421 of his most prized possessions—panties and thongs from his conquests.

When we pulled into the driveway, I could see the lights were on in the living room. Evidently, Rose had watched the election activities on their big screen satellite TV. They were finally free of the Washington frenzy. After I parked the car and opened the door, I followed President Bob inside. I waited patiently in the foyer watching and waiting and silenced by the activity of the moment. As President Bob entered the living room, we could see Rose, who was dressed in a stunning lime green satin chemise. The stereo was playing as her body moved to the musical rhythms, gyrating and enticing onlookers with her every movement and stirring emotions as if creating a witch's brew.

A few minutes later, President Bob instructed me to make myself available to our new President while he did some personal research at home. I dutifully agreed, let myself out and drove home to Cintura.

As I drove, I thought about how fortunate I was to share a special bond with two special people, Cintura and President Bob. Their love is chiseled in my heart and consciousness. They saved me from myself and provided the Lithium and Clinoril that abated my periodic delusions and depression. I've committed myself to insure their safety, and that's why we are the only people we trust.

Cintura and I celebrated her success with a toast and a night of celebration of play, passion and song. My nakedness was only hidden by the shame of Cintura's wickedness. In another month, the President's final term will end, and our Vice President, Spencer Leon, will succeed him. The parts are already in place for a smooth transition…Barton, Vice President, Cintura, Chief of Staff…and me…

TRACI'S EPILOGUE

▼

Several weeks ago, my mother, Cintura, suspected Albee of being disloyal because she had been observed frequently writing copious notes, while sitting inside presidential vehicles. Cintura sent me to check out the presidential limousines. I found the preceding manuscript Albee had carefully preserved in the glove compartment of one of the presidential limousines in which she had faithfully chauffeured President Bob and his friends, family and colleagues. Unfortunately, she had recorded their activities. When I found the manuscript between Homer and The Invisible Man in one of the glove compartments, I wanted to burn it; however, my mother thought that it would be better to save it until after her career was over and then publish it using different names. She said that no one would believe the characters, but the events would speak for themselves. The spotlight of inquiry will reveal the lines of truth, and then the true believers will not be believers at all. As usual, Cintura was right. Reading Albee's manuscript was better than a Shakespearean tragedy. It's ironic that when I read the following words, I realized that she and I loved my mother, but from different perspectives:

"The night I met Cintura, I wrote the following lines that expresses in a few words what fuses us at the hips."

> I found something in her eyes that rocked my soul—
> Her touch, her torch and her passion for that which is
> forbidden.

An unquenchable thirst for adventure spurned by trying the
    unthinkable,

Becoming the impossible and challenging the inevitable.

The spirit of rhythm is not reason,

But the three seasons of life—birth, growth and death

Keeping time to the pendulum's beat.

I'm cursed with the yearning for the flower's nectar

And sentenced to temporal satisfaction.

Yesterday was the beginning of something special,

Today is thoroughly unique,

And tomorrow is the reflection of yesterday's promises.

Because our panties are not our own,

We gave them away with the key to…"

President Bob, yes my loving father, was scheduled to meet his demise by a thorny Rose. Cintura waited for him, tired of his time spent with others and never time for her. She found little comfort in his periodic Manhattan trinkets on Christmas and birthdays for her loyal benevolence.

I often ask myself, 'What is this thing called love? Is it a mask that eludes common sense, a potion that intoxicates the vulnerable or a heavenly experience between mutually consenting individuals…giving all and expecting nothing? The answer is always an echo of the question reverberating against the space of time.'

Cintura realized that the only thing worse than loneliness is the chill from loneliness. She often commented that 'Despair as a result of loneliness could fashion itself into a blade of redemption…purged by the blood of one's nemesis.' Cintura ordered me to lace the thorns of a single yellow rose with a slimy substance that was a combination of arsenic, Dermacentor tick saliva and black widow spider venom and place it in the center of President Bob's bed. Each substance causes temporary paralysis and can lead to death if untreated; however, a combination of the three causes certain death within thirty minutes.'

I chose to be loyal to a father whose love I had never known rather than enjoy the wealth of a woman who gave me life but no love. The flower was left in her bed not his, in between the fitted sheet and mattress. As I lay in bed listening to Cintura and Albee romp in the next room, I felt relief when their sighs of ecstasy ended. I waited a few minutes then crept into their bedroom and saw their spent bodies sprawled limp and exhausted across the queen-sized canopied bed. Cintura's body was stiffening by the second as I came closer. The lethal venom had caused muscle and respiratory paralysis. She looked at me as in disbelief, then realizing my betrayal, tried to utter, 'Why?' Her cold stony eyes remained fixed while no sound could be heard as her life's breath was snatched. Albee was still lying on top face down and thought Cintura was sleeping after a nice rendezvous; however, when she looked into her face, she became frightened and confused. Albee clung to Cintura thinking she had caused her untimely death. I tried to pry Albee's hands loose but couldn't muster the strength. Albee sobbed, lamenting her lover's death. I tried to explain to Albee that it wasn't her fault, that Cintura probably had suffered a heart attack or another physical ailment. However, nothing I said seemed to seep through and after an hour of useless effort, I decided to leave them until the next morning.

As I entered Cintura's sunlit room the next morning, her face seemed to glow as if in a perfect sleep, while the pink satin sheets still covered her body. Albee was sitting up in bed with her firm subtle breast casting a shadow while observing Cintura with a whimsical smile reflecting on a night well spent. At that moment, a single shot rang out from my dart gun hitting Albee in the temple. The asphyxiant from the dart killed her instantly as her final page floated to the floor. It ended with a question, 'Can an observer be an active participant?'

I dressed the bodies and summoned my two security men to assist me in disposing of them. We tossed Cintura in the back of the limousine and Albee in the driver's seat and left the engine running. Cintura's home was in a wooded area and could not be seen from the major main streets nearby. We took a rusted jagged knife and bore a hole in the limousine's security box that controlled the unbreakable glass windows and protective mechanisms in the car. This allowed the liquid nitrogen to escape into the atmosphere and the control box to crystallize. *The windows and doors were now frozen and locked. One of my security men pried off one of the tricuspid hoses that led from the engine's exhaust manifold and let it dangle in front of the vent in the floorboard.*

We called the fire department and Captain Melton, one of Cintura's contacts, came within ten minutes with a fire crew. They used a blowtorch to unlock the doors and remove the bodies. As his crew was packing up their equipment to return to the fire department, Captain Melton told me that his preliminary investigation indicated that the car must have hit a sharp object the previous night. The car's security control box was inoperable, and the windows and doors were frozen in position. However, the doors apparently were accessible with a key. The car's sensors operated on a separate system connected to the transmission. Once fumes were detected in the car, the transmission had immobilized the car. The interior of the car was soundproof so even if the car's occupants cried out for help or banged on the windows, no one could hear them. Captain Melton assured me the report would be done quickly and appropriately. I told him that his professionalism and discretion would be appreciated and rewarded by the end of the day. After I signed a brief statement, Captain Melton left with his crew smiling confidently.

Just as the old patriarch of the Christian Church in agony exclaimed, 'It is finished,' and so it is with Cintura. Her mission is analogous to a pebble rolling down the snowy hill of chance, culminating in a crescendo of power and wealth, after being stopped at an appointed end in time.

978-0-595-30883-5
0-595-30883-X